PRAISE FOR LAUR

'Laura Jane William
relatable wit and bol
Dolly Alderton

'Hilarious, heart-warming and truly authentic
– your modern rom com must-read'
Hello!

'Sexy, fun and full of heart'
Beth O'Leary

'A joyful, romantic and life-affirming love story'
Red

'I can't remember the last time a book made me forget
I had a phone. Pure escapist fiction!'
Stacey Halls

'Joyful and romantic . . . tailor-made for summer'
Cosmopolitan

'Charming and full of warmth.
This is the book equivalent of a big hug'
Sophia Money-Coutts

'LJ's honesty and voice are unique'
Stylist

'Smart, sisterly storytelling . . . You can practically feel modern
romance evolving as you're reading it'
Observer

'A hilarious and brilliantly written story from
one of our favourite writers'
Bella

'This is the feminist rom com of the summer'
Holly Bourne

'A cult hit'
Grazia

'Real escapism with warmth, a lightness of touch
and vivid characters you really root for'
Ella Dove

'OH MY WORD. Such a beautiful read . . . it just
made me tingle with joy'
Elle Cook

'A modern, playful romance with flirty rhyming texts,
real bffs, and mind-blowing sex. So refreshing!'
Lily Lindon

'Simply gorgeous and effortlessly charming. Laura has
created a cast of seriously engaging characters who
come to life like real life pals. I have three words
of advice: ADD TO CART'
Hannah Doyle

'What a book! Sexy, fun, but also heartfelt, real and deep'
Emily Stone

'An absolutely gorgeous, funny and romantic delight
– I adored it!'
Rachael Lucas

Laura Jane Willliams (she/her) is the author of five novels, a novella, and three works of non-fiction. The rights to her international bestseller *Our Stop* have been sold for television and her books have been translated into languages all over the world. She loves romance, being a parent, and Mr Kipling's French Fancies – the chocolate ones are best, but strawberry will do. Laura is currently writing her next book.

Fiction by the same author

Our Stop
The Love Square
The Lucky Escape
The Wrong Suitcase (novella)
One Night With You

Just for December

LAURA JANE WILLIAMS

avon.

Published by AVON
A division of HarperCollins*Publishers*
1 London Bridge Street
London SE1 9GF

www.harpercollins.co.uk

HarperCollins*Publishers*
1st Floor, Watermarque Building, Ringsend Road
Dublin 4, Ireland

A Paperback Original 2022

First published in Great Britain by HarperCollins*Publishers* 2022

A catalogue copy of this book is available from the British Library.

ISBN: 978-0-00-836549-3

Typeset in Minion by Palimpsest Book Production Limited,
Falkirk, Stirlingshire
Printed and Bound in the UK using 100% Renewable Electricity
at CPI Group (UK) Ltd

This book is produced from independently certified FSC™ paper
to ensure responsible forest management.

For more information visit: www.harpercollins.co.uk/green

For Molly Walker-Sharp
thank you for being a dream when
you inherited a nightmare (!)

1

Evie

A movie set is an extraordinary place.

Lights! Camera! Action!

All right, Mr DeMille, I'm ready for my close-up.

The camera department mill about preparing their equipment, loading film and figuring out shots. Grip and electric crew yell as they set up the lighting, sound and video playback, run cables and prepare their carts. Hair and make-up are with the actors in dressing rooms or trailers, exchanging newsworthy gossip or listening to lines. And the sets! To walk through the lot is to walk through history. Who cares that Hollywood is a place where they'll pay you a thousand dollars for a kiss and fifty cents for your soul when over there on Stage 24 is where they filmed *Friends*, and right around the corner is where they did *Jurassic Park*. Marvel as the director goes over the script, deciding what will be shot, and how, with the director of photography. The chatter of sound mixers and assistants, caterers and producers. How many people say they want to make TV or movies? How many people actually get to do it? Everyone there has made it against the odds, and they know it. It's what breathes magic into the air.

Fame, I'm gonna live forever.

The promise of all this – the lights, and the camera, and the action – is probably what made Duke Carlisle become who he is, Evie thinks. She got an extended bio through from her agent once they knew Duke was involved in the screen adaptation of her book. It said that little boy in Sunderland, England, knew that if he couldn't do this – act, in Hollywood, for the whole world to see – then there wasn't much point to anything. Now he's internationally applauded, recognised everywhere he goes, and no doubt has as much money as . . . well, perhaps not God, but definitely a senior royal. He's a working-class northern boy come good, just trying to make his mama proud, apparently. A direct quote from that bio? 'It doesn't get much better than this.'

But . . .

The *reality* of Hollywood is what makes Evie Bird want to avoid the movies for the rest of her life. She grew up on set, watching her dad give instructions to actors speaking the words he'd written – and she knows it's not all as it seems. Abuse of power is real, and everyone works in the knowledge that one false move and they can be replaced *like that*, because there are a million other actors and directors and screen-writers ready and willing to take their place, so the hours are long and the morals dubious.

There's fighting, there's backstabbing, there's torrid affairs . . .

it was par for the course that Evie's father would spend her childhood demonstrating the hat-trick, then.

When your parents are famous in Hollywood, you either want to be just like them, or nothing like them at all.

Evie couldn't stand to end up like her father, and so no. She wants nothing to do with it, not ever.

Storytelling is in her blood, but over her dead body will she work in the movies.

She doesn't talk about her father, or her history. Nobody knows she is Donald Gilbert's daughter and she'd like to keep it that way. She writes books with her mother's maiden name, instead – far, far away from All That – and it's a quiet life that she's more than happy with.

It's unfortunate, then, that she's contractually obliged to fly out to Duke Carlisle's set if she wants to cash the adaptation cheque that she so desperately needs. Unless you're Dan Brown writing *The Da Vinci Code*, book-writing seldom makes you rich, and although money can't make you happy it sure as hell can cover the next ten years of your mother's care home – so what choice does Evie have now it's been offered? Even if the caveat is watching it all get done?

A movie set sounds like a dream come true for most people. But for Evie? Urgh. It's a nightmare.

And she's going anyway.

'Nobody has a face like that *and* a functioning personality,' Evie declares, stood at the mirror in a flesh-coloured bra that's too small and faded high-rise jeans. She has a wardrobe full of stuff and yet lives in a four-year-old pair of Levi's, so well-worn they hold the shape of her even when they're on

3

the hanger. 'And Duke Carlisle?' she continues, noticing a bit of kale in between her two front teeth, left over from lunch. She grimaces at the mirror and tries to rub it out with her finger. 'That's the lamest stage name ever. He sounds like a failed army general with a cocktail named after him.'

Magda, her best friend, shakes her head playfully, which is fair enough. Evie has essentially been performing the same bitter monologue since the summer, when she found out she was being summoned to set to help with 'extra backstage content'. She locates her toothbrush in the bathroom adjoining the bedroom they're packing in, finally getting half a salad out of her teeth. Great. Lunch had been, what, four hours ago? And nobody told her she looked like the Cookie Monster meets Austin Powers, via Whole Foods.

'I'll bet he's a total jerk,' Evie concludes, grabbing a grey roll-neck and holding it up to her body, considering it absent-mindedly, then switching to the ribbed cream one off the bed. Maybe she'll pack both, she thinks, get some wear out of them. She bought them on sale six weeks ago, but they've still got their price tags on. She might even pack some trousers that aren't her jeans. When was the last time she put them in the laundry, even?

She tosses the sweaters over to Magda, for the 'to be packed' pile. God she's grateful for the help – if only to get all the complaining out of her system.

'I know I'm being boring, going on and on about it,' Evie continues. 'But honestly. My whole childhood was watching celebrities on movie sets only being kind to the people who can be helpful to them. It's so screwed up. Although I will

4

admit, up-and-coming actors aren't like that. They're nice to everyone, just in case.'

'I'd hardly call Duke Carlisle up-and-coming though,' notes Magda, helpfully folding the stuff Evie has chosen. 'Even you knew who he was, and you don't know anything about anybody. You basically defy the laws of pop culture. How can anybody be so removed from *everything* featured in the world of fame?'

'You're saying it like it's an insult,' Evie shoots back, searching out a clip for her long blonde mane from the nightstand. 'And yet I receive it as a compliment.'

'How unlike you—' Magda smirks, pursing her lips teasingly '—to edit the script as we go.'

'Consistency is key, oh dear one.'

Evie turns back to the wardrobe now her hair is off her neck – it's heavy work, packing for three weeks in Europe, and she's getting clammy. She decides that she needs a couple of thin turtlenecks for layers. How cold can it be in Germany? She's pretty sure winters on the continent aren't anything like her Utah ones, but she should be prepared. There's no such thing as bad weather – that's what her mother always said – only unsuitable clothing. She runs a hand through the hangers, considering what else she might need, adding: 'Give your readers what they want, with a few surprises. That's plot, baby.'

'The surprise in this story being that you're actually taking the trip,' says Magda, plainly. She shrugs as she says it, as though adding: *God, I never thought I'd see the day.*

Evie holds up a hand. 'Don't. I'm still in denial. I'd rather do a naked fan dance in an old people's home than step foot onto a *movie set*. Not that anyone understands that, of course. Well, except you.' She gives Magda a smile of genuine thanks. 'But, I have an action plan for getting through it. Failing to prepare is preparing to fail, after all – and I am wholly committed to engaging zero shenanigans, and returning with exactly one finished book for next year, otherwise my editor will kill me.'

'I'm all ears.' Magda folds the last of the sweaters and, to Evie's perplexity, moves on to shoes and underwear simultaneously. 'Trust me,' Magda tells her, as Evie issues a concerned look. Magda waves away her interference with one hand, stuffing Evie's sneakers with lace thongs with the other. 'And fill me in on the plan. Let me live vicariously through you. I mean, God, if school was already out, I'd be coming with you. Because I'm one of the naïve civilians who thinks it's all going to be so terribly *glamorous*.'

'Huh,' snorts Evie. 'And anyway,' she adds, not wanting to linger on what's in store. 'Not long to go now. And I'll be back in time for Christmas, just you and me. We can totally ignore that it's even happening, if you want, or make a big thing of it like kids, or be drunk throughout, or whatever. We'll play it absolutely by your ear.'

Magda pauses her methodical shoe wadding – a packing method Evie can already see is just as efficient as Magda had suggested, proving that it was totally right to ask for her assistance – and looks up.

'Just don't get divorced, that's my advice.' Magda sighs sadly. 'It's crappy. Crappy, crappy, crappy.'

She pulls a face, sticking out her bottom lip in a dramatic but, to Evie, totally justified fashion, and Evie pads across to the other side of the bed to hook an arm around her best friend tightly. It was ever thus. There was an Evie and Magda before there was a Magda and Jamie, and there'll be an Evie and Magda long after the divorce papers are finally signed.

'You know,' Evie says, softly, 'six months ago, and you'd have said that through guttural sobs and scoops of Ben and Jerry's from the carton. You've come a long way, baby. I know it hurts, but remember that much. Time, she's a healer. You're doing so well.'

Magda looks at her side-on. 'A divorcée,' she says. 'And for what? I feel like Miranda in the *Sex and the City* reboot.' She blows a raspberry. 'And Just Like That, Magda blew up her life because it wasn't exciting enough, and found herself single in her thirties again.'

'Hey,' says Evie, pretending to be hurt. 'It ain't so bad.'

'You have Carl.'

'Hmm. Do I though?' Evie pulls a face. '*That* isn't . . . that. If you know what I mean.'

'You mean it's temporary on purpose,' says Magda.

'Everything in this life is temporary,' replies Evie, and the comment hits harder than she meant it to. She thinks of her mom.

Evie squeezes her friend's shoulder once more, kissing her cheek, and then they work in companionable silence for a while, each lost in their own thoughts. Eventually Magda announces: 'I've just been thinking lately that I just wish one of us did something really wrong, you know? Committed fraud or didn't disclose a secret family or even had just a simple, straightforward affair with a secretary.'

'You don't have a secretary,' Evie points out.

'Jamie does.'

'Do some digging? Maybe you'll get lucky, and he's been sleeping with her after all.'

'She's a lesbian,' Magda points out. 'But thanks for brainstorming options with me.'

'Any time.' Evie winks.

With a flourish, Magda proudly fondles the expertly folded clothes she's organised, cute sweaters and matching wool hats and festive scarves, declaring: 'At least I'm good at this, if nothing else.'

'You're my hero for getting through it,' Evie says, eyeing her. 'And I don't mean the packing – though it *is* pretty spectacular. I think the fact that you are still standing after what you've been through means we should build a statue in your honour. Seriously. You and Jamie have both been so sensible and nice to each other. It almost makes *me* want to give it a try.'

'You'd have to get married first,' says Magda.

Evie pulls a face. 'A sticking point,' she concedes.

Magda looks skyward – not even God can help Evie engage romance in real life – before taking a break to climb onto the bed. As she crosses her legs Evie's dog, Doctor Dolittle, sees the invitation for snuggles, leaping up to nestle in Magda's lap. Evie needs to drop him at the doggy hotel shortly. She adds it to her growing mental list.

'I'd do it again,' Magda says, ruffling the fur between Doc's ears. 'One day. I think. With somebody more . . . you know. If there was more passion involved, not just a shared interest in a Netflix series.'

'Oh, well then, two for you, none for me. You can have *my* wedding.'

'I don't think they're rationed out,' Magda quips.

'Maybe they should be.'

'But Carl is so nice. Don't you ever think . . .'

Evie tuts dramatically. 'Carl and I have an agreement, and it involves two lives, two nights a week and two hours together. Don't judge what you don't understand, *thankyouverymuch*.'

'Yes, ma'am,' says Magda with an odd raise of the eyebrows that conveys her absolute judgement without another word. Magda *says* she just wants Evie to be happy, to which Evie often replies: *stop hassling me about it, then*. Even in divorce, her best friend still believes in happy endings, which is ironic considering it's Evie who writes the romances.

Evie checks the suitcase still has room for the last bits and bobs that will have to go in in the morning – toiletry bag, chargers, incidentals – by testing it closes. It does, but only just.

'We got side-tracked,' Magda reminds Evie, circling back around to the original point. 'Your plan for survival is . . . ?'

'Oh, yes.' Evie nods. 'Well, basically, I'm on deadline for next year's Christmas book – if I come back here with less than a hundred thousand words to my name you'll have to lock me in the basement and only let me out for pee breaks and thirty minutes of fresh air – so I figure I'll do whatever they need me to do on set and then peace out of there. As far as my agent can tell they just want me for extra content? For social media or bonus material or whatever? Maybe they're making a behind-the-scenes doc for YouTube. I don't know . . . if I think about it too much, I go crazy trying to understand why it's an actual contractual obligation instead of an offer I could've turned down.' Evie pauses, here, closing her eyes and taking a theatrical deep breath. When she opens her eyes, she continues: 'So, once I've done whatever bull they need me to do, I'll just write. At the end of the day, it's a big fat cheque and a weight off of my mind in terms of Mom's care, and as long as I get my word count, I *suppose* I'll survive . . .'

'The Romantic Road *does* have all those Christmas markets and magical castles and ice skating . . .' Magda points out, referencing the area of Germany they're filming in. 'If you're writing next year's Christmas book surely you can hunt all that stuff out to get into the spirit for what you're working on now?'

'Exactly,' agrees Evie. 'And I'm not too proud to admit that it's time to write from somewhere other than the local coffee shop. Freddie's has a soya latte that's hard to beat, but I'm sure there's some quaint Bavarian café that will suit me just fine.'

'So you're going to do the bare minimum for the movie, because movie sets suck and so does everyone working on them . . .'

Evie throws her friend an appreciative nose-crinkle then. Thank the Lord she gets it, where thousands wouldn't: this isn't exciting for Evie. It's an inconvenience.

'And meanwhile, you're going to write your last forty thousand words, drink hot chocolate and eat little German pastries, and call me daily to fill me in on it all, reminding me that the last week of the semester is always the hardest.'

'You got it! And . . .' Evie adds. 'Above all else . . .'

'Yes?'

'I'm going to avoid anyone famous. The director, the

actors, the screenwriter even . . . They can do them, and I'll do me.'

'Of course.' Magda laughs.

'Egotistical, arrogant, fake Hollywood,' Evie nods. 'I'm going to enjoy the days as much as I can – but that doesn't mean I won't be counting them down, too.'

'Got it,' Magda shoots back. Then she thinks about something, her face lighting up as she hits on an idea. 'But for what it's worth?' she adds, mischievously. 'If it's true that Duke Carlisle is now single again, please do pass along *my* number. You might think he's a jackass waiting to be found out, but I happen to think he's hot as hell.'

2

Duke

Duke Carlisle has never heard of a man dropping dead from a broken heart, but that doesn't mean it's never happened.

The pull in his chest tests him – mocks him, even, for being such a fool.

He's been such a stupid bloody idiot.

How did he not see it?

Why did he ever believe Daphne when she said *I love you*? He obsesses over it for the trillionth time as he navigates the walk through Frankfurt airport to his waiting car out front, his Nikes thudding the ground, his designer tracksuit slung low on his hips. The click-click-click of paparazzi cameras and their accompanying flashes act as a baseline to the cries of fans who've been tipped off on his arrival time by some blog or social media account. It's mad, the information super-fans can get hold of. Somebody always leaks it, on nearly

12

every production or media tour. He steels himself. They tell him it's the price of fame. For years now, he's been willing to pay it. He keeps his blue, almond-shaped eyes down, obscured by his designer sunglasses, and raises a large hand to his face to shield himself. He's doing his best not to be grumpy. He really is.

Daphne Diamond, Duke's improbably named co-star, now ex-girlfriend and the woman responsible for said debilitating chest pains, isn't paying the same tax on her celebrity today. They were on the same flight from London, but she's been ushered through the back exit, the private escape designed for high net-worth flyers and movie stars, probably already halfway to the hotel. She's persona non grata with the producers right now, after attracting damning headlines about her cheating ways. Duke sighs. Daphne was caught in a tryst with their married director three days into filming the interior shots for *On the Romantic Road* at Pinewood Studios, photos splashed across every front page of her pressed up against a back-alley wall, her tongue in Brad's mouth and Brad's hands on her arse. And they've still got three weeks of all working together in Germany ahead of them. It's rough.

But, mad as Daphne has made everyone by jeopardising the reputation around the film – she's made investors nervous, and it's put the whole production team on edge – she's being protected by everyone, wrapped in cotton wool, until the team can figure out how to redeem her reputation as girl-next-door Leading Lady, making her a reliable draw for the box office again . . . and keeping the investors on board. Everyone thinks movies are about telling great stories for the world. They're not. They're about making money.

So, even though it's Duke who looks like an idiot to the whole damned world for letting himself get cheated on, for not having a clue, his publicist has him taking the civilian route precisely so that he can be papped looking the opposite of his forlorn and heartbroken self – and save Daphne's cheating arse in the process.

Darling, it's good to be single and happy. The mums will go mad for it. Trust, baby, trust. It makes people fantasise about having a chance with you. That's what he'd been told by Carter, the dazzling American charged with 'Hollywoodising' him.

Duke isn't even sure who he is as a man anymore, such is the attention lavished on him as a brand to be promoted and monetised. *Be careful what you wish for* is Duke's take on all of that. Not to feel sorry for himself or anything. It's a privileged life. It's just, he *thought* worldwide adoration and a brand-new Porsche in the drive of one of his many houses was The Dream until it all started to come true. But then when something like this happens and the press is so intrusive it doesn't feel worth it at all. He's treated like a story, not a human being, and for all his easy charm and gentle swagger in front of the cameras, it wears him down. The fame doesn't cure him of being a person with feelings.

Boohoo, his brain tells him. *Are your diamond shoes too tight, pretty boy?*

'Doook! Doooook!' chant the throngs of German women, mildly mispronouncing his stage name. They're older than you might imagine, but Duke knows from the research commissioned by his management that, whilst it's Gen Z who put on his stuff to begin with, it's parents the world over who keep it on and then replay it again. Hence, the focus on the mums. Wide smile, tousled wavy brown hair, blue eyes described with a folklore-like mysticism last heard geared towards Sinatra – Duke Carlisle is an international movie star who could be your son's very charming university friend home for the holidays with kind words and a secret cheeky wink. Hence being cast in *On the Romantic Road*, an adaptation of Evie Bird's German-set and internationally bestselling romance novel. There are a lot of fisherman's jumpers involved in the role. A lot of bashful looks and stammered sentences and good manners. He's perfect for it.

'Hello, hi, thanks for the warm welcome,' Duke says, lifting a hand and craning his neck so that the women can get their selfie. 'You certainly know how to make a chap feel special.'

His Etonian-esque vowels are exactly as his voice coach trained him, all artificial plums and fake silver spoon. Duke was born and raised in Sunderland, but American audiences don't know what to do with northern accents, his agent said, taking a further five per cent from his first paycheque to finance its flattening. Now he talks like Hugh Grant, which is no small mistake; now that Hugh has five kids and is in his sixties, someone needs to fill his British rom-com shoes. Nice bloke, though, Duke thinks. Hugh has always been very generous with his time towards him.

A pap Duke recognises from his Hampstead house in north London gets close enough to block off his path.

'Careful there, Clive.' Duke smiles, looking over the top of his sunglasses to check the man is okay. He hates the press this afternoon, when he's embarrassed and ego-bruised, but he needs them, too, at the end of the day. That's what Carter always says. And to be fair, Clive is normally one of the better ones. He gets his shot and then buggers off, which is more than can be said of some of the others – they've mounted cars, rifled through his bins, even wire-tapped his phone.

'Sorry to ask you mate, but Daphne? What's the crack?' asks Clive, his camera up to his face, the viewfinder fixed on Duke's reaction. Duke can tell he's stopped taking stills and has switched to video, exactly like Carter said he would. It's almost as if she has briefed the press, organised this whole thing.

'No comment,' says Duke, as per the film publicist's instruction.

'Come on, mate, nothing?' Clive pushes, and Duke plays the game. He's given his rehearsed *no comment* for the production team, now he's to give his rehearsed 'everywoman heartthrob' comment for his personal management, to help with his – God save him for using their word, the word he hates so much – *profile*.

Duke sighs, sticking the book he'd been reading on the flight under his arm and pulling off his sunglasses to rub the bridge of his nose. He feigns trying to think of the right thing to say, something that captures both that he's a decent guy, isn't a pushover, *and* that he still believes in the good things of the world. That's his role, isn't it? To keep romantic hope alive? He has to say this like he isn't worth three to five million a movie, because money can't hide your longing to be loved. It can't even cushion it. He might be Duke Carlisle, but his job in whatever he says next is to make every woman who sees it believe that maybe, just maybe, they could be the next Mrs Duke Carlisle.

If only they could.

He'd kill for real love.

'Daphne and Brad?' Duke starts, careful to look off camera to Clive's other eye and not directly into the lens. 'I'm happy for them. Truth is, we'd actually been broken up for a while. We're still great friends, and I'm happy if she's happy. Everyone's got the wrong end of the stick. I can't speak for Brad's marriage but from our end, Daph and I went back to being friends ages ago. I'm really loving making the movie with her. Any bloke is lucky to have her. But truly, we decided long ago that we're more like brother and sister than anything else.'

The lie comes out easily. He takes a breath and decides to finish on his truth, earnest as it might be.

'I'm very much looking for love myself, though,' he says. 'I'm looking for the woman of my dreams, in case you see her.'

A group of fans issue a collective *aww*, and he waves one last time before ducking outside to the winter chill and into the luxury Mercedes people carrier waiting for him, the windows thankfully blacked out. If he thought the driver wouldn't leak it to a gossip mag, he could almost let himself cry. Everything is a performance for him, even his real feelings. It's enough to send him mad. It's enough to make him feel like the loneliest man in the world, even when everybody knows his name.

3

Evie

The call from the care home comes right as Evie is at the departure gate, boarding pass in hand.

'Ms Gilbert?' a polite-sounding woman says, but Evie can already tell it's Bluebell Assisted Living from her caller ID and the subsequent thudding in her chest. She sees that name and her automatic reaction is to panic, because it's never good. It's never good, and it's also never anything Evie can do much about. That isn't a fair combination.

'Is she okay?' Evie asks, instead of giving a polite greeting back. Every call they give her starts with her heart in her throat, because every call could be the one where they say the worst has happened. She should give them that feedback: *Hey, guys, instead of saying hello when I pick up could you open with 'Your mother is not dead. Is now a good time to talk?'*

'She's okay,' the woman says, understanding the concern. 'This is Polly, Evie. We've met a few times, if you remember.'

'Polly,' Evie repeats. 'Yes, of course. Sorry. I don't mean to be abrupt.' She gulps a lungful of air, trying to tell her body it can calm down. 'And it's Bird. Mom is Mrs Gilbert, but I'm Ms Bird.'

'Of course,' Polly says. 'And don't apologise one bit. I get it. Everyone is the same when they know it's us.' There's a beat. Then Polly continues: 'She's *fine*,' she reiterates, 'but I did just want to let you know that she's sprained her wrist after a fall. She got spooked by one of the new assistants and toppled over a chair. Her wrist is bandaged, but she's anxious, talking to herself, like she does.'

'Yeah, it calms her. She . . . she used to be an editor. Books. Is she telling a story under her breath? Sometimes she makes things up about when I was little, or remembers meetings with her old authors and gives everyone notes,' Evie rambles, knowing that Polly knows all this.

'Yes, that's it. It's been a few hours of it now,' Polly continues. Evie realises she's next in line to board the plane, pointing to her phone and mouthing *sorry* to the air steward checking her paperwork. The man nods, like he understands. 'And she has indeed calmed down – it obviously works for her. We'll keep a close eye on her, but with the injury we just wanted to let you know.'

'Thank you,' says Evie. 'I appreciate that. And just so you know, I'm out of the country until just before Christmas now – I'm actually getting on the plane.' She navigates the air gate, almost toppling over a toddler who randomly stops and sits down in front of her, a grown-up looking mortified behind him. 'So please do keep in touch,' she continues, stepping around the kid, who is now crying. 'Just don't be put off if you get an international dial tone. I did mention it when I came to say goodbye this week, but you never know if it's actually been noted, you know?'

'Good to know,' says Polly. 'I'll double-check. And, erm, Ms Bird, whilst I have you . . .'

Evie knows exactly what Polly is going to say. She's heard it from them so many times before: the slight cough that indicates a segue from pleasantries to a discussion of money. Evie's shoulders immediately tense.

'Oh,' Evie says, trying to save face. 'Sorry to interrupt you, just while I remember. I've left a cheque for you with my friend. She should be dropping it off. It's for the past three months – I've been so slammed with work I've not been on top of my admin. I apologise for the delay. And I fully intend to get all caught up over the holidays, too, so I'll be sure to pay up front from here on out. I should get some help, really, since I'm so forgetful. Ha, ha.'

Evie is painfully aware that she's suddenly talking a dime a dozen, barely pausing for breath lest Polly finds a space between her words to berate her. She *should* be better with money; she knows she should. It's not like she doesn't *make* money, it's just . . . somehow it always seems to leave her accounts as fast as it comes in. It's always been like that, like a compulsion. She should get a financial adviser, especially now her years of hard work are paying off. She's never made an abnormal amount of money, even though her job is to essentially sit at a computer and play make-believe all day. But now her books are getting more attention – thanks, in part, to the news of the movie adaptation – she needs to be more responsible. It's just . . . there's always a reason to treat herself. A good writing day or a bad writing day or the finishing of a draft or missing her mom being fully cognisant or the start of summer or the end of summer . . . Evie buys clothes and make-up and perfume and bags, even though she never really goes anywhere.

She should be saving for retirement – she knows that – especially since her mom went into the care facility and Evie had to start subsidising it. She needs insurance, in case she gets sick and needs care, too. But she never seems to be able to get a handle on things; it's been a struggle since her mom's savings ran out, and Evie doesn't always pay Bluebell on time. Her dad should contribute something, but he hasn't sent money since he left all those years ago. That's why when they got film interest for *On the Romantic Road* she said yes, despite her reservations about the clause requiring her presence on set. The cash is going straight to the home, up front, so she doesn't have to field that *throat clearing* every other month and act like she's a crazy person to buy herself some more time.

'Got it,' says Polly, when Evie finally stops gabbing on. 'I'll make a note of that too. Are you off anywhere nice?' she asks then, right before they ring off. 'For your trip?'

Evie doesn't try to explain. Half the time she doesn't get it herself.

'No, no, not really,' she replies, getting to the end of the walkway to see four attendants welcoming passengers onto the plane. Evie smiles at them. 'Just travelling for work.'

*

The flight is fine. She's in coach, but the seats beside her are empty, so she's able to just about curl up over the aisle and get some rest. Evie tries not to overthink the call with the care home or the fact that her mother seems to be in a state more than she's lucid these past six months. There isn't anything she can do. Not a damned thing in the world. And what is it they say about worrying? You're stealing from the present to think about something that the future cannot even guarantee. Borrowing worry.

Production have sent a car for her, so she's picked up by a smart-looking driver and driven to the hotel in Würzburg, the only irritation being some sort of skirmish with cameras and a VIP by the exit as she tries to leave, forcing the driver to take the long route through the arrivals terminal.

And then they reach their destination.

It's the middle of the afternoon and Würzburg is beautiful. Even in her slightly crumpled mood she sits up straighter in the back seat, taking in the old bridges and tall stone buildings buzzing with people in various states of winter dress: puffer jackets and big woolly scarves in reds and greens, noses pink and breath visible as people speak. Her room at the hotel isn't ready yet, so Evie leaves her bag and decides to pass half an hour taking a walk, stretching her legs and seeing what's what. She has no idea what time it is at home, but it's only 3 p.m. here, so she may as well get onto local time.

The Christmas market is the biggest outdoor market she has ever seen. It's beside the cathedral, a gothic-looking white stone building that ascends proudly into the sky, floor-to-ceiling stained-glass windows marked out in red brick with a grey pointed roof and enormous red-brick bell tower.

Everything is floodlit in golden orange lights, and even at 3 p.m. the sky is thick, weighted clouds making its backdrop a deep navy blue that gets darker by the minute. A Christmas tree the height of two double-decker buses drags her eye away, twinkling with an obscene number of fairy lights, expertly placed equidistantly apart, from bottom to top, where a huge gold star self-importantly sways in the light wind at the top.

There must be a hundred stalls, at least, all lined up in wooden huts and decorated in garlands that smell like Evie's childhood, when it was happier, a more ignorant time, and there are more lights and ornaments, most of which aren't rubbishy little plastic things but rather ornate hand-blown glass and intricate wood. She passes an obelisk festooned with lights too, all trailing down from where they're gathered at the top like a maypole. Traditional wrought-iron lamp posts burn brightly, huge red baubles of different sizes dangling from even more garlands wrapped around, like art deco art installations placed every ten to twenty feet apart.

Almost without thinking, she approaches one of the wooden huts and buys a traditional *Glühwein*, not knowing what it is until the paper cup reaches her lips: hot, spiced red wine. She sips, taking it all in: the stalls with their trinkets for sale, the jewellery, teas and spices, traditional decorations and scented candles and salt lamps. It's mesmerising, and so unlike anything she could reasonably expect to see at home. For her first time in Germany, she isn't disappointed, and as she drains her glass and lets the liquid warm from her throat to the lower part of her belly, Evie finds herself breathing deeply and smiling at strangers as they pass.

Maybe this is going to do me good, she thinks, letting herself acknowledge the moment.

Purchasing another *Glühwein* for the road, she heads back to the hotel. She can do this. She can enjoy the country if this is what it is like. She's not even tired right now – the walk has blown away the proverbial cobwebs.

Yeah.

She's okay.

Her room, when it is ready, is clean and pretty spacious, and she puts on a playlist and unpacks half of her things. The cast and crew will be moving several times over the coming weeks – literally heading down Bavaria's Romantic Road – so it's pointless putting *everything* away. But she finds a home for her toiletries and anything that would crease otherwise, figures out where her nightwear is, finds a sleep mist she likes to use and her work stuff: laptop and charger, notebook, diary, a folder with ideas and research that isn't exclusive to only this project, but more her writing life in general. She keeps anything that strikes her as interesting, without analysing the reason too much. Evie often finds the strangest things cropping up as she types, and it is almost always because she read or watched something about it weeks ago, stashed it away for later use and somewhere in the mental compost of her mind it has served to grow the first bud of a plotline.

As she plugs her phone in to charge, the screen lights up with a couple of missed calls from Carl, as well as texts from him, Magda, and her agent, Sabrina. Carl asks her to call him back, Magda is just checking in, and Sabrina has texted to tell Evie to check her emails asap about a cover brief the publishers are going with for her summer book next year.

She reads them all, one after the other, and then goes back to Carl's message. They hardly ever speak on the phone. Why would he ask her to do so all the way from Germany? Evie hadn't really thought they'd stay in touch at all whilst she is here. That isn't the sort of dynamic they have. When Carl went away for a month over the summer they didn't talk until he was back. Why would they? They're not boyfriend and girlfriend. They're . . . well, like she told Magda: it works for them.

'Hey,' says Evie when he picks up on the third FaceTime Audio ring. 'You okay?'

'Evie, heyyyy,' Carl says, and immediately Evie can tell he's stalling for time. She knows how this goes. His tone. Why can't men hide the pity in their voice when they're delivering a sucker punch? In her experience, both men and women lie: it just tends to be the men who can't keep a poker face about it. She braces for impact. Now she thinks about it, she knew even by dint of him asking for the call in the first place what is about to happen.

She waits for him to do whatever it is he has to do – presumably he's already at work, and doesn't want to talk at his desk. She frowns as she listens to him stand up, the creak of an office chair being rolled from underneath him, the squeak of a door opening and closing. Her gut is an unsettled gurgle, a twisty feeling like everything is pushing upwards and making it harder to breathe.

'Sorry about that,' he says. 'Wanted to slip into a meeting room.'

'Say what you have to say, Carl,' Evie instructs, because she needs to get this over with. They aren't together, so they aren't officially breaking up, but her cheeks burn hot at the imminent rejection.

'Eves,' Carl says, and it's obvious this is a pre-planned speech. Evie stands at the window to her hotel in stocking feet, watching couples hold hands and families laugh at each other's jokes down below. 'You're amazing. Spending time with you is amazing. And I am very, very fond of you.'

Evie cringes at the word *fond*, but doesn't speak. She daren't.

'But . . . I've met someone. And she wants what I want. Something more than . . .'

'I get it,' Evie interrupts. 'Don't worry.'

I hate this, she thinks. *I hate this, I hate this, I hate this.* This is why she doesn't do commitment. Because even when she's only half in, it stings. Imagine the pain if she played to win? Urgh. Not worth it. Not worth it at all.

'Well,' Carl says. 'Just let me—'

'No, no,' insists Evie. She's not going to cry on the line with him. She's not actually going to let herself cry at all. That's the whole point of having *an arrangement*. Precisely because you can't cry over a thing that wasn't ever *something*. 'You're fine.' She makes it come out bright, sing-songy. 'I appreciate you telling me. I've enjoyed spending time with you too.'

'I wanted to tell you before you left, but then we didn't get to see each other and—'

'You're *fine*,' Evie repeats. 'Honestly. Godspeed. No hard feelings.'

'Really?' says Carl, sounding unsure.

'Really,' says Evie, forcing herself to smile so the words sound more genuine than she feels. 'All the best.'

She hangs up, puts her boots back on, and heads down to the staff meeting, the festive Christmas bubble she had not ten minutes ago well and truly burst. Not that she's going to admit that to anyone, of course. Not even to herself.

4

Duke

The drive from Frankfurt to Würzburg takes just over ninety minutes, the dramatic sky lit up in swirling shades of fuchsia against impending darkness, like ink bleeding out on a party dress.

That was great, Carter texts him. *You're already up on the Daily Mail, TMZ and @DukesLewks,* the latter referencing his official superfan account that has almost as many followers as his official page. Carter has attached some links, but Duke isn't interested in clicking through. He's tired.

Daphne says she couldn't help falling in love with Brad, and she's sorry, but Duke can see plain as day that Brad won't ever leave his wife, a woman Duke has never met and who has kept a dignified silence through all of this. But, despite what he said for the cameras, Duke had fallen for Daphne. He's hurting, and he's at the edges of a thought that he's been used, somehow, that Daphne played make-believe for the sake of her own profile. (Urgh, that word again!) He pushes down the notion, afraid that if he thinks too hard on it, he'll never trust a soul again. He doesn't feel safe to be himself in business meetings or at industry lunches, doesn't take phone calls in cars or in the make-up chair – there's so much to keep his guard up against. But with Daphne, he let her in.

He thought she got it, understood how solitary this life is because she lives it too, and together they could form their own little world, just the two of them, an escape from being Daphne Diamond and Duke Carlisle. Together they could just be Daph and Duke, walking the dogs and getting coffee and playing records and board games at home, maybe learning to finally cook instead of having staff do it. But then, now he's thought about it, she *did* want to walk the red carpet together, and she *did* confirm their romance in an interview about her last movie, even though they'd barely been together a few weeks. They shared the same management, but surely if it was a ruse Duke would have been asked up front to be in on it – he's not so desperate for affection that he could be manipulated by a whole team of people. *They* work for *him*. Don't they?

He leaves Carter's text unanswered, as per his MO, and watches the motorway become the town. It's charming. Lots of pointy church roofs and chocolate-box-style buildings in yellows and reds, the lights of market-square Christmas trees twinkling off the river to give the whole place an angelic, magical feel. He catches glimpses of couples and families meandering through the side streets off the main drag, cradling steaming hot chocolates and brown paper bags of chestnuts, their breath visible as they laugh, their love a blanket from the cold. A woman lingers by a bridge, cradling a hot wine, her long blonde hair falling in waves over her shoulders. She looks wistful, pensive. In fact, she kind of looks like Evie Bird, the author of the book. He recognises her from a Google deep dive. He perks up at the sight of her. He can't wait to meet her.

And Duke can see why she set her book here. It's exactly where a person would want to wake up on December 1st, just in time for the festive season. Just as its name would indicate, it's impossibly romantic. Perfect for a person who isn't just *somebody*, but who *has* somebody too.

Duke heads straight to his room at the hotel, to see if his things have been safely unpacked. They have. He's in a suite, and he drops his carry-on in the office nook: computer, scripts his agent has sent to look through, his *On the Romantic Road* script and the accompanying book. He looks at the cover: a hand-drawn couple facing each other, his hair over his eyes, her leg kicked up behind her. They're on a bridge, the top of the cover darker than the middle, like a sort of blue ombre. Evie Bird's name sits at the top, and the title is blocky white characters: ON THE ROMANTIC ROAD. Above it is the strapline: *Love is a journey – is this one they will take together?* He sighs. Doing a romantic comedy was very deliberate: the Nineties classics have been having a renaissance, and where once an actor skipped the genre so as to be taken 'seriously', now everyone needs one in their wheelhouse. But even in his misery, he can see there is a deep-seated irony to the timing here.

There's a knock at the door. He looks through the peephole to see Daphne. She's biting her bottom lip, looking down at her hands. She does that – picks at her nails when she's nervous. It's her one bad habit. Duke has half a mind to pretend not to be in.

'Duke?' she says through the door, like she can sense him. Bugger. He takes a breath, steeling himself.

'Hello, Daphne,' Duke says as he opens it. She looks at him. Those eyes, man. Those eyes are why she's a star.

'I thought you might ignore me,' she says.

'I considered it.' Duke shrugs, and he wants to be serious and earnest, to reiterate, for the thousandth time, how upset he is, but then they hold eye contact and she does her half-smile and he mirrors it and then they're really smiling: awkwardly, but it's there. Not *in* love, but something like it. Friends.

'I just wanted to . . .' Daphne says, and then she looks around, down the corridor, to check there are no listening ears.

'Come in.' Duke steps back and she crosses the threshold. 'Should I call up for drinks?'

She takes in the room. They talked about this, once, because that's what Duke had loved about dating her: that she *got it.* They'd talked about empty, stark hotel rooms, how it can be awful, or brilliant. The blank canvas and new project are an opportunity to be somebody else: sometimes their best selves, sometimes their craziest or naughtiest selves. But when it goes the other way – when a project doesn't jive or drags or is riddled with problems – it's just lonely, and the hotel room is always the most obvious manifestation of that.

You don't always get a choice which way to play it. Duke suspects this hotel room will be the latter more than the former.

'Can we just raid the mini bar?' she asks, settling into an armchair facing the bed. He doesn't have to ask what she wants. He gets two glasses and locates two tiny vodkas.

'Thank you,' she says, when he hands it to her. She looks beautiful, as ever. Bright eyes and smooth skin and a sparkling, winning smile. And she doesn't want him. He can't speak first. He's begged already, when he found out about her affair. He promised himself that here, on the second part of the shoot in a brand-new country, he'd show himself a little more dignity.

'I wanted to . . .' she starts again, and then shakes her head. 'I don't know. Not clear the air, but . . . talk? If that's okay?'

'I let you in, didn't I?' he replies, but they're doing their half-smiles again, because neither can truly be mad at the other. In his imagination Duke can stay cross, but not in person.

'I don't want to insult you by repeating myself. I know I've had my fair share of airtime and I'm grateful you heard me out. I suppose it's just . . . you know. We were such good friends before, and I'd be so sad to lose that. We tried being together and it didn't work, and we have to work together for another three weeks, you know? And after that we have to promote the thing, and I'll bet you get your nomination at the Globes so then there's the awards circuit in the new year . . .'

He looks at her. He blinks. 'I just need some time,' he says eventually, picking his words carefully. 'You say we weren't suited but . . .' He trails off, the silence leaving room for what he's said before. He thought this was it. Isn't that the dream? To finally realise your friend is the one you've been looking for this whole time. After twelve years of knowing her, he'd thought it had all worked out like it was supposed to: the picture-perfect love story for the picture-perfect couple. But he'd been wrong. The thing is, Daphne knows him better than anyone in the world, and so if she thinks it isn't right, he gets that he's supposed to listen. It's just . . . God. It's so hard. He hates being single. He loves love! It's the best thing in the world! And it keeps eluding him.

'This is messy – I understand that,' Daphne says. 'But when you're ready . . . I'd like us to try and be what we were. Before.'

He nods. 'Before,' he echoes.

'I think we can,' she offers. 'If we try.'

He drains his glass. 'You're taking advantage of the fact I can't ever stay mad at you,' he notes, and she winks at him, a risk that pays off.

'Only partly.' She grins, and when Duke pulls a face, she concedes: 'Okay. A bit more than partly.'

'Time,' he repeats. 'I'm not mad so much as . . . sad. I wish it could have been different.'

'I know,' she agrees. 'But I also know there's a huge love out there for you, far bigger and brighter and happier than anything we could have had. I'm never wrong . . .'

Duke rolls his eyes in spite of himself.

'On this occasion,' he admits. 'I really hope not.'

'I've got a feeling,' Daphne tells him, standing up to leave, 'that a great love is right around the corner for you.'

5

Evie

Evie hears his arrival at the team meeting before she sees anything of him. The small crowd of surprisingly middle-aged women who had assembled by the doors of their hotel start to murmur and then whoop, crescendoing with cries of *Duke! Duke!* as he (presumably) exits the lift that faces directly onto the glass-fronted exit.

They probably think he's leaving the hotel again – and she can hear the disappointed mumbles as he instead swerves into the very room she's sitting in. Sat around a large table in a space just off the hotel lobby that's been designated to the crew for meetings, Evie half-cranes her neck before turning back to her coffee as he enters. She spoons the foam into her mouth and arranges her features into as disinterested a portrait as she can manage. Celebrity does not faze her. Being here, in this circus, does not faze her. She's supposed to be at home in Utah, working on her next book, her only concerns being Doctor Dolittle's two daily walks and whether to use the ristretto coffee capsule in her Nespresso or the Treviso.

All of this is the opposite of what makes her heart sing. Evie truly believes that wanting to be famous is akin to a mental dysfunction. She doesn't even use a recent photo of herself on her books anymore, such is her desire to stay under the radar. Evie Bird likes to craft stories that sell, pick up her paycheque, and then get on with her life unencumbered. She loves her work but won't be defined by it, and honestly thinks it's unsettling when people are. When did everyone get job titles over personalities?

'Hey, Duke, my main man, welcome,' says Marnie, the head of production, as the noise outside peaks and then suddenly stops. Duke is surprisingly small, Evie thinks. Hasn't she heard that somewhere? That most actors are shorter than we assume? But God, he *is* handsome: all sharp jawline and honed, glistening arms. That much is undeniable.

Evie doesn't get up, and catches the eye of Daphne, the film's female lead, who also remains seated, casting her gaze down guiltily at her hands. She looks up just in time for her to spot that Evie is watching and gives an embarrassed half-smile. Evie gives a half-smile back.

'Evening all,' Duke says, pulling off a baseball cap and running a hand through his infamously shaggy locks. He's very aware of himself, Evie thinks, watching him as he greets everyone individually and by name – even Daphne. Though she doesn't pay much attention to the headlines, Evie has been filled in about the Daphne-Duke-Director love triangle by the director of photography, who – in the space of one afternoon – has thawed Evie's resolve not to make any friends. Katerina, her name is. Evie has decided she'll be her one ally. She can get through the next three weeks with one ally, easy.

'Oh goodness,' Duke says then, finally reaching her. Evie stands, in spite of herself. She doesn't want to appear deferential or star-struck, but to stay seated would be outright rude. He's actually taller than she thought at first, so she's tipping her chin upwards to see him. And those eyes? Okay, fine. Evie can understand why those eyes get talked about like he's the second coming. But she gets the sense that he knows that too. How can he not? The only thing worse than the trouble a handsome man brings is a handsome man who knows it. That's *double* the trouble.

'Evie? Honestly, can I please tell you right now, I am an incredibly huge fan of yours. I'm so honoured to be able to feature in this adaptation. Truly.' Duke puts his hand to his chest then, as if his heart cannot lie. Evie understands that in showbiz blowing smoke up one another's self-congratulatory asses is par for the course, so she magnanimously chooses not to test him on his alleged fandom and instead tells him he's very kind. She wants this over as quickly as possible.

'I can tell you don't believe me,' he says, doubling down. 'But seriously, I've read all of your books. All sixteen of them. I even have *Half Your Life* on preorder for next May,' he adds, referring to her next release. He must have had his people create a crib sheet on her or something, charming her in case she can be useful to him at some point.

'Well,' Evie says, not breaking the eye contact this man

seems hellbent on maintaining. 'I'm afraid I'd never heard of you before all this.'

Everyone laughs like it's a joke, because, as Evie now knows, Duke is one of the most bankable and lusted-after stars in Hollywood – apparently all that English self-depreciation and the dazzling blue-eyed thing have charmed both his home country and hers. He did a remake of *10 Things I Hate About You*, Magda had explained, with a topless scene coming out of a swimming pool that was made into a meme that went viral. Evie doesn't run her own social media because she has to write two books a year and has found that when you write about love and matters of the heart, people like to confide in you. It's a burden she has no bandwidth for right now, not with everything else in her life – her mother, her father, the shopping habit that she really ought to sort out soon . . . the list goes on. She'd gotten in trouble with her publisher for going on a podcast and admitting that she doesn't even believe in love, and that anyone who messages her for advice is barking up the wrong tree in terms of a sympathetic ear. But nobody here knows any of this, of course, and assume she's as much of a fan as the next girl – and as much of a romantic as the next girl, too.

'Never heard of me? Well, pleased to hear it.' Duke grins, apparently assuming it's a joke too. 'Ghastly business, all this. Ego central, you see.' Evie notices the straightness of his teeth, their bright white colour. *I thought the English didn't have good teeth*, she muses, surprising herself that she knows anything about British dentistry. Where has she been keeping that useless titbit?

Evie exhales as everyone takes a seat, and puts in another

drink order – nobody has alcohol, so Evie doesn't order any either. She takes another coffee. She'll order a red wine up to her room later, she thinks, or maybe a bottle. She feels eyes on the back of her head and turns to see Duke has picked the spot right behind her shoulder. He smiles at her. She looks away.

'So here we are,' Marnie begins. 'Welcome to part two of *On the Romantic Road*. Internal shots at Pinewood were a massive success, and that's in no small part because of the source material Evie Bird wrote – welcome, Evie, to the continuation of our little movie shoot here.'

Everyone titters, because the little movie shoot is costing twenty-five million dollars, give or take, and one by one the folks around the room give Evie a little nod of acknowledgement. She feels compelled to pipe up: 'Veronique did a great job with the script. It's all her.' They applaud Veronique, even though she's not here. Apparently she had a disagreement with the director and refused to fly in – or so Katerina said. Evie doesn't know her personally, but they did have a couple of Skype calls as Veronique worked on the adaptation. Evie wasn't precious about it – she gave her express permission for the practised screenwriter to take whatever creative licence she needed to.

'We're already in editing with what we have, since, as you know the promotion of the movie has been moved up to capture the summer preview circuit for a big Thanksgiving release. We'd also like to capitalise on the fact that *On the Romantic Road* has just entered the *New York Times* bestseller list at number three, which is, I believe, the highest charting you've had yet, Evie, right?'

Evie did not know this. She fights the urge to grab her phone from where it is face-down on the table beside her, to check her emails and see if her agent or editor can verify. Has a five-year-old book really gone into the chart? That feels impossible. Instead, she just offers a brief nod. She doesn't want to create a scene.

'You've all got what you need in your rooms already in terms of info sheets. We're booked out here, so it's just us. Everyone has a per diem spend for food and drinks, and there's security on the door and on each floor. I'm sure you're aware, but so we're all on the same page, the objective for these exterior shots here on location, here on the actual Romantic Road, is to capture the fairy-tale-like enchantment of the place. Duke and Daphne are doing a superb job as George and Hermione, with such chemistry and fondness in the early edits. Everything we need to shoot outside, here, is to really hammer home the *feeling* of what we're creating. The weather is cold – I'm told we're expecting snow – but what we want to make people feel is the *warmth* of this story. The Christmas markets, the lights, the hot chocolates and carols and these magnificent castles that just seem to be everywhere . . . folks should watch this movie and, yeah, fall in love with George and Hermione, but we also want them to fall in love with Bavaria. Germany is the third character in this love story.'

'I'm about halfway in love already,' Duke leans in to whisper in Evie's ear. 'I might even see if I can go out for a walk, later, if you want in.'

Evie gives him a polite smile that is non-committal. Why does he keep trying to charm her? Surely he has bigger fish

39

to fry, the egomaniac. She mostly just wants that wine, in bed, ready to doze off in a slightly buzzed slumber before the criminal wake-up call of 5 a.m. tomorrow. Why she has to get up that early she doesn't know – something about cast morale?

Milling around are about a hundred of the team, and after their meeting Evie makes polite chit-chat as a buffet is unveiled. It's not a *bad* gig, per se, being in Germany on somebody else's dime, staying in a fancy hotel and being fed and watered, it's just her deadline really is looming. She looks at her watch. Maybe she can get a thousand words in before bed.

'I *have* to get you to sign my copy of *Once in a Blue Moon*,' Duke tells her, as she heads back to the buffet table for more poached salmon. He might have even been waiting for her, the creep. He's too eager to please. Too chirpy. It smacks of inauthenticity. 'If you don't mind,' he adds, noting the look on her face.

Evie loads up her plate. 'It's okay,' she tells him. 'Nobody else can hear.'

He blinks.

'You don't have to pretend with me,' Evie clarifies. 'You don't have to kiss my ass?'

Duke nods. 'Ah,' he says. 'You think I'm just saying I like your work because . . . I'm in it?'

'I don't know why,' Evie replies, looking for the herby hollandaise she had earlier. It was delicious. There was lemon in it, capers too, but something else, something she couldn't put her finger on.

'I understand,' Duke says, picking up the bowl she was

looking for like he can read her mind. He offers it up as if to say, *this?* and Evie begrudgingly reaches for the serving spoon to drizzle some onto her plate. 'Why would a bloke be reading romantic comedies in his spare time? Well . . .' he says, setting the bowl back down when she's done. 'It just so happens I'm an unabashed idealist, and I was once on holiday with Adele, who had brought along your *No Stopping Us*, and it got me hooked. She adored it, and so I read it too, my gateway drug. You write about people who meet and fall in love, yes, but there's so much more. You have them end up so wise, and it makes me think that you must be wise. Do you get that a lot?'

'Not really,' Evie tells him, just about raising an eyebrow in amusement. *Of course* he's name-dropping who he goes on holiday with. She supposes Harry Styles must have been there too, maybe Denzel Washington and Dolly Parton. Ridiculous. 'Truly, you don't have to do this. I write boy-meets-girl, boy-and-girl-suffer-setbacks, boy-and-girl-live-happily-ever-after books. "Heteronormative nonsense that could be sorted out with a proper conversation." That's what one particularly memorable Amazon review said.'

'HEA, isn't it? Happily-ever-after is HEA? Isn't that what they say?'

'Exactly.' Evie nods. 'I write HEAs and it gives people a day or two's escape from the real world. But you and I both know half of what I write about doesn't exist. Eighty per cent, even. What I write is as much fantasy as a *Star Wars* movie.'

'You don't believe in a happily-ever-after?' Duke asks her, crinkling his brow in a suspiciously unlined sort of a way.

'Of course not,' Evie retorts, grabbing another bread roll and deciding that, actually, she will have a glass of wine now. 'I'm a grown-up, and adulthood sucks. Life isn't an Ed Sheeran song and a mad dash to the airport to stop somebody getting on a flight. But that wouldn't be a very comforting read, would it?' she asks rhetorically. 'Now, if you'll excuse me.'

She squeezes by him, half-noting his woody scent but mostly just wanting to *not* be playing at networking when she's hungry and still ruminating over Carl and her mother's fall and the fact that she's been awake for many, many hours now.

'Jesus,' she hears Duke mutter as she settles into a seat beside Katerina. 'She's a ray of sunshine, isn't she?'

Evie doesn't give him the satisfaction of letting him know she's heard, and instead tucks into her salmon.

6

Duke

It's dark, it's incredibly early, and the twinkling lights of a lone Christmas tree in the hotel window are currently the only thing switched on to mark the first day of December. Duke sees Evie linger by the door of the hotel and only realises he's been waiting for her to arrive when he feels a lump of disappointment rising in his throat when she doesn't come near him, a feeling of *oh, she's not coming down this way*.

She was rude last night, standoffish. Duke isn't used to people giving him a hard time, which is something else he hadn't realised until after she'd walked away from him at the meeting. He couldn't stand to think she didn't like him, somehow. He wanted to impress her. When he'd read *No Stopping Us*, her book about two terminally ill patients who meet at a cancer support group and decide to make a bucket list of things to do before they die – falling in love along the way – he'd laughed out loud and shed actual tears. That had never happened with a book before. He's been low-key obsessed with Evie Bird's work ever since, and that she's here, on set, is something he's been so excited about. He wants to grab a drink and ask her a million questions. Duke has been fiddling about with a novel of his own, actually, although it's not very good. Anyway, he's hoping for a do-over. Maybe she was jet-lagged yesterday, or overwhelmed. We all have bad days.

Duke pretends to scroll on his phone from where he's stood by the cast and crew bus, bundled up in a coat and Ugg boots and a woolly hat with a bobble on top, looking up surreptitiously to see she's obviously choosing to hang back so that she doesn't have to talk to anyone – he watches the calculation in her eyes, how she sweeps over who is stood where, their proximity to the vehicle, and then casting back to see who is coming out of the door just at her shoulder. His feet start moving in her direction before his head has computed any sort of plan. He looks right at her: hair loose but tucked into a checked cashmere scarf, her breath making clouds as she exhales into the cold. *It really was you on the bridge yesterday,* he thinks, her expression suddenly familiar.

Evie looks up, and he points to the hotel door, opens his mouth and says, barely forming words: 'I just forgot my . . .' He trails off, cursing himself inwardly. Why is he acting so nervous? This doesn't make sense. He hasn't forgotten anything. He wants *her*!

In response, Evie lifts her eyebrows as if to say, *sure, whatever,* and looks back down. Duke grabs the door as the lighting director comes through it from the other side, ostensibly to head inside for the pretend thing he's 'forgotten' before he changes his mind.

'That's a lie,' he finds himself admitting (what is his problem?!), and she looks up again. Her eyes – brown, very dark brown – shift from side to side, like she's confused as to who he is talking to. *Okay then.* She's going to continue to make this hard. *Got it,* thinks Duke. *But I can overcome this.*

'I just wanted to come and talk to you.' Duke smiles, and when she understands he really does mean to address her she creases up her face, bemused.

'I feel like we didn't get off to a great start last night and you were stood here by yourself, so—'

'I'm just trying to get some work done,' she interjects, shrugging. She doesn't say it harshly or nastily, she just . . . says it.

'Oh.' Duke nods. 'Sorry.'

She looks at him again and then continues typing into her phone. He doesn't intend to look over at her screen, but he must have done because his head casts a shadow over her phone so she looks up again.

'Seriously?' she asks him, taking a step back.

He's really messing this up. Again.

'No, sorry, I didn't mean to be nosy. God. You make me nervous. Have you ever been told that before? That you're intimidating?'

She doesn't look up as she says, 'I think that sounds like a *you* problem, not a *me* problem.'

'Right.' Duke nods again. 'Sure. Okay. Well, not a morning person, I see.'

45

He doesn't move. He's gone from wanting to establish some kind of rapport to feeling like *what the hell?* In less than thirty seconds. Is she really not going to even feign niceness? She doesn't even know him; how can she *not like him*? She must be like this with everyone. He feels like he's been conned, somehow. This frostiness is not a character trait that comes across in her work.

'Look,' Evie says, finally casting her eyes back over him. 'I'm sorry, okay? I'm dealing with a ton of stuff here, and I haven't had coffee yet, and I just need to, like, make it to midday and then maybe I can give you the old razzle-dazzle or whatever it is you need from me to stop you from looking like I just stepped on your puppy. I apologise for being . . .'

'Rude,' Duke supplies, when it seems like she can't settle on the word. He doesn't mean to be combative. It's just, well . . . It's the only word that fits.

'Er,' Evie muses. 'I haven't been *rude*.'

'Somebody tries to come talk to you and you tell them to get stuffed? Seems pretty rude to me.'

'Says the man who thinks he's *owed* a woman's attention?'

'I don't think I'm owed anything,' Duke counters. 'I came to try and right our little . . . *interaction* . . . from last night, because we're working together, and it seems like the right thing to do. But I can tell that has somehow rubbed you up the wrong way, and so you're right, you don't owe me your attention. I will back away slowly, now . . .'

He holds up his hands in surrender, shaking his head and heading back towards the bus. Jeez. Some people are just obviously better on the page than they are in person. That's fine. He's misjudged her.

'No,' she says, pulling a face. 'You don't get to make this—' she gestures between them as she speaks '—*my* fault. *I'm* not difficult. *You* are too . . . too . . . *fake*.'

This is ludicrous. Are they really arguing right now? Duke is aware of people starting to look in their direction.

'People are staring,' Duke says, contorting his face into a smile and speaking through somewhat gritted teeth. 'Can we not?'

Evie looks around and seems to take note of the glances in their direction, looking back at Duke and mirroring his pasted-on 'smile'.

Through equally gritted teeth Evie says, 'Let's just call this quits, shall we? Leave each other alone? Like I said last night, we don't have to be besties.'

Duke shrugs, realises it looks hostile to the last of the lingering eyes on him, and so opens out his arms so that his body language seems more congenial. Evie looks at him, horrified, and then inserts herself, putting her arms under his in an awkward collision of their angry bodies. They are hugging, now. They are grimacing and hugging and talking in hushed, snatched whispers.

'Weird,' Evie quietly says, after she's pulled away and folks have started to file into the bus, ready to go to set. She doesn't look at him, but at the ground.

'Super weird,' Duke echoes, letting her walk in front of him as he tries to figure out what the hell just happened. They went from snapping to hugging? In the blink of an eye? Bizarre. She's mercurial, this author. Duke finds himself breathing shallower, unnerved.

Putting as much distance between himself and Evie as he

can, Duke lets a few others onto the coach ahead of him, and then clambers up the steps himself. The thing is packed, a sea of tired faces staring blearily into their phones, so he looks down to his immediate left at the seat behind the driver, the only seat free on the bus. In the neighbouring seat, Evie looks up at him, stony-faced, and then back down at her phone. He sighs and sits beside her. They do not talk. Duke half leans into the aisle to avoid accidentally brushing up against her. He holds himself as rigidly as he can as the bus takes bend after bend through the Bavarian streets.

When they finally pull up at their destination and the doors open, Duke flings himself down the steps to the safety of the land, confused as to how a silence between two people can feel so wordlessly aggressive. He decides, then, to leave her well alone. What a mistake trying to befriend her has been. He's practically got frostbite from her cold-hearted attitude.

7

Evie

The sky turns pink at about six thirty. Houses and shops have orangey glows in upstairs windows, lights turning on one by one, as people begin to wake up and start their days. The river running through the town reflects all of it, a mirror to a thousand lives happening all around them. It is quiet, punctured only with occasional birdsong from little robin redbreasts perching on icy gates kissed by Jack Frost in the night. Evie blows into her gloved hands, her breath visible like a dragon's, and then rubs them together. She's *freezing*.

'Take two,' the director, Brad, says, as somebody with a clapper board snaps it open, closed, then steps away from the camera. Duke and Daphne are in character as George and Hermione. Her heroine is in layered cream knitwear, a lavender scarf and bobble hat with matching mittens – accents of gold jewellery twinkling in the soft light. Her long hair is lightly curled in a way that could be accidental, but Evie saw her call time and knows for a fact she had two hours in hair and make-up.

Looking through one of the monitors it's incredible to Evie how it all works. She'd sworn to herself that she wouldn't let herself be overly impressed, but she has to admit this *is* cool. George and Hermione started out as thoughts in her head, when she was sat at her kitchen table in her pyjamas. And now here they are, walking and talking in exactly the ways she had decided they would walk and talk, a hundred people around them making sure it all goes to plan. She wishes her mom could see this. Evie snaps a photo, but deep down she knows her mom won't fully understand what she's saying when she tries to explain. Not unless it's an especially rare lucid day. There's a Christmas miracle Evie wouldn't mind. She won't hold out for it though. She knows better.

'I don't know,' Duke says in character as George, the collar of his navy peacoat turned up against the back of his neck, a new golden sheen to his forehead that must be make-up but comes off as sun-kissed on camera. Evie doesn't hate him when he's in character. George isn't Duke, and so it's easier to watch in awe. 'It's what I promised my mother and every time I think I'm ready to break that promise I see her face. I can't do that to her, Hermione. I just can't.'

They walk slowly along the wide street that's been cordoned off until 8 a.m. for filming, a camerawoman capturing it all as a man in a puffer jacket walks slowly backwards, pulling her along a train track that means she can keep them smoothly in frame as they move. Everyone is under strict instructions to work fast and use as few takes as possible, because there just isn't the time. Three weeks is a tight shoot, she's been told, and they've got a mountain of restrictions around filming times and locations because of the time of year. Southern Germany wants the movie made here, but not at the cost of annoying their tourists.

The actors pause in front of a small shop window.

'You see that ring there?' 'George' asks 'Hermione', and Evie holds her breath as he does. *She wrote these words.* It's crazy. 'She had one just like it. I wish you could have known her, Herm. I really do. My dad gave it to her after he came back. These little things that remind us – they're everywhere, aren't they?'

It's Daphne's turn to speak. 'George,' she says, and her voice is different than it is in real life. Evie doesn't know why that surprises her, but it does. 'Your capacity to romanticise the past astounds me. It's what makes me love you like I do. But can't you look forward, too? Because the past is over with, and I'm stood right here asking you to think of a future.'

Evie winces at the sentimentality. Those words haunt her, because she spoke them herself, once; the last nail in the coffin of a thing called hope. Back in her twenties her ex, Bobby, had truly broken her heart, but he was one in a long line of heartbreaks, starting with the moment that as a fifteen-year-old teenager she watched her dad pull out of the drive with two suitcases and his raging temper. Having him in the house had been hell, in many ways, because he seemed to resent that although he was *Donald Gilbert, famous screen-writer and director,* out there in the world, in the house he was just dad. It was like Evie and her mom weren't enough for him, like he needed to not only be loved but revered. So he left, ran into the arms of one of his actresses, then left her for another one.

The only time Evie has seen him since is in the occasional arts section magazine feature. Every other man she's tried to love since then has done the exact same thing. They always do, Evie understands. It's just a case of when.

She watches Duke finish out his scene and feels a pang of guilt. She crossed a line with him this morning and the shame of it burns behind her ears, even if she doesn't like him. He was only trying to be nice, smarmy as he might otherwise be. Evie doesn't have to make every man pay for the dismal actions of a few, but Magda has dared suggest she seems committed to trying. No. He might be an actor, but he's not the devil. She should have been kinder. She can't explain why she was so atrociously discourteous to him, only that she was. She feels silly about it, now. Maybe it's the jet lag. Maybe it's the niggling feeling that she's wasting time, here, that she should be writing. Her work can often be like that, reminding her even on a weekend or public holiday that there's still more to be done. Being an author is like forever having outstanding homework.

'And cut,' Brad says, pulling her out of her thoughts. She's missed the climax of the scene. Everyone disperses as the next one is set up. They don't need another take – the second one got it just great. Evie sees craft services setting out a fresh batch of hot drinks and heads over, desperate to warm up.

'Hey. You okay?' Katerina asks her. Evie didn't see her there. She looks up, her vision a bit blurred. She blinks her eyes and realises she's welled up.

'It's the cold,' Evie says, and she almost sounds convincing.

'I don't think I factored in wind-chill when I was getting dressed this morning.'

Katerina takes off her earmuffs and gives them to her. 'Here,' she says. 'Wear these for a while.' When Evie protests, she insists. 'Honestly, I don't need them. I think I have a hat in my bag and this gilet is battery-powered, too. I'm toasty warm. Plus, these will make you look cute for the socials team.'

Later, when they find her, the socials team agree. Two early twenty-somethings, Dream and Willow, have been tasked with behind-the-scenes interviews, wardrobe looks, cast and crew Q&As, the works.

'Make-up say they've got time for you if you want,' Willow-or-Dream offers.

'I'm wearing make-up,' Evie says.

Willow-or-Dream tilts her head to one side, like she doesn't understand. 'Hmmm,' she says. 'Maybe just get them to warm up your complexion a bit, widen your eyes? And let's see if wardrobe can lend you something to break up your coat colour against your skin.'

'What's wrong with the coat colour against my skin?' Evie asks. She feels attacked. 'This is a good coat. It was expensive.'

Of course it was. Her shopping habit is why she can't get the roof of her house fixed. Or help her mom more. Things can't love her back, but they also can't leave, can't disappoint her.

'No, yeah, I get it, totally, black is, like, super versatile for, like, being out and about in the cold or whatever, but I'd say you're maybe a warm autumn? So maybe a lighter brown colour, or a red? Navy even would be great. Then you won't look as washed out.'

Washed out! Evie thinks, but then Willow-or-Dream is already leading her by the wrist towards a couple of trailers cordoned off by a small park area. They knock, wait, and then get invited inside. To Evie's dismay, Duke is in there, and she steels herself to at least smile at him, to literally grin and bear it.

'I'll be okay,' he's saying. 'I'm happy for her, I am. It's cool. Oh . . .' he interrupts himself when he sees Evie.

Evie raises a hand. 'Duke.'

'Evie.'

'Oh!' says Kayla, the make-up artist. 'You're Evie! Amazing! Duke has just been telling us about your book, haven't you?'

Duke looks down with a shrug.

'Called you an author extraordinaire!' Kayla claims, oblivious, apparently, to the frost emanating off them.

Evie narrows her eyes. Are they all making fun of her? She looks from Kayla to Duke in the mirror. He pulls a face that she can't quite grasp the meaning of.

'I just said I liked *You and Me and Us*,' he says, slowly, like he's afraid Evie will yell at him again. 'The ending, especially. You make it seem like everyone is getting everything they've ever wanted but there's a sadness there, too, something bittersweet. That's all.'

He catches her eye for a beat and then looks away. Fair enough, Evie thinks, she really did give him a hard time earlier. And last night. She tentatively offers him something to work with, her way of saying sorry without actually saying sorry.

'Yeah,' she acknowledges. 'Because life doesn't work like that, does it?'

'That's what my therapist says,' Duke quips to the room. Kayla laughs. He continues, looking at Evie more confidently, now: 'That there's no arrival point. The only ending is death, and even then it's the start of something new.'

Evie nods. That's pretty much exactly how she feels. Did he really come up with that analysis of her stuff himself? Surely not.

'Ha,' he says, then. 'God, listen to me, yakking on and on. I don't know how much time you've spent in the make-up chair but Kayla will tell you: I talk a lot trying to keep from falling asleep, don't I? This job isn't a shift down the mines, but they *are* long days.' He yawns for effect, and it strikes Evie as self-conscious, as if he's given her more than he intended to and he's trying to double back.

Kayla laughs again as she does something to his jawline, charmed, and says in her South African lilt: 'I love our chats, Duke. You know that.' And then to Evie: 'He's lending me your book. I'm excited to read it. Do you want to take a seat?'

'Thanks,' Evie mutters, adding: 'They say you need to warm up my complexion.' Kayla motions her over to the chair beside Duke.

'I can do that,' Kayla says. 'I just need two more minutes with Mr Carlisle here and then we're good to go.'

Willow-or-Dream leaves, and Evie takes off her coat to sit back in the make-up chair facing the mirror. She's opposite Duke, and their reflections mean they immediately have eye contact. Evie notices how extraordinarily symmetrical he is, how angular his features are. In contrast she seems doughy and pale. The strip lighting of the trailer doesn't even dim his handsomeness, let alone eclipse it.

'Don't say anything about my eye bags,' Duke jokes, noticing her notice. He says it tentatively, double-checking that she has indeed thawed out and it's okay to converse. Evie gives him her renowned closed-mouth smile, the best she can manage. It's her way of saying: *Fine. Let's tolerate each other whilst we have to sit side by side. Again.* 'Kayla has done her best, haven't you? I'm just not sleeping well right now. Diet, exercise, make-up, it can do a lot, but nothing hides a lack of quality REM does it?'

Evie is unsure if it's a rhetorical question or meant for her and Kayla.

'You look . . . great,' she says. It sounds hollow. She feels his eyes roam her face, perhaps in appraisal of her own eye bags, evidence of that jet lag. She swallows, unsure of the feeling in her stomach as he gives her the once-over, and before she can think of anything witty to say Kayla announces that she's done and he's free to go. There's a knock on the door and a woman in a headset with a clipboard says there's five minutes to go, although to what she doesn't specify. Presumably the next shot, Evie thinks. There's so much happening, so much action and movement and activity all the time, just like she remembers from her childhood.

'So,' Duke presses, lingering behind her as Kayla stuffs white tissues into the collar of Evie's jumper.

'To catch the excess,' Kayla explains.

Evie takes a beat to understand he's addressing her again.

'It's your first day on a set?' he says. 'Katerina said.'

Had he really been talking about her? Odd.

'Pretty magical, isn't it?' he continues.

Evie narrows her eyes. She goes to speak, realises she

doesn't know what to say, and closes her mouth again. Then she takes a breath, seeing him awaiting her words, and settles on: 'Yup. This little old nobody can't believe she's here.'

She's trying to sound gently mocking of herself. Duke issues a heightened guffaw. God, whatever energy is between them, it can definitely be filed under *Does Not Work*. No matter how hard either of them tries, they seem to speak different languages, miss the point of one another.

'You do know it's *your* book we're filming here, don't you?' he asks, one eyebrow raised just enough to be infuriating in its cockiness. 'I hardly think you're a nobody.'

'No, you misunderstand me,' Evie says, regulating her voice to sound calm and rational. 'I *like* being a nobody. I *want* to be a nobody. I'm not here on set because I want to hobnob with the stars. I'm only here because of a contractual obligation.'

Duke nods. He's got the smoothest, cleanest-looking skin Evie has ever seen, like a real-life Ken doll but somehow even more attractive.

'Yeah,' Duke tells her. 'I know. I asked them to put that in. I wanted to meet you.'

Evie blinks.

What?

'*You* made them bring me out here?' she asks. That doesn't make sense. Why would he do that?

'Yeah,' Duke tells her, like it's no big deal. 'Like I say, I'm a really big fan.'

WHAT! Evie sees a red mist, her temper going from nought to a hundred.

'I'm missing my deadline,' she says, the control she had managed before ebbing away with speed. 'Away from my dog,

57

and my house, and my mother and my best friend who happens to be going through a very horrible divorce, at Christmastime, to freeze my ass off on the other side of the world because of *you*?'

Duke gives a little laugh that Evie assumes he thinks is self-effacing.

'Well, yeah. I wanted to meet you, and everyone said you were up for the interviews and the behind-the-scenes documentary . . .' he says, slowly, still acting like this is all one big rational conversation and not the start of the apocalypse. Evie is already getting out of the make-up chair.

'Thank you, Kayla, but I'm all set on the glow. I'm sure I've got more *colour* to my *complexion*—' she says 'complexion' with air quotes '—now that I am *furious*.'

She turns her attention back to Duke.

'You *made* them fly me out here?'

He nods, seemingly unsure of why that's an issue, which only serves to make her even more irate.

'The rest of the world isn't a puppet for you, you know,' she spits, flabbergasted.

She's been building some anger for a while, now, ever since the call from the care home about her mom's fees going up right before she got on the flight. She's been wanting to yell at somebody. She can't yell at her mom. Or Carl. So it may as well be Duke Asshat Carlisle. She's almost grateful to him for providing the opportunity. 'That's so *horrible*. If you want to meet somebody you write an email and *ask*. You don't make it a contractual obligation, like you're Christian Goddamn Grey!'

Duke winces, and Evie swears he's trying to give her a

comic touch. 'Sore subject, that,' he says. 'I just missed out on that role. Bloody Jamie Dornan.'

Evie closes her eyes. He's insane. Actually certifiable. Cracking jokes in the face of her very warranted anger? She shakes her head at him as she tries to put on her coat. She misses the arm and he takes it from her, standing behind her and coolly helping her to put it on as she keeps up the momentum of her rant.

'Thank you,' she says, snatching the material away from him as he moves to try and help her zip up. She does it herself, hurriedly, so fast it almost breaks, then adds: 'I hope it's been amazing to have me here as per your summons, oh godly one, but contract or not, I'm going home. See ya.'

She stumbles down the narrow steps of the trailer as she flounces down them, not sure why she's gone off the handle with *quite* so much vigour except Jesus: she's so over this Duke guy. Screw him. Screw this whole stupid thing. She should never have agreed to it. She'll find the care home money another way – *any other* way. A man like Duke can't just say jump.

She styles out her misstep and slams the door behind her.

Duke Carlisle is an egocentric jackass, she thinks to herself, trying to figure out which way it is back to the hotel. As she walks, she remembers how he helped her with her coat. *Urgh!*

8

Duke

It turns into a cloudless, bright-blue-sky day, and as the sun gets brighter it serves to melt away Duke's thoughts about Evie. It's been less than twenty-four hours and they've butted heads three times. Once can be forgiven, twice is unfortunate, but three strikes? Yeah. He's out.

For a moment it seemed like they might be able to turn things around in the trailer, and then she went postal on him, storming out. The woman is obviously unhinged. Duke had imagined she'd be like the characters in her books, but he's realised something else now: people who make art are seldom 'normal'. Evie must just be another one of those people-who-make-things. Actors, writers, artists, designers, musicians ... when you try to experience the world and then say something about the world, you have to have a paper-thin skin to let the world affect you, to let it run through you.

He's going to have to file Evie into the 'genius-but-volatile-and-unpredictable-with-it' category.

Even though it's freezing the sun shines intensely, in the way it does in Europe. Duke loves his house in London – a rambling townhouse with real working fireplaces and dark, ssumptuously decorated rooms – but the city itself is hard for him. Obviously being British he wants a UK base, but he isn't in touch with his old school friends up north and all his industry friends are in LA, where he also keeps a home. He loves the sunshine there, and the way the weather so positively affects everyone's disposition. The weather in the UK is always somehow damp. In London, he always seems to have cold feet, like the water in the air permeates his bones. Sure, he's wearing thermal socks on set today, and thermal long johns under his costume, but it's not cold like it gets at home. It's crisp and clear, and it makes him feel . . . well, better about things. His broken heart seems less broken here, the change of scene helping to change the way he's thinking about what happened back at Pinewood.

They're set up in the marketplace beside the town hall. It's a wide, paved square with a terracotta-coloured fountain and ten-foot Christmas tree with white lights and a big gold star. Lights are strung through the trees dotted around, lit, despite it being daytime. The timber buildings are three storeys with wooden frames in red and black set against white walls. Everything goes smoothly, with the weather making everyone chirpy and efficient. They get what they need quickly, and Duke knows he's done a good job. He has to admit Daphne is still amazing to work opposite – she gives him a lot, and it means he can give a lot back. The chemistry doesn't have to be manufactured. His tentative okay-ness is sudden, a quick wind change, but since they spoke it's sunk in for him that he and Daphne might really be better as friends. He can see how that might be true.

She didn't have to shag the director, though.

If he's truly honest, his ego might take a bit longer to heal than his heart.

For all her bluster, Evie has returned to set. Duke is aware of her behind the monitors, catching glimpses of her between takes. She's got her sunglasses on now and looks ready for the slopes. Duke wonders if she does actually ski. He's spent time with Kate Hudson and her family in Aspen – they get on like a house on fire, and he loves Kurt and Goldie, they're a real laugh. They'd like Evie, understand her tortured-artist routine.

Okay, that's peculiar. Thinking about Evie on holiday with him is creepy.

He glances across to where she's stood again. She looks up. He turns away. Hmm. He's still going to give her a wide berth. Apparently she isn't off home like she threatened earlier, but still, their worlds should probably remain separate.

'Hey,' a voice says from behind him when they break for lunch. 'Hey!'

He turns. Evie. So much for that wide berth. He takes off his own sunglasses and sees immediately that she's mad. No surprises there, then. It's her default state.

'Hey, me?' he asks, incredulous.

'Have you seen this?' she asks, handing him her phone. It's a text thread, with the name Magda at the top. The last message says: *Erm, okay girl. Talk FAST please!!* Then there's a link to a gossip site. He takes off a glove and opens it. The headline reads: DUKE CARLISLE TAKES A WRONG TURN WITH EXPLOSIVE AUTHOR FIGHT ON THE SET OF *ON THE ROMANTIC ROAD*.

There's a series of photographs of them from six hours ago, outside the make-up trailer, with Evie gesticulating wildly and Duke looking half amused, half pissed off. He moves his body to shield the phone from the glare of the sun, and squints to read the piece:

Hollywood heartthrob Duke Carlisle was pictured having what appeared to be a heated exchange with a colleague on the set of his new movie today.

The Anywhere You Go *star, 37 – wowing in a snug grey tracksuit and form-fitting T-shirt – was said to have entered a war of words that ended in tears.*

Author Evie Bird, 36 – looking pale and unkempt in exclusive photographs taken just hours into filming on location in Würzburg, Germany – stormed out of a trailer after a blazing row, sources revealed. The movie in question is an adaptation of her romance novel On the Romantic Road, *with Duke playing lead character George.*

Handsome Duke clearly isn't known for keeping the ladies of his latest movie happy, as he's also fresh out of a break-up with his co-star Daphne Diamond. She was caught cavorting with married director Brad Beckonoff not long after filming in London commenced, and their affair is believed to be ongoing. Brad is married to Caterina Falange, and they have three young children.

Tension is alleged to be high with bad blood between

*all the stars on set, with Duke working under the man
who stole his girlfriend, the ex who spurned him, and
now the author he just can't seem to get along with.*

*Evie Bird is no stranger to explosive sets herself, raised
in Hollywood by esteemed writer-director and now
estranged father Donald Gilbert. Gilbert was fired as head
writer on his TV show* Let's All Just Get Along *after
allegations of unprofessional behaviour.*

*The argument comes as another blow for the film, a
UK production in collaboration with Starry Night Studios,
as gossip from set continues to eclipse production. The
nature of this argument is unknown.*

*Bestseller Evie has an average 4.2-star rating on review
sites, for novels that feature themes such as palliative care,
teenage abortion, extramarital affairs and chance meetings that lead to love.*

On the Romantic Road *was optioned for film after
the book went viral online, and is slated for festive release
next year.*

'Right.' Duke nods, his nostrils flaring. 'Well, I come across
as a total bloody idiot, don't I?'

He looks to Evie for moral support, since they're in this
together, but if his nostrils are flaring Evie's are positively
tunnel-like. She's gone bright red.

'Duke, you get stuff like this written about you all the
time. *I* am in sixteen pictures! Why does anyone need sixteen
freakin' pictures of me calling you a . . . a . . .'

Duke looks at her.

'A what?' he asks, genuinely curious.

'That's my face, all over the internet! And what's all this about my average star rating for my books, too? Four point two is *good*. They say it like I'm publishing blank pages that still manage to disappoint. A four point two is *incredible*.'

'I agree.' He nods. 'A four point two is like . . . eighty-four per cent on Rotten Tomatoes? In fact, you'd be certified fresh on Rotten Tomatoes for an eighty-four per cent. Not that I'm surprised.'

She blinks 'Thanks,' she says, and he can't read her tone.

'Also,' he adds, because he can't help himself. 'I didn't know you were Donald Gilbert's daughter.'

'I'm not.' She rolls her eyes. 'They got that bit wrong. Duke, what are we going to do about this? No. Wait.' She seems to reconsider what she's asking. 'This is *your* fault. What are *you* going to do about this?'

'Nothing?' he offers, and her face darkens. Duke shakes his head. 'Evie, this is showbiz. The papers write things, and, like you've just pointed out, most of it is made up.'

'But this wasn't made up. We had a fight and somebody here caught it on camera. And who are all of these "sources"?'

'MADE. UP,' Duke reiterates. 'They even gave you the wrong dad! That's how made up it is!' He notices tears threaten in her eyes. 'Look,' he says, trying to be calm. 'I'm sorry if the story has upset you, and I can understand how intrusive it must feel. As you have already pointed out, you don't even want to be here. In fact, I thought you were going home, so, if that's still your plan you can be certain of the fact this won't be repeated. At least not for you, anyway. For me, it's part of the job.'

'I'm not going home,' Evie grumbles, looking at the ground.

'Oh?' Duke says.

'That contract is legally binding, apparently. You've got me here as a hostage. A hostage who is now being photographed against her will.'

Duke considers this. He feels for her – he does! – but the machine is bigger than he is. He can't rewrite the laws of the biz, established a century ago.

'I'll see if I can do anything about the contract, okay? I can't control the paps, but if you really do want to go home, I'll ask how we can make that happen.'

She looks at him from under her lashes then, like she hates having to acknowledge what he's said might be a solution.

'Don't worry about saying thanks,' Duke sarcastically offers, when it's obvious she isn't going to give any words of gratitude for his suggestion.

She scoffs at him. 'I've got nothing to thank you for,' she tells him.

Seriously, what crawled up her jacksy and died? It's like she's incapable of basic niceties.

'This is your world, and you've dragged me into it,' she tells him. 'So I'm not saying thank you for you cleaning up your own mess. Just get it sorted, okay? So we can both go on with our very separate, very different lives?'

Duke sighs. This woman. He's never met a more difficult, stubborn, obstinate human.

'Fine,' he says. 'Thanks for the pep talk.'

She turns on her heel and the way she storms off makes Duke realise he's never truly seen anyone *flounce* before. At least not since this morning.

*

Duke calls his therapist, Phoebe, that night. He's been seeing her on and off for six years now, after Jennifer Aniston told him it was imperative he get a neutral party to talk to if he was going to survive his career. It helps give him another perspective when he's stuck in his own head. In fact, Phoebe doesn't often say much. Mostly he talks, and she nods or makes a 'hmm' noise, exactly like she's doing today.

'So I feel like, okay, we're in the papers. But what did she expect? This is what happens in this world. Although, actually, I suppose she did say she likes being a nobody, in the make-up trailer, when we actually had the fight. So . . . maybe I do have some culpability here. Hmm. Well. I can own that, you know? I can own my culpability. It's just not a good look for any of us, now it's out there. It makes the movie look bad, and God . . . Ben and J.Lo proved that the last thing you want to be known for is your personal life over The Work. Urgh. I can't believe I just said *The Work*. I know it's not minimum wage on a factory line, but it does matter to me. I think. I'm kind of interested in how Evie avoids any sort of public scrutiny at all. I might even be a bit jealous. That's a horrible feeling. Jealousy. And I suppose I feel a bit rejected by her, which is obviously my trigger. She just isn't impressed by me, and after everything with my mum, you know, all I want is her attention, her approval, and it's just this stupid . . . *compulsion* that I have, that everyone has to like me. I want to control the situation so that I am liked, which is actually kind of the opposite of being a good person, isn't it? Not that I'm looking for evidence that I'm a *bad* person, I know we've been through that. But in terms of my behaviour matching up to my best self . . . what do you think? Am I doing okay?'

He waits for Phoebe to speak.

'What do *you* think, Duke?' she asks. Typical. Duke sighs.

'I think that it's manipulative to try and make people like you, so I should try and stop. I think that's what Evie probably represents, or whatever: I got her over here, I expected all these things from her, and now I've really screwed things up because I had no idea she was so private and she's in the press. So . . . I can say sorry, and do what I said I'd do and get her out of here.'

Phoebe makes another *hmm* sound, and then announces, 'Okay then, Duke, well that's time for today.'

Duke looks at the clock. 8.55 p.m. He rings off the call with Phoebe and starts scrolling through his phone for the exec producers of the film, desperate to be a man of his word. He hates that Evie is right: he's abused his power, here. That's a bitter pill to swallow.

9

Evie

Evie is still fuming, even by evening. That's her face, all over the internet. It was basically the middle of the night back in Utah, when Magda saw it, but she hasn't been sleeping, what with the divorce, and was apparently scrolling stupid gossip sites in bed so saw the story literally as it went up. After asking Duke to deal with it (or, rather, *telling* Duke to deal with it) she's come back to the hotel, and she's pacing up and down at the bottom of the bed, letting her thoughts run wild. She doesn't want to be here. Her agent has said she has to be. She just wants to go home.

Evie hates herself for doing it, but she googles her name. The 'story' is everywhere. *She* is everywhere. There are hundreds of search results already.

It feels claustrophobic. It feels invasive. And in the pit of her stomach there's a ball of something close to fear. When she examines it, the most she can figure out is that this fear relates to her dad. 'Dad'. His fame destroyed her family. She doesn't want anything even close to her own celebrity – notorious or otherwise – in case it destroys her. How did they even get hold of the fact that she's related to him? Thank God Duke didn't seem to push the issue. Nobody has. Still . . . she doesn't want her stupid freaking face up there. She tells people she works in marketing at the coffee shop she works from sometimes, avoids literary festivals and bookshop events because people make her nervous. She hates talking in front of crowds. Sure, she doesn't sell as many books because of it, because she won't hop on TikTok or Instagram Live or run a Facebook group with read-alongs. But that's okay. She doesn't know a lot about life, but she does know that if you do what Duke has done – if you do what her father has done – and give the world a tiny piece of yourself, it will never be enough. Better not to give them anything. And besides, the lie she can tell herself is that maybe her father doesn't know how to find her, how to track her down. If she's offline and untraceable, there's a reason he's never been back in touch. But with her face and name all over the news, surely he's going to see it, and then Evie will know for sure that it isn't because he *can't* find her that she hasn't seen him in over twenty years. It's because he doesn't want to.

Her phone beeps. It's her agent again.

Okay, the text says. *Apparently, production have an idea about how to proceed with everything. They want you in suite 304 for a meeting at 8 a.m.*

Evie exhales. A solution. Good.

Sure, she texts back. *Thanks. Any clue what the solution is?*

None, her agent tells her. *But just stay open to hearing it, okay? I think you'll have to stay out there, but at least there will be ways to make it bearable and worth your while.*

Hmmmm. Evie considers this. She hasn't written a word today, and she swore she'd try for a few thousand. She takes a shower to wash the day off her and sets an alarm for 6 a.m. She'll do it first thing, bash out what she can before the meeting.

Tomorrow will be better, she tells herself. It sure as hell can't get any worse than today.

10

Duke

'Absolutely not. No. No way. That's *ridiculous.*'

Duke's had an hour's head start on coming to terms with what Evie has only just found out: that they should, according to the movie heads, fake-date.

'It's for the investors,' Marnie, the head of production, clarifies. 'I cannot overemphasise just how nervous what happened in London made them, and now there's this. Gossip forums are rife with stories about the film being doomed, and you know what? We deserve more than that. I, for one, have worked too hard for this to all be dead in the water. We *all* have.'

Duke watches Evie size her up, eyes shooting daggers.

'As a woman, you honestly think this is okay?'

'Yes, actually,' Marnie tells her. 'Because as a woman I know that gossip is a tool of the patriarchy, a way for women –

because it is mostly women on these sites, and it's mostly women clicking on all the articles too . . . what was I saying?' She appears to lose her train of thought.

'The patriarchy,' Duke supplies, and now Evie's daggers are mentally fired at him. The fury in her face is enough to make it feel like she's actually pierced skin.

'Yes, right.' Marnie takes a breath. 'Gossip is a tool of the patriarchy. If women are gossiping about each other, they're less concerned with altering structures of power. So in rewriting the narrative on purpose, with planted stories, we can use that to our advantage.'

'If you're so hellbent on changing structures of power, why don't you opt out of the gossip in the absolute?' Evie asks.

Marnie nods. 'Because I am one woman,' she says, 'and I've got two and a half weeks left of this nightmare shoot. I just want to get home for Christmas, to be honest. Maybe in the new year I can dismantle the powers that be, but now, here, I've got to hold my hands up and say: I'm just trying to get through this, best I can. Aren't you?'

Duke is impressed. He likes Marnie because she always shoots straight, and he considers this another example of her good character.

'I understand you and Duke really did fight, and Duke has held up his hands to say he accepts the blame for that.' Evie doesn't look at him when Marnie says that, but he can tell by the tiniest movement to her eyebrow that she's registered it. 'All we're asking for is a few snaps over the next few weeks of you holding hands or going ice skating or whatever, so that we can salvage the reputation of the movie. There's a lot of money at stake here, for all of us.'

'You want me to sell myself,' Evie supplies, and now she actually does look at Duke and for the life of him, he can't figure out how she's going to be persuaded. 'You want me to *pretend* I'm *dating* him? Like an escort?' Duke tries not to take the total disgust in her voice too personally. He isn't exactly thrilled either. When he asked everyone to find a way to counter the press intrusion, what he'd meant was to stop it entirely, not encourage it but with a different angle.

'We understand that you don't like press,' Marnie says, and Evie shakes her head, shooting more evil looks at Duke. Duke looks to the window, suddenly the most interesting framing of the sky there has ever been.

'But this could be good for you, too,' Marnie insists. 'Your agent said after Duke was photographed with your book that sales spiked, and that other studios have expressed interest in adaptations of some of your other works. That's amazing! Like, really cool. We can make sure they don't mention Donald Gilbert again, if that's the issue – this will just be Evie Bird and Duke Carlisle, and by the new year it will all have been forgotten about.'

'It's not that I don't like the press,' Evie says, her voice low. 'I *hate* the press. I hate . . . all of this. Putting on a dog and pony show. It's embarrassing.'

'It's lucrative.' Marnie shrugs. 'And we've all got a job to do.' Duke feels Evie's eyes on him, then, and he dares to meet her eye.

'And you're okay with this?' she asks him accusingly.

'I don't know what I think,' Duke says slowly. 'I told everyone it's down to you. I thought you might have some strong feelings about it all.'

'You want *me* to be the bad guy?' she asks him, and without waiting for an answer she says to the group, 'Fine, I'll be the bad guy. No.'

Nobody speaks.

Evie flops down on Duke's bed and stares at the ceiling.

Duke's heart thumps so hard the others must be able to hear it. He feels terrible, but the contract is iron-clad: Evie cannot go home early. So like everyone else, she needs to accept that, and find a way to make it work.

'What I think is this,' Duke begins, not getting up from his seat. Evie props herself up on her elbows and stares unblinkingly. It makes him nervous, but he is able to sound more confident than he feels. 'They've all said they can't make the articles go away, that the press will now be interested no matter what. And now they want to mould the press intrusion into something that helps everyone. The film, Daphne's reputation too, because it'll be a new piece of gossip and a nice neat ending to the drama of her affair with Brad. It helps me, because . . . well, it makes me look more down-to-earth, et cetera, dating a civilian or whatever you want to call it. And you will get a bigger profile, press for your books. That's good, right? Your book is being made into a movie! Like it or not, you're going to have your face known for a little while, so you may as well make the most of it whilst it lasts. Because, please don't take this the wrong way, but . . . you'll just as easily be forgotten. And you don't need to do any red carpets or do your own social media – literally just some public dates whilst we're both in the same place. Nothing confirmed or denied.'

Evie sighs, eyes narrowed.

'Fine,' she says, finally, and Duke can't hide his surprise. But before he can say anything, she looks at him and says: 'But first, we need some ground rules.'

Duke can tell the others are palpably relieved.

'Thank you,' Marnie says. 'We'll make it as painless as we can for you both. And who knows? You might even end up having fun.'

The look on Evie's face lets Duke know that no such turn of events will be possible.

When everyone else has gone, Evie stands looking out over the square at the double window, her hands on her hips, breathing loudly. In, and out. In, and out. Duke waits for her to turn around, but she doesn't. She just stands there. Breathing. In. And. Out.

'I'm trying to relax,' she says, eventually. She's obviously been aware of his impatience. He *has* been lightly tapping his foot – she was the one who called this little *tête-à-tête*. She wants further ground-rules clarification, but in order to do that, Duke is going to need her to actually speak.

'Sure, in your own time,' Duke says.

She turns around. 'Right,' she starts. 'Let's just get on the same page here, okay?'

'I'm all ears,' Duke tells her. 'Hit me.'

'Rule one: no kissing.' Duke bursts out laughing. She gives him that look. That scowl.

'Oh, you're serious,' he says. 'Right, yeah. No. No kissing.'

He had never even put kissing on his mental table, so it was no stretch to take it off. Kissing Evie Bird? It would be like snogging a cold stone statue.

'Or ass-grabbing,' she says.

Duke sets his mouth in a firm line and furrows his brow.

'Absolutely not,' he agrees, trying not to give his internal monologue away. Arse-grabbing? He'd no sooner make a move on her like that than he would put his hand into a viper's nest. Still. Saying all this out loud is obviously calming her down about it all, and so listening is the least he can do.

'Hand-holding should last no more than a minute, but two at most.'

Duke bites his cheek to keep from smiling, now. 'It would be borderline foreplay to pass sixty seconds. I agree.'

'Can you take this seriously?' she says. 'I'm trying to keep this strictly business so there's no . . . well, God, that's a contradiction in terms, isn't it? Keep a fauxmance professional. Jesus. We're really doing this?'

'If it's any consolation,' Duke tells her, 'I'm not exactly over the moon myself.'

'No need to be rude about it,' says Evie.

Duke startles. 'How am I being rude? You just said the same thing!'

'You didn't have to agree so readily,' she says, pouting.

God, this is going to be a rough ride. The woman doesn't even make sense half the time. Duke can't keep up.

'No kissing, no arse-grabbing, hand-holding for less time than it takes to microwave a frozen jacket potato. It's all logged,' he tells her, tapping his temple.

'What do you know about cooking frozen jacket potatoes?' she asks. 'Did you come across something like that when you were researching *civilians*?'

She spits that last word, and Duke realises he used it as a turn of phrase earlier.

'I didn't mean anything by that,' Duke says. 'I'm sorry if that offended you.'

'I'd have to care about what you say or think to be offended.' Evie shrugs.

'Ouch. I think that just hurt *my* feelings.'

In response Evie raises an eyebrow, unmoved.

'I do have one personal question,' he says, knowing she's liable to throw something at his head for it. She blinks. 'If you have a boyfriend, or girlfriend, or whatever . . .'

'I don't,' she says, quickly.

'Oh,' says Duke. It's not like this surprises him, Little Miss Sunshine being single, but he had to check.

'If you did, I was just going to say they'd need a heads up. Just thinking ahead.'

'Your concern for my love life is crossing a line,' Evie says.

'Right.' Duke nods. 'Let's just move on? Anything else you want to say other than don't touch you, don't look at you, don't try and make the best of it?'

'No,' Evie says with a fake smile. 'I think that's about it. This is just for December, and then poof, we can erase it from our minds.'

'Just for December indeed,' Duke agrees. 'What a gift.'

11

Evie

Their first fauxmance date is a disaster, just as she'd assumed it would be.

They decide, up there in Duke's suite, to get it all over and done with as soon as possible by heading out to get coffee, taking a walk around the block, and then heading back to the hotel where Evie can then get on with her work, and Duke can . . . do whatever it is Duke needs to do – presumably go to set, or spend an hour in front of his mirror staring lovingly at his own reflection.

They head out, Evie holding open the door to the hotel for Duke to walk through, and Duke quipping: 'Why am I ninety-nine per cent sure that if I tried to hold the door open for you, you'd shout at me for it?'

Evie pulls down her hat low on head. It's super cold out.

'You seem to think I'm, like, rudeness personified,' Evie says. 'Which is, in itself, really rude.'

If Duke replies, she doesn't hear it. He strides ahead, and she has to jog slightly to catch up.

They round the corner to a little café they've both independently clocked on their explorations, and suddenly Evie realises there's no takeout. Magda had said something about this, about no 'takeout' culture in Europe like they have in America, and it's true – they can either stand at a little bar area for an espresso or take a small table outside under the heaters.

'I'll come in with you,' Evie says, as they slow down outside. 'I'm going to hold on to your arm at the counter for like, five seconds, okay? Do we even know if this is being photographed?'

Duke looks at her, pastes on a pretend smile and says through gritted teeth, 'I. Have. No. Idea. Evie. I. Assume. So. Smile. Back. Please.'

Evie bursts out into fake laughter, throwing her head back and then reaching out to touch Duke's arm.

'You're so funny, Dukey!' she squeals, hamming it up, and a woman with a dog sat on her lap at the table closest to them frowns discontentedly.

Inside, they wait their turn as a waiter takes orders, makes coffees, serves pastries. Duke orders a black coffee, and Evie a latte. The waiter tells them how much it is in German first, then in English when she realises they don't understand.

Duke leans forward with contactless pulled up on his phone at the exact same moment as Evie reaches out with a ten-euro note.

'It's fine,' says Duke. 'It's on me.'

'As a point of pride,' Evie counters. 'I insist.'

She repositions her arm to block his access to the card reader. He bats away her hand but she goes back in again, wherein he tries again to use his card with more force, flinging her arm back and up into the air, making her step back with it – right into a waiter with a tray full of coffee.

It happens in slow motion. The tray somehow moves upwards. It flips. Coffee hurls out in a thousand different directions, including directly onto Evie's chest where it promptly spills down the entirety of her coat and drips to her boots. The waiter screams. Somebody sat at an indoor table nearby moves back in their chair, so it makes a nails-down-a-chalkboard screech. The tray lands on the floor. The six cups that were on the tray also land on the floor, clattering and crashing, splintering into chunks at Evie's sodden feet.

'Oh my God,' says Evie, looking around, totally panicked. 'Oh my God! I am so, so sorry. I am so sorry!'

She spins around to Duke to see if he's okay, if he's been caught in the crossfire too, and though she discovers he is, her concern quickly morphs into anger. She should be relieved he hasn't, she supposes, but it's not that he isn't covered in coffee that bothers her. It's that he's *laughing* at her.

'Seriously?' she says, grabbing paper napkins from the counter and furiously wiping at herself. 'Unbelievable,' she tuts, not so much cleaning the coffee up as simply pushing it around her coat so it smears more, making everything worse.

But Duke keeps doing it – he keeps laughing. In fact, he seems to find the whole thing so funny that the more frustrated Evie gets, the more hysterically she starts trying to clean herself up, the more people loudly talk in German around them, fetching mops for the spills and newspaper for the breakages, the harder he laughs. Right up until Evie says his name.

'Duke,' she snaps, looking at him. 'Duke!'

As she shouts, she hears somebody nearby say, 'Duke? Duke Carlisle!' and then there's even more of a frenzy as word spreads that the movie star is here, in the café, and nobody noticed.

He looks at her, then, and opens his mouth, about to speak. But before he can say anything Evie grabs her latte and hurls it at his body.

'Okay,' he says slowly, holding his arms away from the spreading wet patch, flecks of coffee dripping from that irritatingly picture-perfect face. 'I can see how I deserved that.'

They go back to the hotel in enraged silence.

Dinner is a cast and crew affair in the hotel, wherein Evie stays at the opposite end of the long dining room to Duke for the duration. Their coffee date finished her. She could see what everyone meant about turning the narrative about the movie around, about using it to her advantage. Her photo is out there now – it may as well be out there for the next few weeks if it's going to help sell more books and even more movie rights, her father seeing it (or not) be damned. Fine. She's not going to cut her nose off to spite her face. But Christ, she's up online with these new shots already, live-action pics of the coffee spillage posted for the masses. Fortunately, it looks like her own coffee slipped from her hand when she threw it over Duke. At least, that's what the caption says: *Another disaster quickly followed, when the coffee spilled on the floor made author Evie Bird slip, covering her date from head to toe too.* The truth is, she lost control when Duke laughed at her that way. It's shocking to her how much quicker she's been to anger since she arrived, like the Hyde to her Jekyll has been released. Duke just pushes her buttons. All of them.

When she's eaten, all Evie wants to do is go upstairs to try to write, and yet when she finishes the last of her roasted beef Katerina heads on over to see if she's coming to the 'pub quiz' being hosted in the snug next door.

'Erm, no?' Evie says, confused. Organised fun is her least favourite kind of fun, so much so that organised fun is actually her idea of hell. 'I've got work to do.'

'Noooo!' Katerina intones. 'Impossible! Come on – it'll only be an hour. You can't hide away all on your own.'

'Of course I can.' Evie blinks, and even she can admit how boring she sounds. Katerina pulls a face. Evie's façade melts. 'Oh for God's sake,' she says, perilously close to smiling.

'Is that a yes?' Katerina asks, like butter wouldn't melt. 'There will be wine . . .'

'Fine. But *one* hour, okay? I really do have to get some words down before bed.'

'Sold,' says Katerina, and they head on over to the snug. As they walk Katerina adds: 'This is good bonding. And also, as a hardened on-set DP, I really have to insist that you don't get sucked into survival mode. This job only works if you give in to the cabin fever of it all and become best mates with everyone, if only for the time we're all together.'

Evie lets herself be taken by the arm to the far corner of the hotel lobby. The snug – basically a room cosier than the lobby and smaller than the restaurant – is festiveness person-ified with a roaring log fire, low-beamed ceilings, and chairs upholstered in worn corduroy and velvet, strewn with throws and pillows. There's about twenty people huddled off into groups of two or three, pieces of paper between them and Jerry, a fifty-something lighting guy with a ponytail and a microphone, evidently leading the proceedings.

'Oh, great!' he exclaims as he clocks their arrival. 'We're literally about to start. Evie, can you team up with Billy No Mates there? Katerina, you're with Daphne she says.'

'Daphne has good taste in pub quiz partners,' Katerina quips, breaking away from Evie and crossing the room to a small three-legged table with two wooden chairs, one of which is occupied by a smiling Daphne holding a pen. Evie looks around to see who Billy No Mates is and comes face to face with Duke and the empty chair beside him. She looks to Jerry, who is occupied by flicking through what seems to be a rather extensive collection of questions and answers, and when he finally does look up, he simply gestures again in Duke's direction – who, for his part, has figured out what's going on and seems, to Evie's eye, to be rather panicked about it too.

'Right, there are several rounds to this: general knowledge, movies, history, science – but no sports or music since the cultural divide between the UK and US reference points means I'll only be accused of rigging it one way or the other,' Jerry begins. 'Ready?'

Evie looks around nervously and makes her way over to

Duke. If she walks out now it will feel like he's won, somehow, like she can't hack it. And she can. She can take him on. She will not lessen herself for him.

'I'm very competitive,' Duke says, by way of greeting.

Evie slips onto the low couch beside him, close enough that her knee knocks his as she settles in to see the scoresheet, telling him: 'Me too. So . . . don't mess this up, okay?'

He sets his mouth in a firm line. The quiz begins.

The pair storm through the general knowledge round, surprisingly passing off answers in quick succession.

'What is the world's largest land mammal?' asks Jerry down the mic.

Duke shrugs and says to Evie simply, 'Elephant.' He isn't conferring with her, he's saying it to confirm it with himself, but it sounds about right so she doesn't stop him from scribbling it down. Jerry moves on to the next question.

'Nostradamus was famous for making *what*?' he asks the room.

Evie doesn't know the answer to this one. Duke looks at her and she shrugs.

'Didn't he predict the end of the world?' she offers, and Duke's eyes light up.

'Predictions, then?' he asks her, and Evie shrugs again.

'I guess.'

Duke writes it down with the disclaimer: 'If it's wrong, that's on you.'

'The velocipede was a ninth-century prototype of *what*?' presses Jerry.

Evie is determined to prove her worth now. His suggestion

85

that she could cost them a point makes blood boil under the surface of her skin. She knows stuff! Just because he's terrible at consulting her doesn't mean she can't pull her pub quiz weight.

'I mean, that has to be bicycle, doesn't it?' she says, talking quickly, joining the mental dots of the etymology of the word. 'Velocipede,' she considers again, and he looks at her, boring holes into her skull as a way to motivate her to think faster. Not that he's coming up with suggestions of his own. '*Velo.* Isn't that French for bike?'

'I think so?' he says. 'Sounds sensible enough.'

'Bike, then. Put down bike.'

She watches him write down the answer.

'And hey,' she adds, leaning in to hiss at him. 'If it's wrong, that's on both of us.'

He raises his eyebrows in a way Evie can't make sense of.

12

Duke

As the quiz goes on, it bugs Duke that he's noticed Evie smells like incense and patchouli.

'What?' she snaps, as Jerry pauses his questions to get another beer.

Duke pulls a face. 'Nothing,' he says. 'God. You're so . . . defensive.'

'Just anxious not to make a fool of myself, actually,' she shoots back. 'Here . . . let me write. You're starting to slow down.' She takes the pen from his hand and leans in, ready for the next question.

George Michael, she's written, *'Careless Whisper'.* He hadn't known the answer to that one anyway, so it's just as well she's taken over.

'Who said the lyrics, *When I find myself in times of trouble, Mother Mary comes to me*?' Jerry asks now he's back, and

Duke knows Jerry is getting drunker because he's slurring his words whilst also talking, somehow, faster.

They both whisper, at exactly the same time: 'The Beatles, "Let It Be".'

Duke watches Evie write it down, her loopy handwriting showing up his schoolboy-like scrawl.

'*I've got this feeling in my bones, it goes electric, wavy, when I turn it on*,' says Jerry. Evie looks up at Duke, obviously unsure.

'Justin Timberlake,' Duke says. '"Can't Stop the Feeling".'

'You like pop?' she asks, after she's written it down.

'Don't say it like that,' he replies, 'all judgey. Everyone likes pop. That's why it's called pop, as in *popular*.'

'All right, music police.' She rolls her eyes, and it makes Duke's skin prickle. He wasn't being an arse, and yet she makes him feel like one, always ready to pounce on any little thing that displeases her – which is, it would seem, everything. 'I was just asking.'

'You were just *provoking*,' he corrects her. He looks at his watch. It'll soon be bedtime.

'I write popular fiction, Duke. You act in popular movies. It's called conversation, not provocation. Jeez.'

He eyes her as she half-turns to focus on Jerry, all flushed cheeks from the mix of the warmth of the snug and pure competition. She could be pretty, if she didn't scowl so much.

The next rounds move fast.

'Who played James Bond in *For Your Eyes Only*?' asks Jerry.

'Roger Moore,' Evie hisses, fast off the mark.

Jerry continues: 'Which British actor died whilst filming his supporting role in Ridley Scott's *Gladiator*?'

Evie immediately says: 'Oliver Reed.'

'Which country was the first to give women the vote, in 1893?'

'New Zealand,' whispers Duke, and when Evie looks at him as if she's surprised, he feigns nonchalance. He only knows it because he's recently read a script set in the time period, but over his dead body will he admit that to her.

'What name is given to the 8th of May to mark the unconditional surrender of the German Army at the end of World War II?'

'VE Day,' they whisper in unison. She writes it down.

'Roughly what proportion of their DNA do humans and chimpanzees share? Seventy-seven per cent, ninety-two per cent or ninety-eight point five per cent?'

They look at each other, and, Duke realises, in a way it's the first time they actually have. She stares into his eyes. He stares into hers. They are both searching for the answer to the question within each other, but there's a split second where, for Duke at least, it's almost like it's something more. Like in that moment he can see the tiniest crack in her veneer and a softer, more vulnerable woman underneath. Then she says: 'Looking at you I think the answer is ninety-eight point five. You're basically a chimpanzee who can memorise a script, right?'

'Low blow,' he says, rolling his eyes. 'But also: yes.'

'Who is best known for his theory of black holes?' asks Jerry.

'Stephen Hawking,' Duke says.

'The chemical symbol Y denotes which uncommon metal?'

They look at one another again.

'No idea,' she says, grimacing.

'Same,' Duke supplies.

In the end, it doesn't matter: once they've passed their papers to the next table, every team marking the answer sheet of the team beside them, and then get it back again, they know they must be in with a chance of winning. They only got three wrong in the whole quiz. Not bad given that they guessed a solid third of them.

'And the winners are . . .' Jerry announces, practically falling off his stool. 'Duke and Evie!'

The pair leap up in a fit of excitement, screaming 'Yay!' in harmony and grabbing each other's arms. Smiles wide as the moon, they jump and whoop, before suddenly coming to an abrupt stop. They look at each other then and, instantly, at exactly the same time, both seem to become remarkably embarrassed by such displays of teamwork, and sit down again, quickly and quietly, like it was a close call to ever have been so enthusiastic in such close proximity to one another.

'Well then, goodnight from me,' Duke says, once everyone starts filing out of the room.

'Yeah,' says Evie, standing up too. She opens an arm outward, letting him know to go on ahead. He does. When he turns back around to say something – he doesn't know what, exactly – she's gone.

13

Evie

'The coffee spillage was *not* my fault, just so we're clear,' Duke tells Evie as they play a fairground game of Bottle Stand. They are Trying One More Time re: a fake date, at the behest of both their teams. It's going better this time – at least in the sense that neither of them are covered in coffee. She aims a ball at the row of jam jars. If she can knock one off the ledge, she wins a prize.

'Yes,' she says, after she's missed her shot. 'It was. But whatever. I've been talked into trying again, so . . . I'll just be sure to keep all further drinks out of your reach, and also be my guest: you can pay for everything from now on. I won't even pretend to try and reach for my money.'

'If you'd have let me be a gentleman in the first place . . .' Duke intones.

Evie shakes her head. 'Seriously? I thought we just said bygones?'

Duke bites his bottom lip. 'We did. As you were.'

'You know,' she tells him, pretending the jar is his head and if she hits the target she knocks it clean off, 'what's insane about this is that I can't tell if anyone has even clocked you at all out here. If there were photographers around, wouldn't we know? Can anybody even see this charade playing out?'

'You'd think they'd be easy to spot, wouldn't you?' Duke says, handing her another ball and pointing to a jar as he says, 'I know the instinct is overarm for this, but you might be better off with underarm.'

She issues him with a glare.

'Or not,' he adds, holding up his hands in surrender.

Evie misses her third and final shot, a pulse of frustration passing through her. She really wanted to prove Duke wrong. It feels strangely apt though, given that this whole thing feels similarly out of her control. And she knows it's not just the bottles making her mad at Duke now. Even if she did let money trump her morals and agreed to the fauxmance, she feels compelled to blame someone, to have a concrete body to channel her misgivings towards, and tough luck, Duke Carlisle, you're in the line of fire.

Filming has moved further down the Romantic Road, now, and the schedule has been arranged so that Daphne does her solo scenes today and Duke does his tomorrow. So, making the most of Duke's rare free day, after checking in to their Rothenburg ob der Tauber hotel, they headed out to the Christmas market. It's only 2 p.m. but the sky is heavy and grey, the blue skies of the morning giving way to clouds filled with the threat of snow. There are fairground games and food stalls, fried doughnuts and bright, glimmering lights.

Duke and Evie have been tasked with simply moving through it for a few hours as if it's a real date, with Duke's publicist even going as far as to say that if they did a little cheeky kissing, too, it wouldn't be such a bad thing. Fat chance of that, thinks Evie, that goes well against the rules of engagement. She'll take in the sights and even talk a little, if the mood takes her, but she's not for sale in anything close to the biblical sense. The only thing she intends to let anywhere near to her lips is juicy wurst off of the *Schwenkgrill*.

'Hungry?' she asks Duke, as she spots a place selling sausages and mulled wine.

'I've not been allowed to acknowledge my hunger since 2009, but sure,' he replies. 'I can buy one to hold and fake-eat, as we fake-date.'

He pays for their food and, as Evie waits for hers to cool down, she asks, 'Is that true? That you've been on a diet for over ten years?'

Duke nods. 'Camera adds ten pounds,' he tells her, patting his belly for emphasis.

'God,' Evie snorts. 'Next you'll be telling me you've had three nose jobs and can't eat ice cream because your veneers are too sensitive.'

'Oh no,' laughs Duke. 'My dental work is second to none. My dentist could win awards for the work he's done on my smile.'

'Show me,' Evie teases, finally taking a bite of her food. 'Give me the *People Magazine* smile.'

Duke looks away, over his shoulder, and then whips his head around to look at her and grin. Even though she's expecting it, it still unnerves a part of her. His cool blue irises, his strong, Roman nose, the way he can speak with the subtlest of expressions – it's all too much. No one human should be that attractive. And his skin? It's like the man doesn't have pores. Where does his sweat go?

'How's your . . .' he says, dropping his voice to a suggestive lilt. 'Sausage? Everything you hoped for, little lady?'

Evie chews and rolls her eyes at the same time. Everything is just so ridiculous that it's actually not hard to slip into the role of woman-falling-in-love-with-him, because it's like an out-of-body experience. Not so long ago she boarded a flight to Europe as regular old Evie Bird, and now she's playing for the international cameras. Not that she can spot them. When he talks to her like that – playful and silly – it would be *very* easy to think this was real. She has to keep her wits about her.

'I can see why they don't let you write the scripts,' she jokes. 'Your dialogue is very clunky.'

'Hey!' Duke laughs. 'Don't knock my dreams!'

Evie uses a napkin to wipe her mouth. She could eat more, now. The fairground food isn't filling her up, it's opening a void in her that asks for more and more. She wants those little hash brown pancakes, too – *Kartoffelpuffer*? Is that what they're called? – and she's seen people with little bowls of mushrooms in some sort of white, garlicky-looking sauce. She wouldn't mind that, as well.

'I could eat a horse,' she announces. 'And I smell garlic. Let's follow my nose.'

'God,' Duke says. 'The way you say that is enough to tempt me, too. It's erotic, the way you talk about *Knoblauch*.'

'Don't mock me,' Evie warns. 'Not when there's food involved.'

They meander through the crowds some more, making idle chit-chat until Evie forgets once again that this is all manufactured, all just for show. In a strange way it's actually fun, looking at the little stalls selling salt lamps and decorations, traditional treats and wooden games. In fact, she can't remember the last time she did something like this – wore lipstick, laughed with a man. Her last date was years ago, real or fake. She'd thought she'd been fine with that, but there's a stirring in her lower pelvis, an awakening.

'Oh my God, look!' she cries, pointing at a merry-go-round. 'It's so cheesy.' She chuckles. 'Shall we? I can just imagine – getting our photo taken as we giggle with glee on a merry-go-round, leaning in to whisper sweet nothings . . . Makes it almost worth it, getting to be *that* absurd.'

Duke cocks his head at her, like he's trying to find where her tone lands on a scale of one to sarcastic.

'I mean, I'm game if you are,' he says, slowly, and Evie nods.

'I'm not joking,' she insists. 'Merry-go-round! Merry-go-round!' She claps her hands with the rhythm of the words. They pay for tickets and wait for their turn in companionable-enough silence. If it was a real date Evie would wonder if she should fill it, but as it goes she isn't actually trying to impress Duke, so when the conversation naturally ebbs, she doesn't force the flow. They shuffle forwards, and then suddenly she feels something land on her cheek.

'Duke,' she says. 'I think I just felt snow!'

They both look up to the sky.

'I did! Look!' she squeals, holding out a mittened hand to reveal the tiniest snowflake. 'This is incredible. I can't believe this. Like, is the crew here trying to make this as much of a Christmas cliché as possible?' She tips her head back then, cackling. She might be high on the saturated fat of all those snacks, or it might just be that she's got no choice but to lean into the production of it all. She's trying to trick literally the whole world into thinking this Adonis of a man is sleeping with her so that she can sell the film rights to some of her other books and what? Take some time off to relive it all as one psychotic dream? She hasn't filled Magda in yet, but when she does, Evie knows she's going to FREAK. OUT. This doesn't happen to people like them. Even Evie, the crowned Queen of Cynicism, can admit that this is awesome.

'We're up,' says Duke, pointing to where the man in charge has opened the gateway to let them through.

'You should sit on the pink one.' Evie giggles. 'What did you say in that meeting? That "dating" me would make you seem down-to-earth? Well, what says mere civilian like sitting on a pink pony?'

Duke frowns and then hoists a leg over a unicorn-esque horse in shades of ruby glitter. It's far down to the ground, having stopped on a 'down' instead of an 'up', so he has to tilt his chin to look at Evie, and it takes her aback, when he does so, how vulnerable he seems.

'You look absurd,' Evie tells him, happily.

'I'm very aware of that,' Duke grumbles back. 'Thank you.' The ride begins.

'If we are being papped, they'd better be getting my good angles!' yells Evie over the din of the fairground music.

'What good angles?' Duke shoots back, and it takes Evie

by surprise. He's good at keeping her at arm's length, but Duke is seldom outright mean.

'You're insufferable,' she says, shaking her head. She doesn't need an actor reminding her of her plainness. 'And also, you might look good on camera but in real life you've got a very unnerving nose, so you're no oil painting either, buddy.'

Duke raises his eyebrows, opens his mouth, and then snaps it shut. They don't talk after that, and Evie enjoys the ride, the wind lightly in her hair, the lights blurring as she lets her focus soften.

'I've had enough now,' Duke says, when it's done.

'Oh . . .' replies Evie, struggling to hide her disappointment.

Duke laughs.

'What?' she asks.

'Nothing.' He shakes his head and does something with his brow – crumples it, like he's very tired.

'No, go on – what?' Evie presses.

'I was just thinking,' Duke tells her, 'that maybe you've missed your calling. You're a good actress. You almost sounded genuinely upset to be going home just then.'

Evie is stunned. He's being mean, again, and it's clear that earlier wasn't a one-off when he was cruel about her looks. He actually doesn't like her, really does think he's better than her.

'Fine,' she says. 'Go home. I'm going to do one more turn around the fair. Have a good night,' she snaps, sauntering off.

He's a pig, she thinks to herself, meandering through the crowds. *He's got no idea how he makes other people feel, the self-centred dweeb.*

She turns around, then, for no discernible reason than she feels compelled to. And there he is: Duke, looking after her, watching her walk away.

Evie throws her arms up, asking him wordlessly: *What?!*

Duke shakes his head, jaw slackened, expression wounded, which is a bit rich considering he's the buffoon. Evie decides to stare him out; she will not cower from him, will not pander to his moods. She didn't even want to be here, remember? And now she's a central player in this farcical few weeks and *he* has got the nerve to have attitude!

She wins. Duke turns away. And Evie hates herself for noticing the curve of his ass and the confidence to his walk as he does so, the curl of his fingers at his sides, his width, everything.

So he's hot, she scolds herself. *So what? What's hot when it's all window dressing?*

But she still doesn't look away. She keeps one eye on that window dressing until he's out of sight, and even then the thought of him lingers in her mind.

14

Evie

Evie can't help herself. All day she has been trying to write, to get her book ever closer to being finished, and yet somehow all her love interests are suddenly being written as though they've got Duke's blue eyes or wide shoulders. In the café where she went to work this morning, on set this afternoon, and now in the hotel bar, still a thousand words short of her target, she keeps thinking about her fake date with Duke last night.

Frustratingly, considering she hates all of it on principle, it went so much better than the coffee shop – until his mood changed, anyway. Before that point she'd been perilously close to enjoying it. When Duke relaxes and forgets to be 'on', he's okay company. Not that he does that often, of course. It's odd. She woke up thinking about the closeness of his arm when they were walking, the flex of his forearm muscles when he grabbed the pole of the merry-go-round. It must be tiredness, or ongoing jet lag, but it's on a loop in her head, annoyingly, and she can't stop playing it. So she googles him, just to distract herself, and before long is reading feature after feature on him, including in one of the Saturday arts sections in *The Times*.

She reads:

Duke Carlisle isn't your average Hollywood rising star. After a decade and a half in pursuit of his dream, he tells Sally McVitie what he's learnt about love, laughter, and the importance of honesty onscreen . . . and off.

Duke Carlisle sits across from me in a central London hotel lobby; arms resting on his knees, baseball cap pulled low on his forehead. 'It's not like I'm Bieber or anything,' he tells me with a sardonic smile. 'People do recognise me, but it's all about context. When I'm suited and booted it's obvious I'm on the clock and it's okay to approach, but when I'm like this I mostly get left alone. It's the paps, really, who don't have any boundaries.'

I tell him that must be hard – I don't even like it when I get tagged in a mate's Instagram photo without prior permission.

'Thanks for saying that,' he tells me, those famous blue eyes sparkling with mischief. 'I know it's a bit like complaining my diamond shoes are too tight – I'm aware of that. But equally, when did we collectively decide that making movies means I'm allowed to be followed down a dark alleyway at night, or photographed putting the bins out with a hangover?'

With his distinct clipped vowels and wry, disarmingly straightforward demeanour, he's not what you expect from a man tipped as award season's front runner for his guest appearance in The Marvellous Mrs Maisel, *the face of Chanel's new men's fragrance and seller of tabloids simply by dint of being alive. Today, he sips his green tea as we chat, pausing to consider each question before launching into an eloquent, discerning and refreshingly frank response.*

'I know it's possible to be in the public eye without the constant scrutiny. This is going to sound like a major name-drop, but I'm mates with Stormzy and it's incredible to me how he gets left alone. He gets to make his music, have his life, and then pop up out of nowhere to release an album and perform Glastonbury, and then it all gets pretty chill for him. When I got photographed on that paddleboard a few summers ago, he thought it was awful, but we laugh about it now. He's put me in his phone as Anaconda, apparently.'

Ah yes. I'm glad Carlisle is the one to raise this (so to speak). The paddleboard photographs he refers to broke the internet in summer 2020, when unbeknownst to him he was snapped cavorting on a lakeside beach with a mystery blonde – stark naked. Twitter had a meltdown over the size of his manhood, with everyone from The Late, Late Show with James Corden *to Boris Johnson passing comment. He seemingly took it in good humour at the time, but months later went viral once more with a blogpost he wrote about the invasion of his privacy.*

'I just had to say something,' he explains, in a sudden

bout of seriousness. 'Like fair play, I had my knob out in public. We were in France, and I was in love and feeling happy and free. And then the media, and social media, made one of the happiest, most romantic days of my life into a sort of joke, and it took me ages to work up the courage to say it made me uncomfortable. I just kept thinking, if it happened to a woman, would people have been sharing it like that? Or would it have been unfeminist?' And that's exactly what his post explored. 'Like, okay, we know what the male gaze is and how it makes women feel, but surely the definition of equality is not that we then adapt a sort of female gaze that reduces men to the size of their . . . whatever. Equality is saying hey, let's not make anyone feel this way. Let the man paddleboard in peace! And maybe buy him some new swimwear!'

He breaks out into a charming chuckle at that, doing what he's become so well known for in his movies: pushing his audience to an emotional edge, and pulling the rug from under them with his humour and delight.

'Because you just can't make it up, can you, how weird life is. And I know that me and my friends, we don't sit around crying too much. I don't mean that in a blokey way, like I'm too much of a man for that. Maybe it's being Northern: you choose to laugh rather than cry. I guess that's often what I try and bring to my work. To me, that's humanness. Walking that line.'

I can't help but wonder how he came to be this way. Little is known about his childhood, except that he was raised by a single mother in Sunderland and didn't show an aptitude for theatre until relatively late.

'Yeah,' he tells me, stroking his chin thoughtfully. 'I had a really great teacher, Mrs Steinenberg, who told me about an audition happening. I've never asked her why she pushed for me to go – it was right as we were leaving school and then the audition became my first gig, moving to London, and, bam, here we are all these years later.' He shakes his head fondly. 'Do you ever get freaked out by how fast life can move? Like, wasn't I just a kid? It's mad.'

Life must feel fast when you pack in as much time on set as Carlisle does. Last year alone he featured in four major movies and his guest spot on Mrs Maisel. 'Ah, yes,' he says, in typical self-depreciating style. 'But that was only three episodes of the show, and two of the movies were supporting roles. But when Olivia Wilde asks you to play back-up to the great women-led stuff she's been making, you make the time, you know? Same with Greta. When she called, my head exploded. I can't tell you what an honour that felt like.'

The Greta he's referring to is Oscar nominee Greta Gerwig, and his role in her newest movie is why we're meeting today . . .

Evie pulls herself away from the article. *Focus,* she reminds herself. *Just get this first draft done!* She has had to turn her phone off because she's suddenly become Ms Popular, with people reaching out left, right and centre, from college friends of friends to her old high school English teacher and her editor to her cover designer. Photos of their fairground date have been published, with more rubbish about their 'growing love' for one another, with yet more fake sources from set. It's too much. She just needs it to all blow over. This is exactly what she has spent her career trying to avoid! You can't create good work when you're distracted by noise! She hates it. Hates, hates, hates it. She opens a new browser and idly types in *Duke Carlisle paddleboard*.

'Crafting your next masterpiece?' Duke asks, casting a shadow across her screen. She looks up, horrified, snapping her computer shut faster than a teenage boy with a sock in his hand. Duke is fresh from the shower, his wavy hair damp against his face and neck, looking casual in grey jogging bottoms and a T-shirt that on mere mortals no doubt hangs loose, but on Duke Carlisle clings to rock-hard biceps and solid abs.

'*You*,' Evie says, darkly.

'I know,' he replies, smiling with only one side of his face to convey his contrition. 'I've ruined your life. I'm fairly confident it will all be tomorrow's fish paper before you know it, but still . . .'

'Fish paper?' Evie asks.

'It's a British thing, I suppose. From when we used to wrap our fish and chips in yesterday's newspaper. So: today's news is tomorrow's fish-and-chip paper. Ergo it becomes old pretty quickly . . .'

'I see,' Evie says, not bothering to reopen her laptop. She needs to admit defeat. She hasn't published sixteen books in ten years by working when the muse doesn't show up. Evie knows she can sit here for the next two hours and get maybe five hundred usable words, or she can wait until she's had a good night's sleep and let five thousand pour out of her in the morning. 'Well, they say the internet has a long memory, so . . . It all remains to be seen, doesn't it?'

'Can I join you?' he asks.

'Isn't that just asking for trouble? We're fighting, we're too cosy together, we're sleeping together . . . What next? Plotting to ruin the world . . . ? Plus, I thought you'd had enough of me last night. You stormed off.'

He looks around. It's quiet. Most of the crew have gone out into town tonight.

'I had had enough of you,' he says, but he's smiling, the handsome prick. 'You drive me potty. But there's nobody else here to have a drink with and I don't know – I think I'm just a glutton for punishment.' His voice is mischievously low, and it makes Evie smile in spite of herself.

'Fine,' she tells him. 'I was going to order another anyway.'

Duke calls over the waiter and Evie admires the space. The bar is wood-panelled with red leather banquette seats and low lighting, and piano renditions of festive favourites play softly from a speaker above them. Coloured lights from trees in either corner dance slowly, reflecting light onto strategically placed tinsel. Garlands hang from the ceiling, and Evie only just realises that they must be made with real fir tree branches because the smell of pine permeates the air. Their red wine comes, and Duke looks at her.

'Cheers,' he says.

'Cheers,' Evie echoes. They clink, touch their stems down to the table for good luck, and drink. It's heavy and full, berries and promise staining her lips.

Duke takes another big gulp from his glass. 'My trainer

would kill me for this,' he says, nodding to the wine, but Evie can't relate.

'I've been thinking,' Evie says, then. She's already had a large glass, so she's loosened up. It's easier to voice your opinion when you feel loose. 'You said it was you who put it in my contract. That I had to be here. But I don't think you ever said why.'

'Why did I want you out here?' He pauses, and Evie rolls her eyes at his dramatic delivery. He's such an actor. 'Because I really am a fan,' he says. 'I've honestly read everything you've written, and I even tried to get an advance copy of next year's, but I got told they're not ready yet.'

Evie pulls a face. It's the equivalent of: *yeah, okay, whatever*. 'My best friend isn't even that eager,' she tells him. 'Not that she should be or anything. It's not like I go and stand in the back of her classroom and applaud her teaching, so why should I expect her to read everything I write for work?'

'Not the same thing,' he says. She blinks. Duke narrows his eyes. 'You *still* don't believe me, do you? You don't believe that I cried when Max and Sinita had to get on separate flights in *Fly Me to the Moon*. Or at Luther's scene, where he finally confronts his dad so that he can lay his demons to rest and move on with Rochelle in *Hope and Ghosts*? I cried for like, an hour after that one. It was cathartic. Not to mention George, in *On the Romantic Road*. Why do you think this movie even got made, Evie? I read the book and made it happen. I took this to Stu at Independent, got Marnie involved; I attached my name early so we could get funding. Me.'

Like a goddamn sweeping saviour, Evie thinks, darkly. But then, her jaw slackens. He seems genuine. She goes to speak, but then finds she doesn't actually know what she wants to say. She settles on: 'I didn't know that. I don't know how this all works.'

'You do understand that you're brilliant, though, don't you?' he asks her. She shakes her head. Brilliant? No. Brilliant is a bit strong. Competent. She's competent.

'I'm not Shakespeare,' she says. 'I have a committed group of readers who like my style, and I try to tell the emotional truth of things, even if I do fudge a happy ending. But it's just stories. Just words.'

'Words that help people,' Duke says. 'Surely they must tell you that, at book signings?'

'I don't do signings,' Evie counters. He knits the tops of his eyebrows together. 'I'm not very good . . . publicly. I don't like it. I told you. I'm a private person.'

'Emails, then,' he pushes. 'DMs.'

She shakes her head. 'Somebody else takes care of all of that for me.'

'Reviews?'

'Nope.'

'Whoa. You literally have no idea what your work means to people? You don't have a relationship with the people who buy it?'

She shakes her head. She writes it, and what happens after that is none of her business. That's what she's always told herself.

'You're changing lives, Evie. You should fire your people if they aren't making you see that. That's why I wanted you here. You've *helped me*, Evie. The way you see the world helps *me* to see the world. I don't care that your books aren't even for me. I'm a dude who reads romance! So what! I bloody love them. They give me *hope*, Evie. Do you know how incredible that is?'

Evie can't compute the passion with which he's talking. It's hyperbolic, all this. He's an actor; he's paid to be dramatic. And she isn't this great inspirational figure he's making her out to be. She's a mess.

'I don't write to tell other people how to live their lives,' she tells him, once he's calmed down. She takes a breath, knowing what she wants to say but hesitating. Can she trust him? She decides that she doesn't care. The truth is the truth. 'I write to escape my own.'

Duke stops smiling. He looks at her, intently. For a moment, the air feels charged, like if she leans forward he'll be pulled into her orbit too, right until their lips collide.

'That's exactly why I act,' he whispers.

He reaches out a hand to her, and for a split second she lets herself enjoy it. The feeling of being understood. Seen. Heard. Appreciated.

Then she pulls away.

Men leave.

Don't trust anybody.

She could never be enough, anyway.

This isn't real.

'It's my bedtime,' she announces. She's rattled, the wine sitting heavy in her stomach. She can't buy into what he's saying – not to mention how he's saying it. Okay so she's googled some articles about him and had some thoughts about his arms. The fact remains, though: this? This 'relationship'? It's fake. He's a damned good actor, though – she almost reached out a hand back to him, almost laced her fingers through his. Is this why actors on sets always end up together when they're filming? Because fact and fiction get so easily blurred? She picks up her laptop and shoots him a closed-mouth smile, and before he can say anything else she gets the hell out of there.

It's maddening, then, that no sooner has she fallen asleep than she dreams about him.

15

Duke

'Can I put my arm around you? Would that be okay?' Duke asks Evie, shyly. They're out and about after filming again, at the Christmas market, happy to be photographed. *Hoping* to be photographed! Marnie, head of production, has already reported back that the positive headlines about Duke and Evie are reassuring the investors, so everyone is pleased all around. They just have to keep doing what they're doing. And actually, Duke can't put his finger on why that feels better than it did, but yeah. He's not *hating* the situation like he did. Evie seems to be more relaxed, now. Last night they even came close to a moment, before she bolted. Evie Bird is a mystery to him, and the more time he spends with her, the more he wants to unravel that mystery.

'I think that's realistic, don't you?' he adds. It's an incongruous feeling, asking permission this way. But they do have their ground rules, after all, and this could almost break the 'no unnecessary touching' one.

Evie twitches her nose at the suggestion as if she's displeased, and Duke expects her to decline. It shocks him, then, when she affirms that yes, he may. It's not the way he'd like to be embracing a woman – none of this is exactly 'fun' when it's forced – but if this has to be happening with anyone, there could be worse people than Evie Bird. She's prickly, but he's starting to sense the sweet centre to her.

'I'm actually a bit chilly,' Evie says, and so he loops his arm over her shoulder and she reaches up her far hand to hold his. They walk more slowly than they did before – both because the place is busier than ever, and because arm in arm and walking in step they physically can't move as fast. If it were a real date, Duke would be pleased with the market as its backdrop. Everyone around them is in good spirits, and it's a pretty sweet deal to be here shooting a Christmas movie surrounded by actual Christmas. He's heard stories of summer blockbusters being filmed in late winter sun, and friends of his having to act freezing during heatwaves. He doesn't have to do much work to feel festive when his actual job is to be festive, and vice versa: the full immersion festivities make him all the more cheery. He's come a long way from the Duke who landed in Germany only a little under a week ago. Daphne who? His mood is much better than it has been.

'What shall we do now?' Evie asks.

This close to her, he can smell her shampoo. It's coconutty.

'Maybe it would be nice if I bought you something?' he suggests. 'You can pick out a bracelet or something – they sell those leather woven ones. It could be a moment, me tying it to your wrist?'

'You've done this before,' she titters, and Duke understands that he's oversensitive, that the way she's mocking the arrangement upsets him in a way he can't articulate, but to infer that all his dates are manufactured hurts his pride.

'Ouch,' he replies. 'I know you're on a sugar high, but I do have feelings you know.'

She tugs on his hand. 'I keep upsetting you, don't I? I don't mean to.'

'No,' he insists, though he's quietly impressed that she'd be so direct. It inspires him to be as frank in return. 'I just know you don't want to be here. I get it, and it's silly of me to feel rejected by that, but my therapist, she says rejection is my whole thing . . .'

'Hell of a job to have when you don't like rejection,' she tells him, but that just proves she doesn't get it.

'The feeling when it all goes right though,' he counters, 'there's nothing like it. Even when you know it's empty and hollow and could all go away tomorrow, it's like being addicted to heroin – I spend my whole life trying to top my very first high.'

'Duke,' Evie says, 'you don't mean that. Do you?'

She's looking at him with those big brown eyes, circling something close to pity.

'No.' He smiles, changing his tone. Why did he think he could be honest? Why is he so desperate to feel seen by somebody, anybody, that he would say something like that to a virtual stranger? It's her books. He meant everything he said about loving her books, loving their insights. But the author isn't the work – that's what he's coming to comprehend. She's beautiful and sharp and has a very specific sense of humour, and some of that goes into her work, but that isn't *her*. Maybe it's parts of her. The other parts are here, mocking everything he's dedicated his adult life to, and actually, that's not okay.

They get the bracelet and by the time Duke's back at his hotel, citing a headache and a need to run his lines, the photos are online. Just as they'd hoped, there was a photographer there the whole time. He hates that he checked, and hates even more the sad, heavy feeling that develops in his stomach as he scrolls through. There they are eating, riding the rides, looking into each other's eyes. There's a photo of him gazing almost adoringly at her as she looks off to one side, and then perplexingly, considering she had a wry smile plastered to her lips for most of the afternoon, a photo of her looking at him in quite the same way. He's reading a menu, or a pricing list, and her face is open and wide, her expression playful and sweet. It really does look like she's into him. Duke wonders if she hasn't missed her vocation. Apparently she's quite the actor too. *I want that look for real,* he thinks to himself, before deciding he doesn't mean that, that he needs to sleep, that he'd never want to be with a woman like Evie, forever feeling like he can't keep up.

So why does he keep thinking of her?

'You seem blue,' Daphne says to him after their final scene, a physical comedy moment that involved an ice rink, a fall, and an almost-kiss. 'I'm here, you know. If you need me.'

Duke looks at her. It's late. He's not really been able to

mull over his 'date' yesterday, how unkind it felt to be the butt of Evie's distaste for their *fauxmance*.

He was up early to get one of his solo scenes, which went fine – not great, but fine. The snow had frozen into ice, so it was pretty chilly, and it's hard to focus when you're that cold. But as the sun came out and the ice melted, he was able to finally lean into the thing he's best at. He's really proud of what they're making together. It doesn't happen on every set – hell, it doesn't happen on most sets. It's some sort of magical alchemy where cast, crew, story, and set are all aligned. This won't be a contender for the awards season but that was never the point of taking the role.

The point of the role was . . . well, when he read the book he *felt like* George. Every thought and feeling and worry. Duke's mother isn't dead, but she's seldom present. What Evie said, about him being a little boy, it's played on his mind. He can hear Phoebe's voice ringing in his ears: of course he's like a little boy, because little boys need parents to help them become men, and nobody guided him through that. Since he was eleven years old, he's more or less raised himself – his dad never known and his mother drunk. It's a romance, this movie, but for him George is a talisman for a man holding himself back because of his relationship with his parents. For George, it's supposed to be positive: he loved his mum so much and she's gone. What does he do now?

For Duke, he wants that chance to love his mum so much; it's simply always been impossible. And yet, he keeps trying. Does that make him a fool? What does Duke do now? Where is he supposed to put this love he has to give? Nobody seems to want it.

'I'll be fine,' Duke tells Daphne. 'I will.'

They head to her trailer, and he sits on her sofa as she takes off her make-up, transforming from Hermione to herself. She throws him a wipe so he can do the same. His dermatologist says wipes are the devil's work, but he'll cleanse properly at the hotel. It comes away orange. It's incredible how much stuff they have to put on your skin to make you look 'normal' in 4D. Nobody actually looks like Duke Carlisle, not even Duke Carlisle. No wonder nothing is ever good enough – he's comparing himself to an apparition. A myth of his own creation.

'Brad said the photos of you and Evie are everywhere,' Daphne says, throwing her hair up into a high messy bun. 'So that's good. It's not lost on me that you could have said no, because it helps me too. I appreciate it.'

'Just doing what I'm paid to do,' Duke says to the ceiling.

'Poor little superstar,' Daphne says, plopping herself down on the sofa next to him. She reaches out a hand to his and holds it. Her tone changes. 'You'll get what you're looking for, you know. I know it doesn't feel like it, but you will. I see it for you.'

'Yeah?' Duke says, looking at her.

'I see a doting wife, and an army of kids all with that hair of yours – happy beach vacations and huge Christmases. It's just . . . well, are you accepting unsolicited advice?'

'If I say yes,' Duke retorts, 'by definition doesn't that then mean it's actually solicited?'

She rolls her eyes. 'Look. I adore you. I do. You know I do. And so when I say this, I mean it with all the love in the world, and I'm saying it to help, not hurt.'

'Why do I get the feeling you're kissing my forehead right before you skewer me with a sword?'

'It's the *trying*, Duke. You try so hard to make a relationship what you think it should be in your head that you don't let it unfold as what it actually is, and that's why it never properly feels real.'

He was right: that feels like a sword to his heart.

'I am who I am, Daphne,' he tells her. 'I'm a trier.'

'Absolutely.' Daphne nods. 'I just mean . . . be who you are and trust that that's enough.'

He looks at her. That's just it, isn't it? The thing he talks about in those sessions he pays hundreds – thousands! – of pounds for. Being enough. Feeling enough.

'My therapist says nobody will see past my celebrity to the real me until *I* start to accept the real me and stop hiding behind my status,' Duke says. 'Which is embarrassing, because it's a bit like complaining my mattress is stuffed with too much money, isn't it?'

'No,' Daphne says emphatically. 'This business is screwed up. Everyone thinks they know us, but when we let people in, we get screwed over. And then when we keep our circles tight, we get accused of being aloof and stuck up. It's mad. I want you to know, though, that you are enough, and the man I've seen at 6 a.m. making scrambled eggs in the kitchen and singing into his toothbrush before bed, he's remarkable. And my Christmas wish for you is that *you* get to see that. You're a good actor, pal – but you're an even better human.'

When they've said goodbye for the evening, Duke tells his driver he'll walk to the hotel. It's almost midnight, so the market is closing up and the crowds are non-existent. He'll be fine, getting some fresh air. It's not exactly dangerous in a tiny town in the middle of Bavaria. He just wants to feel normal. With his hat on and hood up, he should be okay. The trick is not to make eye contact with strangers – keep looking down; that's what Owen Wilson taught him.

He's in trainers and joggers and watches the cobblestones underfoot as he puts one foot in front of the other. He doesn't know where he's going. It's a common misconception that filming all over the world means that he's visited all over the world. He hasn't. He's seen the same trailers and craft services and hotel rooms the world over, but doesn't often get time to truly explore a place. By the time he's done on set, he often just wants to head to London or LA to have food he knows, beds he chose, and catch up with the few friends he has.

He ignores the shout of his name the first time it happens. It's a woman's voice, and he worries he's been spotted, will have to make polite talk and take a photo. He's trying to get just five bloody minutes to himself. Just five minutes! That's all he wants! But when the voice comes again he recognises it.

'Evie,' he says, confronted by her open, pretty face.

'Hey,' she says, not-quite-smiling. 'Looks like we've had the same idea.' She gestures to the empty streets.

'A midnight walk to mull over the complexities of being human?' he offers, and she laughs. He gets a feeling again, a feeling of pride at the accomplishment. He wasn't even trying to make her laugh that time, like he has done before. And yet.

'Something like that,' she replies, eyeballing him. It looks

117

like she's been crying, now he can see her properly. Her eyes are red-rimmed and her cheeks are blotchy.

'My mom,' she says, gesturing to her face, when she clearly realises he's noticed. 'I hate being away from her. I've been having a *moment*, as my best friend Magda would say.'

Duke aches with envy. What must it be like to miss your family so much it makes you cry? To have a best friend, even? He feels a pang of guilt that she's away from everyone she loves. It's his doing, after all.

'She's lucky she's got a daughter who cares so much,' he offers. 'That's lovely. It will be nice to get back in time for Christmas, I bet.'

She changes the subject, and Duke assumes somehow it's for his benefit. She pulls a small silver flask from her coat pocket and takes a swig instead of speaking, coughing when she's done.

'It's good stuff!' she hoots, holding out the flask for Duke. 'Comes recommended,' she adds. He reconsiders his earlier assessment. Maybe the eyes were from crying but the blotchy cheeks were from booze. No judgement.

He takes it, drinks, and she tells him the view is great from up the hill she's just come from.

'Do you want me to show you?' she asks, and the way she says it is like a peace offering. They haven't seen each other all day – Duke hasn't even spotted if she's been on set or not – and when they said goodnight after their date it was terse. Almost unfriendly. Duke had wanted to alleviate the pressure of pretending once they were back at the hotel. He didn't need a jovial friend hug again. He knows where he stands.

'You don't have to,' he tells her. 'I should probably get back to the hotel anyway.'

'Don't wanna risk those eye bags?' she quips, and Duke pulls a face like *well what can ya do?*

She looks at him – like really, properly looks at him. It makes Duke uncomfortable. What is she thinking? Does she *pity* him somehow? She's such a tough nut to crack. It's ironic: he's desperate to be seen, and she's an expert at hiding.

'Come on,' she says. 'Another half hour won't kill you. It's worth the late bedtime, I promise you. And besides, I *want* to.'

She takes another swig of whisky and offers the flask back to him.

'I can choose sleep deprivation or a hangover.' Duke smiles. 'But I can't do both.' She tucks it back into her pocket. They walk.

Evie is right about the amazing view. They hike in silence, climbing a set of steep steps and then rounding a corner and winding between some bigger, more luxurious houses until they find themselves in a clearing beside a small stone square with a statue of a man on a horse. There's a wall, and Duke assumes that at the other side of it is a steep drop, because the closest thing he can see is the river, far below – its promenade lit up with wrought-iron lamp posts glowing amber – and across the way an expanse of winding streets just about visible because of more streetlamps. It's quiet, and Duke finds solace in that. His brain moves at a million miles an hour but, right now, a shot of bourbon in his veins and his lungs working hard after the climb, the peace extends through his ears into his entire body. He takes a big breath.

'Same,' Evie says, softly, moving to rest her forearms on the wall. Duke mirrors her.

Eventually, Duke says, 'So the missing of your mum – you okay now?'

'Oh yeah,' she says, 'I'm fine. I'm so fine.'

Duke smirks. 'So says every fine person in the land. I'm totally buying it. You're fine.'

'Okay, not *fine*,' Evie concedes. 'She's in a home. She has Alzheimer's. Most of the time she has no idea who I am, and I rang to see how she's doing, and the answer is: not great. She's agitated. Won't cooperate. I couldn't do anything if I was there. I'd still be crying. I wish I was stronger, I guess.'

Duke feels a wave of sympathy. 'Urgh.' He nods. 'I'm sorry. That must be very hard.'

'It is what it is,' she says, wafting a hand. 'Like I've said before, life sucks. Most of the time at least.' She takes in the view again and Duke follows her gaze.

'Yeah,' he sighs. 'And then there's a view like this.'

'And then there's a view like this,' she repeats.

16

Evie

The truth of her life slips out easily to Duke. She didn't mean to tell him about her mom – the Alzheimer's is yet another secret she keeps; even Magda doesn't know the full extent of her mother's illness. He listens kindly, as in: he doesn't interrupt her, and empathises with the weight of it all without offering solutions or acting like he can be her hero. She hasn't realised that's what she's been in need of: a witness to it all. She doesn't need somebody to rescue her, God no. It's another person nearby who soothes her. His presence helps. Him just standing beside her whilst she acknowledges her truth is . . . oddly healing.

She's not sure what's happening. They're fake-dating, and she *did* hate him . . . But the more she seems to lean into it, just for the heck of it, the more he pulls back, like he is worried she doesn't understand it is all a game. Evie doesn't see the harm in trying to find at least a shred of fun in it, since she's already busted through so many personal reservations to reach this point. She's kind of in *yolo* mode. She mostly stayed away from set today, taking calls with her agent about book sales and movie option updates (the short version? Everything is on the up, frighteningly so). But she was restless tonight, and she isn't sorry they've ended up in the same place. She hates being around him, but hates *not* being around him more.

'What about you? Are you close with your family?' she finds herself asking. She's going to ride this wave of sudden conversational intimacy whilst he's apparently open to it.

'No comment,' he replies, shaking his head.

'That bad, huh?' she pushes.

'You've got no idea,' he tells her. 'Seriously.'

'All evidence to the contrary,' Evie counters. 'In case you've already forgotten, my mother doesn't know who I am anymore, and just so you have the full picture: my dad is a cheating asshat who left. I have seven half-brothers and sisters I've never met because of him.'

'Oh,' Duke says. 'That's horrible. I'm sorry you're part of the Shit Dad Club too.'

Evie turns her back so she's no longer facing the view, but leaning against the wall instead. She crosses her feet at the ankles and stuffs her hands in her pockets.

'Should we get T-shirts made, or . . . ?' she jokes, and when they lock eyes it's loaded. It really is a special kind of club, Evie thinks. You don't know unless you know. 'You seem remarkably well adjusted anyway,' she adds. 'So my compliments to your therapist.'

'Ha.' Duke smiles. 'I'll be sure to let Phoebe know.'

'Phoebe?' echoes Evie. 'That doesn't sound like a therapist name. Patrice, or Monica. Those are therapists' names.'

'Jonathan.'

'Jonathan!' exclaims Evie. 'Yes. Maybe they should get a name change with their diplomas. I'd trust a Jonathan. Although, jeez, I don't know how they do it, listening to everyone's whining all day. I'd throw myself out of a window. Shall we walk? I'm freezing my nuts off.'

They decide to see if there's a path back down to the main town at the opposite end of the opening to where they came, each emboldened by the other to explore.

'So therapist is off the list of alternate careers for you I take it?' Dukes enquires, as they find a very dimly lit passageway that could take them to exactly where they need to be, or end in their untimely mutual deaths by way of an axe-murderer in the shadows.

'At this point, I am absolutely unemployable,' Evie quips. 'Who's gonna give a job to a woman likely to use it as plot?'

'Do I need to be careful what I say?' Duke asks over his shoulder. He's leading the way. Evie strains in the dark to get a good look at his ass before she's really aware of what she's doing. She catches herself. Why is she looking? It's not like she's into him or anything.

'Always.' She laughs. 'I can make no guarantees.'

'Duly noted.' Duke chuckles, and Evie feels the need to clarify.

'For the record,' she tells him, 'I am absolutely serious. There are two things as a writer that I know to be true. One is that even if you, as the author, don't believe a thing your character says, people will assume that it is your truth and act accordingly. If your protagonist thinks *live, laugh, love* signs are basic, everyone assumes you think they are basic too, and by extension that you're an uppity bitch. If your antihero hates olives and thinks anyone serving them at a party must have been born without taste buds, nobody will ever offer you a pitted kalamata ever again. Very few people can separate the book from the author, and it pisses me *off.*'

Duke chuckles again, and it's not lost on Evie that she's on a bit of a roll with making him laugh. It does something to her chest, the notion of amusing him.

'What's the second thing?' he asks.

'That I don't mean to be a magpie or pick over the carcasses of stories that belong to other people, but it just sort of . . . happens. I write about humans, and also interact with humans on a daily basis. Well . . .' She reconsiders this. 'Mostly daily basis.' There are stretches of time when she's on deadline where she stays home, unshowered, only pausing to let the dog out into the backyard. But besides that, she does find it helpful to write in coffee shops, listening in to the conversations of others, or lingering in the locker room after a weights class, eavesdropping on small talk.

'My seventh-grade crush once made an appearance in a novel, and I only realised I'd been imagining him as a grown-up and using all his characteristics *after* the book was published. The mannerisms of my hairdresser, I've used them before too. The bad behaviour of exes . . .'

He turns around at this. 'What about fake exes?' he asks. 'When our fauxmance is a nomance, are you going to write about it?'

Evie rolls her eyes. 'Be wary of the man who directly asks if you're going to write about him,' she says, but she means it good-naturedly. It's her way of saying no. Honestly, not if she can help it. It's too embarrassing. Something tells her that saying as much won't go down well with him though, so she doesn't.

'What about you? Any unlived lives?'

They're back down on the flatter terrain of the main city now. Right as Evie wonders what the time is – it's too much effort to pull off her gloves and unzip the top part of her coat to retrieve her phone – a church bell strikes with three tolls. Three a.m. She's been walking for hours.

'For a while I thought I might do something in science – I love working out how and why things work. But I didn't qualify for a bursary at uni because technically our household income was too high, even though . . . well, Mum drinks. Please don't tell anyone because I don't want anything in the papers about it. I asked for this life; she didn't. But yeah. In theory we were this mother-and-son middle-class family, so on paper I didn't need any help, but behind closed doors she was barely functional, mismanaged all her cash, all her bills, things like that. It was my secondary-school drama teacher who said I could try auditioning, see if I could get some cash-in-hand gigs as an extra for a couple of projects she knew were local. And it all started from there. As soon as it clicked that you can make a living from saying stuff on camera – like, come on, let's be honest, how is that real? – I didn't want to do anything else. Mum seemed to drink less for a little bit after my first appearance on this BBC show, as the friend of the main guy. I had maybe ninety seconds of screen time over four episodes but it's the first time she acted like she was proud of me. Sorry. I'm talking a lot, aren't I? Always did love a monologue.'

Evie can tell he suddenly feels awkward about how much he's revealed, so she doesn't press him. The small back streets give way to wider roads, guiding them back to the centre, the lights making the damp cobbles glisten and ever so slightly slippery.

'Gah!' Evie shrieks, as she skids on a stone. She rights herself sheepishly. 'Spot the attention seeker,' she jokes. 'Sorry. I was literally just about to say that I am enjoying your monologue. I feel honoured that you trust me. Because you can. I know what I said earlier, but I can be a vault when I need to be.' She motions locking her lips and throwing away the key, and he sniggers.

'I absolutely believe you,' he says. 'Thousands wouldn't.'

Evie gives a fake beam and flutters her eyelashes.

'To round off my sad tale,' he continues, and they're walking closer to each other now; there's room to meander side by side. If they were on the clock as fake lovers Evie would be tempted to slip her hand into his. He has big hands, she's noticed, with long thick fingers and perfectly rounded, short nails. 'Surprise! It didn't last. But Christ, I think I've dedicated my whole career to trying to impress her enough to get her to stop drinking again. Surprise number two: it has, so far, been a complete and utter waste of my time.'

'Duke . . .' Evie says, softly, stopping. She touches his arm, and he looks down at it, then back up at her. She forgets what she was going to say. It doesn't seem fair that he has to hold in so much pain. At least Evie's mom doted on her

126

whilst she still could – although maybe that makes it worse. If she'd be an awful mother, it might not hurt so much to lose her. As it stands, it feels like a death without a body to bury. Sometimes Evie wonders, in the absolute dead of night, if she isn't just waiting for her mother to die, so they can both be released from purgatory.

They're stood still now, Evie and Duke, and she hasn't taken her hand off his arm. She can't be sure who has instigated the lack of distance between them, but the gap has closed. They're maybe a hand's width apart, and she didn't realise the depth of his eyes before, how they tell so many stories without a word. She could melt into those eyes. She could do nothing else for many more days except look into those eyes. Is that too much? She doesn't care. He's *beautiful*. Not handsome. Beautiful. And she's misjudged him. She assumed he had it all, this fancy actor in the lead role of her book's movie, assumed that cartoon birds dressed him and his pavements were paved with gold. She's been unfair. Even with the fake-dating – it seems to be causing him pain, somehow. She can see that now. It's just another role required of him by others.

She's ninety-nine per cent sure that he is one hundred per cent out of her league, but she thinks, in this moment, as they continue to get, minute millimetre by minute millimetre, just a little bit closer, that she could kiss him. So she leans in, caution to the wind and taking her chance, willing to risk it all in case she's wrong and he might just kiss her back, and she swears he leans in as well. He's not repulsed by her, he doesn't hate her. Actually, he might want this too . . .

The church clock chimes again, and Evie leaps back, coming to her senses.

What was she thinking?

She can't fall for him, can't kiss him, can't be feeling any of this.

'We should head back,' she announces, clearing her throat with a cough. Duke frowns, just a tiny amount, and then murmurs agreement.

'Okay,' he says, and they head back to the hotel in silence, exactly as they seem to have done many times before.

'Coffee,' Evie says. 'I cannot face this day on no sleep without coffee.'

They're only just getting back to the hotel at 5 a.m. Evie can't believe that the time passed by so quickly. Even when they took a wrong turn and ended up looping around town in the opposite direction to the one they'd meant to go in they were chatting and laughing. But they're here now; they've figured it out. Everyone must have a later call time than Duke, because it's quiet. Evie expected to have to avoid inquisitive looks and impertinent questions but, like so much worry is, it was misspent. The place is deserted.

'I'm going to need a triple,' Duke agrees, looking around like he's noticed the eerie calm too. 'I don't think I've pulled an all-nighter since the 2015 Emmy's.'

'He says, offhandedly,' Evie quips, rolling her eyes.

'Good morning, Mr Carlisle, Ms Bird,' says the barista behind the bar. 'I thought you'd left already with the others.'

Evie is already requesting a double-shot latte as Duke says, 'Sorry, what? The others have gone already?'

'Yes,' the barista says, a pretty thing with long brown hair pulled back into a ponytail and delicate, elfin features. 'The

128

actress, she said there was an emergency schedule change, I think. Last night.'

Duke looks pointedly at Evie, who is aware that his spine has straightened and his shoulders have become broader.

'I'll still take that coffee to go,' she tells the barista. 'And one for him, please.' But she's already lost him. He's pulling out his phone and the look on his face means, Evie can surmise, that something has happened.

'They've gone without us,' he says, shaking his head and reading off his phone. He thumbs through his missed call list – reams and reams of calls from what Evie can see – and then tells her: 'I'd been on set all day so nobody told me – I hate being bothered by logistics when I'm working. It's distracting. So they packed up my stuff and were expecting me to get back to the hotel after the shoot but I went for a quick walk and my driver didn't know, I suppose . . . my phone was on silent, and . . . Did I really not check my phone this whole night?'

The barista sets down their coffees, and Evie fishes out her phone too. It never occurred to her that she hadn't checked it. She often switches it off and puts it in a drawer when she's working, so it's not unusual for her to go hours or even days without it. If the nursing home needs her, they have her emergency home phone number, and whilst she's here they have the number to the hotels.

She takes a look. She also has several calls from the producer, and Katerina, the DP, and her agent, all of whom probably assume she's made a break for it like she threatened to. Ah.

'So . . .' Evie says. 'Oops?'

'Yeah,' says Duke. 'Oops. Okay. Let me call my driver. You'll just get in with us, right? I mean, you kind of have no choice.'

'I'd like to ride with you, yes,' Evie replies, slurping from the coffee that has been made to a pleasingly drinkable temperature. 'Did they really leave you behind?' Duke looks at her. She says it laughingly, and the look on his face demonstrates that he agrees that it is pretty funny. 'You're a pretty expensive valuable to head off without.'

'Let's just get that coffee. My head feels scrambled.'

By 6 a.m. they're in Duke's luxury people carrier, upholstered in leather that Evie notes is softer than butter. They both had time to quickly shower, and Evie packed her own bags, on account of the fact that as a lowly author nobody had done that for her, as they had Duke. They threw down a breakfast sandwich and another coffee as they waited for Duke's driver to fill up on gas and so far, now they're on their merry way, Duke has spent most of the time on his phone.

'Budgets,' he grumbles, as they fly down the autostrada at a speed Evie has never travelled outside of a jet before. Apparently Germany doesn't do speed limits. 'They're trying to shave two days off the production because Brad needs to make sure he's under budget. That's why the schedules and corresponding locations got moved so suddenly.'

'Does that really matter?' asks Evie, trying to watch the world go by out of the window but struggling to get her eyes to adjust to blur after blur. 'The budget?'

'Yes, it matters,' Duke snaps, half looking up and seemingly deciding she's not worth the effort and so immediately going back to his phone. 'It impacts what he can negotiate for his next job.'

His tone is sharp, and Evie decides to write it off as a mix of embarrassment and frustration. All she meant was that surely two days would hardly make a budgetary difference, when you consider the amounts of cash everyone is dealing in. But maybe that's naïve. What does she know? This isn't her industry. All she knows is that in order to write *On the Romantic Road* she spent a lot of time googling all the picturesque towns and castles, and to actually visit the Schaezlerpalais in Augsburg is an opportunity she never thought she'd get. It's the one thing she managed to get even slightly excited about when she signed her contract, and now she's staying, and even trying to do it in good humour, she doesn't want to miss it.

The blurs outside the window become more focused, then, and Evie becomes aware of trucks and other cars and vans. They slow, at first, and Duke finally looks up properly from his phone.

'Traffic?' he asks the driver, and the driver replies, 'Accident, I think.'

They stop completely.

Flashing lights from emergency services light up behind them, doggedly requesting everyone move out of the way to let them through.

'Must definitely be an accident then,' Evie observes.

'You think?' Duke snaps, tapping his foot in erratic rhythm.

Evie shoots him a look. 'Hey,' she says. 'You can be anxious to catch them up without being an asshat to me, buddy. Cool it.'

Duke sighs irritably. 'I think I can be afforded a little wiggle room on being an asshat,' he tells her. 'When this is your fault.'

Evie thinks he's kidding to begin with, so laughs before quickly noting his serious face. 'Oh, for real?' she asks.

'It was your idea to go up the hill,' he says.

'And the gun I held to your head that persuaded you,' she retorts.

'You'd been crying! What was I supposed to do, leave you?'

Evie's jaw drops in temporary bewilderment. 'So you walked around with me all night because you . . . what? Felt sorry for me?'

She holds his eye, bold and defiant. She doesn't need his pity. This is exactly why she doesn't tell people about her mom. She's fine. She thought he *wanted* to take the stupid frickin' walk. She was already making her way back to the hotel when she saw him. She'd only meant to smooth things over and make nice; she could have easily not bothered.

'Well?' she pushes, when he doesn't reply right away.

'Forget it,' he says, turning his attention to outside, craning his neck to see what's happening.

They wait, the air between them full of resentment. Evie isn't sure what turn they've taken, but she sure as hell knows she's seeing a side of Duke Carlisle that she doesn't like. The sooner they get to Augsburg the better. She can see this isn't anything close to what she thought, or if it was, she's had a lucky escape. His moods are dark. Is it because he's not used to having anything but a smooth, easy time? What is it they say – you can tell a lot about a person by how they handle lost luggage or a sudden downpour of rain? Apparently Duke can only be charming when everything is going right, and that isn't real life.

More blue lights flash, more cars move to the hard shoulder to let them through, and they wait ten minutes, fifteen, thirty, Evie long having put in her AirPods and Duke continuing his effort to make his thumbs fall off from scrolling.

Forty minutes. Forty-five. It starts to snow. An hour. They still don't move.

Evie sees the driver turn around to talk with Duke, so she pulls out an AirPod to listen.

'What do you mean, closed until the morning?' she catches Duke saying. 'Can't we take another route?'

The driver nods, signalling he understands the request. 'The smaller roads,' he says. 'Even if I could get to them, in this weather? It's no good. It's very dangerous. This is a big car, and the snow . . .'

They both turn to look out of the window the driver is gesturing out of. It's windy – really windy. Inches of snow have fallen even in the time they've been stationary, and it's now being picked up by the gale to make a blizzard.

'The radio,' the driver presses. 'They say not to move.'

Duke argues, listing all the reasons why it's impossible, why he's a special case whom the weather should not affect, offering more money, a little extra if the driver can just sort it all out, and Evie can see that the more he talks the less impressed the driver is becoming. The more he speaks the less impressed Evie is becoming, to be honest.

'Duke,' she says finally, when he pauses for breath. 'Nobody can control a snowstorm. It literally needs to just blow over. Look!' She points out of the window. 'People are leaving their cars *in the road.*' She gives a little clap in between each word for emphasis. 'Two hundred pounds can't stop that.'

Duke flares his nostrils, his breathing heavy. He's upset. Like really upset. Evie doesn't want to suggest that it's disproportionately so, but the shoe fits. She lets the reality of their situation sink in for him. He watches a family in the next lane get their two kids out of the back, each parent carrying one as they all tuck their heads down.

'There's a service station just up ahead,' the driver says. 'We have to go.'

Duke looks to Evie for confirmation, and she nods as he zips up his coat.

17

Duke

It occurs to him that if the blizzard is so bad that they have to abandon their car, surely filming will have been halted too. Small mercies, then – any further delays won't be his fault. Thank God.

Duke wishes he'd worn better shoes, since the snow takes seconds to seep into his trainers and turn his feet to ice. Evie thought to grab spare socks, jumpers and her toothbrush from her suitcase and stuff them into a bag to bring with her, but Duke is stranded with nothing. He wonders if petrol stations sell socks.

They walk for maybe ten minutes, passing the accident where nobody seems to have been seriously hurt, but two cars block the road in its entirety. The ambulance is snowed in now, as is the police car, and so it doesn't take huge imagination to figure out that the tow truck was too late to make it through the snow.

'I've never known weather like this!' Evie exclaims, as they reach the services. It's a medium-sized squat building that thankfully has power. There's a couple of fast-food restaurants, toilets, paid-for showers and two coffee shops. There's a subdued atmosphere, like the snow has insulated the collective volume.

'No,' Duke says, carefully moderating his voice to compensate for snapping earlier. 'Me neither.'

The driver excuses himself and tells Duke he'll text when he knows anything, leaving just the two of them. They stand side by side surveying the service station, and when Duke has cast his eye over the place once, twice, twenty times, he goes to say, 'Shall we find something to warm us up?' but right as he does Evie announces: 'I'm going to explore. Catch you later.'

She's gone before he can stop her. Damn. He's screwed this up; he shouldn't have been so short. He was getting it from all ends, though: production, Brad, his team – even Daphne had made a throwaway comment about him being away with the fairies. *Who doesn't look at their phone for five hours after they've disappeared from set?* was the general gist. How does he explain that whilst hanging out with Evie he forgot that the rest of the world existed, let alone his phone? And that deep down, he's not sorry about it?

He hadn't wanted their night to end. Something was different with her – she opened up to him. He hasn't known her long, but he knows enough to understand that that occurrence is a rare one. *Serendipitous*, that was the word. That he was there, and she was there, and they both felt like being together was better than being alone. So they'd walked and talked and laughed and she'd made him think, too. Everything he takes for granted, she challenges and questions. It makes him aware that if he's been unhappy, he's got more control over it than he's given himself credit for. She's been more effective in holding him accountable to himself in a night than Phoebe, his therapist, has been in six years. The way Evie sees the world makes his own vision clearer.

He unzips his coat, but keeps it on for now. Maybe there's a heater he can leave it on, or at the very least a coat hook. His feet are like ice, so he heads to the store where he's delighted to find a modest selection of winter essentials: socks, gloves, wellies, little gel packs that you crack to warm up. He buys a veritable smorgasbord, just in case this thing goes on for longer than he'd like. He heads to the biggest window at the far end to take a look at what's going on. It's still going strong. Bugger.

Three laps of the space and a toilet trip later, his feet have warmed through in his new climbing socks and horribly plastic-looking rain boots, and he spots her in the café, sat with a man. It can't be her, he decides, at first glance, because she's not alone – but it is. Her coat is over the back of her chair, her hair tucked into her polo neck, her hands wrapped around a big blue mug, as if she's the actor, not him. Nobody actually holds a cup that way. What's wrong with the handle? She keeps touching her cheek and laughing. No, not laughing. *Tittering*. The guy is maybe early forties, all salt and pepper hair and strong jaw. Duke notices the jawline of every single man he sees, because he's had to work hard for his. He chews rubbery weights to help with the definition. He already hates this guy for being so sharp.

Should he go over? Interrupt? He can't decide. Evie isn't his property. She can talk to whoever she likes. Flirt with whoever she likes. And yet there's a feeling in Duke's lower belly, his gut, he supposes, that doesn't like what he's seeing and wants it to stop. She looks up before he can decide what to do. They lock eyes. If panic response is fight or flight, Duke doesn't know where he'd fall since he finds himself frozen stuck to the spot. She lifts a hand. He doesn't know if that is acknowledgement or a welcome over. She goes back to chatting with her man. Duke can't stand it, he decides. Even if he just goes over to know what they're talking about, what's making her look up from under her eyelashes that way, that's enough.

'You look like you're settled in for the duration,' Duke says coolly as he reaches their table. With his coat still on, ridiculous petrol station boots and laden down with bags of his discounted stock, he looks ridiculous. This meathead Evie is sat with is all thin layers and fleecy fabrics and effortlessly Bear Grylls.

'Duke,' Evie says. Is she happy to see him? 'This is Markus. Markus thinks we're going to be here for a few more hours yet.'

'I work at the national news station.' Markus smiles. 'So I have a meteorologist on speed dial.' He has an accent, but perfect English.

'Shame you didn't call him before you set off this morning.' Duke smiles back, but the humour he thought he'd injected into the joke doesn't translate.

'Yes, I thought so too until I met Evie here.' He's smooth. Too smooth. Duke will not be leaving her alone with him. Nope. No way. Duke sets his bags down and turns around an empty chair from a nearby table.

'Mind if I join you?' he asks, but he knows they can tell it isn't really a question. 'Another hot chocolate for everyone?'

Evie narrows her eyes, evidently weighing him up.

'What?' Duke blinks, because he's not going to bring up their fight if she isn't.

'Marshmallows and no whipped cream,' she says, evading his prompt.

'Cream and no marshmallows,' Markus says, and instead of going to the counter – because Duke will be damned if he's leaving them alone for one more second.

He waves at a twelve-year-old kid nearby and says, 'Hey, do you speak English?'

'Of course,' the kid says, in English as good as all the other Germans Duke has met.

'Want to make fifty euro?' Duke says, and he knows it's somewhat of a dick move but he gives him a hundred-euro bill and the kid goes to buy their drinks.

'You're unbelievable,' mutters Evie, but her eyes are crinkled at the edges, betraying her tone. Duke knows he is hazardously close to the fine line between eccentrically charming and douchebag, but given the crinkles . . . he thinks he's on the right side.

They talk amiably enough, and Duke hates that Markus isn't overawed by the fact that they're here, in this tiny pit stop largely in the middle of nowhere, the last place you'd expect to bump into *People Magazine*'s Sexiest Man 2018. He takes everything in his stride, and if it wasn't for the way he keeps looking at Evie, Duke would almost want to be his mate. Except, Markus *does* keep looking at Evie that way and so Duke needs him to piss off.

'What are you doing?' Evie hisses at him when Markus excuses himself to answer a phone call. 'There are no cameras here, Duke. The show can break for intermission.'

'I don't know what you mean,' Duke replies. 'I'm talking with our new friend. There's nothing else to do whilst we wait, is there?'

She shakes her head. 'What about all of that massively important texting you were so busy with before? Or some more sulking? You're very good at passing the time that way.'

God, he really does find her sexy, he thinks, quickly followed by: *Oh, hell. What? Where did that come from?* He looks at her properly then. Her pointed barbs sharpened and designed to kill, her flushed cheeks, the tiny bit of cocoa powder near her nose – she's amazing.

'Look, I *am* sorry about earlier. I was . . . distracted. Would you like me to get on my knees and apologise one thousand different ways?' he says. 'Because I can.'

'Getting on your knees sounds perfect, actually,' Evie counters, calling him on it. Duke takes a breath. Well, if that's what the lady wants . . .

'Oh, Evie!' he cries, pushing back his chair and falling to the floor. He's on bended knee, but when a dad two tables over nudges his partner Duke realises that it looks like a proposal, so drops the other one.

'Evie Bird, bestselling author, lady of midnight-walking knowledge and endless hurtful-but-strangely-provocative jibes, I offer thee my most sincere apologies! Thou art a fair maiden and I but a rude, indignant ogre, and all the days and all the nights could not add up to enough time to truly give you the sorry you most truly deserve! Evie! I beg for your mercy! I beg for your grace, oh benevolent one!'

Evie looks at him and with a perfectly straight face – all the more impressive considering almost everyone in the café is looking at them – and says, 'Forgiven. That was a very proficient apology. Well done.' Duke had hoped to make her laugh. He'll settle for getting to return to his seat at the table.

'Your not-so-secret admirer hasn't come back . . .' Duke says, and Evie raises an eyebrow.

'Is that surprising?' she asks.

Duke purses his lips. 'I don't know what you mean,' he retorts quickly – too quickly. 'I thought you two were perfect for each other.'

Evie doesn't reply, simply busies herself with putting some lip balm onto her perfectly kissable lips and popping a mint.

'Want one?' she says, and Duke smiles. 'Is that a hint?'

What he meant was, was the lip balm and mint a hint that a kiss might be imminent. She knows that's what he meant. Instead, she pushes his buttons and tells him, 'Honestly? Yes. You've got breath like a sewer.'

Duke suddenly panics that that's true, practically ripping the mints from her hand. He takes two and chews quickly, and when he looks back at her sees that she's laughing. A lot.

'You're a funny one, mister,' she says to him.

He swallows the Tic Tacs.

'Is that so?' he says.

'Yup.'

'Hmm.'

'My sentiments exactly,' she clucks.

Then the penny drops. She's not going to make this easy for him. It's his turn, now, to push the needle forward on whatever *this* is. Last night, it was almost like she was ready to kiss him. Could it be? Is it possible that they've reached a place together that promises potential?

'Evie?' Duke prompts, needing verbal confirmation. She chews her lips and raises her eyebrows at him in response. 'It's my move, isn't it?' He grins.

She grins right back, and just like that they're on the exact same – and unexpected – page.

'Oh yeah,' she tells him. 'And you'd better make it a good one.'

'Hey,' Duke whispers, as close to her face as he can so as not to wake anybody else. 'Wake up, Evie. Psst.'

She looked so peaceful it felt borderline mean to nudge her, but she laid down the gauntlet with such provocation that Duke has to act before he loses his nerve. He doesn't know what it is about her exactly, why she can unnerve him so deeply. It might be her wildly obvious lack of regard for his work and his fame. She acknowledges it, but pushes him to show her what else there is. It terrifies him and exhilarates him. It's an addictive rush. She's calling him on his bull: he wants to be truly appreciated for who he is, and she's daring him to show her who he is, without the fame, first.

He watches as Evie lifts her head from where she'd been resting it on a café table. It's the middle of the night. They're

142

still in the service station awaiting word that it's safe to go back to the car. Traffic northbound is moving, but it won't be until sunrise that the debris from the car crash on the southbound road is lifted, and that's after the snow has been cleared. It's stopped, now, but there's a lot of it out there. Inside, the only lights come from the covered fridges in the food outlets and the Christmas decorations. The music has been turned off so people can rest, as if they're all on a flight somewhere over the Atlantic and will be awoken with lemon-scented wet towels by a smiling air hostess when it's time to think about their destination. There's fifty or so people stuck with them, so it's not too crowded – luckily so, since that's what sparked Duke's plan. This is the most public privacy he's had in years.

'Hey,' Duke says, as she eyeballs him. 'You okay?'

'I was,' she mutters quietly. She wipes some drool from her mouth and sits up. She's got creases down one side of her cheek. Duke wants to reach out a hand to them, to caress her face and cup her chin, but he doesn't.

'Yeah,' he whispers back. 'Sorry to wake you. I was just wondering if you wanted to go on a non-fake date with me.'

She quasi-smiles. 'What?' she asks. 'Now?'

She says it like it's a joke, but Duke nods. 'Yeah. Come on.'

He holds out a hand for her and with a puzzled expression she takes it. He leads her to the other end of the services and behind the counter of one of the outlets. Fingers entwined, palms touching, he takes her around another corner and holds back a curtain. He lets go of her hand to step aside and reveals what he's spent the past few hours working on.

'Ta-da!' he says.

He's assembled a small round table and two chairs. There's a dark red tablecloth, a small poinsettia in the middle, and tinsel wrapped around the backs of the seats. Light comes from hundreds of fairy lights, looped in varying levels of tightness around exposed beams above, so that some bits hang lower than others. On a bench fixed into the wall is beer, water, some sort of cold meats selection, bread, and cheese. Duke finds the lighter he's been hiding in his trouser pocket to light a single red candle.

'I didn't want to leave an open flame unattended,' he explains, waiting for Evie to say something.

'What the . . . ?' she comes out with slowly. He thinks it's a good what the . . . 'Are you serious? Duke!'

She scooches around to take a seat, her eyes wide and jaw slack as she takes it all in. 'This is very cute.'

Duke takes a seat as well in their grotto for two. 'Well,' he says. 'I heard you. I know the showmance stuff has been . . .'

'Not great,' she supplies, holding out a glass for him to fill it.

'Not great, yes,' he echoes, and once she's got her beer, he fills his own glass with a taste too. 'But I figured here, in this very bizarre German service station, in the middle of the night, when everyone is asleep, we might just get enough undocumented alone time for us to try normal. As an apology, maybe? It's all a lot. I know.'

'Cheers to that, Duke Carlisle,' Evie says, and they clink glasses.

'Just call me Duke,' he says. 'Or Derrick, if you want my real name.'

'OMG.' Evie laughs. 'Duke isn't your real name? You're called *Derrick*?!'

'Derrick Jones,' Duke admits. 'Derrick James Jones.'

She cocks her head at him, appraising this new information. 'How many people know that?' she asks him.

'Not many.'

She nods, like she understands the significance of his revelation to her.

'For the purposes of transparency, you should know that my name really is Evie. Evelyn, actually, like my mom. No middle name, just Evie Bird.'

'It suits you,' Duke says. 'Classic, with a twist.'

She pats her hair like an old-time starlet. 'Why, thank you very much,' she says, in a silly accent. 'I absolutely did not choose it myself.'

They laugh.

'Do you date much?' Duke asks her, bracing himself for the answer. She might have said she's single but that doesn't mean she doesn't have a friend with benefits, perhaps, or something on the back burner.

'Who, me?' she retorts. 'Unabashed starry-eyed, silly, playful me?' She raises her eyebrows like he's just asked her if she likes to poop on the front lawn as her preference or the back. 'No,' she says. 'Not anymore. What's the thing Einstein said? Doing the same thing over and over again and expecting a different result is the definition of insanity? Well, yes, hi, hello. That was me until I was thirty-two.'

'How old are you now?'

'How about you don't ask a lady her age?'

'I wasn't, I was asking you.'

'Ha, ha.'

They drink.

Duke decides to keep the conversation going. 'You know I have to ask what happened at thirty-two, don't you?'

'Ask all you want.' Evie grins, finishing her beer. 'But if you think ex-lovers is good first non-fake-date chat, I can see why you're still single.'

'Ouch.'

'Somebody has to help you out, buddy.'

More staring. More smiling. More loaded, heavy air.

'Go on,' Duke challenges her. 'If this was ten years ago and you were still dating . . .'

'I'm not forty-two, you asshat.'

'You keep calling me that!'

'You keep being one!'

Staring.

'What is acceptable date chat for you, Ms Bird?' he asks then.

She makes a gagging sound. 'Oh God.' She laughs. 'I don't know! I told you, I'm so bad with people, and . . . I don't know. I am aware I can be prickly. It's just who I am.'

'I am enthralled by you.' He says it like the queen, rolling his r's. It takes the edge off the truth in it.

'You and Magda, then. That's it. The two people in the world who think I'm interesting.'

'Surely not.'

'And my mother,' she adds. 'When she remembers.'

'Do you wanna talk about that?'

Without missing a beat she replies, 'Nope.'

They chuckle, and she picks up the empty beer bottle and picks at the label.

'I've just read a novel that features parental dementia,'

Duke says. 'I can lend it to you? It's in my stuff at the hotel.'

'Thank you,' she says. 'I'd like that. And thank you for being kind to me,' she adds, when Duke decides to let the silence play out. It's nice, sitting here with her, shooting the breeze, nobody with any proper idea where they are. He feels safe, and comfortable. He tries to think of anybody else he could pass twelve to eighteen hours stranded with, and he can't.

18

Evie

This is incredible of him, Evie thinks to herself as she steals a glance at Duke's angular face. She loves that he has kitted out this space this way, taking the time and effort to be sweet. No man has ever been this thoughtful. Her friends, yes. Magda is basically her surrogate partner when it comes to birthdays and holidays and small everyday celebrations. Magda is the person Evie texts when her flight lands, or she has work news, or she wants to complain about a bad day. And Magda does the same for her, too. They've taken trips together, dressed up for BFF date nights together, nursed the other when they've been sick – but in terms of a *man* going the extra mile? Nope. Never. That's why she makes it all up and writes it down in her books. That's what she meant when she told Duke her stories are as much fantasy as lightsabres and other-worldly dimensions. This kind of stuff just doesn't happen, and definitely not to her.

He's partway through telling a story about Jennifer Lawrence falling into his pool fully clothed when he threw a housewarming at his LA house as she considers him. She had him wrong. She can own that much. She thought he was an ego, an actor who thinks the world revolves around him. But he isn't. He's like the moon, reflecting the rays of the sun. He doesn't put himself at the centre of the solar system, which demonstrates character. Maturity.

She arches her back a bit, like she's uncomfortable after sitting for so long. She isn't, but she has a plan. She cricks her neck, and then shuffles in her seat, surreptitiously picking it up and moving it a few inches in Duke's direction as she does so, just to see how it feels. It makes him pause in his story like he's not sure if he's getting this right. He must have women throw themselves at him all the time, right? He knows how this goes, she thinks. Not that she's making a move, per se, it's just . . . the nearness of him. And yet he seems nervous, swallowing hard when Evie flicks her hair over her shoulder slowly and bites on her bottom lip again. What is she doing? Dare she?

'Sorry,' she says, her voice soft and her eye contact strong. 'I didn't mean to interrupt.'

Duke juts his chin out a little, and she gets that flash of a little boy again. And then almost immediately, he's back to his nervous, awkward self.

'Yes, you did,' he tells her, his voice wavering.

'Yeah,' she says, 'I did.'

And then they're greeted by the glare of a flashlight, the Spanish inquisition come to life. It's a security guard.

'No candle,' he says in a gruff, accented voice. 'Fire hazard,' he adds.

Duke leans over and blows it out, standing up and saying, 'Sorry about that. I didn't think. Quite right.'

Their moment is lost.

When the lights go back on, they're dozing next to one another on the floor, back in the main lobby area with everyone else.

'Morning,' Duke says to her, awkwardly.

'Morning,' Evie says back, just as awkward. Last night comes crashing back to her. Had she really thought she wanted to kiss him? She shudders at the memory. What an inexplicable moment of madness. She resolves to act extra normal with him, lest he get the wrong idea. Thank goodness the security guard interrupted when he did.

They pass Markus as they try to seek out their driver, who looks between them and nods, his lips set in a firm, unemotional line.

'Good morning, Mr Carlisle, Ms Bird,' their driver says when they approach him. 'As you can see, we are free to go. The snow has stopped, the roads have been cleared, and we should arrive within the hour.'

'Great. Thanks so much,' Duke tells him. 'Coffee for the road?' he asks. Evie wonders if he is being 'extra normal' to compensate for her stupidity last night too. Had he clocked what she had been about to do? 'Three lattes?'

'Please,' she says, with a big smile that doesn't quite reach her eyes.

They buy pastries and water, too, and chewable toothbrushes. Who knew such a thing existed?

Evie climbs into the people carrier and sits at the far

window, like she did yesterday. Duke gets in behind her. They head off the autostrada and into Augsburg. ('Founded by the Romans' their driver tells them. 'In 15 BC. This is the oldest city in Bavaria and the second oldest in Germany.')

Augsburg has buildings much like they've seen so far on the Romantic Road – all different colours, two or three storeys high with pointed, angular roofs. They pass two big white churches with red roofs and turrets, and pull into a huge cobbled square to a long grey building with attic windows and flags outside.

'The hotel,' the driver announces. 'Ms Bird, I'll follow with your things.'

It's brighter than their last hotel, which had a lot of dark wood. The Maximilian is all polished marble floors and pillars, very luxurious, and the sitting room-cum-bar area is laden with deep sofas and plush velvet chairs. They check in, and the concierge tells them they'll let the producer know they've arrived safely.

'This is for you,' the concierge says, slipping Duke a piece of folded paper. Inside, it says there's a cast and crew meeting in the restaurant at 6 p.m., attendance mandatory.

'I'll just go and get that book for you?' Duke asks.

'Sure,' Evie says. 'I'll come with you, if that's all right?'

See. Normal. Normal, normal, normal.

'Fine,' he replies.

His suite is on the top floor, with views over Maximilian-strasse and the Schaezlerpalais. They enter with a key card to find themselves at one end of a series of rooms, each closing off to the next with a pocket door that disappears into the wall. First is a lounge area, with a widescreen TV, sofa, a low wooden chair and a huge knitted rug over a chevron-laid wooden floor. The bedroom is next, with a bed that must be the size of two kings combined, and the fluffiest bedding Evie has ever seen. Then there's the bathroom, all shiny brass taps and marble tops, a huge wet-room shower, and then a wardrobe at the far end, where somebody has already unpacked Duke's clothes, his designer suitcases stacked neatly in the corner.

'Whoa,' Evie says. 'So this is how the other half live, huh?' she marvels, padding through to get a proper look.

'You say it like you're not one of us,' Duke retorts, doing the same. He hangs up his coat.

'I'm not,' she says, watching him peel off his jumper. He sees her, and she looks away immediately.

'What do you mean?' he asks.

'I meant that I could never afford a hotel, or a room, like this, myself,' she says, like it's obvious.

'But you're a bestselling author,' he says. 'Isn't this your world too?'

She scoffs, thinking he's making a joke. Everyone knows you don't get into writing for the money. 'You know I didn't write Harry Potter, don't you?' she says. 'Most of us earn just about enough to get by.'

'Oh,' he says. 'I didn't know that.'

'No reason why you should,' she says.

'Hmm. But how can a person be a *New York Times* bestseller and sell the rights to multiple books for screen, and not be . . .'

'Rich?' she supplies.

'You know what I mean.'

'Why are you so interested in my finances?' Evie asks, annoyed. 'I thought Brits were shy about money talk?'

'I'm not *interested* . . .' he tells her. 'I was just curious.'

'Curiosity killed the cat.'

'Okay,' he says, shifting so he can look at her. 'Sorry to ask. My bad.'

She shrugs. No way is she going to tell him about the flow of money through her bank account. That the more she earns, the more she spends, mostly on stuff she doesn't even need. Scented candles at a hundred dollars a pop. Handbags, even though she doesn't go anywhere. New coats, jackets, trousers, cashmere jumpers every season, which get worn to the coffee shop or Magda's house, maybe even a restaurant or bar during the daytime, and that's it. The stuff with tags still on that hangs in her closets because there aren't enough outfit changes in the day, or the car she has in the drive with less than ten thousand miles racked up in two years. Not to mention the soft furnishings, the smoothie machines and coffee makers in the kitchen. She knows it's a problem and has been for years: she doesn't feel worthy of the money, so she spends it on physical manifestations of *stuff*. Stuff she can look at, a physical thing that acts as an object to represent that she's doing well. She doesn't *feel* like she's doing well at anything. So she's sold a few hundred thousand books – so what? What does that mean when she goes to bed alone, when she's spine-less in the face of life because she's tired? Evie is so, so tired. Yeah, fine, she cashes the cheques, she pays the care home monthly – most of the time – and then she gets rid of the money as fast as she can. It's a compulsion. A stupid, embarrassing compulsion, and he's just not going to understand, is

153

he? Absolutely no way. And she's promised herself that the next big cheque won't go to her mom's nursing home to cover a month, or the next six months. Her spending is getting so bad that since May she's not been able to pay them at all. She's going to pay them for the next ten years when the movie money comes in, to avoid any problems. She's getting more and more reckless, and nobody has any idea because she has a Canada Goose jacket and a fancy watch and nice nails.

'Anyway,' she says. 'The book?'

'Right, yes. Hold on.'

Duke busies himself finding the novel he wanted to lend her, and Evie idly takes in the rest of the room. And then she sees it, poking out of the pile of papers. It's an information sheet. And it's about her.

She moves two paces to the left to angle her body away from Duke and tugs the paper out the tiniest amount more. It's her name, a general bio, and what looks like facts and figures for her books. It takes a breath, but then the penny drops: she had it right all along. None of this is real.

Duke doesn't care about her at all – her brain or thoughts or even her books. He's got a crib sheet on her, exactly as she suspected when she met him. And she nearly fell for it! All that talk about what her work means to him, and she'd started to believe it. He must think she's so stupid, just another groupie desperate to be wanted by him. Urgh.

When he comes back into the room, she silently takes the book from him and leaves.

'See you later?' he asks to her back.

Suddenly, she hopes not.

19

Evie

They're in the Schaezlerpalais later that afternoon, filming a dramatic and beautiful ballroom scene that serves as a climax for Hermione and George, who've attended after meeting a countess by accident, when they saved her and her dog from a wayward bicycle that had gotten out of control. It's deceptive outside – Evie counted seven windows across, and three floors up, but that was only the front façade. The Baroque palace extends far back from the street, with dozens of rooms, courtyards, and gardens. She takes a leaflet about the place and reads that the gilded mirror ballroom was built in the late 1700s and survives mostly intact. When she was researching the book, that was the thing that struck her imagination the most: that it could still exist. What dances must have been held there over the years, what secrets exchanged. It's like a set from *Bridgerton*. She spots Duke, in costume as George. He's in a tailored navy suit with a pressed white shirt, and it all looks like it's made to measure, which, thinking about it, it probably is. Daphne is in a long teal-coloured tulle gown, her feet in Uggs to keep warm. Her hair is piled in dramatic curls on the top of her head, her neck bare and perfect.

'My money is on them getting back together,' Katerina says, appearing out of nowhere. 'Look how they gaze at one another like that. There's a lot of love there if you ask me.'

'Oh . . . Katerina, hey,' Evie says, doing her best to look absolutely not bothered at all by the suggestion. 'Everything going okay today? I can't wait to see the ballroom.'

'It's . . . going,' sighs Katerina. 'Brad is in *the worst* mood. It's affecting the whole set. Well, almost the whole set. The lovebirds don't seem to be minding.'

Evie follows Katerina's gaze again. The pair *do* look cosy. They're just chatting, but there's an obvious familiarity between them, with the way Duke laughs and Daphne reaches out to hold his wrist as he does so.

'Am I allowed to go through to the ballroom before you shoot?' Evie asks, suddenly aware that the words feel foreign in her mouth, like she's trying too hard to act as though she's on film sets all the time. 'Or however you say it. Before you start filming,' she self-corrects.

'Yes, sure,' Katerina says. 'Just through there. It's stunning. It's going to look like a scene from *Bridgerton* when we're done, I swear.'

'I was just thinking that!' Evie exclaims. 'It does already.'

Evie walks through several doorways with rooms displaying art in ornate gold frames, and then she's there.

It's magnificent. The floor is a golden beehive formation in shades of golden syrup, dark in the middle and lighter around the edges, over and over again and polished so well it could practically be a mirror. It's a double-height room, with one set of sweeping windows down one side, and a second level of windows above to let in twice the light. The duck-egg blue panels that make up the walls are slim, and each is set with complex gold carvings, meaning that at first glance she almost thinks one side of the room is windows and the other simply dripping in gold.

As she gets closer, she can see the level of detail everything has. It's extraordinary. Several crystal chandeliers hang on long glass chains and, as she follows the lines upwards, Evie gasps, actually, truly gasps. The ceiling is painted with a series of elaborate murals in shades of lavender and mauve and lilac, depicting sunset and faith. There are some powder pink chairs with more gold around the edges, and a piano in sublime walnut wood in the corner, where Evie didn't at first see that a man in full morning suit is sat. He starts to tinkle on the keys, warming up. The sound reverberates around the room theatrically, and tears involuntarily prick at Evie's eyes. She's here. She can't believe she's here. She wishes she could call her mom. Magda won't be awake yet, but Evie will have to try her later. Somebody needs to know she's experienced this. They're going to have to remind her if ever she forgets.

Although . . . she's not mad at Magda, but she is a bit miffed: it's unlike her not to reply to a text, especially when Evie says she wants to catch up, but the last three messages yesterday went unanswered and it's made Evie feel a bit needy.

This feeling is evidence of why it's so horrific to reach out and say you need help, she thinks to herself. If she'd never asked, she'd never have to feel resentful at the radio silence.

Watching them film in the ballroom is amazing. The outdoor stuff has felt so . . . big? Like, outside, in the elements, within the context of the wider world, she has felt so far away from it, couldn't imagine how it will translate on screen. But here, everyone working within the same room and the lights and boom mics and all those extras, dancing, dressed in finery that Evie imagines could out-fancy even the poshest dress on the red carpet . . . She's truly in awe.

It's hard, though, knowing Duke really did have that crib sheet on her. She'd looked at it when she was in her room, a list of her books and accolades, a photo of her from her website and information her agent had obviously sent through ('Sarcastic but kind, media shy, bit of a lone wolf'). He'd said he was a genuine fan – and he'd lied. Evie is pretty sure she can trust the connection they've been building, but it's a red flag to her. She reminds herself that he might be an amazing actor doing a great job, but all this off-set stuff is still work to him. *Just for December.* That was the agreement, wasn't it?

'I'm still in negotiations with Scott Free and Columbia Pictures,' her agent Sabrina tells her on the phone later. 'And you're still storming the charts. The photos of you with Duke at the Christmas market, and that midnight walk? Perfection. I know you don't follow the tabloids, but the long and short of it is that it's playing out great – people love a rom-com within a rom-com, so get out with him again if you can, or maybe send your social girl a photo for her to upload to

Instagram. Doesn't even have to be to the grid – even just to stories is great, so it disappears within a day.'

'Wow,' Evie says. She's stepped outside for some air. It's baffling that everything outside on the street is so normal. She's become used to crowds waiting outside, but the world has kept turning today, like nobody is any the wiser they're about. 'Okay. God.'

'We're up to mid-six figures right now, just shy of a full half million.'

'Dollars?' Evie exclaims.

'Dollars,' echoes her agent. 'I'm telling you: this is your moment, darling. We have to seize it!'

Evie nods, then realises her agent can't see her do that down a phone line. 'Right,' she says. 'That's nothing like what we got for this deal. That's so much money,' she says. 'I don't know what I'd do with that kind of money. It makes me feel a bit sick, actually.'

'Pay off your house, for a start,' her agent says, gleefully. 'And spend the rest, baby. You've worked hard for this. You should enjoy it!'

'Right, yeah, okay thanks,' says Evie, her chest getting tighter. She's hot in her face, and the back of her neck too, despite the temperatures being freezing. She can see the hotel across the way, and doesn't even realise she's heading in that direction until she's searching for her key card, using it to take the elevator, pushing through to her room to rip off her coat and jumper and then standing in her bra in front of the bathroom mirror, desperately splashing her face with cold water.

She looks at her reflection. She cannot have that money.

That money will kill her. She can't have half a million dollars – more, if her agent keeps pushing. God only knows what the royalty cheques will be if she's charted in multiple countries, with several other countries having put in foreign rights bids too. She doesn't want that. She doesn't deserve that. It's too much. She comes back to that thought again. *It's too much, it's too much, it's too much, it's too much.*

She thinks of her father leaving, the last thing he said to her: *This isn't enough for me. This wouldn't be enough for any man.* She thinks of her mother in the home. And here she is about to get a freaking lottery win for books that aren't even that good. She just got lucky. But this is more luck than any one person needs. Her breathing gets shorter. Duke springs to mind, but she doesn't trust him. She likes him, but she doesn't trust him. Somewhere in the back of her mind she can see that she's gone pale, really pale, and she stumbles to the bed and looks at the hotel phone and she thinks to herself: *But there's nobody I can call. There's nobody here to help me.*

20

Duke

Duke pulls out his phone to see where Evie is so they can get another fake date underway, but as he goes to type her name into the search bar he realises he doesn't, actually, have her number. He's never had to use it before, since they've always been in the same space on set, or in snow blizzards.

He decides to burn off his excess energy in the hotel gym. Maybe he'll bump into her at dinner or in the bar. He doesn't want to chase or seem desperate. He grabs his workout shorts and vest and heads to the state-of-the-art gym in the basement. He has his AirPods in and is scrolling emails as he walks, so it's not until he practically bumps into Brad that he looks up and sees he's not alone. He pulls one headphone out. Daphne is there too. They're arguing, and he's interrupted.

'Oh, hey – sorry,' he says, looking between them both.

'Hey, man,' Brad says, and it takes Duke a beat to process what he's seeing. There's nobody else in the gym, Daphne's eyes are red-rimmed but she's forcing a smile, and Brad is breathing heavily and unevenly, like he's agitated about something. He's been in a foul mood all day, so Duke doesn't blame him for coming down here to burn off some steam, but the way Daphne is rubbing her wrist doesn't seem right. She sees him notice and looks away quickly, and when Duke looks to Brad, he does the same, like he's been caught.

'You okay?' he says to Daphne, looking from her wrist to her face once more, and pointedly so this time. *I know something has just happened,* he wills her to understand through the way he looks at her. *Let me step up for you. I can handle this.*

'It's just a stupid fight,' she says, not even bothering to try and deny it. 'We're both tired. It's fine.'

Duke can tell by her tone that it isn't fine.

'Did you put your hands on her?' he says to Brad, through gritted teeth and trying very hard not to simply pin him by the neck to the wall, because nobody touches a woman that way. Nobody hurts a woman.

'She was pushing my buttons,' Brad says, looking at Daphne as he says it. 'We were pushing each other's buttons. That's all.'

'So you . . . what? Laid your hands on her to stop her?' Duke presses. His heart is thumping wildly. Brad is his director, and losing his temper at him won't play out well for the rest of the shoot if he flips his lid, but that's no reason not to.

Brad sighs. Exasperated. Dramatic. Dismissive.

'You of all people know what she can be like, bro. Don't walk the moral high ground. You get it.' He stops short as

162

he sees Duke's undoubtedly changing face – the tension in his jaw, the flare to his nostrils – and softens his voice, man to man. 'Nothing happened, dude, okay? Come on, Daphne, let's go.'

Daphne winces, just slightly, as Brad grabs her by the very spot she's rubbing like it's tender. Reflexively, quicker than light and sound, Duke punches his arm away so he lets go. There's a beat, a moment, where nobody knows what to do. It was a violent, deliberate move. There's a faraway part in Duke's brain that knows nobody can get any visible bruising because of their jobs, but another part has Duke take a quick step towards Brad like he might actually deck him. Brad dodges in fear, and it's pathetic. Brad is scared of Duke. It makes Duke laugh out loud.

'Scum,' he says, taking a step forward, leading with his chest. 'Don't you dare ever – and I mean ever, ever, ever – hurt her again. Do you hear me?'

Brad rolls his eyes. Duke takes one more step to close the gap between them and screams, louder than he has screamed anything in a very long time: 'DO. YOU. HEAR. ME?'

He can see in the gym mirror that he's gone purple. He waits for his answer.

'Yes,' Brad tells him. 'I hear you.'

He walks off then, and as Daphne tries to go after him, reaching out, he shrugs her off and says, 'Not now, Daphne. Fuck off for a minute, why don't you?' Daphne's face falls to hell. She can pretend it's a misunderstanding all she likes, but now Duke has heard him speak so nastily, the jig is up.

'He's just stressed,' Daphne says, almost pleadingly, like she doesn't want Duke to think badly of him. 'What with the delays, and he's got the producers on his back, his wife calling him every hour of the day . . .' She trails off, embarrassed. 'He's never done it before,' she says. 'I swear. I wouldn't stand for it if he had.'

Duke looks at his friend, the woman he thought had broken his heart. He sees that her own is breaking, too, and it's Brad who has done it.

'You deserve better,' Duke says.

Daphne nods. 'I know.'

'Come here,' he says opening his arms when it looks like she's going to break down into tears. She doesn't even reach his chest before she issues a sob. 'I know, darling,' Duke coos, stroking her hair. He closes his eyes and says it again. 'I know, darling. I know.'

Duke and Daphne are the lead story on TMZ, Mail Online and @DukesLewks, which means the photos have already become memes and gone viral. Somebody photographed them laughing on set yesterday and then hugging in the gym – Daphne's face buried in Duke's chest, his arms wrapped protectively around her, his eyes closed. Speculation over whether they're getting back together is rife – although one anonymous source claims they were never really over in the first place. The production team don't seem to care one way or the other, as long as their movie keeps making headlines and getting clicks. As long as Duke is dating somebody, they're happy.

Duke is livid.

'There's a rat,' he spits to Daphne in the breakfast hall, where they've sat opposite each other at a middle table so that they can demonstrate to anybody who might care that they've got nothing to hide. 'It goes against every law on set. We're supposed to be a team. On set everyone is equal – that's how it should be.'

Duke shakes his head, feeing partly responsible. Hadn't Evie asked who could be the 'sources' on set? And he hadn't done anything about it. He'd brushed it off, acted like it was made up, and now look. The call is coming from within the house.

Daphne looks tired. Duke hasn't asked about her and Brad, knowing that if he pushes it, he risks making her withdraw entirely. She needs to be the one to bring it up, so he can be a willing listener. He's aware Brad isn't in the breakfast room though. Hopefully they didn't share a room last night. Duke knows how it looks in the photos, like they really are having a moment, but all the love he has for Daphne, somehow, even in less than a month since they broke up, is genuinely platonic. His feelings run deep and true, but they're deep and true in the spirit of friendship. He can thank Evie for that. No matter what happens there, something has shifted in his expectations of romance. He can't wait to bring it up with Phoebe when he's next in therapy: he's circling around something about greater vulnerability bringing greater rewards. He didn't get that with Daphne, because exactly like she said he played the role of boyfriend without ever properly opening up. He gets it, now, though.

'It might not be crew,' Daphne offers, focusing on her fruit plate. 'It could be staff from the hotel . . .'

Duke has considered this, but it doesn't account for the photos of him and Evie back in Würzburg. Unless staff everywhere along the Romantic Road make it their business to photograph their guests, which, in his experience of the German people just doesn't seem right. Everybody has been kind, deferential, and generally unbothered by their star power: they've just provided great service and gotten on with their days.

He sees Evie, then, walking across the room to the bread station.

'Evie!' Duke calls out, and when he waves it's as though she looks right through him. She's seen them. He excuses himself to go over to her.

'I tried to find you last night,' he says, standing beside her as she slices from a sourdough loaf and puts it on the small toaster. 'They wouldn't tell me what room you're in at reception. Got to love that dedication to guest privacy.' He's making a joke, but he can't even tell if she's heard it.

'Are you okay?' he asks. She looks a little . . . peaky.

She picks up and puts down some little pots of jam and marmalade, adding two sachets of salted butter to her plate and peering over at the progress of her toast.

'Evie?' he prompts.

She rubs at her eyes. 'Yeah,' she says, absent-mindedly.

Duke pauses. 'Okay,' he replies, as she puts the toast on her plate. 'Well, do you want to join us?'

'No, thank you,' Evie tells him. 'I think I'm just going to take this up to my room. I've got a bit of a headache.'

She disappears.

That was weird, thinks Duke. He wonders if it's something he's said.

21

Duke

They're filming what Duke thinks of as an outdoor 'frolicking' scene today, over at Naturschutzgebiet Seeholz, an area of natural woodland with winding paths and a small lake that, with a fresh sprinkling of snow, is a grander and more dream-like set than even the most talented designer could concoct. His costume for George is the warmest thing he's been put in this whole trip: it's basically full skiwear. In black padded salopettes, snow boots, thick gloves and a fitted black gilet over a black fleece jumper, he's snug as a bug in a rug. The sun is bright and the skies blue, his favourite kind of weather. He stands outside of the hair and make-up trailer getting some fresh air, taking it all in . . . and looking for Evie. He saw her get on the crew bus earlier, so he knows she made it.

'Duke, hi! How are you doing?' the director of photography, Katerina, says. 'Delays aside, the shoot's all going great, huh?'

He doesn't know Katerina well, and hasn't spent much time with her on set aside from at a small drinks gathering when they wrapped at Pinewood on the internal shots, before they flew out to Germany. He tries to rack his brains for some common titbit of information he remembers about their chat, but he comes up blank. Pinewood already feels so long ago, and he was a mess at the time, with news of Daphne's liaison so fresh. He goes for a different tack instead.

'Great, yeah,' says Duke. 'And look at this! It's gorgeous, isn't it?' He gestures at the expanse of snowy fields and pine trees, a veritable winter wonderland.

She nods enthusiastically in response. 'Well . . .' Katerina says, when it becomes apparent they've not really got anything else to say. 'Break a leg today.'

'Yeah.' Duke nods. 'You too.'

He breathes it all in again, but barely takes five breaths before Willow, from content, interrupts him.

'Hey Duke,' she says. 'I've just been on the line with the head of PR at the studio.'

'My favourite way for a sentence to start,' Duke quips, rolling his eyes.

'I know,' she says. 'We're always asking you for something, and I'm afraid today is no different. Just to give you a heads up, we know there are paps here today – I mean, we might have tipped off the paps, truth be told, but I cannot officially confirm nor deny that – and re: you and Evie, and you and Daphne . . . we just wanted you to know.'

'What's the play?' Duke asks.

'We're going to have Daphne and Evie take a walk between takes, so there's no suggestion of rift there or that they're fighting over you. Half the internet are shipping you with one, half the internet with the other, but the studio doesn't want to play into the cliché of great men being a scarce resource – *especially* since Evie has gone on record to say that will never be the case in her books. Does that make sense? Basically people can ship whoever they want, but we want the narrative to be that no man is so great that he can come between two new friends.'

Duke crumples his brow. '*Are* they two new friends? I don't think I've even really seen them speak.'

Willow shrugs. 'They are now,' she trills. As she walks away, Duke asks her, 'Hey, speaking of which – do you know where Evie is?'

Willow points. 'Isn't that her?'

Duke follows her finger with his eyes. Evie is in the middle of a field, her face upturned to the sun, eyes closed, spinning in small circles. Duke smiles. 'Yeah.' He nods. 'It is.'

She doesn't seem to hear him approach. Duke isn't sure if she's doing some kind of meditation; she seems to be in a bit of a trance. He mirrors what she's doing, self-consciously sticking out his arms too, standing beside her and getting a look at the peaceful expression on her face. He gives it a go for himself, closing his eyes and turning his face up to the warm, low winter sun. It's nice. He takes a breath, inhaling through his nose and then exhaling a big breath through his mouth. When he opens his eyes again she's staring at him, one eyebrow raised.

'Just wondered what all the fuss is about,' he tells her sheepishly.

'What's the verdict?' she retorts, smirking now. He'll take a smirk over a catatonic glazed-over nothing, though.

'You've defrosted since breakfast,' Duke says, closing his eyes again and keeping his arms wide to reassume his meditative stance. He hears her move in the snow and, peeking through one eye, sees she's done the same, and so that's how they converse, stood like two Angels of the North, side by side, in the middle of a field in Naturschutzgebiet Seeholz.

'Bad night,' she says, simply.

'I'm sorry to hear that. Are you hungover?'

She hits him. 'No,' she says. 'I had a panic attack, actually. I mean. I think that's what it was. A freak-out? Meltdown?'

'Oh hell,' Duke says. 'No wonder you felt rough this morning. I . . .' He trails off. Is he going to tell her? He can trust her, can't he? 'I know how that feels,' he concludes. 'After my first Marvel movie I started to get them. I don't even mean on set, or after, on the press tour. I mean after I landed the role, before I even got the full script. The *idea* of being in the Marvel universe sent me . . .' He doesn't have the word, so he makes a honking noise instead, hoping that gives her the gist.

'Oh,' she says. 'Well, I am very sorry to learn that. Last night was the first time I've ever properly felt like I was out of control of my body, and it's a hard pass from me, a hard do not recommend.'

'Do you know what caused it?' Duke asks, knowing it's not always that simple. He can be triggered by specific things, still – especially doing seventeen-hour press days in foreign countries and having to be 'on' all the time, since one bad interview out of fifty good ones will be the one to go mad online, sinking a movie even if it's the best thing that's ever been made. It's a big weight to carry. But also, he can feel like the floor has been pulled out from under him, just sat in his car at a red light or at home watching screeners.

She doesn't speak. He peeks at her again. Her eyes are still closed.

'I'm not sure,' she says. 'I had a call with my agent, and it was all good, and then . . .'

'Bam,' Duke supplies.

'Yeah,' she says. 'It was so unusual. I googled it, and I found a website that said to get outside as quick as possible. They call it nature-bathing? Just . . . being in nature, letting it wash over you and reminding you of your place in the world?'

'You say it like you're cynical.' Duke laughs. 'How unexpected.' Obviously he means the opposite. Cynical is just about her middle name.

She hits his arm again.

'Ouch!' he exclaims. 'Can you not?'

He can almost hear her smirking.

'Question,' Duke prompts then. 'It was after *good* news that it happened? Like when I got the Marvel role?'

'Yup,' says Evie. 'I don't claim for it to make any sense.'

'Oh no,' he insists. 'It makes perfect sense. My therapist calls it acclimatisation. Like if you hike Everest, the air thins and you need time to get used to it. When we experience even the best stuff, or our reality gets heightened or altered dramatically, our air thins and we need time to get used to it before digging in. Extreme good can be as mind-blowing as bad stuff happening, physiologically speaking.'

She reaches out then, searching for his hand. 'Thank you,' she tells him. 'Just . . . thank you.'

As they head back to the trailers, Duke gently tugs Evie to a stop. 'Hey,' he says. 'Is there anything I can do to help?'

'You're cute,' she says, dismissively.

'Don't push me away,' he says, calling her on it. 'I mean it. Telling me what's up when I ask you is one thing, but I'm rapidly learning that you don't actively ask for help very easily.'

She pulls a face.

'Evie,' he says. 'You don't need saving – I know that. And I also know if I tried to rescue you, somehow, from your own humanness, that you'd hate me. But girrrl?' He uses a silly voice now too, like he gets the only way she'll be able to hear him is if he takes out the emotional weight. 'You gotta use your *words* to tell *other people* how they can be there for you whilst you're busy rescuing yourself from this humanness. Okay?'

She giggles, another distraction for him.

'Well?' Duke presses. '*Is* there anything I can do?'

She pauses, clearly mulling it over. 'I don't think so,' she says. 'You're right though – I should ask for help more. I was just thinking I wish Magda was here, so maybe I can text her to ask if we can FaceTime a bit more, so I can share all this as it happens.'

Duke smiles. 'More FaceTime with Magda sounds very doable,' he says.

'Yes,' she says. 'It does. I'll text her, ask if we can talk tonight.'

22

Evie

Evie shadows the content team of Willow and Dream all morning and features on camera herself a little too. She talks about the idea for the book, how it feels to see it get made, and then Duke, Daphne, and Brad are all interviewed with the cameras and equipment for that afternoon being set up in the background, talking about their roles and how exciting it is to all be working together. They finish with all three of them laughing about the mad dash to finish before Christmas so they can all get home to their families, but when Dream says she's got everything she needs their three faces fall, the smiles slip away, and the director can't leave quick enough.

'Brad—' says Daphne, but it's already to his back.

'No, thank you!' Brad shouts over his shoulder, and it makes Evie furrow her brow in question. It's none of her business, and yet . . .

'Stress,' Daphne says to them all: Evie and Dream and Willow. But the way she exchanges a look with Duke betrays her. It's just a flash, half a second, but Evie sees it. They're in cahoots somehow.

'Understandable,' offers Evie. 'I suppose it's his job to keep this train on the tracks.' Duke looks to the ground and Daphne lets herself down with the worst fake smile in the history of all of smiles. Yup. There's definitely something afoot.

'Duke!' calls one of the producers then, and when he's gone it's suggested that now would be a good time for Evie and Daphne to take a short walk up the lane.

'And if you're papped, you're papped.' Dream-or-Willow shrugs with a smile. 'Does that work?'

Evie and Daphne look at one another.

'I don't have anywhere to be,' says Evie, with a laugh. Half the time she still thinks it's ridiculous that they paid to fly her out and put her up in all of these hotels, just so she can pinball between trailers and monitors, not doing much besides occasionally giving a thumbs up to the content team and saying, 'Yes, it's all such a dream.' It's so unnecessary. If Duke wanted to meet her, he should have just invited her for coffee. Although, if she's honest with herself, she would have probably said no. Hmm. *Well played, Duke,* she reflects. It's still inappropriate that he exercised his power that way, but she's less mad about it now she's enjoying herself properly.

'Great,' says Daphne. 'Let's boogie.'

There's a wide, pretty straight path just around the corner from the set, lined with snow-topped trees. They walk in silence until they're steadier on their feet, testing where is safest to walk and where there's hidden ice.

'Here,' Daphne instructs, as she finds her rhythm on the left. 'Look.'

Evie follows her footprints until they're side by side, both in padded coats, hats, scarves, mittens and sunglasses to guard against the sun's glare. Admittedly, Daphne looks eighty times more glamorous because her outfit is her Hermione costume, whereas, in a bid to keep warm, Evie looks more like a little boy who dressed in a hurry. Daphne takes Evie's arm, like they're just a couple of gal pals heading out for cocktails. She's deceptively strong. Evie assumed that a woman so tiny would be frail, like a little sparrow, but she's got a grip like a vice and steers them determinedly.

'Good core workout,' she says, as they fall in step. 'Walking in snow is like running on sand – you don't realise how sore it's gonna make you.'

Evie deadpans, 'Running on sand. Yes. I've heard of that.'

Daphne laughs. 'Duke said you're funny.'

'Did he now?' Evie quips. He talks about her?

Daphne grins as she looks at her. 'Aren't you going to ask me what else he's said?' she teases.

'Nope.'

'Because I'd tell you.'

Evie raises an eyebrow. 'Remind me not tell you *my* secrets then,' she says, and Daphne laughs again.

'You're no fun!' she mocks, and Evie hears it, then, the sound of a camera button being pushed. *Click, click, click.* The guy isn't even trying to hide – although to be fair, where would he? It isn't the same man from before, the one Duke said is called Clive. This is somebody else.

'Afternoon, ladies,' he says, in a British accent. 'Don't mind me.'

It surprised Evie when Daphne says, 'Afternoon, Billy. Get my best angles, won't you?'

Evie is learning that nothing about this business should surprise her, and yet it takes her a second to comprehend that *of course* Daphne knows the photographer, in the same way Duke knows some of them too. What had he said? That he needs them, sometimes, and it's just best to work with them? Magda will be so shocked by the fakeness of it all when she tells her. Obviously Magda would have to answer her phone first though – Evie has sent three texts in a row now, all unanswered. The last few days of the semester at school must really be kicking her ass.

They continue for about half a mile, and Evie doesn't know when the clicking stops but at some point it does and as mysteriously as he appeared the paparazzo is now gone.

'So, seriously,' Daphne says, as they stop at a snow-covered brick wall and admire the expanse of white fields and forest. 'You and Duke? I ship it.'

Evie pulls a face. 'Apparently only half the internet do,' she says. 'The other half ship *you* and him.'

Daphne waves a hand. 'We're not a match,' she explains. 'We've known each other years – we have the same management. I think they would have loved for us to become some sort of Brangelina power couple, but it wouldn't have been real. He thought he loved me but honestly? I've never seen him look at me the way he does at you. And, truth be told, I never looked at him in the way you look at him.'

'Er, what?' says Evie, stunned. 'If you're going off the photos . . .'

'I'm not,' Daphne insists. 'I'm going off real life.'

'Hmm,' muses Evie. 'Okay.'

'Okay what?'

'I mean . . . well . . . We get on, that's true. We didn't, at first. But relations have . . . thawed. I've made no secret of how hard I find all this—' she gestures around her, meaning *Hollywoodland* '—and I was willing to give him a chance, but . . .'

'But what?' Daphne asks.

'This sounds like I'm upset about him not being a fan of my work, and that's not it at all,' Evie starts, and Daphne furrows her brow in question. 'He said he loved my books, but then I found a crib sheet he has on me, and I get the feeling that everything he tried to say was from his heart was actually just a brief from his people. So now I feel like I can't trust him? Even though I want to?'

'A brief?' Daphne asks, blushing slightly. 'Like an information sheet?'

'Exactly.' Evie nods. 'Yeah.'

Daphne puts her hand on Evie's forearm.

'I hate admitting this,' she tells Evie, 'but that was mine. It's me who asked for the information on you. I didn't know your books before. I know for a fact Duke really has inhaled your back catalogue. Honestly – he hasn't been lying.'

Evie considers this. Is Daphne just covering for her friend?

'If you say so . . .'

'I do!' she insists.

Evie doesn't say anything else about it. She doesn't trust herself to. Instead she changes the subject.

'How long have you been acting?' Evie asks her. 'I never expected you to have read my stuff, obviously, but I'll admit

I've seen you in a few things – the one with Olivia Colman, and I honestly thought you were superb as Joan of Arc. Like, whoa. I think there were people in the cinema actually applauding at the end? And, I was one of them . . .'

Another laugh. 'Thank you,' Daphne says. 'Yeah, that one was a doozy, but I loved it. I grew a lot from it, and that's all I ask for really. I just want to learn something new about myself and what I'm capable of on every job. That must be a bit like writing, I imagine?'

A bird swoops low in the sky, almost colliding with them.

'Gah!' Daphne screams.

'Jesus!' says Evie. 'That felt like it was coming right for me, like, ON PURPOSE! Did you see that?!'

'At least it didn't poo on us,' says Daphne. 'Wardrobe weren't very happy at me coming out in costume, but in winter it makes you colder, getting dressed and undressed, doesn't it? I said I'd tag them both on social later, send some followers their way as a thank you.'

'Ahh bribery, works every time.' Evie sighs.

'Story of my life,' says Daphne. 'There are some real diamonds in this industry, but I can't lie: there's a lot of people who want something and everything, too.'

'Duke's said the same, yeah.' Evie nods. 'I'm sure publishing can be that way as well, but I try to keep myself to myself, living my tiny little life out in Salt Lake.'

'The lives we call tiny can actually be some of the biggest,' notes Daphne. 'And also, can I just point out: you were the one to bring Duke up that time.'

Evie sticks out her tongue.

*

By the next morning the photos of Evie and Daphne's walk are published – not widely, but they're up, with several more feminist websites saying exactly what Willow-or-Dream had hoped: that no man is worth coming between two women. A few 'anonymous sources' are featured, saying how hilarious the two women find their alleged love triangle portrayed in the media, when behind the scenes the real love affair is between them, as friends. 'Seriously,' the source says, 'outside of filming they're normally just propping up the bar, drinking cocktails and putting the world to rights.' *The Cut* even runs the headline THE ONLY ROMANTIC ROAD COUPLE WE SHIP ARE THE AUTHOR AND THE REAL STAR, and Evie doesn't even hate the photo they've chosen either. She really is laughing hard and free, and it actually does look like Daphne and Evie are BFFs.

She gets sent the link by her agent, who tells her of two more foreign rights offers that have come through for some works in her back catalogue – Poland and Brazil. It's not huge money, but it all contributes to the growing snowball of buzz around Evie and her work, the mounting total of cash her agent says is coming her way. She breathes deeply. *It's okay for all of this to be happening,* she tells herself as she arranges her hair into two French braids that will fit under a hat. *Isn't it?* she thinks, when she's done.

She's working on the self-worth thing.

'That's nice,' Duke says, nodding at her hairdressing skills at breakfast. 'You look like you should be called Heidi.'

He's in his off-duty uniform of skin-hugging T-shirt and low-slung grey joggers. Evie's eyes flick to the waistband, the easy-going and idle way it sits just on his pubic bone.

'I wonder what today has got in store,' he says to her, and she drags her eyes away quickly, ashamed at her mind in the gutter.

'Hmmm,' answers Evie in between chews of a pain au raisin. 'More smouldering glares and meaningful glances for you, and more hanging about watching your smouldering glares and meaningful glances for me, I'd imagine,' she says. 'And maybe pasta salad at lunch.'

'Your imagination is limitless,' Duke quips back, finding some watermelon and loading up his plate as Evie stands and watches. 'I can see how you've managed to make a career out of storytelling.'

'Your compliments sound so sincere.' Evie grins. 'I can see how you've made a career out of acting.'

'Ouch,' Duke says, smiling and grabbing his heart like that's where her sass has landed. 'You got me.'

She looks at the clock on the wall. 'Well,' she tells him, popping the last of the pastry in her mouth. 'You don't got me. I've been summoned to reception for 8 a.m. by Daphne.'

'How is it that Daphne has your number and I do not?' he asks, faking a pout.

Evie smiles cheekily and as she's halfway out of the door tells him: 'Because you've never asked for it.'

In the lobby, Evie searches out Daphne. Her text didn't say what she needed to talk to her about, only that if she was free, Daphne would love it if Evie could come down for a coffee with her – *and it's not a photo op. I promise!*

She picks a spot in the corner: a small round coffee table with two big, cosy leather armchairs. Perfect, Evie reflects, as a little reading nook. Urgh. Reading. Thinking of reading makes her think of writing, which makes her think of her MacBook lying untouched upstairs. To some people, 65,000 words sounds like chapter and verse but to Evie, who needs 100,000 words, it's pitiful – and haunting. She's never asked for a deadline extension in her life. Is this book going to be the one she pleads for longer with? Her editor won't be happy. You don't get to publish in a regular spring and winter slot year after year if you don't deliver your manuscript on time. And yet, despite what she's promised herself, there seem to be so many interesting distractions that she finds herself struggling to commit to her work.

She hears somebody say, *'Oh no, don't worry, I've got it,'* and it sounds like Magda. Her heart pines for her friend, then – she can't remember the last time they were apart for this long.

Evie sits back in the armchair, promising herself she'll do it later and absent-mindedly admiring the lobby. And then she sees her, stood by the automatic doors, waiting to be noticed.

'Magda?' Evie says, too stunned to stand.

She waves. 'Thought it was time for me to take a little trip,' she says, grinning. 'Shake this place up a bit.'

Evie squeals then – full-on, top-of-her-lungs screams, getting up and launching herself at her best friend.

'What the hell!' she says, excitedly. 'How are you here? How the hell are you actually here? Why didn't you say?'

The friends hug, and it's so powerful, so full of love, that Evie actually manages to knock Magda to the floor, which makes them *both* squeal then, and then they're laughing, lying on the carpet runner of the five-star hotel, just giggling and giggling. Evie turns her head.

'I can't believe you're here,' she says, and before Magda can reply she sees Duke's face loom into view, hovering above them, amused.

'You got my surprise then,' he says to Evie. 'You must be Magda,' he adds, and in return Magda squeals again.

Evie and Magda sit in the corner Evie picked out earlier, two empty coffee cups apiece and neither of them showing any signs of easing up on the talking any time soon. Evie still cannot believe her best friend in the whole world is sat opposite, in the lobby of a Bavarian hotel with her, telling her Duke flew her out here.

'I honestly thought it was a joke,' Magda says. 'He has one of those blue ticks on Instagram, so I'm like, okay, it's not a fan account but maybe his real account got hacked? Or maybe I'm misunderstanding everything? But his assistant got him to record a video of him *verbally* telling me that he'd love to get me out here because he knows how much you want to share it with me.'

'True,' says Evie. 'I did tell him that, yes.'

'They sent a car, and I turned *left* on the plane, which is *insane* by the way. They have proper glasses in first class! I ate better on that KLM flight than I have done in most restaurants! And the whole time I'm telling myself *this was paid for by Duke Carlisle.* Like . . . seriously?'

'I'm starting to see that he's very kind like that,' Evie says. 'I'm sorry he couldn't stay. He doesn't get to decide his schedule, but we can all go for dinner tonight, maybe, if they're done in time?'

Magda waves a hand. 'If he was here, we wouldn't be able to talk about him,' she whispers conspiratorially. 'And I am *desperate* to talk about him.'

'Come on,' Evie instructs. 'Let's put your stuff in my room and see the sights. Have you ever had *Dampfnudeln*? Because quite frankly when it's my time to go I'm going to need you to bury me with a bunch of them. They're my heaven.'

The women meander around the town, chatting and giggling and taking it in turns to exclaim, 'I can't believe this is happening!' over and over as they pass the Perlach Tower and Augsburg Cathedral. After lunch they head to set, where Duke and Daphne are filming a George and Hermione kiss, after a build-up of half a book's worth of tension on the will-they-won't-they make it. After they get their passes and make their way to the designated area, they watch the scene unfold – first a rehearsal, and then a take.

'When this is on TV one day, we'll be able to say we saw it filmed live,' Magda marvels in a whisper. 'That's so cool!'

They watch a couple of takes before Brad declares they've got it, and Magda shakes her head in awe. 'Duke is coming over. Do I look okay? Do I have sauerkraut in my teeth?'

'Why hello.' Duke smiles as he approaches. 'Are you two having a lovely time?'

Magda opens her mouth to answer him, right as Duke reaches out to tuck a stray hair behind Evie's ear, and the tenderness of it catches even Evie off guard, making her heart beat in quickstep and cheeks flush. They swap coy smiles. Evie is painfully aware that her best friend is staring, mouth agape, but she refuses to ruin the moment by acknowledging it.

23

Duke

Duke thinks that Evie's best friend is the funniest person he's ever met – and he's spent five weeks on set with Jack Black before now.

'Magda, ohmygod!' Evie shoots her best friend a look after she's made her third joke about oral sex, and then turns to Duke and Daphne. 'Please pardon my best friend's disgusting mouth,' she says, and Duke is trying to figure out how somebody so serious and focused like Evie can be BFFs with somebody as filter-free and hilarious as Magda.

'I love your best friend's disgusting mouth.' Duke laughs, shrugging.

'I kind of do too,' echoes Daphne.

'Traitor,' Evie faux-scolds them, narrowing her eyes first at Daphne, then at Duke. 'You too, mister.' She points, accusingly, and Duke holds up his hands like he's been caught in the crossfire innocently.

'I regret nothing,' he says.

'That's just your problem,' Evie chastises.

They could have eaten in the restaurant to the hotel, which would have been fine, it's a great place, but Magda had been told about a little bistro off the beaten track and had insisted that nobody cared who they were and that if they were bothered, she'd protect them. Her enthusiasm is contagious. They'd relented.

'This is fun,' Daphne says, smiling. 'I've been wanting to explore a bit. I'm always just so tired after filming, and Brad never wanted to do anything . . .' She trails off, and Duke wonders if this is the moment she's going to tell them they've broken up – not because he wants her back, but because Brad seems as close to scum as it's possible for a man to be.

It isn't lost on him Daphne's just used the past tense to talk about him, though. He looks at Evie. Has she noticed? They've seemed friendlier since their photoshoot, maybe Daphne has told her all about it. Women open up to each other easily that way, don't they?

'I came just in time to liven things up then, didn't I?' Magda quips. 'Seems intense, being on set all day.'

'Yeah,' Daphne says. 'It's a lot of waiting around, and getting cold, and we're the ones on screen but really we're just a cog in a movie-making machine. We don't even have that much power, to be honest – I mean, I feel that way, I don't know about you, Duke.'

Duke nods. 'Yeah,' he agrees. 'I think the studio heads have the most power.'

'How so?' asks Evie.

'They hold the purse strings.' He shrugs. 'And when you control the money, you control everything else on the movie too – both for making it, and marketing it. A great movie that doesn't get marketed won't get seen, or you can be really clever with marketing and get a mediocre movie a good return. And as studio head, you're the one everyone is answerable to, so you're the one with the most agency.'

'I'd have thought that was directors,' Evie offers, as their main courses arrive.

'They certainly *act* like they're the puppeteers,' says Daphne. 'I mean, not always. Sometimes. The men more so, to be honest.'

Duke shrugs. 'Sorry,' he says. 'For my people.'

'Here's to that,' Magda says, raising a glass. They clink glasses and drink.

'I wouldn't mind trying it, though,' Daphne adds. 'Directing. Maybe once I've established my own production company.'

'God, ambition is hot.' Magda winks. 'Good for you.'

They eat, drink, and generally get merry at dinner, and by pudding Magda is trying to convince everyone to go to a local bar for a nightcap.

'Come on,' she says, happily drumming her fingers on the table. 'Just one,' she says. 'Just one!'

Duke is almost tempted. He's been having such a great time – just chatting, hanging out, being around people and doing something as normal as having a meal in a public place has been so refreshing. And Magda was right: nobody has recognised them. Or, if they have, they've left them well alone, which is wonderful. Duke thinks the people of Augsburg are *very* cool.

'Oh, look,' Magda suddenly interrupts herself then. 'Sorry,' she announces to the table. 'I made friends with that woman at the airport. She gave me a Kleenex in the arrivals hall after I spilled my drink on myself. She was the one who told me about this place, actually. Let me just go and say hi.'

Duke carries on chatting as she goes, telling Daphne and Evie that he's going to have to call it a night.

'Do you mind? Or do you prefer to go out in the presence of a big burly man?'

'Actually yes.' Evie giggles. 'Do you know one?'

It's only as he's rolling his eyes that he shifts his gaze from the table, and then, even though he's telling himself there's no way she can be here, not here, in Germany, in this restaurant with these people, he knows she is. He doesn't know how, or why, just that it is so. She's gesticulating with her hands and tipping her head back laughing as Magda points to their table and she looks over and their eyes lock. She looks brighter than normal, more functional, and there's a man with her. An unremarkable man – he has eyes and a nose and a mouth and a jumper and trousers and a coat. She says something to him then, and Magda looks across and then Duke stands up.

'Hello,' she says to him as she approaches the table.

He blinks. He might be on the verge of crying. He might be crying already.

He swallows. 'Hello, Mum.'

It transpires that the unremarkable man is Roger, her new boyfriend.

'We met in AA, pet,' she tells him, as they settle into the same corner Magda and Evie gossiped in earlier today. Already that feels like a year ago. The past twenty minutes – paying at the restaurant, deciding to get back to the privacy of the hotel, taking off their coats – has felt like a week. His mother is here? In Germany? To see him?

'He's ever so kind to me. Really patient. Got two kids himself, though he's out of touch with one of them. I told him I know what that's like.'

If it's an attempt at bonding, it falls flat for Duke. He's doing what he has practised with Phoebe so many times: breathing, saving his response until he knows what he wants it to be, picking out the facts that he knows to be concretely true, not hysterical manufactured worries from his imagination.

This is his mother. She is here. She is not drunk. She has a boyfriend.

His mum looks at him expectantly. For a while he called her by her first name, Anna, as a way to articulate that she's no mother to him. Never to her face, but privately, in sessions or to friends. But it felt forced, like he was trying to be madder than he was. Mostly he's just always felt sad about her. Sad and lost and hurt.

'I'm just struggling to connect some dots here, Mum,' he says, when she sighs contentedly, like she's over the moon to be here, with him, together. Roger has excused himself to go to the bathroom, but he's been gone ages already. Maybe he's giving them some space. 'How did you know I was here? How did you even *get* here? Why didn't you tell me you were coming?'

She nods along, like she gets why he'd be confused.

'Uh-huh,' she says. 'Well . . . You've been in the papers a lot, you see, and they said you were filming in Germany.

When I googled it, there was a fan site that speculated on what locations you might use – is it adapted from a book? Some websites used clues from a book? And you don't answer the phone when I call anymore, and I know why that is. I know I haven't been a very good mum to you, pet, I do. But I'm in AA. I'm almost three hundred days sober. And I've come to say sorry. I used the money you sent. I don't normally spend it – everything you send is in an account, ready to pay you back. I don't need your money, not anymore. Everything is different now.'

Duke nods. He's played this conversation in his head thousands of times: the fantasy of hearing I'm sorry. Except, in his imagination he leaps up, at this point, and they hug and say they'll never fall out again, and his mum swears she'll be everything she should already have been, and Duke says yes, okay, he'd like that very much. But here, confronted with the reality of it, he doesn't feel like saying any of those things. He doesn't feel like saying anything at all.

'Where are you staying?' he asks her, and she fishes out the card to a three-star hotel a few miles away. 'Here,' she says, handing it to him. 'This is us.'

Duke nods.

'Do you know your room number?'

'Two-twelve.'

He nods again. 'I'll call you tomorrow,' he says. 'In the morning. About 8 a.m., okay? I have to go to bed now.'

His mother stands up as he does, and Duke sees Roger approaching and gives a little wave.

'Nice to meet you,' Duke says, and he goes up to his room. He gets his phone out of his pocket, and then puts it back again. He's not sure if he wants to talk about his mother being here, making it real, or to go to bed and close his eyes and pretend it's not happening. The hotel phone on his bedside table rings.

'Hey.'

It's her. Evie.

'Can you come up?' he asks her.

It takes her less than three minutes. He opens the door to her and she looks at him, and it isn't pity, he doesn't think, like she feels sorry for him. It's real, proper concern.

'I won't ask if you're okay,' she says, opening her arms wide, asking permission to hug him. He lets her. She smells like watermelon and green apple. Citrusy. 'Did you have any idea?' she presses, holding his hand and leading him to a chair in the corner. He sits in the chair, and she sits at his feet on the woven rug, her arms draped over his legs, her eyes inquisitive.

'None,' he says. 'I've not seen her since, like, three Christmases ago when she ended up in A&E from drunk driving. I was so mad at her, Evie. She could have killed somebody. I mean, by all means she can drink herself to death but there could have been a kid, somebody's uncle or father or sister . . . She says she's sober now.'

Evie nods. 'Do you believe her?'

Duke sighs. 'I really, really want to,' he says, 'But honestly? I don't know how much hope I have left in me when it comes to her.'

He moves to the bed and sinks down, exhausted.

'Okay. You asked me once what you could do to help. My turn to return the favour . . . What do you need?'

'I . . . don't know.'

'Well, how about I go grab my laptop and I sit here and write? Then if you need me I'm here and if you don't, no worries.'

He nods. 'That's kind,' he says.

'Of course,' she tells him. 'You can even fall asleep, if you want. I'll just . . . be around.'

This is the Evie Duke thought he'd meet all along. He knew she was in here somewhere. Not an Evie to look after him, but a thoughtful, careful Evie. One without armour. It makes Duke reveal more of himself, too. It feels human. Empathetic.

Duke remembers getting to the last page of the book Adele lent him on that holiday together, stretched out on the sun lounger with tears pricking at his eyes, a lump in his throat that might have been sadness or might have been optimism. Evie's words tread a fine line. He'd read her acknowledgements, short and sweet, and then on the inside cover was her photograph. He'd looked at her wide eyes and arched eyebrows, the almost-smile on her lips and her serious, earnest gaze. The bio underneath said, simply: *Evie Bird is a writer from Utah. She has been nominated for the Romantic Writers' Award six times and won three.* No Stopping Us *is her eighth book. She is currently writing her ninth.*

He googled her, but not much came up – a webpage with her book covers and links to buy, no contact page or email box to write, and a social media page that stated in the bio that it was run by a social media manager. He'd brought the book home with him to London, put it on his shelf and ordered her back catalogue. For the past few years, he's had her next publication on auto-buy, and when *On the Romantic Road* was released, just before yet another Christmas his mother ended up in hospital, he knew it needed to be a movie, and that she needed to be involved. Her words saved him, and she'd had no idea.

Evie nips back to her room for her laptop, and when she's back Duke feels a swell of gratitude.

'Hey,' he says, suddenly remembering something Daphne had mentioned.

'Hmmmm?' she asks.

'I just want to say – Daphne said you found an information sheet on yourself? It really was hers, you know. I don't want you to think I've been putting on a front about how I relate to your work . . .'

She looks at him and smiles. She seems pleased.

'Okay,' she says. 'I think I believe you.'

'Think?'

She shrugs. 'Ninety-eight per cent, yeah.'

Duke shakes his head. 'You're impossible.'

'Correct,' she says, and smiles again. 'Anyway. Tea? Or I can call up for some food . . . ?'

He shakes his head. 'No, I'm fine,' he replies, and then he thinks of his scenes tomorrow, how he'll probably look terrible, all things considered. It's very late. 'Maybe just grab me a mineral water from the mini bar?' He can at least stay hydrated.

She gives him a bottle and takes one for herself, settling into a chair.

'Want me to talk or type?' she says, and then she yawns. 'Sorry,' she adds.

'I was just thinking of how I googled you after I read *No Stopping Us* and found, like, zero information on you. I was so eager to know who was behind that story.'

She shrugs. 'Well,' she says. 'Now you know.'

'Yeah,' he says. She's waiting for him to say more about his mother. He can tell. But what is there to say?

'I'm going to call my mum in the morning,' Duke opts to say. 'I mean I told her I would, so I don't really feel like I've got a choice.'

Evie nods. 'Well,' she tells him. 'You've always got a choice.'

'Do I? She came all this way. She says she's sober. She has a boyfriend? Apparently? I was too stunned just now to ask her everything I want to ask her. If she's going to be here, I want her to answer my questions.'

Evie tips her head, absorbing everything he's saying.

'Well, that's good, isn't it? Getting a lucid conversation out of a drunk parent . . . the chance for some closure? Pretty rare.'

Ah. Of course. Evie's dad drank. She'd said so in passing.

'Is all this making you think of . . . ?' Duke starts, but Evie holds up a hand.

'No,' she says. 'This isn't about me. But for what it's worth, I suppose if my dad did show up, I'd hear him out too. Do you want me to come for moral support?'

'I'm okay,' he says, and then he thinks to himself: *because even you asking helps.* Something stops him from saying that out loud, though. 'I'm going to try and get some sleep now.'

'Good plan. I'm right here at the foot of your bed if you need anything.'

He falls into a dreamless sleep almost instantly.

24

Duke

At his request, his mother comes to meet him at his hotel, so that they can talk in relative privacy. Nobody asks him who the older woman with greying hair around the temples is, but it's probably obvious: they have the same nose, the same hands, the same feline eyes. Daphne passes by with Katerina, the DP, and then Brad, who seems to be distracted by yelling at someone down the phone. Duke doesn't introduce her. Nobody approaches them. The atmosphere must be apparent.

'Thank you for this,' his mother says, as she sits down and orders a tea. Duke can't eat. His stomach is in knots, wrapping around itself in anxiety. Evie was gone when his alarm went off this morning, a note on his coffee table wishing him luck. He'd searched online for what to do with a newly sober parent, but even as he typed it out, he struggled to believe

194

it. He wants her to prove it to him. He's here to look into her eyes to see if they're as glassy and glazed over as he remembers from too many days, and too many nights, when it felt like nobody cared, like if he slipped out of the front door and never came back, somehow *then* she'd be happy. Why couldn't he make her happy?

Nothing he did was enough, so he must have been the problem.

'I know I've ambushed you,' she continues, as her tea is set down in front of her. 'Like I said – I didn't know what else to do. I didn't even know if this would work, but I had to try. I sort of can't believe we were in the same restaurant . . .'

Duke blinks. He can't find it in him to be pleasantly chatty, but really, why should he? 'Yeah,' he says. 'Ain't fate funny?'

His mother bites her lip, understanding his tone. She sips her tea. Duke watches her.

'I am an addict,' she tells him. 'And I can't imagine how hard that must have been for you.'

Duke keeps watching her. His breathing gets shallow, and he's aware, in the back of his mind, that he can see the quick rise and fall of his chest in his peripheral vision.

'There's no excuse for what I've done. I won't try to find reasons for letting you down, and I don't need you to say it's okay or that you forgive me. I broke your trust over years, and so if you ever decide to let me try to build it back up, I will commit the rest of my life to that. They say relapse is always possible, but I'm not going back to who I was. I'm really not. I don't need you to do anything for me. I don't need you to help me through this. I'm fine. I've got AA, and

Roger, and a job, now, too. I'm just so glad you even called this morning, that I get to see you, your handsome face, pet . . . My love has not been enough,' she tells him, and she's welling up, looking up to the ceiling like somehow that might stem her tears. 'But it's all I have. So . . . I'm going to try, okay?'

She breaks off and reaches for her handbag on the floor, rifling through it, presumably for tissues. Duke closes his eyes and sighs deeply. Can this really be it? Just like that, his mother has changed? It feels stupid to trust it, naïve. Immature. He had to grow up fast, having a mother who loved booze more than him. He's used to life without a mum. And yet . . .

'Was it my fault?' he asks then, his voice wavering on the edge of cracking. He hates himself for needing her to say no, for being a thirty-seven-year-old man who needs Mummy to give him a big hug. He's done so well without her. So, so well. It might even be *because* of her that he's done so well, if not in spite of. She couldn't love him but, look at that, now the whole world does. But . . . it isn't enough. 'If I had been better,' he presses. 'A better son . . . done better at school or did more around the house . . .' He is openly crying now. Bugger. Bugger, bugger, bugger. His mother hands him one of the tissues she found.

'No, Derrick,' she says, using his real name. 'No. Is that what you really think . . . ?' And now her tears are falling harder, and faster, and she reaches out a hand across the coffee table and Duke looks at it, and then takes it. He grips her tight, and then stands up to hug her, because even if he can't trust her, he believes in this moment. He believes that she's really here. He's needed her here for so long. Better late than never, maybe. He doesn't know what comes next, in the future, but he can hug her now if that's all they have.

They stay like that, his mother sat, Duke leaning down over the table, arms wrapped around each other, crying and letting it all out. They're probably quite the sight, but what can be done? Emotion can't be timed, can't be neatly arranged to be convenient.

It might be five minutes they stay like that; it could be ten or fifteen, but eventually the crying stops. Duke sits back down and takes a big gulp of water. He feels purged. Tired.

'I don't know what happens now,' he tells her. 'I don't know what I want to happen next.'

His mother nods. 'That's fair,' she says.

'You can't just . . . be in my life because you've decided it's time to get yourself together. You know that, don't you?'

She nods, wincing the tiniest amount, as if it hurts to hear him say that. But so what, Duke thinks. He's hurt for decades.

'I know,' she says. 'And I really will prove it. From near or far, things are different now. That's why I waited so long to make sure – well, nearly ten months. It's the longest I've ever gone, and it's because I told myself that I'd come find you, if I could do it. I want to know you, Derrick. I can't tell you how much shame I have,' and she starts to cry again, now, taking big gulps in between her words. 'How much shame I have,' she repeats, taking a shaky breath, 'that I don't get to see my son. I want to know you. I know I don't have a right to anymore but I'm hoping that maybe one day things will be different again.'

Duke nods. 'Okay,' he says. 'Let's just see, okay?'

'Okay,' his mum tells him, wiping her eyes with a damp tissue yet again.

25

Evie

'God,' Magda says over a traditional Bavarian breakfast of *Weisswurst, Brezel* and *Bier* – literally, white sausage, pretzels and beer. 'I mean, Duke seems like a cool, well-adjusted guy but can you imagine your newly sober mother turning up out of the blue when you're essentially at *work*? And not to make myself a main character in this when I am, at most, a peripheral observer, but isn't it crazy that I met her at the airport?'

Evie shakes her head. 'It's stuff like that that makes me believe in fate,' she says. 'We were at that restaurant because *she* told you about it, to be fair. But what were the chances, even then?'

'Infinitesimal,' agrees Magda. 'I mean. I wonder what her plan was – was she simply going to ask around about where the nearest film set was and . . . wait?'

Evie shrugs, dipping her pretzel into some hot mustard. She isn't hungover, but having been up late with Duke and then waking so early, the sleep deprivation makes her feel that way. In fact, she's had less sleep on this German trip than she even did at college. She's too old for this. There's not enough eye cream in the world.

'That's what the fans do, I think,' Evie says. 'Get wind of what city we're in, share the info online, on blogs or whatever, and then hang around waiting to get glimpses of everyone.'

'Another world.' Magda sighs. 'Although, if I was born in the Seventies, I totally would have been a music groupie. Trying to sleep with Bowie or the Beatles or whoever, following them around from gig to gig.'

'If you'd have been a teenager in the Seventies,' Evie jokes, 'you wouldn't have made it to the Eighties.'

Magda shrugs. 'I'd have had a great time, at least.' She smiles. Then, changing the subject, she says, 'And, hey. Just checking in to see how Duke's alcoholic parent showing up like this makes you feel about your dad? We don't have to talk about it, but I have to ask. You okay?'

Evie considers it. She *has* been thinking about her dad a lot, considering she's back in his world – not to mention the newspaper identifying him as her father. Any hope she had that he'd reach out is dashed, if it was even there. But still. She can't lie. He's occupied more of her thoughts than usual.

'I suppose I've been thinking of him a bit, yeah,' Evie admits. 'More from, like, an empathetic point of view. Like what would I do if my dad showed up like Duke's mom has.'

'And?' Magda pushes.

'I honestly just don't think he would. I don't exist to him.

He has this whole other family, but I don't know if he's sober now, or still drinking . . . I mean, if his other kids know about me, surely they'd let me know if he died or whatever. But other than that . . .'

Magda nods. 'And that's . . . okay with you?'

Evie raises an eyebrow. 'This doesn't put me in the mood for some big fuzzy reunion, if that's what you mean,' she says drily. 'If Duke gets to patch things up with his mom, then I'm happy for him, but, no, it doesn't inspire me to track down my dad. I don't think he wants to hear from me anyway.'

'Hmm,' says Magda. 'It's interesting, isn't it? You're both the children of alcoholics and both do very public work. You make each other laugh, you seem relaxed with him . . .'

'What's your point?'

'Lots in common, I suppose is my point.'

'Right.'

Magda stares her out, refusing to say anything else until Evie relents and gives her a bit more to work with, presumably.

'Shall we get the cheque and do some shopping?'

Magda shakes her head like Evie has told an especially unfunny joke.

'Unbelievable.' She laughs. 'I'll tell you something: I don't ever worry that under torture and duress you'd give away my secrets to the government. You never talk about *anything* you don't want to.'

Evie laughs too. 'And this is news to you?' she says.

As they exit the café, they bump into an irate, shouty man on his cell phone, pacing in the cold without a coat, his breath raging in front of him like the fire coming from a dragon.

'Jesus,' Magda says, 'American tourists are the worst, aren't they? It's a shame the Germans speak English so well. Dude needs to *chill*.'

Evie shakes her head at the stream of f-thises and f-thats that the guy is screaming. She can't even tell who he might be talking to: a partner, a colleague, a poor customer sales rep. And then he turns around enough for her to see that it's Brad, the director.

'Whoa,' Evie says, lowering her gaze and tugging on Magda's sleeve. 'Stop staring now. It's the director.'

The pair hurry across the square and around the corner from their café and the hotel, and thus the hustle and bustle of anyone from the movie. Up a small side street strewn with fairy lights and with a big Christmas tree at the end, Evie explains: 'He's wild, man. Like, so super nice to your face, really Hollywood, really showbiz, and he was okay on set at first, but then something happened with him and Daphne . . .'

'Well, they're together, right?' asks Magda. 'She was with Duke, she cheated on Duke, you started to be photographed in a fake romance with Duke so everyone would lay off her a bit . . .'

'Yes.' Evie nods. 'All of that is true. But in terms of Daphne and Brad still being together, I don't know. Duke hasn't ever told me what happened the night he got photographed hugging her, but something did. Set has been ice cold since . . .'

Magda stops to look in a shop window displaying two winter outfits on headless mannequins. 'I like that jumper,' she says, pointing, and Evie hums in mutual appreciation.

'Hard colour to wear though – red,' she says.

'Needs a red lip for balance,' Magda agrees. 'Then you're getting into lipstick on your teeth at a Christmas party . . .'

'Or wearing that stuff to coat it so it doesn't come off, and ending up with lips drier than the desert,' agrees Evie.

'Better to stick with a nude lip and neutral clothes palette.' Magda laughs. 'Never mind. I don't like the jumper after all.'

They continue to walk, Magda slipping her arm into Evie's.

'You don't think . . .' Magda starts, and Evie can sense the tone shift immediately.

'What?' she says, with trepidation.

Magda scrunches up her nose, as if to say: *Don't get mad at me, I'm too cute.*

'It's definitely finished with Daphne, isn't it?'

'For Duke?'

'Yeah.'

'I'm pretty sure, yeah. What do you mean?'

Magda shrugs. 'Just that those photos of them hugging . . .'

Evie can't figure out what Magda is getting at. Does she think that Daphne and Brad have just been a musical interlude in the ongoing love of Daphne and Duke? And is that Evie's business?

'Well,' Evie says, 'I appreciate you looking out for me, since you think, apparently, that me and Duke might . . . well, I don't even know.'

'Looking out for you is indeed all I'm trying to do,' inserts Magda. 'I'm just checking everyone's intentions are clear and good, here. You seem to maybe . . . possibly . . . like him? And you haven't liked anybody properly since . . .'

'If you say Bobby's name, I'm going to guide you to the nearest body of water and push you in.'

'Why can *you* say his name?'

'Same reason I can bring up my dad being a bastard and you can't – it's my business.'

'Fair,' says Magda. 'Very fair. And yet . . .'

'As a best friend you're still going to push that boundary?' supplies Evie.

'You got it!' Magda retorts. 'It's part of the job description. Not always, but when the situation necessitates.'

'And you think this situation necessitates it?'

'We're mere mortals, on an all-expenses-paid trip to Hollywoodland. None of this is normal. I don't know how seriously to take everyone, you know? That director being off his rocker back there, people photographing you secretly, pretend romances and secret hugs, not to mention how those are two very good-looking people. You are a solid ten in the real world, you really are – but have you seen Daphne's hair? It's like there's a light box behind her at all times. Even in the restaurant she glowed. And her boobs? That's some rack.'

Evie narrows her eyes at her friend. 'Sounds like *you* like her, let alone Duke.'

'Out of my league,' Magda says with a laugh. 'Which is entirely my point.'

'Whoa!' Evie giggles. 'Thanks, babe.'

'What about *that* sweater?' Magda asks, nodding in the direction of another storefront. 'It's very Cameron Diaz in *The Holiday*, no?'

'Yes,' notes Evie. 'You'd look good in it.'

The pair push through the door of the boutique, still laughing loudly enough that the sales assistant looks up.

'*Guten Morgen*,' she says, a serious-looking thirty-something with pale pink hair and a diamond nose stud.

'*Guten Morgen*,' the friends echo back, stifling their giggles. They move around the store, picking things out, making appreciative noises, the beady eyes of the assistant following them from behind the counter.

'Evie?' asks Magda from the other side of the rack. 'What about *this* shade of red? It's more flattering, right? I could do this?'

'For sure.' Evie nods. 'Yeah. You know I saw a woman at the restaurant last night who had a silk scarf around her neck even though she was wearing a high neck like that, and I thought it looked so chic. Maybe I'll look for that shape, too.'

'You need help?' the sales assistant asks.

'Erm,' Evie ponders. She's kind of scared of the woman. Aren't customer service representatives supposed to be more congenial? 'Sure,' she settles on. 'Do you have any sweaters with the high necks, like the one my friend is holding? Maybe in cream, or grey?'

The woman nods and bustles around the store. As she hands Evie exactly what she has asked for, in both shades, she says, 'Evie Bird, yes?'

Evie is so stunned to be recognised in this tiny shop that she simply nods. It's Magda who appears by her side and speaks for her. 'The famous novelist? Yes, this is her!' she supplies.

'Oh my goodness! My friends won't believe this!' the woman suddenly cries, her excited face in direct contrast to the sternness from seconds ago. 'We love you! We have all your books. *The Sun in My Sky* is my favourite book ever, I think. I can't believe you are here, in my store. Can I get a selfie?'

'Oh...' Evie stammers, unsure how to respond. She doesn't want to be childish, but she hates that kind of stuff.

'Get your phone,' Magda says, knowing full well that Evie doesn't like it but that it means too much to the woman to turn her down. Who is going to see it anyway? It doesn't matter that much.

They take the picture and Evie buys the sweaters, plus two pairs of trousers, a camisole and three pairs of earrings, and when they leave, she feels strange.

'You did good in there, friend, letting yourself be appreciated. I know it's not your thing.'

'I just find it so awkward,' Evie admits. 'Like . . . they're just books.'

'Books that mean things to people. Didn't you say Duke read you before he met you? That he just likes the way you see the world?'

'Yeah,' says Evie. 'So he says. What's your point?'

'So when are you gonna let yourself enjoy this success? You coop up in that house, you don't do press or events, you're getting a freakin' movie made for Chrissakes, with more on the way by the sounds of it . . . I just . . . I don't get it. I really don't.'

Evie goes quiet. She thought her friend understood her.

'I just . . . don't deserve any of it,' Evie settles on. 'I really don't. I'm not worth anything. Not worth sticking around for. None of it is real, and everybody leaves. This will probably all end soon enough. Everything does.'

'No,' coos Magda. '*I* don't leave.'

'Everybody except you, then,' concedes Evie. 'I guess the point is: if I don't have expectations, I can't be upset when they're not met. So . . . here I am. Expecting nothing, from anybody, ever, not even nice people who pay money for my stories. I don't even trust them. Hell, most of the time I don't even trust myself.'

Magda shakes her head like she can't believe what Evie is saying. 'That's the saddest thing I ever heard,' she says. 'We have to fix this.'

'I've tried,' Evie tells her, her face impassive and serious. 'I'm broken. The lady ain't for fixing. Just let me get on with my life.'

'Hmm,' Magda says, concerned. 'I just don't think I can do that.'

'You look awful,' Evie tells Duke as he opens the door of his trailer up to her. 'I came to see how you are, but . . .'

'But you thought you'd rub salt in the wound a bit instead? Marvellous. Thank you.' He's not exactly smiling as he says it, but he sounds light-hearted enough. He does look terrible, though, with dark circles under his eyes, and sadness etched into his features. Like he's exhausted and carrying something heavy – which, Evie reasons, he is. 'Come in,' he adds.

His trailer is shades of cream, with a big sofa and a few vases of fresh flowers and a small kitchen with a coffee machine and kettle.

'Can I make one of those?' Evie asks, pointing.

'I'll do it,' Duke offers, and Evie thanks him as she shrugs off her coat and takes a seat.

'It was bad?' Evie asks.

'No,' Duke replies, and it comes out as a strange laugh. Evie's confused.

'I know it makes no sense,' he continues, noticing the expression on her face. 'Although maybe it does. I don't know. Everything feels underwater today. Blurry and a bit slow, you know? Even when people talk to me, I feel like it's coming from far away, like I can't even hear properly.'

Evie drinks her coffee. 'It must be a big shock,' she tells him. 'I told Magda I can't imagine my dad ever tracking me down, let alone showing up, but honestly, if he did . . .' She doesn't need to finish the sentence. The implication is that she'd be a goddamn mess. 'You're handling it really well.'

They exchange a meaningful look.

'Can I do anything?' she says, predicting the answer is no, but goddamn it, he's so handsome, and kind, and so incredibly lost . . . It's not often Evie finds herself feeling more grounded or rooted or sorted than the person opposite her at a table, but today, on this occasion, she can see it plain as day: Duke is beat.

Tears start to pool in his eyes. 'Bollocks,' he says, wiping the tears away with the back of his hand. 'Sorry. Urgh.'

'No, please don't apologise,' Evie insists. 'Cry! Let it out!'

'Kayla will kill me. My eyes are going to be impossible.'

'Fuck Kayla,' Evie says, and it makes them both laugh that she'd say something so strongly. 'In the nicest possible way,' Evie tempers it with.

They sit, and Duke lets the tears flow, and eventually Evie tells him: 'I'm honoured you'd let me in, you know.' He looks at her. He's got questions in his eyes, but they don't make it to his lips.

'What?' Evie adds.

He shakes his head. 'I like you,' he tells her, and it gives Evie a funny feeling, how he says it. She's desperate for the confirmation that whatever is happening is worth taking note of, but as quickly as that feeling comes, something else washes over her, too. Fear. Panic. The urge to crack a joke.

'You're okay,' she tells him, shrugging a shoulder. 'I guess.'

He drinks his coffee, too, but he's not crying anymore. She offers him a stick of gum and he takes it.

'I'm mad at her,' Duke admits, as he chomps down on it. A couple of coffees and a bit of bad flirting is what it has taken him to relax and start talking properly. Evie receives the compliment of it. 'Because she's chosen to sort herself out, and so breakfast was nice. She didn't even expect me to pay – I can't tell you the last time somebody close to me has picked up the tab.'

'Lunch at craft service is on me, then,' Evie says, and he rolls his eyes.

'May I continue?'

'I insist. Sorry. I'm still trying to figure out what emotional wavelength we're tuned in to today.'

'You and me both. Christ,' Duke says, and then: 'The thing, I'm sat there, a grown man and his mother, and I'm listening to her saying all the things I've ever wanted her to say. All of them! And then I think, half my life is already over, and she only just shows up to it now? She's my mother, for God's sake. She shouldn't be showing up at the bloody half-time show – she doesn't get to have been so bloody absent and then change her ways right when it suits her. Which isn't kind, or forgiving, but it's like the thirty-seven-year-old in me can feel one way, and then there's a five-year-old boy who watched telly on his own on his birthday, and a fifteen-year-old who had to put her to bed after she'd wet herself on the sofa – the list goes on, and on – and for them, I want to flip a table and scream and scream and scream. How dare she, you know? How *dare* she?'

He delivers this as one big long speech, like it's all been in his head, building and building, and Evie's asking means he's finally got somewhere to put it.

'I know,' Evie says, shaking her head. 'No kid should have to do those things, Duke. You know that, don't you?'

He doesn't say anything.

'And you know it isn't your fault, right? She's got a disease, Duke. It's no more your fault she's an alcoholic than it would be if she got cancer.'

He shakes his head. 'I just don't believe that, you see,' he says. 'Because when I think about having a family, when I imagine my own children, whenever that might be, I do not believe that for one second I would let *anything* come in the way of that. She chose a bottle over me so many times, and I don't care if she's *sick*—' he says *sick* like it's in inverted commas '—she never even tried. And this morning we talked, and we hugged, and then I walked away and felt like I wanted to . . .'

Evie holds her breath. What did he want to do? 'Go on,' she tells him.

He takes a breath. 'I hate how somebody else can make me feel this bad,' he says. 'I want to forgive because I don't want to hate her – I don't want to hate my own mother. That's poison. But I can't forget what she put me through,

210

and so . . . I don't know. Maybe I don't want her in my life.'

Evie nods. 'I get it,' she says. 'And whatever you think is the right thing to do for you is absolutely the right thing.'

'Yeah?' he says, looking at her hopefully.

'Of course,' Evie says. 'But I do think you should tell her all this. Not even for her – for you. Not to play the Alzheimer's card but at least your mom is cognisant. And I'm really not trying to play the misery Olympics here . . .' Evie notes Duke's puzzled face, like he doesn't know what she means. 'Misery Olympics? Like I'm not competing for the "I-Have-It-Worse" trophy, I'm just using my life to maybe give a different perspective on yours, and you can take it or leave it, but . . .'

'But at least my mum can process what I'm saying,' Duke offers, and Evie nods.

'Having an alcoholic mother is an unfair and unjust hand to have been dealt,' Evie tells him. 'And it's up to you how you play it. For what it's worth, all I'm saying is: tell it to her straight. Don't disappear on her, or just stop answering her calls. She needs to hear what you just told me – it won't be anything she's not already heard from you in her mind before. It will probably be a relief to hear you say it, because then it's out there: you're mad at her and don't know if you will ever not be. And once you've done that, once you've given her the full truth of how you feel FOR YOU, so you can release it, then you'll be better able to decide on what to do next. A relationship, just a Christmas card every year, family counselling. It starts with being honest with yourself – which, my compliments, you're doing beautifully – and then telling the person you need to. So. There. That's *my* monologue for the day.'

She feels embarrassed now, like she's hijacked the conversation and said too much and interfered. The feeling intensifies the longer Duke stares at the floor, blinking, moving his head from side to side just enough to demonstrate that he's not totally frozen up but not enough to mean anything. Yes? No? Maybe?

'Duke?' Evie says, eventually, because she can't take it any longer. For all she knows, he's fallen asleep with his eyes open.

'It's just . . .' Duke says, his eyes scanning the floor like he's reading an autocue at his feet. 'This is exactly what I meant about the wisdom in your books. You're a prophet, Evie. And I cannot believe I get to know you in real life.'

And then he looks at her, and she knows what's going to happen before it does. She parts her lips and takes a gulp of air, the tip of her tongue slowly running along her lips. He gives her a half-smile, but he is serious. Earnest. Beautiful. He takes a step towards her.

'Evie,' he says, and then his hands are in her hair and their mouths are clashing together and they are kissing, and kissing, and kissing.

26

Duke

Duke feels better for talking with Evie. Okay. It might have been the kissing that has made him feel better. Both? It felt good to say those things about his mum, to release the hold it has on him. And it was like in doing so, he was suddenly able to see something that's been in front of him: her. Stubborn, mouthy, irritating, funny, kind, wise Evie Bird.

Against the odds he's in the zone today, and there's that magic again, that *sensation*, the thing that lights up his whole body, when the cameras are rolling. Which makes it all the more surprising when Brad yells cut and proceeds to have the most epic tantrum Duke has experienced in his entire working life.

'What the HELL is THIS, you BUNCH OF FECKLESS AMATEURS! No. No!' Brad walks with such purpose towards where Duke and Daphne are standing that Duke can't tell where he intends to stop. Brad marches right past them, turns on his heels, and then roars. Not roars as in shouts loudly, roars as in like a child would do when playing scary dinosaurs. He roars like it's the only way to exorcise the feelings out his body, and he does it for so long and at such volume that the whole set drops absolutely silent, everyone completely still, in shock at what is happening. They are witnessing the melt-down of a grown fifty-something man in real time, the man in charge of this movie, essentially, and nobody knows what to do about it.

Brad roars, and roars and roars, and then, in a total switch, very quietly says to the ground: 'I am going to my trailer. I am not to be bothered.'

'What. The. Hell?' Daphne whispers, when Brad is fully out of sight. The colour has drained from her face, and Duke wonders if she's seen him behave like that before. After what he saw in the gym, and the fact that they very much don't seem to be together anymore, Duke is suddenly sure that what he witnessed wasn't a one-off.

'Hey,' he says, stepping towards her. 'You all right?'

'Yeah,' she says, quietly, like she's trying to convince herself first and foremost. 'Yeah, are you?'

Duke shakes his head. 'I have never seen anything like that in my life,' he says. 'What should we do? Should somebody go after him?'

'I think they're trying to figure that out,' she says, gesturing to a corner, and Duke sees that she's pointing at some very panicked-looking producers. She looks around the set. 'I guess that's cut, guys?' she says to the crew, and so they cut and linger around set for a moment, in case anything else happens.

214

'Hey,' Evie says, coming over to them fifteen minutes later, Magda by her side. 'Are you both okay? We just heard what happened.'

She looks at Duke. Making eye contact with her stirs something in his chest. He smiles, coy. She permits him a half-smirk in return, and it might be in his imagination, but he feels Magda look between them. He gets a flashback to their kiss earlier, the feeling of her in his arms, the flushed, excited look on her face when a knock at his trailer door interrupted them and the spell wasn't so much broken as made into something else: a new secret, just for them.

Duke nods, coming back to life.

'Yeah,' he says. 'He just flew off the handle. It was so mental.'

'We saw him do that yesterday, too. He seems like a very angry man,' Magda comments, pulling on her fluffy earmuffs to brace against the cold of the day.

'What do you mean?' Daphne asks. 'When did you see him?'

'After breakfast, near the hotel,' Magda says. 'Right, Evie?'

Evie nods, looking between Daphne and Duke like she doesn't want to be caught gossiping. 'Yeah,' she admits. 'On the phone. I mean, I'm just an outsider here,' she adds, 'but it kinda feels like he's been getting worse and worse as production goes on?'

Duke nods. He's been circling the same thought. When they started at Pinewood last month, doing all the internal shots, Brad had been charming and given great notes, great direction. Within a week it came out that Daphne was seeing him, and Duke realised he'd been positively overcompensating to hide it, which he continued to do in a way that

Duke came to brush off because he just wanted to get through the shoot, so he didn't have to be around Daphne. But then he'd met Evie, here in Germany, which, now Duke thinks about it, is when Brad seemed to unravel a little more. His moods have dictated set, and set has become icier and icier as time has passed.

'I thought he was just under pressure,' Daphne starts, almost like she's apologising for him. 'But I wonder if it's something more . . . ?'

The four of them let the question hang. Nobody knows anything, and it's cold, so they decide to head back to Duke's trailer with some hot chocolate – Daphne and Duke waiting to be called back, Magda and Evie because, they say, they'd rather stick around to get the warts and all movie-making experience than disappear and go shopping again.

'Not that there's anything left here to buy,' Magda quips as they walk. 'We've shopped till we've dropped.'

'You did?' Duke asks her, and he swears that Evie blushes a bit. 'Hey,' he adds. 'Don't be embarrassed. When I was last in Rome I blew so much at the Gucci store that I also had to buy another Gucci luggage set to get it home in. No judgement here.' He holds up his hands.

'I bought like, two sweaters,' Evie mumbles, and Duke decides not to try and bond over tales of shopping again, since it seems like an oddly sore topic. They reach his trailer, and he stands back to let the women go ahead of him, Daphne first, then Magda, then Evie. Duke can't help it – he reaches out a hand to brush her fingertips with his own.

'Hey,' he says.

'Hey,' she replies, with a coy smile. God he wants to kiss

her again. He daren't say anything else, but it sates him to see the glint in Evie's eye. He feels vaguely like a schoolboy with his first crush.

'So this is the inside of a Hollywood trailer, is it?' Magda observes as they all disrobe from their winter warmers and pile hats and coats and gloves high on a chair in the corner. 'I don't mean to sound rude,' she continues, 'but I expected something more . . .'

'Glamorous?' provides Daphne, and Magda pulls a face. 'Me too,' she continues, laughing. 'But if I say that, I get called a diva.'

'God, I don't know how you do it,' Evie says, as Duke texts his assistant for the hot chocolates. He doesn't have anything to make them with here, and they'll be nicer from a proper little German café or market stall anyway.

'What, slum it in a bad trailer?' Daphne quips.

'No.' Evie laughs. 'Moderating yourself all the time in case you get a reputation.'

'Oh,' Daphne says, with a big sigh. 'You don't know the half of it. Although I deal with it better than you do, don't I, Duke?' She self-corrects, then. 'Well, not better. I mean – you struggle more. You don't like it, do you?'

'Nope,' Duke says. 'But that's what therapists are for.'

'Quite,' Daphne agrees, taking the hint that he doesn't really want to talk about that.

'Do you think this thing with Brad will delay the shoot at all?' Evie asks, taking the hint too. 'It's so close to Christmas . . .'

'No,' Daphne says, shaking her head. 'The cost of it, if nothing else. The producers will sort him out. Although, Duke, at this rate, it's going to be up to us to be one-take

217

wonders, I suppose, if we have any hope of staying on schedule.'

'Well,' Duke says, taking the chance to give the compliment. 'I've been meaning to say how much I am enjoying sharing this with you. I can't believe only a month ago that . . .' He trails off. Should he really be saying this? Probably not, considering Evie is here. But too late, the words are out of his mouth.

'That only a month ago I stomped on your heart, and now we're mates again?' Daphne supplies, and Duke smiles.

'Something like that, yeah.'

Duke looks at Evie without meaning to. She holds his gaze, like it's okay that he just clarified that, that she understands he and Daphne are friends. He feels the heat rise at the back of his neck.

'I saw that,' Magda says, smirking.

'What?' asks Evie, looking up.

Magda looks at Duke, waiting for him to explain, and Duke waits for a hole to open up in the ground so he can disappear. He doesn't want to talk about what might be growing between him and Evie. Not just yet. He isn't even sure himself.

'Let's just say,' Magda tells Evie, 'that my little theory yesterday has been proved wrong. These two genuinely are just best mates, I think. Our friend Duke here is smitten with someone else, I'd say.'

'Magda!' Evie cries, and Duke goes to defend himself but then, confronted with the horror behind Evie's cry, finds that he can't.

Daphne fills the gap for him. 'Wait, you thought there was something going on between us?' she asks Evie.

'No,' says Evie, hurriedly. 'Not me. Magda.'

'Sorry,' says Magda. 'It's just . . . you're both very attractive, and were together like, ten minutes ago, and also have very good chemistry on camera, et cetera.'

'It's called acting,' Duke says, and it comes out a bit cross. But he is cross. He's angry that Magda would posit such a thing to Evie: the person he *actually* likes. In fact, Evie is precisely *why* he can be so friendly with Daphne. Daphne had it right all along: they're better as friends and he was in love with the idea of her, more so than her. He certainly didn't feel the way he does now, with Evie . . . It's been one kiss. But dear God, it was a great kiss.

'Yes,' Magda says, agreeing. 'I misspoke. Evie said so yesterday, anyway.'

Duke looks at Evie. Why does he suddenly feel like this is a bad sixth form party and everyone is talking about him?

'Knock, knock!' a voice comes then, and Duke assumes it's the hot drinks arriving but it's not his assistant. It's the head of production, Marnie.

'Hey,' Duke says, standing up to shake her hand.

'Hey,' Marnie says, shaking Duke's hand and waving at the three women. 'Listen,' she presses. 'Can we have a little three-way meeting here? Sorry Evie, and . . .' She trails off, unsure who Magda is.

'A guest of mine. Magda,' Duke supplies, and Marnie nods politely, obviously wanting to discuss something sensitive.

'We'll pop to the café on the corner,' Evie announces. 'Leave you all to it. Break a leg, won't you?' she adds, fumbling through all their coats and jackets to find what belongs to them. 'If that's . . . Is that what we say? Okay. Well. Whatever . . . it is. Bye.'

It's the first time Duke has seen her flustered and unable to articulate herself properly.

'Right,' says Marnie, once they've both gone. Duke looks at her. She's a calm woman, with a kind and patient demeanour, so it's unnerving to see her sweating and tapping her foot with nervous energy. This must be bad.

'Is Brad okay?' Daphne asks, slowly, and Duke looks at her. Trust Daphne to be compassionate, even in the face of rude, dickish behaviour.

'Physically?' Marnie says. 'Yes. Mentally? No, to be frank. He's off the project. So is the assistant director.'

Duke is shocked. Off the project? Halfway through it? That is not a thing that can happen. This is *serious*.

'I know,' Marnie continues, and she motions to an empty chair. 'May I?'

'Yeah,' Duke says. 'Of course.'

They watch her get comfortable, take a big gulp of air, and then continue, calmer now: 'Speaking confidentially, there have been . . . allegations.'

'What kind of allegations?' Daphne asks, and Duke can hear the alarm in her voice.

'Sexual harassment,' Marnie says. 'Intimidation. Bullying.'

Daphne sets her face in a hard line. Duke has a very fleeting thought – is she the accuser? And then it disappears. If she is, it's none of his business unless she tells him directly.

'What happens now?' Duke asks. 'Are we done?'

'No,' Marnie says. 'Financially, we just can't do that. The investors are insistent. But, so close to Christmas, right now, finding somebody else . . .'

'We'll do it,' says Daphne. Duke looks at her. She doesn't meet his eye. 'We'll self-direct.'

Marnie nods. 'I was going to suggest as much.'

'We'll do it,' Daphne reiterates. 'Won't we, Duke?'

Before Duke can answer – direct? A movie? Between them? – Marnie interjects.

'I need to make something very clear though,' she says. 'We can't credit you. We can work something out – a first-look pass for future roles, a development deal or something. Daphne, I know you're interested in producing too, so maybe there's something we can do there. But for the good of the movie – the press, all of that – this needs to be you scratching our backs for now, and later we'll scratch yours.'

Daphne nods. 'But *you'd* know what we did, wouldn't you?' she clarifies.

'And I wouldn't forget it in a hurry,' Marnie replies. 'I can assure you.'

'Duke?' Daphne asks.

Duke nods, slightly.

'Is that a yes?' Marnie asks.

Duke nods again, clearer this time. Daphne gasps.

'Yes,' Duke says. 'But we're not doing a thing until we've got what you've just said in writing. Daphne gets a credited directorial debut, somehow, and I get a first-look pass or development deal.'

'I'll get legal on it now,' Marnie says. 'Hold that thought . . .'

She leaves, and for a moment Daphne and Duke simply stare at each other. Eventually Duke says, 'Crikey.'

And then they burst out laughing.

27

Duke

Duke and Daphne don't pause for breath until breakfast, working through the night. They've got some catching up to do, and so, despite the fact Duke is desperate to be alone with Evie again, now is not the time.

'I've never felt this alive in my life,' Daphne says, leaning back from Duke's MacBook Pro. 'My blood is pumping faster, I swear. I'm like, energised by being energised. Does that make sense?'

Duke laughs, because he knows exactly what she means. They've been looking over the rough edits that have already been done to the internal scenes, figuring out what's left to shoot and how to do it, agreeing on some rules and boundaries for working together. There's three more locations left – Pfaffenwinkel, Schwangau, and Füssen, all happening in very quick succession – and so they need to be razor-sharp and clear as day with their intentions and scheduling.

'I'm not worried,' Duke says. 'I think we're going to be totally fine. Like, this is going to be fun. It's an amazing opportunity.'

'I'll say,' Daphne hoots, crossing and uncrossing her legs. She lifts up an arm and smells her pit. 'Urgh,' she says. 'Okay. I'm going to go shower. Meet in my trailer in an hour?'

'Done and done,' Duke says. 'And, Daphne? Well done.'

'You too,' she says, smiling, and when she's gone Duke considers calling down to Evie's room, but it's still early and he doesn't want to wake her. It's the first time he's thought of anything other than the movie all night. And this needs his focus: he can't blow it. Not for his sake, nor for Daphne's. Between the directing, now, which will carry on into the new year with post-production, even after they've done filming, with edits and sound engineering and everything it entails, and then his mother, who is still here . . .

Ah.

She texted him, and he hasn't replied.

He doesn't know what he wants to say. Evie gave clever, sound advice, but he knows that to explain everything he wants to explain to his mum, he needs emotional bandwidth – not to get all 'therapy speak'. But he's going to cry, at the end of the day, because that's what he does. He's a crier. And then he's going to have to pick a coping mechanism, and since working with Phoebe he's been able to manage his undereating and overexercising, and luckily precisely because of his mother he's seldom had more than two drinks a night and doesn't ever do drugs.

223

After a shower and a change of clothes, Duke calls his mother at her hotel.

'Mum,' he says, when she answers. 'I'm so sorry. I've been working all night. I didn't mean to leave you hanging.'

'No, no,' his mother insists. 'I know you're working, pet. It's fine. We've been exploring and seeing the sights.'

'Okay,' he says, and there's a pause. 'I'm on set all day today, too,' he tells her. 'We're taking over some directing duties, actually, so there's loads that needs to be done.'

'That's nice, love. Congratulations.'

Duke isn't sure she means it. There's something hollow about the supposed compliment.

'Are you okay?' he asks her.

'Yes, yes,' she says. 'I am. I'm just wondering . . .'

And there it is. Duke can feel the blow before she issues it.

'I think we should probably go home. You're busy, and I've said my piece . . .'

Duke doesn't say anything. She wants to go home again? It's been two days.

'Right,' Duke says, his heart thumping like he's being kicked from the inside. 'Well, that's up to you, isn't it.'

He's met with silence.

'Mum?' he pushes. Suddenly, he realises that she's crying. 'Mum,' he repeats, firmer this time.

'I just thought this would be different,' she says, her voice wobbling. 'It's my fault. I expected too much. Roger says he hates to see me like this, waiting by the phone for you.'

'Oh, Roger doesn't like that, does he? Well, I'm very sorry for *Roger*,' Duke says, and it's harsh, and he doesn't censor

224

how mad he is that she's said that, but also: she should count her lucky stars that he's not gone full postal on her, because he easily could. Bloody ROGER? What's he got to do with anything? Jesus!

'He cares about me,' his mother counters, and the way she says it fills the gaps between her words with something else. The spaces leave room for the other truth: *and you don't, Duke.*

'Well,' Duke retorts. 'It's nice that he's in your life.' The space between his words suggests another truth: *because I haven't been, and that's your fault.*

'You can't keep blaming me, Derrick. I've said I'm sorry.'

Before he can think, he says back: 'And you also said you didn't *have* any expectations, so it's interesting that now you suddenly do, and I don't meet them. This is so bloody typical, Mum. YOU chose the time to reach out, YOU set invisible expectations and denied they were even there. You're not being fair.' And then there it is: he cries too, exactly as he always does. 'Urgh,' he adds, upset with himself for letting her do this to him again. They both sob down the line. Eventually Duke says, 'Look. I know you love me. But the way you love me, it isn't enough. The love I deserve is bigger than the love you can give. And that's going to have to be okay. And I love you too, but, Mum: it hurts me. So I think I just need to . . .'

'What?'

He's got two choices. He can hit the nuclear button, or he can give himself room to have more complex feelings.

'I need time, Mum. Let's spend some proper time together, when I'm not working, somewhere neutral.'

'Hmm,' comes her voice down the line.

'Hmm?' he repeats. 'Come on. Give me something. You're the parent, remember?'

'Yes,' she says, then, and Duke suspects that Roger is beside her listening to all of this unfold, coaching her through what to say. Does he mind that? He can't decide. God, the box he's stuffing everything into won't be able to get the lid on soon enough. There's a lot being left to figure out later.

'Well, I love you, and I'm sorry if my coming here has felt like an attack out of the blue. That wasn't my intention. I accept that you need time. The next move is yours to make. I won't bother you again.'

'You haven't *bothered* me, Mum . . .'

'I do love you. I keep saying it, but that's because I mean it.'

'I know you do, Mum. We move to the next location tomorrow, so I imagine we'd be saying goodbye anyway. Do you want to come to set today? We're close by, and we should hug, at least, before you fly. I won't have long, but . . .'

He can hear himself doing it: extending an olive branch and then in the same breath issuing a rebuttal, taking it back, giving her a get-out clause.

'We'll come,' she says, before he can rescind the invitation altogether. 'Is there a time that's best?'

Duke stops himself from saying that no time is a good one, really. Instead he decides: 'After lunch. I'll send you the details.'

He isn't crying by the time he rings off. He splashes cold water on his face, looks at himself in the mirror, and tells himself he's loved, and loving, like Phoebe taught him. He thinks of Evie's face. For the first time in a long time, he chooses to believe it.

In the hotel lobby, he bumps into Evie and Magda.

'Hey, hey, Mr Director!' Evie says to him, giving a playful punch to his upper arm. 'You ready?'

'How did you know?' Duke asks, standing proud.

'Katerina said.' She shrugs. 'Congratulations!'

'Thank you.' He nods. 'Yeah. It's pretty cool.'

'It's amazing,' she says, grinning. 'But also: you ready to go? I need to be on set too apparently. Let's walk and talk.'

'Yeah. I'm ready. But whilst you're here I have a favour to ask.'

'Okay Duke, yes, I'll be in the movie. FINE,' Magda jokes, and Evie purses her lips like *of course* Magda wants to be on film. Of course she does.

'It's about my mum,' Duke continues, and Magda, clearly understanding that maybe she shouldn't be privy to this, demonstrates her ability to read the room by announcing, suddenly, that she's just going to get a coffee to go and she'll be by the front doors getting some air when Evie is ready.

'Perfect.' Evie nods, turning her attention back to Duke. 'What can I do?' she asks. 'What do you need?'

'Well . . .' Duke explains. He knows this is a big ask, really. 'She's coming to set. I imagine she'll have Roger with her. They're coming to say goodbye, just quickly. The thing is I don't want everyone knowing my business, and who knows what she might say to who . . .'

'You want me to play babysitter?' Evie asks.

'Host,' Duke corrects, adopting a funny voice. 'Would you *host* my mother on set? Also known as babysitting, yes.'

Evie nods. 'Of course,' she agrees. 'When's she coming?'

'After lunch. I told her one, and she'll be by the barriers, and knows to wait to be met by somebody. I didn't say who, though I assume she'll recognise you.'

'Keep it light, keep it charming, find you for a hello and then get the heck out?' Evie clarifies.

'You've understood me perfectly.' Duke smiles, relieved that she is who she is – that she gets it.

'Magda can occupy herself too, so it really will just be me.'

Duke smiles, reaching out a hand to her wrist. He feels ... heard. Cared for. And it's such a small thing to feel such disproportionate gratitude for, but he's aware that this woman in front of him – this beautiful, funny woman – never makes it about her. She has her issues too, but she's here for Duke, and it's so easy to let her in. She's not being kind and deferential because he's Duke Carlisle, international movie star. She doesn't need anything from him. He's just Duke, and she's just Evie, and he really would like to kiss her again.

'Not here,' she says, reading his thoughts. 'Eyes everywhere.'

The *not* doing it causes Duke a physical pain.

'Got it,' he says. 'But. Soon?'

'Soon.' She smiles.

28

Evie

'So, sorry,' Magda says, when Evie rejoins her. '*Where* are we going tomorrow?'

'Pfaffenwinkel,' Evie repeats. 'I think that's how you say it, anyway.'

'That's a lot of f's,' Magda says.

'Pleasing use of *winkel*, though,' Evie notes.

Magda laughs. It's so wonderful, having her best friend here. Evie knows she could stand to loosen up a little, and Magda makes it easier to give in to enjoying it all. She feels less angry with the world when her friend is around. She's still on her guard, but less so.

They're walking to set. Evie's social media manager has asked her to get some images of what it's like behind the scenes, so they can post about it on her account when the movie is out next year. She asked if Evie might even consider actually being *in* the photos, too, since, considering the international press her fauxmance with Duke has had, her stance of total anonymity has evidently wavered. They haven't had a fake date in a while, actually, although Evie has a feeling that with the directorial changes she might be called upon as a distraction technique again. She doesn't mind. Between this and his mom, Duke has had a lot on his plate. She'll welcome the excuse for some one-on-one, whatever the circumstance. And he *has* suggested more kissing might be involved, which isn't a terrible thought . . .

'So . . .' Magda begins, and it's in *that* voice. They walk through the city, having turned down the offer of a private car, taking in today's dark sky, threatening snow again, and the contrast with the twinkling white lights and red ribbons that festoon almost every single building. It's a chocolate-box city, perfectly picturesque.

'Oh God, what?' Evie groans, passing a roasted chestnut stand, a woman in fingerless gloves pushing them around a huge smoking pan, a smile on her face.

'Well, look, I know we talked about not feeling worthy yesterday, and honestly, I am so honoured you'd share that with me because in all the years I've known you, you've never actually articulated yourself that way. That was the most openly I've heard you talk about your dad, ever.'

Evie feels her tummy contract and her throat get hot. Where is this going?

'Am I about to be punished for that . . . ?' Evie says, and she's only half-joking. The other half is dead serious.

'Nooo,' Magda says, tutting. 'But I did just want to keep that conversation going? If you're open to it?' Evie doesn't say anything, and Magda apparently takes this as permission to continue. She takes a breath, and the seriousness of it makes Evie furrow her brow. Everything seems less pretty now. But somehow she *is* more open to this conversation, more open than, as Magda said, she's been in years. The thought of Duke's face floats into her imagination. Odd.

'Because I couldn't help but notice that after that salesgirl noticed you, you spent a lot of money. And look, I don't know your *exact* situation, but I am your friend, and I do know when something isn't right.'

Evie would rather talk about her heart than her bank balance out loud.

'I was treating myself,' Evie says, waving a hand.

'And that's totally allowed,' Magda replies. 'Obviously. It's just . . . it wasn't a small amount of money. And I know you say about it being so expensive for your mom's care, and you've always kind of skirted around the issue when your credit card has bounced or whatever. So I'm only thinking that . . . you know . . . if you're good for cash, why does the card bounce?'

'I keep the limit small,' Evie says. 'So I don't get in trouble. So small that sometimes it gets maxed out. But rather that than have a big limit and overspend because of it.'

'Uh-huh,' Magda muses. Evie starts to think that that's the last of it, when her friend adds: 'You said something about being able to pay for all your mom's care without worrying because of the new foreign rights deals, too?'

'Nursing homes are expensive!' Evie says, defensively. 'The good ones, anyway.'

Magda makes that noise again. 'Uh-huh.'

'I'm fine,' Evie says, when she realises Magda isn't following up with anything. 'Money comes in, money goes out. I write two books a year, Magda. I don't travel much, or even go out very often, but I do buy nice cashmere to do my work in, and nice candles to burn as I do it. I think I deserve that much.'

'Totally.' Magda nods, and they're near to set, now. Evie doesn't want to be talking about this with everyone else around. Evie doesn't want to be talking about this at all. 'But I want you to know – staying in your room, I've seen the other shopping bags, and I've seen the clothes in your wardrobe with all the tags still on.'

Evie tries to protest, but Magda won't let her interrupt.

'And I've seen the same at home, too. When I've stayed over. I've never pried, but when you've told me to help myself to a sweater when we're watching TV or whatever. I'm just not stupid is the thing. It'd be a worse thing if I didn't ask you about it. People would kill for the paycheques you get – I know you're not a millionaire, but it's clear from those phone calls you've been having that paying your mom's fees shouldn't be the struggle you say it is . . .'

'Magda,' Evie warns, colour rising to her cheeks, her breath shallow. 'That's enough.'

'But—' Magda starts, but Evie holds up a hand.

'I said, that's enough.'

The women walk in silence through set, past the trailers to where everyone is working on a scene where Hermione and George have an argument that starts out playful, but quickly gets serious and threatens how they can move forward. Evie

232

can see Daphne and Duke stood side by side, pointing at something on a monitor, deep in conversation.

'Can you get me doing a thumbs up with them in the background?' Evie asks Magda, trying to move on from the heated exchange they have just had.

'Sure,' Magda says, holding out a hand for Evie's phone. Before the new directing team call action, Evie is photographed in a series of shots: she pretends to look through one of the cameras, holds the clapper board and, as Katerina passes, corrals her into posing too. They take a fun few as mirror selfies in the make-up trailer with Kayla as well, and then Evie's reminder alert goes off, and it's time for her to go and collect Duke's mom.

'I'll see you later?' Evie says to Magda. 'At the hotel?'

Magda says yes, of course, and that she's sorry. Evie doesn't reply. She doesn't want to say it's okay, and she doesn't want to say she's sorry too, because both those things threaten to pop the lid off the can of worms and that's not what she wants. But also, she's tired of hating herself so much that she won't even let herself accrue savings. It could be a relief to tell Magda. Maybe Magda will understand. Maybe Magda can help.

'Hey – are you Duke's mom?' Evie says, approaching a neat-looking woman in a sleek wool coat and surprisingly youthful black leather boots. The woman looks up.

'I am, yes,' she says, and then she laughs. 'Although it's always so strange to hear him called that. We called him Ricky growing up. Derrick – after my father-in-law.'

Evie smiles. The woman seems nervous. Anxious.

'He told me that not many people know that,' Evie tells

her, and she sees the woman mentally calculate if she's just made a faux pas. Evie drops to a stage whisper. 'But I knew . . .' she adds, and the woman looks relieved. 'I didn't know it was after his grandfather, though. Just that Duke is a stage name.'

'I suppose it must help,' Duke's mother ponders. 'Being one person on stage and another in real life.'

'It's a good job Duke knows the difference.' Evie smiles. 'I'd imagine it's very hard for actors to remember.'

His mother looks at her, then, with slightly narrowed eyes. 'Yes,' she says, and then holds out a hand. 'Anna,' she says. 'Sorry, I should have introduced myself properly.'

'Evie,' Evie says, holding out a hand too. 'We met, actually, just briefly.'

'At the restaurant that night.' Anna nods. 'Yes. I thought your face was familiar.'

Evie waits for the penny to drop.

'Were you the girl in the photographs with him? Sorry – are you Derrick's girlfriend?'

Evie starts walking, motioning for Anna to come with her. 'No, no,' she says. 'Didn't he tell you? It's all for the cameras.'

'He didn't mention,' Anna says. 'No.'

'Well . . .' Evie replies. 'We've become friends, at least. I actually wrote the book the movie is based on. They're doing a great job with the adaptation. Did you know Duke is doing some directing now too?'

They arrive to the main area where the activity is taking place, and Evie notices Anna's eyes widen. It's a full crew today, a hundred people dashing about purposefully in bobble hats and battery-heated gilets, cameras and tracks and lights and boom mics everywhere. It strikes Evie how quickly this has become normal for her again: a film set. Seeing Anna marvel so openly reminds her how lucky she is, how totally crazy it is that this is her life. Magda is right: most people would give an arm and a leg to bear witness to something like this.

'I've never visited him at work before,' Anna says, and Evie can see there's a tear in her eye. 'Look at him.' Anna points to where Duke and Daphne are walking through their scene, Duke listening intently as Daphne explains something. He shouts over to the cameraperson, and the three of them start hashing something out. Anna and Evie are far enough away that their staring isn't a distraction – they're just another couple of people on set.

'Do you want a tissue?' Evie asks, gently, when she sees Anna's tears are flowing more freely, now.

Anna nods. Evie takes off a glove and fishes around in her pockets.

'Here,' Evie says. Anna takes it. They watch, and Anna continues to cry.

'It's fun to watch, isn't it?' Evie says, eventually. Softly, too, since she can tell Anna is feeling a lot right now. 'I can't believe I'm here.'

Anna nods. 'I just can't believe what he's made of himself,' she says, shaking her head. 'I'm sure he's told you I wasn't a very good mother.'

Evie doesn't say anything. She doesn't know how to reply to that in a way that doesn't do an injustice to Duke. He can say what he likes about his mother, but Evie can't join in. She settles on: 'My father drank.'

She says it neutrally. As coolly as she can.

Anna nods. 'Do you still see him?' she asks.

Evie shakes her head. 'He left when I was a kid. He's never tried to say sorry like you have.'

Anna nods tearfully again. 'Do you think he'll ever forgive me?' she asks. Evie shrugs – again, unwilling to overstep.

'I really don't know him all that well,' she says, and she surprises herself to think: *yet.*

Anna wipes at her eyes. She's stopped crying, now. Silence hangs between them, and Evie continues: 'What I do know is that he is kind, and thoughtful, and generous and funny. He's got a good heart, you know? Many a man with a face like that could get away with being horrible, and the world would still forgive them.'

Anna laughs. 'Yes. He's always been a looker,' she says. And then, looking at Evie, she adds: 'Thank you. I'm sure you've got better things to do than look after a doddery old woman and her tears.'

Evie smiles. 'Nah,' she says. 'I love doddery old women and their tears.' She says it with a wink, and Anna gets the joke. 'Come on. I don't think there's going to be a good time to interrupt, so let's just go for it. I'll take the blame.' They head on closer to where Duke is working, and he senses them now, looking up and giving a little wave before whispering something to Daphne and coming over to meet them.

'Hey,' Duke says to his mother. 'You made it. No Roger?'

Anna shakes her head. 'I asked for some mother-son time,' she says, and then Evie gets the hint and goes to excuse herself.

'I . . . just need to make a call,' Evie says. 'I'll come back in five?' she asks, to Duke. He nods.

'Thanks, Evie,' he says.

Evie walks away, ostensibly to check in with her agent about the other film deals, but she's still within earshot when she hears Anna say to Duke: 'She's nice.'

'Yes,' Duke says. 'She is.'

Evie's agent picks up on the fourth ring.

'Evie,' she says. 'Thanks for getting back to me. I've got news. Columbia have just made their final offer for the movie rights to two more of your novels. Long story short is this: we're coming in at just over half a million dollars.'

Evie pulls the phone away from her ear and makes sure she's got full signal. She has.

'Sorry,' Evie says. 'I can't hear you very well. It's my signal. Can you repeat that?'

Her agent clears her throat and takes a breath. 'Evie. We've just been made an offer for six hundred thousand dollars. I'll send it you in writing, but that's the top line. Six hundred thousand dollars for the option on two books, and they've already got actors in mind. They're meeting with Reese Witherspoon to see about co-production with Hello Sunshine as well.'

But Evie doesn't hear her anymore, because she's got her hands on her knees, bent over, dry retching to the ground. By the time Duke and his mum have seen what's happening and come over, she manages to finally bring up her breakfast, all over Anna's boots, the ones that only ten minutes ago she was admiring so much.

Evie's rich!

29

Evie

The Litzauer Loop near Burggen, Pfaffenwinkel, is a horseshoe-shaped piece of land with the river wrapping around it at such an angle that it is almost a river doughnut with a snow-covered tree-topped bit of land in the middle. Duke and Daphne went into painstaking detail about the type of shots they're after today when Evie and Magda had dinner with them last night, but it's only now everyone is here that the true majesty reveals itself. When Evie wrote *On the Romantic Road* she used Google to travel to all the places featured in her mind. To be actually on those stops, and now on this particularly incredible one, makes her feel as nauseous as she did after talking to her agent yesterday.

'I'm going to need your help, yes,' she'd told Magda, after she'd fainted and generally caused a fuss yesterday. What a thing – six hundred thousand dollars? Reese Witherspoon?

Two books under film option? She still gets dizzy thinking about it today. 'But not yet. Just give me time.'

To her credit, it's been almost twenty-four hours and Magda is doing exactly that. Giving Evie time, and space, to process her fortunes.

'This is beautiful,' she marvels, as they let themselves feel tiny against the imposing skyline. The crew is reduced today, and tonight there's a party for everyone to help, as Duke and Daphne had explained, keep morale high. There's only a few days of filming left – but it's enough that Brad's departure needs an energic clear-out and collectively they could do with blowing off some steam.

Evie doesn't actually need to be here today – the content team have shifted focus to capture Duke and Daphne working together as directors, in case the producers decide to play up to that publicly in the run-up to release – it depends how everything shakes out. But if Evie's here, she's not in town, doing what she really feels compelled to do: somehow get rid of all her money in preparation for another big cheque dropping. She doesn't want the temptation of the boutiques and shops, and doesn't want the quiet that she'll fill by telling Magda everything, so they're here, bearing witness to Mother Nature at her most showy-offy.

'Hey,' Duke says, coming up behind her after she's wandered off to the edge of the water, the brisk cold making her nose feel like an ice cube. He touches a gloved hand to her mitten, just enough to send a spark straight to her stomach. She turns.

'Hey,' she says. 'How's it going?'

'Okay. Fine. Is it strange if I tell you I miss you?' Duke

asks, and she looks at him, eyebrows raised, because of all the things she was expecting him to say when she realised he was there, that wasn't on the list.

'Oh,' she says, embarrassed. 'No,' she adds, quickly. 'I know we haven't had a minute to . . . you know . . . there was . . . the thing . . . that happened.'

'I liked that it happened,' Duke tells her. 'Just FYI.'

She dares to smile.

'I know things have been crazy,' he says. 'We kind of started to have this really nice time, and then . . .'

Evie knows what he means, but can't find the proper words to explain it either. This is a whirlwind: filming, pretending to date, the kissing, but then his mom, Magda being here . . . It's only been two weeks yet it feels like enough has happened to fill two months. And they only have one week left, too. Six days, to be exact. Time is passing at the speed of light.

'Life,' Evie supplies, and he nods, smiling.

'Life,' he repeats.

They look out to the water, to the trees looping around at the other side.

'I'll make sure to find you at the party later, okay? Not party – the producers say we can't call it that, it makes people get too out-of-hand they say – but celebration. Production celebration or whatever it is we're actually allowed to say.'

Evie nods. 'Yes,' she says. 'Come and find me. Maybe we can sneak off for a walk again.'

'I'd like that,' he says, and for one dazzling moment Evie is on Cloud Nine.

And then she reminds herself to get a grip.

*

By 6 p.m. there's been a raffle, a mini-quiz, and an adult game of musical statues. They're at the hotel, which is smaller and more boutique than the other places they've stayed at, with low wooden-beamed ceilings and chairs tucked away in corners, mistletoe conspicuously abundant. Everyone is in good spirits – it's been a needed outlet. There are trays of pizza coming from the kitchen at regular intervals, and baskets of fries, too. Magda is laughing hysterically with Katerina, the DP, and Evie is having fun too, talking with Daphne and Duke and some of the crew, playing a game of Never Have I Ever.

'Never Have I Ever . . . peed in Keanu Reeves's swimming pool,' Daphne offers to the group, and Duke is forced to down the last of his beer.

'What?!' exclaims Evie. 'That's foul!'

Duke shrugs, nonplussed. 'A guy's gotta do what a guy's gotta do,' he says.

'Never have I ever been caught arguing with Duke Carlisle by a national newspaper,' offers one of the art directors, and Daphne is forced to drink now. Duke looks to Evie, and she concedes that he's right: she must drink too. Gosh, how long ago that feels now. She hated him that day. Really, truly hated him! And now look. The ice between them has thawed, they've kissed . . .

It's as if by mentioning it that Dream-or-Willow appears, then, an apologetic look on their face.

'Hey,' she says, and looking between Evie and Duke, Evie knows what's coming. Wasn't she just thinking yesterday how they've not been requested to do any more showmance shots with the press? 'I'm so sorry to interrupt . . .'

Duke turns his shoulder so he and Evie are effectively shielded from the others, who pause for half a second to listen in before deciding it's much more fun to keep playing. Evie hears somebody say *never have I ever had an on-set romance* . . . but she can't see who drinks.

'There's a pap loitering outside,' Dream-or-Willow says. 'Can we give them something? I know you guys don't like it, but especially with Brad gone, it helps the movie . . .'

Duke looks at Evie. The way he does it, she gets a flutter between her legs. This is the most relaxed and silly she's seen him, as though with the directing, and after seeing his mom, even, internal dots are being connected for him and he knows it's okay to be himself. And Evie likes that self. After he told her he missed her today, she's kept thinking about it. When she was getting ready for tonight, she did her bikini line in the shower and moisturised her whole body, slowly and deliberately, and found herself daydreaming about his hands over her body until Magda banged on the door and said, 'Evie! I need to shower too! What the hell are you doing in there?' She couldn't well admit that she was thinking that she'd like to go to bed with Duke. She hasn't even told Magda they've kissed. It feels too sacred to do that. Too delicate.

Evie shrugs. 'Fine,' she says. 'We can go get some air, can't we, Duke?'

Duke grins. 'Sure,' he says, like he's doing everyone a favour, but Evie knows that tone of voice. She throbs again. Her body is making it known that she's hungry for him.

Outside, he loops an arm across her shoulders and pulls her in close. It thrills her. They see the pap at the same time, nod at him, and then resume the make-believe story that they think they're having a private moment.

'Alone at last,' Duke says, and Evie laughs.

'Should we ask him to join us?' she says.

Duke shakes his head. 'I gave up group sex after an *Eyes Wide Shut* party at the White House.'

She laughs again. 'Which administration?' she teases.

'I couldn't possibly say,' Duke says with a straight face. 'I signed an NDA and it's more than my life is worth.'

Evie pulls away to look at him. 'I honestly can't tell if you're joking anymore,' she says, and Duke pulls a face. What kind of life has this man lived?

'My mum liked you,' he says, as they head down the steps and around the corner to a quiet little cobbled path with the fuzzy lights of yet another market at the far end.

'Not something I hear a lot,' Evie admits. 'I'm normally not the kind of girl you introduce to your parents.'

Now it's Duke's turn to peer at her with an uncertain expression. 'I don't believe you,' he says. 'You're always alluding to being some sort of hands-off, unlovable ice maiden, but I know the truth, Evie Bird. You're none of those things. You're the opposite of those things, in fact.'

'Oh, because you know me so well?' Evie fires off without thinking, though inwardly she kicks herself. She's sick of it – sick of how she can't let him in. She's thought of him all day, craved him, even, and he's being kind and she's saying things she doesn't mean. What the hell is wrong with her? 'Okay fine,' she adds, noting the wounded look on his face and trying to recover quickly. 'You know me a *bit*.' She pulls her own face then, letting him know she's aware she's been prickly. 'I'm trying, you know,' she tells him. 'I'm doing my best to live up to this idea you have of me.'

Duke stops walking and turns her to face him, his hands on her shoulders. He sighs.

'I need you to stop this,' he says. 'I can't convince you that you're amazing, and that I like you, and that I'm not going to change my mind every single time we talk. I'm too tired, Evie. I just want you to be in this.'

Evie looks to her feet. Why does he always have to be so articulate, so clear about what he wants?

'Okay.' She pouts. 'No need to cry about it.'

He playfully hits her arm. 'For pity's sake.' He laughs, visibly frustrated by her *in*ability to be clear about what she wants. She finds the courage to look at him.

'I'm hot for you, is that what you need to hear?' she asks him.

He takes a step towards her. 'Ooh,' he says, a smirk playing on his lips. 'Actually, yes. Say it again.'

'I'm hot for you,' she repeats, mocking him.

'Say it like you mean it,' he instructs, and it's harder for her to stay playful, now. She can't be cheeky when he's licking his lips that way, looking at her like he could take her right here, right now, right on the street.

'I'm hot for you,' Evie whispers, and he's inches from her, now, and it's Evie who is licking her lips this time. 'I'm hot for you,' she repeats again, turned on by the nearness of him, his obvious lust. She's scared to want him as much as she does, but it's way sexier to let herself desire him than it is to withhold just how much she needs his lips on hers, his hard, muscled body pressed against her.

Before she knows what's happening, he's pushed her up against the wall behind her, one hand steadying her at the waist, the other snaked up under her hair to the nape of her neck, where he tugs, just enough to force her chin up so that their mouths can meet. It's been days since they were last together alone, days since he muttered her name into her mouth between kisses, and she's missed him too.

'Take me back to the hotel,' Evie tells him, and he goes one better, lifting her up in his arms so that she squeals. 'What are you doing!' She wraps her arms around his neck, and he carries her back the way they came, putting on a caveman voice to say: 'Me, Tarzan Duke. You, Evie Jane. We, have sex in my room, right now.'

Neither of them even care that the photographer is having a field day. Evie just wants to be upstairs, in his bed, naked – and as soon as possible.

Duke Carlisle is an exquisite lover. As soon as they are in his suite, he has her pressed halfway up the door, and Evie's legs are wrapped around him, her ankles locked under his ass so she can pull him in. He grinds against her, the bulge in his trousers obvious and delightful. His mouth is on her cheek, her neck. He appears to have set his own personal challenge to let no inch of her décolletage go unkissed.

'Yes,' sighs Evie. 'Yes, yes, yes.'

He carries her across to the bed, depositing her with such ease it's like he's placing down a bag of feathers. He's strong. Really strong. Evie lies back and he climbs on top of her, and what comes next is carnal, filthy, and long overdue.

'Yes,' Evie says again, when she's come so hard she thinks she might have pulled a muscle in her back.

Duke grins, and credit to him: he's panting.

'God, that was . . .' starts Duke, and in between her own panting Evie agrees.

'It was,' she agrees.

He looks at her. He's golden and chiselled. No man should look that good.

'Shall we go again?' he asks, his hand rubbing her thigh lightly, threatening to slip between her legs.

Evie hoots an involuntary laugh. 'Absolutely not,' she shrieks.

He looks at her, eyebrows raised.

'At least not until we've ordered some food. I need to recuperate.'

He comes closer, rubbing his nose to hers, almost – but not quite – having his lips meet hers.

'Lightweight,' he teases, and Evie laughs.

30

Duke

Duke isn't sure when it starts to happen, but it's definitely whilst they're still in the act. Evie is on top of him and has just moaned his name over and over and over again as she writhed around, before switching to repeating the fact that she was coming – over, and over, and over again. The sight of it – hell, the feel of it – was enough to make Duke follow suit not long after, but somewhere in between admiring her boobs, the crash of release through his body, and the feel of Evie's skin on his, he has started to cry.

'Are you okay?' Evie asks, and it's not the breathy, hey-that-was-so-sexy *are you okay* a person might expect after what they've just done. She actually sounds really worried about him. He can't really see her very well and then he feels her fingertips underneath his eyes wiping something away and for a second he can see again, before it all gets blurry once more.

'Urgh,' he says, when he comes to his senses. 'God, this is mortifying. God. I'm so sorry.'

Evie moves off him and he sits up, and from there she starts to rub his back. Apparently he can't *stop* the crying. This is horrific.

'It's okay,' she says, and her voice is kind and light. 'I think I'm actually quite flattered.'

Duke lets out a snotty laugh. 'I swear this has never happened before,' he says. 'I suppose I'm a bit emotional, and . . .' He can't finish the thought, because the tears are in the way.

'Sssh,' Evie soothes. 'Take your time. I know it's been a big month for you. I can't say this has ever happened to me before, but truly, I can empathise as to why.' He steals a look at her, and she gives him a lopsided grin. 'It's because I'm a spectacular shag, isn't it?' The word *shag* sounds funny in her American accent, making Duke shake his head and do another breathy, mucousy chuckle.

Evie gets up, butt-naked, and he watches her go to the mini bar and pull out bottles of water, a can of Coke, and some crisps from the gift basket the producers have left for him. She's got pendulous breasts that swing hypnotically, and a round tummy with small hips and a generous bum. Duke has been with people from within the industry for almost as long as he's been in it. He doesn't mean it horribly, only as a statement of fact, but hers is the first 'normal' body he's seen in a long time. She has stubble under her arms and hair on her toes and her skin is smooth but imperfect. He can't say it out loud – he never, ever would – but he likes it. He likes that she's not plucked and preened and tanned and smoothed and whatever the heck else Hollywood does to women – people! – to make them more desirable to audiences.

And he's complicit, obviously, with his two nose jobs and veneers and injectables. He's been asked before, in interviews, about unrealistic body standards, and he's given vanilla 'nothing' answers about having access to the best chefs and trainers in the world, but that's only a part of the story. Being with her makes him feel like he doesn't want to lie anymore. He's been co-director for two days and already his head is swimming with ideas about what happens next, where he can go from here. What if he sets up that production company with Daphne or starts directing more, or even leaves Hollywood altogether? Maybe he could write – maybe he could write with Evie. Something about real people and how they live.

'Here,' Evie says, handing him the water. He takes it with one hand and then stretches out the other to her left nipple, running a finger over it.

'I think you might be the most gorgeous human being I've ever cried to after sex,' he says, when she cocks an eyebrow.

'Is that so?' she whispers, and instead of climbing in beside him she clambers on top, straddling him so that he can issue a kiss to the chest he's just been admiring.

'This is like a form of worship,' he says, running his tongue down from her neck.

'It's not bad, being worshipped by you, like this,' she says, and he pulls back on her hair like he did outside, in the cold, nibbling at her neck and then holding her head so her gaze is steady with his, staring at her.

'I'm serious,' he whispers. 'I feel like myself with you.'

She smiles, and he can't read it.

'Have you ever thought about writing a screenplay?'

She shakes her head. 'Nuh-uh. Why?'

'No reason,' he tells her, kissing the exposed skin. She wriggles in pleasure, and he holds his grip even firmer. 'Do you like that?'

'Yes,' she says, and he isn't crying anymore.

'Did you think this would happen when you got me out here?' Evie asks, when they catch their breath. She's under the crook of his arm, and they're holding hands. Duke feels happy. Contented. He's starting to understand something about himself – about who he is and what he wants.

'Who could have guessed?' he tells her. 'No way.'

'Hmmm,' she says.

'You?' he asks, curious now.

She laughs. 'No. I did not,' she replies. 'Obviously. Mostly I was just furious I had to be here at all.'

'Ahh, yes,' he says. 'How could I forget?'

'Nice way to end the year, though, I have to say. I don't think I realised how much I needed to get away. I mean, it's been peculiar, with the photos and the fake-dating and then whatever this—' she uses her free hand to gesture at him '—is. But being on set has felt invigorating. I'm on deadline for my next book, and I've done nothing whilst I've been here, not really, but I still feel in a better place with the manuscript than I did when I left. I'm confident I can write quickly and cleanly when I get home now. I think I was hiding from some truths for my characters and somehow I'm tapping into that here. I can't explain it.'

'The magical creative process,' Duke says, putting on a silly voice.

'Something like that, yeah,' she replies. 'And Magda being here – I don't think I've thanked you enough. It was a very sweet and kind thing for you to do.'

'I'm a sweet and kind man.' He shrugs.

'I told your mom that,' she replies, adding: 'I hope that's okay.'

Duke bristles at the mention of his mother, but more from habit than anything else. When she said goodbye, when she came to see him on set yesterday, he felt something very close to forgiveness for her. He was pleased she'd come alone, and there was a vulnerability to her when they spoke that made Duke think that, honestly, she really is trying her best. Her best might turn out not to be good enough, but to know she's trying felt comforting to him. He's searched online some more about what to expect and read that the real work starts once a person is sober, almost like getting sober in the first place is the easy part. Staying that way and learning to live with yourself is the kicker, whether the people you hurt along the way forgive you or not. He's going to try to be patient. Deciding that is as much for him as it is for her. It's like he's been holding pain in two clenched fists, and now he can release it there's room to hold on to something else. Like, for instance, love.

'Sorry,' Evie says, clearly noticing his visceral response. 'Should I not have brought her up?'

'No, it's okay,' says Duke. 'I'm still trying to wrap my head around the fact that she just showed up, but I get it. She felt like there was no other way. She didn't even have my phone number anymore. It says a lot that she went to all of this effort.'

'I think so too,' Evie says. 'I know I was harsh about addicts and the black hole they can pull you into, but that's easier to say in theory, when the person you're talking about is a hypothetical. When I met your mom, I was kind of struck by how normal she seems? And how proud of you she is. I felt like I wanted to give her a hug to stop her bursting from pride when she was there yesterday. That must feel nice.'

'Yeah,' Duke says, and it's nice to feel understood by Evie. His instinct was right. She really does 'get it'. He doesn't know what 'it' is, but she's there. She speaks his language. 'And she has my phone number now, so she can call or text instead of randomly showing up next time. We've said we'll start with FaceTiming once a month and take it from there.'

'The privilege of your phone number!' Evie teases him, and he's glad she's brought this up. 'Imagine such an embarrassment of riches!'

He laughs. 'Well,' he tells her. 'I was thinking that we should finally exchange numbers? It was cute at first, but now I think it's silly.'

'Nahhh,' says Evie, and he thinks she's kidding, at first. It takes a few beats for the air between them to sour, just the tiniest bit, and Duke needs to clarify what, exactly, is happening.

'You're not serious,' he says, moving to look at her. She looks around the room – everywhere except at him – like she's trying to decide what words to use next.

Finally she says: 'Well, yeah, I am, actually.'

'I don't get it.'

She swallows, takes a breath, then looks at him. The way she does it makes his stomach drop.

'I just think having your number would mean I would want to use your number.'

'That's the general idea, yes,' Duke responds.

'And I don't want to be, like, pathetically waiting by the phone.'

'Well, you won't,' he says. 'I will call. And hopefully see you. I mean, I assumed . . .'

What did he assume? That she felt how he felt? That she was falling too? That beyond here, in Germany, for the movie, they would spend some time together, hang out, see where it went . . . ?

'Don't get me wrong, I'm having fun,' she says. 'Getting to know you and everything. It's been really cool.'

'Past tense,' Duke says.

'What?'

'It's been really cool, like it's already done.'

'No,' she says, but there's something prickling under his skin, now, a funny feeling that started in a corner of his brain and is bleeding into every part of him, like poison. *It's happened again.* He's been used, once again. She's here, passing the time, filling the minutes before she goes and so she's played along with the stupid fauxmance the producers asked of them and taken it a bit too far – got her press and her books on the bestseller lists and even another movie deal. Good for her. It's all come up roses. Meanwhile he's done exactly what he always does and made a total fool of himself, giving too much of himself like the desperate little boy he is, and she's just not bothered, not interested.

'We still have time . . .' Evie continues. 'We said this was for December, right? I didn't mean . . .'

'*Just* for December,' Duke corrects. 'And don't worry, I know what you meant. I get it absolutely.'

He climbs out of bed, then, and pulls on his underwear. He doesn't know where he is going, since this is his room. He tries to find the words in his throat to ask Evie to go, thinking about the best way to do it: saying he needs some proper sleep, saying outright that he's upset, telling her to go screw herself even. But he can't. He doesn't have it in him to be confrontational; that just isn't who he is. So instead he pulls on his trousers and trainers, grabs his phone and his coat, and leaves without saying anything at all. Then he changes his mind, opens the door again, and sees her sitting up in bed, exactly as he left her.

'Sorry,' he says. 'I just . . . I can't . . . I can't do this,' he sputters. 'I think I've made a mistake.'

By the time he gets back, half an hour and a drink at the hotel bar later, she's gone.

31

Duke

It's like Groundhog Day, waking up to a flurry of texts from both his teams in LA and London, with links to the internet on fire with photos of Evie and Duke down a dimly lit alleyway, his hand up her top and his tongue in her mouth. What's different this time, though, is that the headlines have become personal. DUKE CARLISLE'S WRITER GIRLFRIEND LEAVES GRAVELY ILL MOTHER ALONE IN CARE HOME SO SHE CAN NIBBLE SCHNITZEL ON GERMAN FILM SET is the *Mail*'s choice, with many others offering a variation on that theme.

What the hell? This is where Duke's relationship with the British press sours. He can stomach the odd staged shot or even let the occasional genuine candid pass by if it goes on to afford him some peace, but what's all this about Evie and her mum? It doesn't even make sense – if her mother is ill, it goes without saying that Evie would leave her behind in a care home. This is her work. You can't be expected to bring a sick parent (a sick anyone!) to work. It was likely only a matter of time before they found some way to demonise her – she is a woman, after all. Duke doesn't get much of that. They've never touched his family history and mostly only cover his shirtless beach pics or whoever he happens to be talking to on a film set, which, of course, is exactly how this whole thing with Evie started.

He doesn't have her number to call and see if she's okay, as per their fight last night. He's mad. Humiliated, really. It was immature to think that life changes just like that – he might be the leading man in many a fairy tale, but they're on screen, like Evie says, for entertainment. It's officially time to become more realistic about love, because he can't keep going on this way, falling head over heels and thinking every next woman is the one who is going to save him from the loneliness of his own making.

Something else has shifted for him, too, this morning. Evie is the straw that broke the camel's back: he's not going to keep on this way, held hostage in his golden cage. His stardom is getting in the way of him being able to live how he wants to live, which is to say it's in the way of him being free. *Maybe I'll call Ashton Kutcher,* he thinks, remembering that last time they bumped into each other Ashton was waxing lyrical about ethical investing, about having his money make money instead of being on a film set. Or he could do a Clooney and star in some coffee adverts and make his money that way, and then focus on producing. All in all, there must be another way for him to do this life.

What did he reveal to Evie? That really, it was all for his mother's attention? Well, he's got it. She's sober. She seems happy. She wants a relationship with him. He doesn't need the world to applaud him if he has his mother back. Suddenly, ever wanting that seems ridiculous to him.

'Daphne,' he says, as they ride to set together later that day. 'Ages ago you said you wanted to set up a production company. I don't suppose you'd want a partner in crime for that, would you?'

She's been staring out of the window, lost in thought, which suits Duke because his head is swimming too.

'Yeah,' she tells him, nodding. 'I could be into that. I'm enjoying this,' she adds, wagging a finger between them. 'We work well together, don't we?'

'I think so,' he tells her. 'I think I want to try some screen-writing. And like you said at that dinner we had with Evie and Magda – it's where the power lies, having your own company, isn't it?'

Daphne raises her eyebrows then and wiggles them sugges-tively. 'Ooh,' she says, lowering her voice. 'Speaking of Evie's friend Magda – I have an itty-bitty bit of gossip, if you're in the market for such a thing.'

Is he? He doesn't really want to talk about Evie. His ego is still sore over it, how he thought it was more than it is. Either way it doesn't matter, because Daphne continues to speak.

'Guess whose bedroom I saw her coming out of this morning. And I'm talking at, like, 5 a.m. I was going down to use the gym, and they were definitely only just saying goodnight . . .'

Duke shrugs. Most of the time what happens on set stays on set – people get close when they work so intensely together, for such long days. As Duke well knows.

'Katerina! The DP?'

'Oh,' says Duke. 'I thought Magda had just gone through a divorce with a man?'

'I think she did. But that doesn't mean she's not into women too, does it? And she was definitely with Katerina last night . . .'

Duke returns to looking out of the window. 'At least somebody is having a bit of luck,' he says, glumly.

Daphne looks in his direction.

'What's happened?' she asks. 'Duke?'

He shakes his head. 'The Evie thing,' he explains.

'There's an Evie thing?'

He blinks at her.

'Okay,' Daphne admits. 'I figured there was an Evie thing. What happened?'

He sighs. 'I don't even know. I thought she was different, but . . .' He shakes his head. It's a horrible feeling, disappointment. He just can't tell if he feels disappointed with Evie, or himself.

'Oh, Duke . . .' Daphne commiserates.

'I'm okay,' he presses. 'Onwards and upwards, right?'

Even as he says it, he knows his words are falling flat. Much as he wishes he could just shrug off his misplaced trust, his heart isn't in it. It's not how he operates. The bruise is going to take a while to heal.

'That's what's working for me,' says Daphne, as close as she's got to admitting that things with Brad are over. She hasn't once brought up his departure, or any of the reasons why, and Duke knows she's ashamed, somehow, but he feels like he can't tell her not to be without bringing it up, and he knows Daphne well enough to understand that that's not a great idea. So instead, he's sitting back as she figures it out for herself, running wild and free on set, and he can see how it makes her feel good, how much she's been in her element these past few days.

'Who'd have thought when we signed on for this that this is where we'd end up?' Duke asks, as the car pulls up to set. 'We've gone from a couple on the rocks to friends running the damned show. That's impressive, I think. We need to take a moment to appreciate all this.'

Daphne smiles. 'Life, huh?' she says. 'It'll catch up to ya in the end.'

'Won't it just.' Duke sighs.

It's his American publicist who tells him the news when it comes: Duke has been nominated for a Golden Globe.

'What?' he says, as Dream, one of the content producers, holds out a phone for him. Being so close to Christmas, and awards season, and because he insisted it was just a short shoot for the external shots, there's nobody from Duke's team out in Germany with him. It would have felt extra, needless. For most people December is a time to start winding down and planning how to spend the holidays with loved ones. Duke normally flies out to Bermuda and stays with Simon Cowell and his family, or else does Bora Bora, coming back in time for new year skiing or just after, ready to walk the red carpets – normally as a presenter or plus-one, though.

He's had a few nominations for smaller awards in categories he'd been briefed he'd never win, and things he's been in have won awards for direction and the like, but a Golden Globe has always been the goal. Now it's here, though, and happening, it hits differently.

He just feels empty, uninterested.

'Best supporting actor,' his publicist says. 'And we think you're in with a really good shot. We're already talking to *Vanity Fair* and the *Wall Street Journal* magazine about some in-depth profiles with you, positioning this as a turning point in your career that people need to be taking note of. The relationship with the author – it's really helped your credibility, man. Actors dating actors is so Nineties. An actor dating an author makes your brand more prestigious, my man. We're going to exploit that.'

Duke leans into the speaker phone held at his mouth. 'But I'm not actually going out with her,' he begins to protest, but Carter cuts him off.

'You are for the next six to twelve weeks. We'll get her people to organise her as your plus-one for the big event. Maybe she can do the SAG Awards and Critics' Choice? We'll circle back. But for now, congratulations! This is what we've been working towards!'

Carter hangs up, and Dream takes the phone, congratulating him again and telling him that he deserves it. Duke doesn't know what to do with himself. It's strange, but the person he wants to tell is Evie. He knows that's stupid. She's been using him to pass the time. But that doesn't make it any less true: she's the one he wants to hear saying well done.

He heads to make-up to see if she's been through there,

but no one has seen her today. He should be prepping for the next shot, and he can see Daphne on set already, talking to Katerina, the DP, explaining something about the lighting. He heads over.

'Katerina,' he says, calling her name. 'You don't know where Magda is, do you? Or Evie?'

She looks confused, and her cheeks colour.

'Why would I know?' she says, defensively, and Daphne shoots him daggers as if to say, *What the hell, dude?* Ah. He isn't supposed to know. Right. Well, that was indiscreet.

'Daphne?' he says, as if he's asking everyone. 'Have you seen them?'

She shakes her head. 'No, Duke. And we're setting up for scene 53, when you're ready.'

'Right,' he says. 'Yeah. Sorry. Of course.'

He walks over to the monitors to see how everything is looking, and then picks up the annotated script he's made notes on with Daphne. He's got eleven million thoughts racing through his mind, and not one of them he can hold on to.

'You okay?' Daphne says, coming over to him. 'I need your head in the game, pal. Teammates, remember?'

'Yeah,' Duke says, and his voice sounds far away. 'It's just ... I just found out I've got a Golden Globe nomination. For the guest role I did in *The Marvellous Mrs Maisel*.'

'WHAT?' Daphne says, her eyebrows practically leaping off her face. 'WHAT? DUKE! A GLOBE NOM! OH MY GOSH! Well, that changes *everything*! Go do what you need to do! We'll wait.'

'Thanks, Daph.' Duke tries to muster a genuine smile, and

then he goes to his trailer to pick up his phone. Who can he call? Who can he share this moment with? He hits the number for his mother.

'Darling!' she slurs, and he can tell immediately that she's drunk.

'Mum,' Duke says, cautiously. 'Hey. You all right? Have you . . . have you had a drink?'

'Me darling?' she asks. Somebody knocks on his door, an assistant from production, but when they poke their head in Duke shoos them away with the wave of a hand and a scowl. 'Well, a little. I had just a little-tiny-little-drop to get me through the morning after Roger left.'

'Roger left.' Duke doesn't say it as a question.

'Couldn't hack it I suppose,' his mother says. 'Scared him off, just like all the others.'

Duke starts to sweat. His breathing is all shallow and strange. He knew it wouldn't last. He tries to remember what the websites say. *It's a disease. It isn't her fault.* He doesn't realise he's actually muttering it out loud until his mother says, 'Are you talking to me?'

'Mum,' he says. 'Do you have a sponsor? You need to call them. You don't want to do this to yourself. Can you call Auntie Patricia?'

'That cow,' his mother retorts, which Duke takes to mean she cannot.

There's another knock on the door.

'I said I'm busy!' Duke yells, and he hates himself immediately, because only arseholes yell at juniors on set. It's unbecoming. He adds, in a lighter voice, 'Just two minutes, please.'

There's silence at the other end of the line.

'Mum?'

Still nothing.

'Mum!'

The line goes dead.

32

Evie

Evie doesn't have anything official to do on set that day, save being available if any of the actors decide they want character help, which seems unlikely on account of the fact that they haven't so far, and they all know their characters better than her now anyway. That's why, when she gets back to her hotel room after breakfast and Magda is stepping out of the shower, there's nowhere to hide when Magda says: 'I feel like I'm losing my authority by announcing this in a dressing gown, but I'm staging an intervention. We need to talk.'

Evie looks at her friend. Magda wasn't here when Evie came down after her fight with Duke last night and hadn't returned by the time Evie, who had tossed and turned all night, left for a very early morning walk. She looks tired. There's a tiny bit of mascara still clinging to the side of her eye, and her skin is pink from the heat of the water.

'Are *you* all right?' Evie asks, kicking off her shoes to lie on the bed. Seems like neither of them slept much last night. Thoughts of Duke kept her staring at the ceiling. Why did he disappear like that? It's so freaking *odd*.

'I think I know a . . . thing,' Magda says, slowly. She sets her mouth in a firm line and then blows air into her cheeks so they inflate.

Evie frowns. 'Your ability to communicate clearly is top-notch. I understood every word of what you just said,' she says, sarcastically.

Magda perches on the edge of the bed. It's not a big room, especially for two women with bursting suitcases and a week of shopping behind them, but it doesn't need to be. Their college dorm was smaller than this, and they survived. In fact, look how far they've come, baby.

'Does this have something to do with where you were last night?' presses Evie.

'Oh, well,' Magda says. 'Yeah. I ended up crashing in Katerina's room. I can't even remember why we went up there to be honest – I'd drunk a lot. But then we watched *Parks and Rec* on her laptop and I fell asleep.'

'Oh,' says Evie, her bubble burst. 'I thought maybe you'd hooked up.'

'What!' Magda laughs. 'No! I wouldn't do that to you, get unprofessional on your work trip!'

'I would have forgiven you,' Evie tells her.

'Anyway,' Magda says, reorientating the discussion. '*You* disappeared last night, and I have an incredibly big suspicion as to where, and with who.'

'We're talking about you right now!' Evie says, because

she can't get into it. It was amazing with Duke – natural and fun and somehow it felt like what everything had always been leading up to. There was an inevitability to it. She's still processing that he got cross in the way that he did. She didn't mean to upset him, pointing out the shelf life of their dalliance.

'Well, only because you derailed my intervention!' At this, Magda hesitates. 'Have you seen the news today? Or rather, the gossip sites?'

'No,' answers Evie. 'What's that got to do with the price of fish?'

Magda goes to her laptop and pulls up a story about Evie and Duke, but there's no cute headline about them frolicking in the European winter – it's a cutting and horrible piece about Evie's mum being in a home. DUKE CARLISLE'S WRITER GIRLFRIEND LEAVES GRAVELY ILL MOTHER ALONE IN CARE HOME SO SHE CAN NIBBLE SCHNITZEL ON GERMAN FILM SET.

Evie reads the article, getting increasingly horrified. How do they know all this? And how are they able to print it when it's her – and her mom's – private business? It's like a leech has been stuck to her carotid artery and is draining her dry. This isn't fair.

'. . . Evie?'

'How do they even know all this?' Evie says, her voice barely audible. 'This is my life. Not tabloid fodder. My LIFE.'

Magda scoots over and puts a hand on Evie's knee.

'Why didn't you tell me how sick she'd gotten?'

'I didn't want you to feel sorry for us.'

'Evie,' Magda says, mouth agape. 'I'm your best friend. I'm here to *help* you. Not pity you.'

Evie shrugs. What must it be like to just . . . ask people for help? To tell them your secrets so they don't weigh you down and make you feel like you're drowning? How do people get to be that way? Evie loves Magda with her whole heart and doesn't know what she'd do without her. And yet. Even Magda gets the edited version of her life. Everyone does. It's safer that way. Then when she's inevitably rejected, it's still on her terms. She can never be left for who she really is. A tear rolls down her face. She wipes it away. For crying out loud.

'Dammit,' Evie says.

'Come here,' Magda insists, and as they hug she says: 'I think it's Katerina who's feeding the press.'

'Wait, what?' Evie asks, pulling away.

'I heard her on the phone when I went to pee this morning, after I woke up. She was talking about you and Duke, and then said something about a link. And then this story hit.'

'Why would Katerina feed the press?' Evie asks. 'She's supposed to be my friend . . .'

Magda sighs. 'No idea. I could be wrong – I don't have proof. When I asked who was on the phone, she said *nobody*, and I didn't want to accuse her without proper proof . . .'

'Yeah,' says Evie. 'I wouldn't have said anything in that moment either.' Her tears are drying now. She's over it. It's her superpower: she gets sixty seconds to be upset, and then she gets the hell on with it all. 'Is that the intervention then?' she asks.

Magda shakes her head. 'Only partly,' she says. 'I wanted to talk to you about everything, to be honest. Being here, Evie, I can see there's a lot you've not been telling me – from your mom to the money stuff. I've been thinking, and your self-worth is, like, in the toilet. Sometimes it's self-depreciating and droll. You're funny, Evie, and you know you are. But Christ if that humour isn't the strongest, best defensive mechanism I've ever seen. And now I know you don't even let yourself enjoy your work, that you have to get rid of all the money you make because it makes you feel . . . well, I'm still not sure.'

'Like crap,' Evie supplies, playing with the hem of her jumper so she doesn't have to look up. 'I know I need to sort it out. This big movie money – I'm going to get a financial adviser. I'm going to face it head on. I've decided.'

Magda softens. 'Okay,' she says, slowly. 'Well, that takes the wind out of my fighting sails, then. That was basically what I was going to suggest.'

'Beat you to it,' Evie says.

'You always have.' Magda shakes her head, but she's smiling wryly when Evie dares look at her. It's very embarrassing, being thirty-six and terrible with money. She's not proud of it. She's mortified, really.

'If you have any resources or whatever,' Evie says, 'I'll take them. Spreadsheets or anything.'

'I do,' Magda says. 'And I can. You need several savings accounts, a proper retirement plan, a way to pay your mom's care that is sensible and sustainable – don't just give them all your money at once. And you can invest, too. Wealthy people don't get wealthy by earning money, they get wealthy by having their money make money.'

'Now there's a soundbite,' Evie quips.

'And you can set up recurring donations to charity, too. If you want to give your cash away, at least make it count.'

Evie nods. 'Yeah,' she says. 'I should do that.'

'And I'm going to help you go through your stuff, see what we can sell and for how much. It's so easy to put stuff up online, and between us we can manage the post office runs or courier pick-ups.'

'I can hire somebody to do that,' Evie starts, but Magda shakes her head.

'We'll do it together,' she says. 'Because you're going to let me help you. Even if I have to elbow my way in! Surely after all this time you know I'm your ride or die, Evie. It's you and me.'

Evie looks at her and blinks. 'I think I blew it with Duke,' she says, sadly, her voice wavering. 'I don't know how, but I know I have.'

'Everything is fixable,' Magda says. 'And actually, first and foremost what we need is one last fake date – and a bit of misinformation to Katerina, too. Let's try to catch her out. We can't do anything about what's already up there, but we can play her at her own game, right?'

Evie nods. 'Okay,' she says. 'But you might have to talk to Duke first. He's soft on you. You make him laugh.'

Magda smiles. 'The man's got good taste. What can I say?'

33

Evie

'This is unbelievable,' Evie marvels, as they snake up the big winding hill that Neuschwanstein, a mediaeval castle that looks like something straight out of *Game of Thrones*, sits upon. 'I don't think I've ever been anywhere so beautiful in my life.'

She's in a people carrier with Magda, Daphne and Duke, who has barely said a word since they got in the car forty minutes ago. Now isn't the time to push him, not when they're with the others. He's agreed to be photographed one last time with Evie, though she hasn't explained the real reason behind it yet: so she can know if Katerina really is the one selling stories to the papers. If she is, Evie hasn't quite figured out what she'd like to do about it, but they can cross that bridge when they get to it. For now, Duke thinks he's simply continuing with their fauxmance for the good of the movie, which he has an even bigger investment than ever in as director. And so here they are, ready to be papped. Evie will explain to him later who the leak is, if Magda's suspicions are true.

If the Disney logo was a real castle outside of a theme park, it would be Neuschwanstein. White stone turrets of various heights rise and fall in peaks and troughs, with a solid stone block of a base at the bottom, then another big stone block above that, but set further back, so that it almost looks like the castle is set *into* the hills from a distance. Up close it serves to simply make Evie feel teeny-tiny, but in a good way. She doesn't mind being reminded every so often that her place in the universe is actually minuscule, that the world does not keep turning on every breath she takes. She's just a person, with lots of other people, on a planet that has sweeping landscapes and snow-covered trees and hills as tall as giants.

'Shall we get this over with?' Duke grumbles when the door is opened by their driver, and Evie's heart drops just enough to let her know that she's hurt by his mood. If she thought they could gloss over whatever happened the other night, after they slept together, she was wrong. Although, Daphne *had* said something had happened with his mom. Maybe Evie doesn't need to take this so personally. Maybe she can just be there for him, as a friend, all sex aside. She's been enjoying that – the friendship bit. As they file out of the car, Evie doesn't need any instructions about where to go or how to play it. She's a dab hand at all this by now: she knows that if they walk and talk for long enough, Carter, Duke's PR, or the producers, will have planted a pap who will catch it all.

'This way?' she suggests to Duke, pointing towards a path looping around the lower part of the castle. He nods. They set off.

'You must have seen some amazing places in your time,' Evie says congenially as they navigate the path. Even under the snow she can see that the place is manicured to perfection. She wishes she'd brought her sunglasses, though. This much snow is blinding.

'I suppose,' he says, and then holding out a hand. 'For the cameras?' he asks. She slips an ungloved hand into his. His skin will keep her warm. She puts her other hand into her pocket.

'Daphne said something about your mom being unwell – is everything okay?' she asks, relishing the breadth of him, how safe it feels to be guided by his sure footing.

'Relapse,' he says, gruffly, looking out over the fields with a squint. 'It happens,' he adds.

Evie nods. 'I'm sorry, Duke,' she says. 'I know it's not easy for anyone.'

'No,' he says, and he almost looks at her then, before seemingly changing his mind. 'My aunt went over and helped her. We got her into a good clinic where she can get some help for the next thirty days, so she's safe. I'll go over in January and see how she's doing.'

'That's good,' Evie says, softly. She tries to catch his eye again, tries to find the Duke she knows, that common ground. The Duke who couldn't wait to meet her, and paid a kid to go get them hot chocolate when he thought she was interested in somebody else, and was kind to her when she was upset about her own mother.

272

'I don't know if you heard,' she presses, wondering if a different conversational tack might help. 'But a couple more of my books got optioned because of the press from all this, so . . . thanks for getting me out here in the first place. I don't think I've ever formally said that.'

'You haven't,' Duke says. 'But I'm glad I was of use to you.'

Evie doesn't get what he means. 'I mean thanks for more than just the book sales, you know. Thanks for . . . everything. All of this. You knew what I needed when I didn't. I'm grateful. I . . . care about you,' Evie says.

'I'm sure you do,' Duke counters, and it's colder than the weather, the way he says it.

Evie hears the *click click click*, then, the sound she's become so accustomed to. Sure enough, Clive is on the path behind them, stood off to one side so as not to get in their way and keep everything as natural-looking as possible. Duke hears it too, looks back, looks at Evie, and then pulls her in close so that they're stood facing each other. As he pushes her hair from her face like he might kiss her, he says: 'This has been useful for everybody. Let's call a spade a spade.'

She feels the touch of his fingertips on her cheek, smoothing out her hair to her ear. She could melt at the feel of him, physically melt, right there, into a puddle.

But it's all for show.

This fauxmance! Whose idea was it anyway? She just wants him to kiss her, and mean it. And, honestly, she might have orchestrated this, but she wants the cameras to bugger off so they can talk properly. What kind of grown man spends his life stalking people with a camera anyway? It's disgusting, even if Duke says it is part of the game. It shouldn't be. She wishes Clive would just disappear into a cloud of paparazzi smoke.

'Duke . . .' she says, readying to make some bold declarations, and then there's a scream that chills her blood.

Duke pulls away, looks back to where Clive had been stood, and then runs to look over the edge of the steep hill.

'Jesus!' he says, and he disappears, then, over the hill as well, and Evie runs. She can't see them, can't see either of them. It's all just white, white, snow, and then she hears a voice shout up from down below, somewhere in amongst the trees, 'Evie! Call an ambulance! Clive has fallen!' and she sprints, as fast as she can, back to the others.

'Evie,' Magda says, in a low voice, that night at the hotel. 'There's a very hot man staring at you. Evie!'

Evie looks up into a pair of twinkling baby blues, a strong-set jaw and a wide smile.

'I was trying to decide if it was you,' he says, smiling.

'Markus!' Evie exclaims. 'Oh my gosh, what are you doing here!'

Evie introduces Markus to Magda, who says she can't believe that they met in some random gas station, back in the snowstorm, and are now in the same place at the same time again.

'My sister,' Markus says. 'She runs the hotel.'

'And a great job she's doing too! It's fantastic here,' Magda enthuses, and Evie would recognise that look on her face anywhere. She's flirting. The woman can turn it on like a light switch.

'How long have you been staying here?' Markus asks. 'Do you need anything? Drinks? Some food?'

Magda flicks her hair off her shoulder and smiles, holding deliberate and *smouldering* eye contact.

'Well, aren't you a gentleman,' she says, and Evie has to give it to her, she's not backwards about being forward.

Markus laughs. 'I do my best,' he says, and he doesn't look away. Evie suddenly feels like a third wheel, like she's intruding on something private. She waits for them to stop mooning, but that moment never comes. They're just stood, smiling, not saying anything, not even the smallest bit shy that they're each undressing the other with their sexy eyeballing. How do people do that? Just decide they're hot for somebody and then make it so clearly known? The confidence of it! It chills Evie to the bone. She'd no sooner put herself out there with such abandon than she'd shave her head and ask people to start greeting her with the name Moonshine.

'Oooookay then,' Evie says, not even sure if they can hear her. 'I was actually just about to take a walk to stretch my legs, if you don't mind.'

'I don't mind.' Magda grins, looking at Markus.

'Enjoy.' Markus smiles, looking at Magda.

Evie doesn't bother saying goodbye – she's sure neither of them would hear her over their respective boners anyway.

She meanders down some corridors and out into the cold air. It feels fresh, and it's still the last of the afternoon light, so the sun keeps her warm enough. She does a circuit of the parking lot and then finds a bench to flop down on, pulling her phone from her pocket. She pulls up her emails, but there isn't anything beyond a few pre-Christmas sales emails from her favourite brands, and then, inexplicably, she pulls up a web browser and googles her father's name.

What am I doing? she vaguely asks herself, and she hits the return key. She changes tack, and instead googles herself. Image after image comes up from her various fauxmance dates with Duke. She can see the progression: the pained faces from the coffee shop, the coyness from the fairground, the pictures from the alleyway the other night – a passion that could never be faked. Nothing from today, of course, for her ensnaring of Katerina, because of Clive's fall.

He was okay, after his fall. Duke saved the day. Evie half wonders if she's come outside to see when Duke gets back to the hotel, so she can catch him. She waits. He doesn't come.

She is disappointed, yet again.

Men leave.

Don't trust anybody.

She could never be enough, anyway.

This isn't real.

34

Duke

Duke takes a moment to breathe deeply. He knows the saying about there being years for questions and years for answers, meaning there are times when we have to figure out who we are in this world and other times we get to enjoy it. But for Duke, this whole winter has been a time of growth so rapid and intense that it's actually painful. He doesn't know if he can take much more – even the Golden Globe nomination feels like too much. It's like there's no room in his brain for any other surprises, even a good one.

But the way Evie was before Clive fell, looking at him with those massive freaking eyes, her nose pink from the cold, like she means it, like she really did want him to kiss her, wasn't for the camera. How is he supposed to know the difference between reality and make-believe when she looks at him like that? And how can a person look like that if their feelings are going to be temporary? It doesn't make sense to him. Either she wants this, or she doesn't. There is no in between. Not with burning, aching stares like that.

'Hey, Duke,' a voice says, and it's Katerina, the DP. She's holding two paper cups with steam escaping through the lid. They're working late, Clive's tumble pushing things back. 'Tea? Best way to stay warm is not to get cold, after all.'

'Yeah,' Duke says, stretching out a hand to take one. 'That's great, thanks, Katerina.'

'You're so welcome,' she says, smiling, and Duke is surprised when she doesn't walk away. He braces himself for her wanting a favour. He doesn't mean to play the big-star card, but that's typically what happens when somebody lingers around him on set towards the end of a shoot, like if they don't get the photo for their sister, or video for their son or whatever, they're going to miss their chance. How is he supposed to refrain from feeling sorry for himself when literally, even in the one moment he steals away, somebody else finds him, and asks something from him yet again?

He can't keep doing this. He doesn't mean to feel sorry for himself but genuinely, he really feels empty, in so many ways. He's not talked to his people about what he's thinking, but the longer he sits with the idea of starting a production company with Daphne, of doing the deals of getting great movies made without walking the red carpet or being in front of the camera, the more he feels that it's the right thing for him. Especially now his mum has relapsed. God, that was the worst two and a half hours of his life, waiting for confirmation from Auntie Patricia that she was there, she'd gotten into the house, that his mother was fine, if not having been on quite the bender.

He's one of the most well-known people on the planet, and for half a second, he thought that would cure his mother, and now he knows nothing will – not if she doesn't want it. He's spent his whole life thinking it was him: that being better, nicer, funnier, more charming, more well known, more loved by the world would eventually mean she'd love him too. He understands now that her drinking isn't anything to do with him, and that knowledge is both tremendously upsetting and, at the same time, totally liberating.

'I just wanted to let you know . . .' Katerina pushes, and Duke braces himself for the ask '. . . a bunch of us are going out later. Tomorrow is a lighter day, and when we wrap everyone flies home so quickly for Christmas that there won't be time to have a proper goodbye, so we thought tonight could work. I wasn't sure if you'd been formally told. You disappeared at the bar the other night . . .'

Yeah, he did. He disappeared with Evie.

'Oh,' he says. 'Okay. Great. Have somebody leave the details in my trailer then, could you?' He could do with a bit of a party, a bit of a blow-out.

'Yeah,' Katerina says. 'For sure.'

He nods. He has a sense he's supposed to be making better conversation but there's nothing to say and he really does just want those quiet five minutes.

'See you there.' He smiles, forcing himself to sound bright and friendly.

'See you there.' She smiles back, and for a moment it's like she might say something else, but then she laughs, shakes her head like she's being silly, and repeats: 'See ya.'

Duke watches her walk away. Just a few more days and the

shoot will be done, and he'll be jetting off to . . . well. He hasn't decided. He might check in at The Hotel Bel Air, if he can get a room this late, and just think about how next year looks, what he wants and how to make it happen. He'll need to juice-cleanse before the Globes, and up his workouts, so it makes sense to be in California. Will he still have to juice-cleanse as a producer, or if he starts writing screenplays? God, now there's a thought. Imagine eating a proper British Christmas dinner with all the trimmings and not feeling guilty about it. Imagine kids waking him up at the crack of dawn, eventually, and not having to worry about sleep quality impacting his complexion.

None of this has been real. He's been building his house on sand and wondering why it all keeps crumbling. Well, no more. Bollocks to PR and diets and being a brand, a commodity that makes everyone else rich. Sure, he makes money too, but at what cost? It's done. Over. Finished. Out with the old and in with the new. Bring. It. On.

Okay. Well, this might not be going *too* well. Duke can see three of himself as he pees, a mirror at head height forcing him to squint with one eye, and then the other, because he's been doing shots. It was Katerina's idea. He's having fun, but a glass of water might be nice. Two glasses of water. An aquarium, even.

'Ayeeeee, here he is!' Katerina claps as he stumbles, just slightly, through to the dark basement bar that everyone has assembled in. It's not a private event, so there are other people, locals and tourists alike, but so far he's been unbothered. It's a nice feeling, hanging out like an everyday kind of a guy. Evie isn't here though. He wishes she was.

'I like this!' Duke says to her, leaning into her ear because at some point the music has gotten louder and some people have started dancing.

'This bar?' Katerina shouts back.

'This everything!' he says, and they're interrupted by the barperson asking what they want, and Duke yells, 'How do you say water in German, dude?'

The guy looks at him.

'We're speaking in English, dude.'

Duke bursts out laughing. 'Oh, yes, we are!' he cries, and it makes Katerina laugh too, although she doesn't seem half as drunk as Duke is. How is that possible? She's tiny, and she's matched him tequila for tequila. 'A water please, my man,' Duke adds, asking Katerina: 'You want anything?' She shakes her head. All night, she's been laughing at his jokes and telling funny stories and asking him about himself like she might actually care. It's a nice escape. He doesn't *like-like* her, but it's nice to be blowing off steam with somebody cool. She's good company. She asks a lot of questions, listens really well too. He's probably given her half his life story without meaning to. It's all pouring out tonight.

'Hey, man!' a guy in a hoodie says then – an American, judging from his accent. 'Hey,' he repeats, and Duke looks at him, glassy-eyed. 'Are you Duke Carlisle?' The stranger tugs on his friend's sleeve and says, 'Look! Duke Freaking Carlisle is here!'

Duke holds up a hand and shakes it, and mutters, 'Nah. I get that all the time though.'

The American insists, though. 'Hey, can I get a photo, please? My girlfriend will freak out! She loves you.'

'Sorry, not right now.' Duke can feel the anger rising in his chest. He just wants to dance, for crying out loud, and enjoy this moment, and now here's some tourist thinking he can just whip out his phone and point and shoot a private, off-duty moment? He's sick of it – sick of everyone feeling like they deserve a piece of him to use as they please.

The tourist holds up his phone in selfie mode and puts his head close to Duke's.

'I said *no*,' Duke says, pushing the American away from him. He doesn't mean to do it so hard, but the tourist stumbles and looks at him with shock and hurt. Duke regrets it instantly. This isn't about this guy in the bar, it's about everything else. The guy is just bearing the brunt. Duke takes a breath, readying himself to apologise. But then the guy squares up to him.

'You don't have to be a douche about it. It's just a photo.'

The man reaches out a hand, then, like he's going to push Duke back, and Duke can't explain it, but even with drinks in his system something tells him to get the first punch in, otherwise he's gonna get got.

The tourist fights back, throwing his weight back in Duke's direction, and then Duke is on the floor, and the other dude is on the floor, and they're not throwing punches, exactly, they're more scuffling, grabbing at each other's hair and groaning a lot. And before Duke really knows what's happening, the tourist gets leverage and manages to throw one almighty punch that lands square in his jaw, and just as suddenly as it all started his mates pull him away and Duke is sat there, already feeling the blood trickle. He looks up for somebody to help him – for anyone to help him – and yet they're all just staring. Some people have pulled out their phones, videoing what's happening.

Duke looks from face to face to face, searching for someone familiar, someone to pull him up, and that's when he sees her. But instead of helping him, instead of checking he's all right, Katerina is photographing the whole bloody thing too.

35

Duke

'Not to sound unkind,' Malcolm, one of the producers says to Duke when he lays eyes on him back at the hotel. 'But that face could cost me a lot of money if the swelling hasn't gone down by morning. Let's go to the on-site medic, buddy.'

Getting half-pummelled certainly went a long way to sobering Duke up, but he's not fully there yet.

'I just need some sleep, okay?' he says, and Malcolm raises his eyebrows. 'Maybe some ice. I'm in trouble, aren't I?' Duke asks, but Malcolm doesn't answer, simply sets his mouth into a muted line and hands Duke an ice pack the concierge has procured.

Duke is definitely in trouble.

'Duke!' Evie cries, leaping up as she spots him across the lobby. 'Jesus, what happened? Are you okay?' She turns to the producer. 'What happened to him? Oh my God.'

Her voice is loud, panicked, and Duke is embarrassed.

'What are you doing here?' he asks. Isn't it the middle of the night?

'One of my late-night walks,' she says. 'I couldn't sleep. Now seriously, what happened?'

'A stupid thing,' he says, not wanting to admit the truth: he got too drunk and took his increasingly frustrated feelings out on a guy who didn't, at the end of the day, deserve it. He's furious with himself. But he feels lonely, too. He keeps thinking about Katerina taking his photo when he was down on the floor that way, how not-sorry she seemed about it. Why would she do that? She disappeared right after, so he couldn't even call her out on it. He'd found his own way back to the hotel. He has the niggling feeling that he was set up or fell for a trick somehow, that Katerina invited him out with the exact notion of gaining information on him. It's an awful thing to consider, but he's sure he isn't wrong.

'Let me look at you,' Evie says, reaching out for the ice pack. Duke pulls away.

'It's fine,' he says.

Malcolm pulls a face and says, 'Imagine if that nose is broken. We've got mere days left. So what, for the last scenes of the shoot he's going to look like the Mummy, all bandaged up?'

Evie looks horrified. 'Not to mention making sure you're actually okay,' she says pointedly, and Duke shrugs.

'That's showbiz, baby.'

They fuss around, all taking seats near each other until Duke sees Magda walk into the lobby too, arm in arm with a man who is staring at him. Duke stares back. The man lifts a hand.

'Markus,' he says. 'We met in the snow blizzard.'

Markus? Duke realises with a drop of the stomach that it's the guy from the service station that day. It feels like a lifetime ago. He'd thought Evie was flirting with him and iced him out, and then eventually had been able to have Evie all to himself, setting up for that date in the store cupboard . . . He steals a look at her. She looks away, too quickly for Duke's liking. He needs to talk to her. Something has gone wrong, here – because of his own stupid ego – and he might still be able to rescue it from the gutter.

Clive is suddenly there, too, coming out of a side room where the cast and crew doctor sees people.

'Jesus,' he says, bandaged up from his fall earlier. 'You look worse than I do, Duke. What happened?'

'Off the record?' Duke says. 'I have no idea.'

Clive chuckles.

'You okay, man?' Duke asks.

'Just about,' he says, wincing. 'Gotta say though, I think this was my last hurrah. My whole life flashed before my eyes as I fell down that mountain.'

Duke thinks 'mountain' is a bit of a stretch – it was a big hill at most – but doesn't interject with as much.

'I think I lost consciousness, because I don't remember you coming down to get me, but Evie says you didn't even hesitate, didn't even think twice about risking your own life.'

Risking his own life? Okay. Duke gets that Clive is a bit shook up, but he's being more than a smidge hyperbolic about it all. He slipped down a grassy bank and bumped his head, he didn't snowball down a mountain peak in upper Nepal.

'Clive . . .' Duke starts, but Clive shakes his head.

'No,' he says. 'You've been good to me, Duke. And I've been a bloody gannet, a bottom feeder, making a living off of you, and people like you. I know it's not nice. I know I've invaded your privacy – and Daphne's, too. It was me who got the photos of her with Brad. I knew it wasn't right, selling them, and at the very least I should have told you what I'd seen so you didn't find out in the papers. I don't know. I just know I want to get home to my wife and kids and get out of this game whilst I'm still bloody well alive. I've had an epiphany. Is that what you call them? When you have a big sudden realisation?'

The group nods in unison, everyone listening to this man spill his guts over Duke's lap.

'You didn't have to come after me, Duke, and you did, and you saved my life, if I'm honest. So, how can I go back to sitting in bushes outside your house or accepting tips from people whilst they're stabbing you in the back? I've seen the error of my ways. I have. And I just want you to know that.'

Duke doesn't know what to say. Thanks? Cool? Clive reaches out a hand for Duke to shake, and Duke takes it.

'Cheers, mate,' Clive says. 'Goodnight, everyone.'

'I'm going to make some calls to the west coast for ten minutes, if you'll excuse me too,' Malcolm says.

'Is it just me,' Duke asks, when they've both gone, 'or is everything he just said all a bit . . .'

'Dramatic?' Evie supplies. 'Yes. When I went to check on him before, he was like this too. But, in case you're interested,

I know for sure now who took those first photos of us, and who has been selling stories. They've been working together, it seems. He's confessed everything to me.'

Duke winces again as he adjusts the ice pack.

'It's not Katerina, is it?' he says, once the pain subsides, and Evie nods incredulously.

'How did you know?' she asks.

'I . . . had a feeling,' he replies. 'I don't know what to do about it though.'

'Me neither. I had this whole half-developed plan in my head to catch her in the act, but . . .'

'But who's got the time for that?'

'Exactly.' She smiles.

And then they're doing that thing that they do, where she looks at him with her mouth open just the right amount, and her tongue snakes up to the top corner of her lip, and it's like she's going to say something but doesn't, and it drives Duke crazy because he wants to know every thought in her head, he doesn't want to miss anything. He should say something. He was hot-headed the other night. He's always being hot-bloody-headed lately, but he can say sorry, he can ask to talk it out.

'Duke? The hotel medic is going to look at you now,' says Malcolm, reappearing suddenly.

He looks from Evie to Magda to Markus, who appear to only have eyes for each other, strangely. How do people do that? Meet, and get on, and own the obvious connection they have? Duke can only dream of such a thing. Maybe there's something in what Phoebe has said about how he *says* he wants to be seen, wants a relationship, and yet still hides behind being 'Duke Carlisle'.

'Duke?' the producer prompts him.

'Yes, yeah,' he says, and it's almost dream-like.

'See you tomorrow,' Evie says, as a statement, not a question. He likes that. It feels like an invitation.

'Yeah,' he tells her. 'I'll find you.'

'Okay,' she says, and she nods. 'Look forward to it.'

So there's that, and it's not nothing.

Duke has avoided any major damage, says the medic, and back in his room, after a good night's sleep, a hot shower and a close examination in the magnifying mirror, he feels confident that although it's tender and sore, Kayla will be able to work her magic in the make-up chair and the show can go on. He's received a cursory text from the producers, but it's about as warm as the winter weather outside. He checks in with his Auntie Patricia, seeing that his mum got into the rehab facility okay, and gets a text straight back to say she has, and thanking him for sorting it out. *I'm her son,* he types back. *It's the least I can do.* And then downstairs, in the lobby, he sees Evie sat with Magda eating breakfast, and she tentatively waves at him.

'How's the patient?' she asks, in between bites of an omelette.

'Walking and talking,' Duke says. 'If a little mortified.'

Evie looks at Magda, and then back at Duke.

'What?' he says, but he knows what she's going to tell him even before she says it. It's what all the texts and emails from his people say, the ones he's left unopened because honestly, he doesn't have bandwidth for this right now. He has run out of craps to give.

'Katerina must have sold the pictures,' she says. 'They're out there.'

Duke nods. 'Unbelievable,' he mutters.

'She seems so normal,' Magda says. 'What's the angle there, do you think? We've just been talking about it, and we can't figure it out.'

Duke shakes his head once more. 'Heck if I know,' he says. 'But I tell ya, if I see her on set today . . .'

'You'll what?' Evie says, with a smirk. 'Go for her?'

Duke shifts his weight from one foot to the other uncomfortably. 'Well, no . . .' he says. 'But she has to be held accountable, doesn't she? It's just a matter of how.'

'I'm just going to ask her outright,' says Magda, buttering her toast. 'I don't have time for games.'

'And you think she's just going to tell you?' Duke asks.

She takes a bite. 'Crazier things have happened,' she replies, like it can be that straightforward. 'I'll let you know.'

36

Evie

Evie takes a long walk over lunchtime, starting on set where she sees Daphne and Duke working out the shots for an argument scene in which Hermione and George fight in the street, to the gasps of horrified onlookers, and Hermione storms off. Evie has never had a dramatic, public argument like that in her – albeit very limited – love life ever, and yet it felt right to put it in the book. She remembers exactly where she was when she wrote it: the coffee shop on the corner, Freddie's, sat by the window with her MacBook at a strategic angle to avoid the sun across the screen. She'd written quickly that day, the words just flowing out of her as George and Hermione processed their feelings for one another almost like-for-like with how she'd processed her break-up with Bobby, and it had felt like an exorcism to get it all out on the page so that it didn't have to live in her head anymore.

Even now, years later, watching the words she wrote unfold in live action in front of her is hard. She knows she doesn't want to be with Bobby, and ultimately that it probably wasn't ever right, but God, she'd opened her heart to him, and to hear that he didn't like what he saw dented her confidence in a way she's probably never recovered from.

Nobody notices her watching, and so she heads on out.

It's too painful to be around this scene today.

She's not sure why, only that it's best to keep moving.

It feels like a feat to walk past the little boutiques and stores that previously have lured her in. Everything she's talked about with Magda has landed with her this time: that it's okay to be successful, it's okay to feel proud in her work. She's been thinking about it a lot since she found her dad online. He's still alive, and for all intents and purposes still a drunk, and still angry. She found three articles about three separate arrests, and it hits her, as she walks, that he must have been a miserable son of a gun to tell a fifteen-year-old that she was worthless. A normal person does not do that. A sane, rational person, who you might be inclined to listen to, does not do that.

She sits on a bench by the Christmas market and watches a small merry-go-round with kids wrapped in warm coats and thick gloves sitting in little red cars or pink aeroplanes going around and around, their grown-ups clapping excitedly every time they circle back and come into view. She doesn't hear the women next to her at first, when they say her name. They have to repeat themselves to get her to look up.

'Are you Evie Bird?'

She looks at them. They're about her age, mid to late thirties. One has long wavy hair down past her shoulders, with a lilac bobble hat and hopeful eyes. The other is wearing earmuffs and has a nose ring. They have their arms looped through each other's, like how Evie walks with Magda. And it's the damnedest thing, but instead of shying away, lying, or acting small, she looks them both in the eye and says, proud as she can muster: 'Yes. I am. Hello.'

'AH!' says Bobble Hat. 'We read online that you were part of the filming! We've been to set, but you know – it's a lot, waiting to see your favourite author. Like stalking!'

'We're huge fans,' says Earmuffs. 'Honestly. Your books . . .'

The other ones supplies: 'They're our favourites. I can't believe you're here!'

Evie smiles. They're so enthusiastic!

'What are your names?' she asks, and Bobble Hat says she's Ingrid, and Earmuffs is Petra.

'Can we join you?' Petra asks, sweetly. 'Just for a moment.'

Evie finds herself nodding. 'Of course,' she says. 'I was just admiring the market. It's so festive.'

'We love Christmas,' Ingrid says. 'You're part of our Christmas tradition! We . . .' She breaks off here to ask Petra something in German, and Petra says: 'Buddy-read'.

'We buddy-read your Christmas book every December, when it comes out,' she says. 'And in the summer, on vacation, we take turns with your summer book.'

'That's so nice to hear,' Evie says, and she means it. 'Your English is good – do you read me in German, or do you get the American copy?'

'German.' Petra laughs. 'I don't want to miss anything.'

Evie likes talking to the women. They're warm and friendly and laugh a lot.

'Your book *To the Moon, the Stars, and Back Again,*' Petra says, as they all watch the ride nearby stop, a bunch of kids climb off, and then a new set who have been waiting patiently climb into their spots. 'It changed my life.'

'That's kind of you,' Evie says.

'No, honestly, she's serious,' interjects Ingrid.

'The protagonist,' Petra muses. 'Her best friend says something to her and look.' She rolls up her coat sleeve to reveal a tattoo in German. 'It says *cite your source* in my language,' she explains. 'Like Lisa's best friend says to her.'

Evie thinks back to the book. It's a love story, as always, but the sub-plot is about how Lisa, the main character, is a small business owner in a small town, lobbying against developers who want to build luxury flats on the grounds of the local park. It would stand to make a small number of locals very rich, for various reasons, but a lot of other locals would be worse off. Lisa starts to believe the horrible things people are saying about her – the ones who don't think she should be getting involved – and her best friend tells her to cite her source. Does the protagonist have to receive the criticisms on her personality or motivations from the developers? Actually no, because that is a faulty source. They don't know her. Does she have to receive the affirmations and love from her best friend, and the people whose interests she is trying to protect? Well yeah, actually, because that's a source close to her, and so it is more valid. There's a second line, once she implements this, where she says: *I get to decide which sources to cite in my own goddamn life!* Evie hasn't thought of that in ages. How interesting to meet these strangers who make her reflect back on her own words. She could almost believe she's quite wise. Or, at least, her characters are.

'I don't get along with my mother,' Petra says. 'My sister does. But me? I never have. It's like we are aliens to each other, and we make each other quite unhappy. And she has said some unkind things to me before, and I believed them, and then I read your book and I thought *cite your source*. She might be my mother, but we haven't had a proper conversation since I was still at school. She doesn't know me. So I am not going to cite her as a source!'

'It was like a magic sentence for her,' Ingrid adds, nodding in agreement. 'A sort of freedom, really, I think. Petra?'

Petra nods. 'I met my wife six weeks after I got it tattooed on me. And *she* is a source I cite often, because she loves me and knows me and sees that I am good.'

'Whoa,' Evie says, and she can't quite believe what she's hearing.

'So thank you,' Petra says. 'And thank you for listening. I'll bet people tell you their stories all the time,' she says. 'I know many people must feel how I feel.'

Evie holds a hand to her heart, and then takes the hands of both women.

'I really, *really* appreciate you coming over and saying hi,' she says, her heart swelling. She doesn't want to run away, or make a silly self-effacing joke. She believes she wrote something that meant something to these women, and she is going to be gracious enough to let them tell her. It's only later, once they've hugged and said goodbye, that she appreciates that they didn't ask for a photo, or a social media tag, or anything like that. They just wanted to chat, and that, to Evie, feels like magic. *Cite your source,* she repeats to herself.

And then it hits her.

She's lucky her dad is still a piece of shit.

He's such a piece of shit that he doesn't get to be a source that Evie cites.

Just like Petra gets to disregard her mother's feedback, because her mother doesn't really know her, Evie doesn't have to be held hostage to those words her father spat at her when she was still so young.

How sad, how unfair, that she has carried around his self-hate, his self-loathing, as her own, for all these years.

What he said, it wasn't about her. How could it be? That was all him.

And it's the craziest thing: Evie starts to cry. The relief of it all, of understanding that her dad can go screw himself, because he doesn't get to bring her down too. He can destroy his own life as much as he wants. Evie doesn't know him. And he doesn't know her, and that is his loss.

This time when she pulls out her phone, she googles local tattoo parlours. Before she can question it, she follows the little blue dot, pushes through to the door, and asks the artist if he speaks English. He shakes his head.

'*Nein,*' he tells her.

'Okay,' she says, slowly. 'Erm . . .'

She mimes holding a pen, and he gets her a sharpie and a piece of paper. She draws out what she wants, shows him her forearm, and he writes the number 150, which she takes to mean the price. It hurts, getting it done, and she assumes he's trying to calm her because he says lots of things that sound sweet, but are, to Evie's untrained ear, ultimately unfathomable. There's a poetry to it, really, communicating with smiles and nods and grunts. When he's done, he wraps her arm in cling film and gives her a big tube of cream and holds up a hand.

'Five,' he says. 'Every day.'

Evie looks at him. 'Use this five times a day?' she asks, and he nods.

She shows it off proudly to Magda when they meet for drinks later on, thrusting it in front of her friend's nose as she announces: 'I did a thing!'

'What!' squeals Magda. 'Oh my gosh! A tattoo?! This is very not Evie Bird! Wow! But wait.' She squints, trying to see what it says through the recently applied cream and cling film. 'I can't see it properly,' she tells her. 'I don't want to touch it in case I hurt you.'

'It says,' Evie says, a smile so big it could fall off her face, 'Cite your source. I have a whole story to tell you.'

'I can't wait to hear it. Wine?'

'Wine,' confirms Evie.

As they try to capture the attention of a waiter and then put in their order, Magda furrows her brow. 'Hold on,' she says. 'Cite your source. That's from one of your books, right?'

'Yes, it is.' Evie grins, and the pride in her voice – the pride in her very bones – comes shining through.

The morning after the night before, where Evie had two glasses of wine and a very galvanising chat with Magda, Evie and her new tattoo are on Operation Tell-Duke-She's-Sorry. Which first involves finding Duke, which is apparently harder than it seems because he's nowhere to be found.

'Daphne,' Evie shouts from across the set. They're at their final destination now: Füssen. They have three nights here and then fly back home, just in time for Christmas. It feels bonkers that three weeks ago the shoot seemed like a life sentence, and now Evie doesn't want it to end. At least not without facing Duke head on, and all the fears that come with it: he's going to let her down, laugh at her, use her vulnerability against her . . . the list goes on. It's not personal: Duke is a lovely man. But one lovely man cannot undo decades of telling herself that love never works. The years of being let down, or rejected, or left behind, over and over again.

She might be able to try, though.

Daphne waves at Evie as she hears her name called, and Evie heads over.

'You've not seen Duke, have you?' she asks, noting how beautiful Daphne looks in her hair and make-up. They're filming a horse-drawn carriage scene today, through incredibly picturesque streets, and Daphne looks every inch the girl-next-door leading lady. It's unfair, really, that she should be so gorgeous and so smart that she can direct, too.

'I haven't lately,' says Daphne, trying to do a million jobs at once – look gorgeous, hold a clipboard, not ruin her costume. 'He's due on set soon, so just wait around, maybe?'

'Okay, thanks,' Evie says. 'Break a leg! You look great.'

'Thanks,' Daphne says smiling. 'It's non-stop here!'

Evie goes to say hi to the make-up girls, since she's here and nobody seems to be in their trailer, and by the time she comes out, Duke is preoccupied with filming and it feels creepy to just stand and watch. She'd only be another set of eyeballs on an otherwise busy set, but she'd be the only person there without a specific purpose and to loiter makes her feel like one of his many adoring fans waiting by the set barriers, just hoping to get a glimpse. Instead, she calls Magda.

'Hey,' she says. 'I wasn't expecting you to answer. I thought you'd be balls-deep in—'

Before she can finish, Magda interrupts her in hushed tones and says, 'I am. I'm with Markus. I just picked up to make sure you're okay.'

'Me? Oh yes. I'm fine. Just waiting to pour my heart out to a man I've been willingly keeping at arm's length, but I've realised I owe him a lot more on account of him being incredibly decent . . . but I'm fine. I can hold all that in for another . . . ooh, I don't know? Five minutes, at least.'

'You sound very emotionally healthy,' Magda retorts, drolly, and then she can hear something in the background, giggles, and a muffled whisper akin to *Markus! Stop that!* or similar.

'Things sound like they're going nauseatingly well with Mr Service Station,' Evie notes.

'I can't possibly comment on that,' Magda says, and it's obvious Markus is listening. She's stayed behind to spend some extra time with him, and Evie can't fault her. Magda deserves it. 'But listen, you need me and I'm there in a shot, okay?'

'I know,' Evie replies. 'But it's all good here. Enjoy your man while you can, and text me later, okay?'

'Okay,' Magda says, and before she hangs up Evie can hear more delighted squealing. Other people's happiness is gross – even when that other person is your best friend.

'Right,' Evie says to herself, clapping her hands together and looking around. 'Okay then . . .'

In the end she burns off her nervous energy by walking to the hotel and grabbing her laptop. She takes it down to a coffee shop next door to the hotel, telling herself she'll just reread the last eight thousand or so words she got down and then jot down a few ideas about moving forward. It's a gorgeous little place, with two window seats and a real log-burning stove and the heavy smell of cinnamon in the air. She gives a self-conscious *guten tag* and orders a double-shot latte and a muffin, with a seltzer. There's ten or so tables, half of which are occupied, all with groups of two or three people full of festive cheer, apparently catching up before the holidays.

She sets her stuff – her coat and bag – on the chair one side of the table, and then hops up into a window seat, legs crossed underneath her, laptop literally in her lap, so that she's like the proverbial doggy in the window. Anyone who passes by can see her, but it makes her feel part of something, to write that way. She knows so many writers prefer the quiet of home or a rented office space, but Evie has long sought inspiration by being out and about in the world. The thing is: it's always as an observer. She's so seldom been a partici-pant in her own life, lately. She looks down at her new tattoo. She makes a quiet promise to herself to participate more, to be spontaneous, to make leaps. This trip has opened up something in her, an appetite to *try things*, at the very least. To stop being so damned careful.

To stop being so damned careful.

Huh.

Evie opens up a new Word document instead of the file she's been working on. On the first page she types: UNTITLED by EVIE BIRD, as is her tradition. She makes sure her settings are right – that it's in Times New Roman, twelve point, double spaced, that the shortcuts for chapter headings are in place and the page numbers are in the bottom right-hand corner, just how she likes them. And then that's what she types. She thinks of the women she met yesterday, and goes with that as a name, and that's where she starts with her next novel:

Petra Egerton had decided to stop being so damned careful with her life.

She doesn't stop writing for the next three and a half hours.

37

Evie

The rush of finding the rhythm of a story is the reason why Evie keeps doing what she does. She won't ever be on social media documenting her life, or out on tour going from bookshop to bookshop, nice as she now knows it would be to meet her readers. Because *that* isn't *this*: creating, writing, going in hard and deep on a story that feels like a compulsion to get out of her head and through her fingers onto the screen. That is her offering to this world, that is how she makes sense of things. When the café closes and she's forced to down tools and head back to the hotel to dump her bag, her mind is racing, her blood positively humming with creativity – it's something she's not felt in several books. She's always written what she cares about, but she hasn't felt this specific feeling for a while, and now it is back she wants to hang on to it for as long as possible.

In fact, when she gets back to her room, she sits at the small table by the window and decides to write one thousand more words, because she can. She's not even sure that this book is a romance, like she's done before: there's something else she wants to say, something about a woman taking control of her narrative, taking it back from the outsourcing she has been doing, a thing that has been keeping her small. *What happens,* she thinks to herself as she folds one leg up under her, biting her lip and using the elastic on her wrist to tie up her hair, *when a woman finally gets tired of her own bull?* She almost can't bear it. She's asked herself the question, and now the character of Petra Egerton is going to seek out the answer.

It's 11 p.m. when she finishes. In the space of eleven hours, she's written almost ten thousand words – a tenth of a new book. Ten thousand words is often her own personal barometer of the tone of a manuscript, and so when she finally pauses and that feeling is still there – that light-headedness, that adrenaline – she knows this is it. The other idea has to go out of the window, even though it's almost finished. This new one is exactly the story she wants to tell.

She gets up to pee and stretches a little. There's a masseuse she sees back home in Utah who has never been able to fully get the knots out of her shoulders because Evie never fully commits to seeing her often enough. But she's been given exercises to do, to help, and so she swings her arms loosely from one side to the other, and then puts her hands on her shoulders and circles forwards, then back.

She was supposed to talk to Duke today. It's late. She's

sure filming will be done, so he's likely to be in the hotel. She thinks of her character. *Go find him,* she tells herself. *Go be brave.*

She dabs on some lip balm and goes to the lobby. There's a few of the crew in the bar, Katerina included, but she can't deal with that now. At the front desk, she asks if they can tell her which room Duke is in so she can knock for him. They've moved around so many hotels she realises she doesn't even know which room is his in this one.

'I'm afraid we can't give that information out,' the young man with big brown eyes says to her, and to his credit he does seem sorry. 'We've signed paperwork of the highest order declaring we will not breach any safety standards.'

Evie sighs. 'I get it,' she says.

The man smiles sadly. 'Sorry,' he says. 'Although, what I can say is . . . the more high profile the guest, the higher floor they are probably on.'

Evie smiles. 'That helps a lot,' she says, understanding that if Duke is the top talent he must surely be on the top floor. Why hadn't she thought of that before? The best rooms are always on the top floor.

She takes the elevator up, wondering to herself if this is right, whilst simultaneously telling herself that she is brave, she is beautiful, she is badass. She taps her foot as the elevator goes up, floor one, floor two, floor three . . . Has time slowed down? She turns and looks at herself in the elevator mirror. Brave. Beautiful. Badass.

A little tinkle of a bell lets her know she's on the top floor, and she steps out. It's quiet. There are four rooms up here, all named suites rather than numbered rooms, with sleek gold plates on their heavy oak doors. She looks around. Right. She's just going to knock, and when he answers she's going to say . . . what? I love you? No, that would be *insane*. She's going to say: I'm scared but I like you? That's more her speed. Okay. Brave. Beautiful. Badass. I'm scared but I like you.

She knocks on the first door, and there's no answer.

She knocks on the second door, and Marnie answers, dressed in a robe, another one of the producers in there with her, also in a robe. It might even be Malcolm. Evie has interrupted something.

'Oh shoot, sorry,' she says. 'I was looking for Duke.'

Marnie doesn't say anything, just points, her face impassive.

'Thanks,' Evie says. 'Sorry to . . . intrude.' She lifts a finger and points between her and her guest, and it's more indiscreet than interrupting in the first place. Marnie cocks an eyebrow. She still hasn't spoken.

'I'm going now,' Evie says, and finally Marnie tells her: 'Yes. Goodnight, Evie.'

When she's shut the door Evie is left in the hotel corridor once again, only this time she knows which door to knock on next.

Brave.

Beautiful.

Badass.

I like you and I'm scared.

She knocks and waits. She can hear his voice and his footsteps as he gets closer to the door. He must look through the peephole, then, because she hears him say, 'Oh!' like he's surprised she's there. He coughs, and then opens the door.

'Evie,' he says, and she swears he sounds happy to see her. He's happy to see her! Okay, this is good. Great, even.

'Duke, I . . .' she starts, and then she senses a movement behind him and there is Daphne, wearing one of his T-shirts and not much else. They lock eyes.

'Evie,' Daphne says, and Evie looks at Duke. He's fully dressed but looking down she sees he's barefoot. He's also got a kind of bedhead thing going on. Urgh.

'Never mind,' she says quickly, turning on her heel and heading for the stairs. She practically runs back to her room. Duke and Daphne? Well of course. *Of course* they were always going to get back together. Working together so closely, Brad gone, Evie cast aside like she was always going to be. He can deny it all he wants, but as soon as Evie saw his toes she knows the truth: they've been in bed together. Why else would he be sockless in company? It's a detail she'd put into her own stories, a little feature to prove a point.

Right then. She's brave, beautiful, and badass. And she's also somehow relieved to have proved to herself that her first instinct was right: Duke is a fake player, not worthy of her time.

38

Duke

'Well, I can only imagine what that looked like.' Duke sighs, looking at the space Evie was just stood in, right before she bolted.

Daphne comes and stands behind him, her face contorted in a way that overeggs the definition of *whoops*.

'I'll talk to her?' she offers. 'Explain that it's literally a case of me being a klutz. We're friends now. She trusts me.'

Duke issues a hollow laugh. 'I don't think she trusts anyone,' he says sadly, dejectedly closing the door. 'Bugger.'

'Do you want to go after her? I can keep working on this . . .'

Duke is torn. He wants to set the record straight, wants to talk to Evie, but he doesn't even know what he'd say. *I'm not sleeping with Daphne*, but then what? And there's so much to do here – with edits to review from the past two days, and today's rough footage.

'Seriously,' she says, putting her hands on his shoulders so he looks her in the eye. 'Just keep it quick?'

'Are you sure?' he asks.

'Yes!' she says. 'Literally we're only going to get three hours' sleep as it is, what's a few more minutes? Crack on, fix it, then get back. Although . . .' she adds, shaking her head. 'Look, I know what me prancing about in your shirt and no trousers looks like, but I'm the least of your worries. You both need to sort yourselves out and say you want to be together. It's like you're looking for excuses not to, and I've got no idea why.'

Duke opens his mouth to protest, but finds he doesn't know what he'd protest to, exactly. It's like a slap around the face.

'You're right,' he says, shaking his head with new understanding. 'You're so right! I lost my temper with her the other night, flew off the handle really . . . but what I didn't do is just say what my problem was. Like a grown-up. And I think I'm on the edge of something here, some really radical thought, so bear with me, but . . .' He's smiling now, knowing he's been ridiculous. 'I think,' he says, eyes wide, comically so. 'I'm supposed to *talk* about my feelings and trust the other person will receive them and not run away from them.'

'Duke,' Daphne says, blinking slowly and shaking her head once again. 'I'm glad I could be here to hear the penny drop. Jesus, Mary, and Joseph, I think you've just discovered the meaning of Christmas.'

'Love,' he affirms, and he's actually semi-serious now. 'Is the meaning of Christmas to offer love, without expectation? Am I supposed to offer *trust* without expectation . . . ?'

'Until proven otherwise,' Daphne says. 'Yah. You *say* you like her, but how is she supposed to believe that if you don't offer up your whole self, doubts and worries and all? It makes you look like a . . .'

'Liar,' Duke supplies. 'If I don't tell her what I'm scared about, as well as that I like her, it's a half-truth.'

'And how could anybody trust a half-truth?' Daphne says.

'When *we* were together,' Duke continues, 'that's what you were trying to tell me, weren't you? When you said to be honest with you, I thought I was being honest because I wanted it to work so much . . . but I never told you about my mum, or my worries about all this, or my freaking nose job—'

'It's a great nose,' Daphne offers. 'I figured.'

'Thank you,' Duke says, temporarily off-track. He considers all this. 'Evie knows all those things,' he says. 'She just doesn't know this one last piece of the puzzle.'

'And what's that?' Daphne asks, smiling.

'That I've fallen in love with her,' he says, simply. 'I'm scared I don't deserve her and have spent years – decades – thinking I don't deserve love at all, not unless I'm perfect, and that's why I don't let the mask slip . . . but I am done. I am so, so done. She's seen more of me than anybody. I want to be with her, Daphne. I want her, and me, and warts and all, just to see. Just to know what it's like to really, truly try.'

'Well then,' Daphne says, her face serious. 'I've only got one piece of advice.'

'What's that?' asks Duke, desperately.

'GO!' she squeals. 'Go! Go! Go!'

*

It's not until the lift opens downstairs into the lobby that Duke realises he's not wearing any shoes. When Daphne had dropped that Diet Coke it had spilled directly onto his Nikes, which had been annoying, yes – but then as Daphne went to pick it up and it exploded all over her, all was forgiven because Duke hadn't laughed that hard and that long in ages. The way it happened in slow motion – she dropped it, it spilled, he kicked it slightly right as she went to pick it up, and how they both saw their paperwork and both laptops at the same time, Duke registering the look of sheer terror on her face as she sacrificed herself – and her clothes – in the name of preserving what they'd been doing. She got *covered*. All Duke had to do was take his socks off.

He's about to hit the button to go right back up to the top floor to get some shoes when he sees her. She doesn't see him, and so he doesn't move except to stick out a hand to stop the lift door closing, staying glued to the spot as she stands chatting to Magda and that guy from the service station blizzard, Markus. Markus has his arm around Magda, and everyone is laughing, and then Markus gives Magda a kiss and leaves, the two women watching him go. Magda leans into Evie, giving affection easily, like women often do, and one of them says something that makes them both laugh. She's incredible. Her tiny, short legs and baggy jumper and her hair piled on top of her head like an afterthought. Duke racks his brains for a killer opening line, for something to really capture her attention . . . but nada. Nothing. Then Magda spots him.

'Duke!' she cries, and Evie turns, looks at him, horrified, and then whispers something with her head bowed to Magda, who looks puzzled and then pulls her waving arm down in a hurry. She looks away too.

'Evie,' Duke starts, and that's it, he's walking through the hotel with nothing on his feet, right towards her, even though he can see that there's nothing she'd like less right now – but she doesn't understand, that's all. She will do in just a second.

'That was totally innocent,' Duke says. 'Honestly. You'll laugh about this when I explain. You see—'

'I don't think she wants to hear this,' Magda says, looking cautiously at her friend for confirmation.

'Evie, please,' Duke begs. 'Just listen.'

'*Duke*,' Magda warns again, and she's serious, holding his gaze, and it makes Duke's blood freeze in his veins. Heaven have mercy on the man trying to fight a woman's best friend – holy hell, she could control the weather with that glare. Duke gulps. He stops talking. They stay like that, in vignette of a pleading man, a scorned woman, and the friend protecting them both from each other with arms outstretched. He glances between Evie, who is gazing fixedly at the ground, to Magda, who is gazing past him, now, with her head tipped to one side, computing something. Her expression – focused, confused, doing some mental maths – makes Duke turn to see what she's clocked, and it's bloody Katerina, with her phone up to them.

Duke thinks of the improv games he's played with acting coaches or on cast get-to-know-you afternoons over the years. It's like the narrator has put them into a tableau, and they have to hold their pose. Then, when the narrator has issued new instructions, they say, *Okay go,* and everyone continues the movement they were captured in. Somebody must be

311

saying *okay go* right now, because Evie turns, Duke and Magda see her clock Katerina, and then all at once the three of them are lunging towards her – Evie going for Katerina, Magda holding Evie back, Duke being, on reflection, not very helpful at all but generally flapping and flailing.

'YOU!' Evie screams at Katerina, who has entered her own freeze frame as the three bodies come towards her. She looks each one of them in the eye, then down at the floor, pulling her phone into her body like she couldn't possibly have been doing anything wrong. 'What the hell is wrong with you?' Evie presses on. 'You're a freaking vulture. A vampire! Why the hell would you be taking our PICTURE?'

Evie reaches Katerina and seems to realise she doesn't know what to do next. Duke thought she might go for her throat but she reins it back in, standing literally toe-to-toe and nose-to-nose, breathing like a dragon, waiting for Katerina to say something.

'I wasn't—' Katerina starts, but Evie cuts her off with a sharp 'NO'.

Duke is one side of her, at her shoulder, and Magda the other. It's intimidating, and he can see that Katerina is cacking her pants at being confronted by them. Magda looks at Duke as if thinking the same thing and then says, quietly but firmly, 'Let's just take a breath, everyone.'

Evie steps back, not taking her eyes off Katerina for a second.

'Speak,' she instructs, harshly.

Katerina squeaks, like a mouse in a chokehold. Then a tear escapes.

'For God's sake,' Magda says, under her breath, and it's not totally unkind. Duke is struck by a sense of defeat, understands how pathetic Katerina must feel, because he's been there. He's had that realisation himself, confronting an unpalatable truth about how he's behaved. *We all screw up,* he thinks, *and Katerina knows this is her turn.*

'I needed the money,' she says. 'For my dad. For his care home.'

Magda and Duke automatically look to Evie.

'You've got to be kidding me,' Evie says, her mouth falling open. She rolls her eyes and shakes her head. 'Seriously?'

'Yeah.' Katerina nods. 'I'm sorry. I didn't mean to . . . those first photos, they were so innocent, I didn't even think they'd be worth anything. And then it just . . . snowballed.'

'I'm aware,' Evie says, and she's severe with it, despite her shoulders having softened.

Katerina finally looks up. Evie stares straight back.

'What's wrong with your dad?' she asks, and then she adds, realising she's being just the wrong side of abrasive, even though Duke thinks she's every right to be. 'If I can ask.'

'Parkinson's,' she says, wiping away another tear. 'I've really screwed up. I know I have. But I can't stop. The home,' she pleads. 'It's just so expensive.'

Evie sighs deeply. 'Tell me about it,' she says, drily.

Duke tips his head at Katerina, a signal to go. She looks at him gratefully, and then he has a second thought.

'The photos,' he says. 'Delete them.'

Katerina pulls out her phone and scrolls through the images she just took, the three of them – Duke, Evie, and Magda – watching her.

'And then from your trash,' Magda says, and they watch her do that too.

Katerina slinks off into a lift that opens its doors to reveal Daphne. On spotting Duke she waves him over, her iPhone in her hand.

'I've got Independent on the line,' she says, with a grimace. 'They've got some suggestions for an edit they've seen? Apparently it can't wait.'

Duke sighs, and despite what Magda has said, addresses Evie directly.

'We need to talk,' he says. 'I'll find you. I have things to say, Evie, and I need you to hear them.'

She issues a shifty glance, side to side.

'Okay,' she says, and Duke takes Daphne's phone off speaker to get on with his work.

39

Duke

The next day at breakfast, Duke comes down to see Daphne already sat with Magda and Evie. He hasn't had a *second* these past few days, but he is showered and in desperate need of some food, and he tentatively approaches the table to see if he's welcome. They're all laughing together, after all. Evie must know Daphne is no threat if she's sat having breakfast with her.

'Sit,' says Evie, when she sees him. 'Daphne says you've had a crazy all-nighter again. I come in peace.' She holds up her hands to emphasise her point.

'I've cleared the air,' Daphne tells him. 'If that wasn't obvious.'

Evie shrugs, as if to say *oooops!*

'Our girl here gets her exercise by jumping to conclusions,' Magda jokes, winking at Evie, who scrunches up her nose and takes the hit.

'I've got issues,' she says, but she's smiling.

Duke tucks into his fruit salad, and conversation ultimately turns to yesterday, and Katerina's great uncovering.

'I mean, jeez – she had better be telling the truth; that's all I can say.' Evie chuckles darkly as she spears a piece of asparagus with her fork. 'Because right up until she said it was to pay for her dad's care I was ready to . . . well, I'm not sure,' she admits. 'I was mad.'

'I have known you for almost twenty years and have never, not once, seen you erupt like anything close to that,' Magda agrees. 'I was like, scared.'

'I've only *heard* about it from Duke.' Daphne giggles, 'And I'm still scared. Someone in production said you threw a punch! But Duke says it was more of an *almost*. So I'm pleased about that. What she did was awful, but we don't condone hitting people, do we, Duke?'

Duke accepts the pointed barb.

'We don't,' he says.

'Thanks for setting the record straight,' Evie tells him, and they steal a glance at each other before Evie looks away. Duke would kill to know what she's thinking. He was all primed to make a grand declaration and then . . . it didn't happen. He's running out of time. By mid-morning tomorrow they'll all be on buses – or in a private car, in Duke's case – to the airport.

'Well, I'm envious at your self-control,' he quips, pointing at the very faint bruise still left under his eye. 'I've still got a lot to learn about how violence is never the answer.'

'And this is the part where I say never, in all the time I've known you, Duke, have I known you to lose your cool enough to throw a punch,' Daphne offers.

Duke closes his eyes briefly and reflects on his bad behaviour. 'There's no excuse,' he says. 'My therapist is going to have a field day.'

Magda chomps on a hash brown and says, 'This has all been cray-*zee*.' She makes the word sound French with a roll of the tongue. 'Is every movie set like this? So full of maniacs?'

Duke looks at Daphne and she pulls a face.

'Yup,' says Daphne. 'To varying degrees, but . . . essentially, yes. Although I think this one was particularly heightened.' The way she says it makes Duke think she's alluding to him and Evie, and he's willing to write it off as paranoid until Daphne looks at Magda and they both smirk.

'What?' asks Evie, uncharacteristically oblivious.

'Nothing,' says Daphne, too quickly. Evie looks to Magda.

'Seriously,' Magda says. 'Nothing.'

They chew in companionable silence, before Duke asks: 'Should we verify Katerina's story do you think? I could have some people make some calls.'

Magda adopts a funny low voice to mimic him. '"I could have some people make some calls",' she repeats. 'Have you heard yourself? The shoot's finished. Katerina is scared half to death. It's done. Do as we little people do and build a bridge for yourself.'

Duke doesn't get it.

'She means to get over it,' Evie explains in a stage whisper, and everyone laughs at him.

'Got it.' Duke nods. 'Getting over it right . . . About . . . now.'

At that, Magda starts to push back her chair. 'I have somewhere to be,' she suddenly decides, looking at Daphne in a funny sort of way.

Daphne cocks her head, and then decides the same.

'Me too!' she declares, and Evie furrows her brow and is about to say something when Duke catches Magda tip her head towards him with big eyes. Ah. They're finally being given some alone time.

Duke smiles.

Evie almost smiles.

He sighs.

'I have a million things I want to say to you,' Duke tells her, figuring that that's as good a place as any to start.

Evie nods. 'Yeah,' she agrees. 'Mostly I am *very* ashamed by my over-reaction last night.' She pushes food around her plate self-consciously. 'I'd been writing all day, and I was wired . . . Daphne explained everything. I don't know why I lost it that way. I was scared, I guess.'

'I know a little bit of something about that,' Duke admits.

Eye contact. Nervous smiles. Almost-words.

'Go on,' he prompts her. 'Say it. You can tell me.'

Evie smiles. 'I like you and I'm scared,' she tells him, and Duke's heart explodes with the melodies of one thousand symphonies.

'Well, hell,' Duke says. 'Spot the writer.'

'Yes, my most eloquent phrasing yet,' she self-mocks, and Duke raises his eyebrows.

'No,' he says. 'That's honestly it. Because I like *you* and *I'm* scared.'

'Yeah?' she asks, and the way she sounds so hopeful makes Duke want to throw aside the table with his bare hands, right there and then, so that there's nothing between them and he can take her and hold her and kiss her.

'Yeah,' he says, and she lets out a little *oh*.

'So,' she says, and her eyes dance like they're trying to settle on something with a more concrete conclusion. 'See you tonight? At the wrap party?'

'It can't come quick enough.' Duke smiles, and he practically floats to set.

That morning Duke and Daphne shoot their last scenes, but by mid-afternoon they sit and look at what they need to get done before flying home for Christmas, and it feels insurmountable. The solution starts with: work through the night, work in the car to the airport, work on the flight, and don't stop working right up until the deadline, being methodical, decisive, and where they need to, breaking off to divide and conquer instead of each having to co-sign every decision.

'You've gotta trust me, and I've gotta trust you,' Daphne says, as they look at the tasks they've yet to fulfil scrawled out on a piece of A4. After wrapping on set, they got back to the hotel as quickly as possible. The party downstairs has already started, everyone exited to get home and proud of the work they've done. The pair plan to go down for a toast shortly and then keep on.

'That's the easy part.' Duke shrugs. 'The hard part will be finding the sheer force of will to keep pushing through. I was *not* expecting this when I was budgeting my energy.'

'I know.' She laughs. 'I mean, if we have to be roped into anything at least it's this, right? If we pull this off, it could be the start of something really huge for us. It's like how

319

Reese did *Wild* and what, ten years later had a billion-dollar company?'

'Okay, well when you put it like that . . .'

'But let's pop downstairs now? This is a good time to break?'

'Great,' Duke agrees. 'Although I've heard there's karaoke, so we might have done ourselves a favour by excusing ourselves.'

'Yikes,' Daphne says, and they head out.

Downstairs, the mood is merry and bright. The place is packed, with everyone from cast and crew in high spirits, and gloved waiters carrying trays of drinks and hors d'oeuvres, but he instantly sees who he is looking for. She's resplendent, dressed up in a way he's never seen her. She's wearing a calf-length beaded skirt – it might be sequins – in silver, with a matching silver top that ties at the neck and falls open to show off her back, so that with one false move, it would be boob city. Duke thinks about those boobs. Actually – one false move and all his Christmases might come at once. Her hair is piled high on her head, and she's got a simple pair of studded earrings in. Her lips are festive in red, and when she sees him too Duke thinks: *This is how it is supposed to feel, spotting your person across a crowded room.* He waves, and then is accosted by Malcolm, an arm across his shoulders and a hot, heavy breath laced with vodka saying things urgently about margins and windows of opportunity.

'Yes,' Duke agrees, panicking as he loses sight of her. She's all he's here for. *See you tonight,* they'd said. She knows they're on a tight deadline. She knows what is happening – he made sure to get the message to her. Kayla, in make-up, said she'd find her and tell her personally that he was with Daphne working, but he'd be down when he could as promised.

'Hey, can we circle back on this later?' Duke interrupts Malcolm, weighing down on his shoulder, right as the producer says, 'In fact, let's see if we can get LA on the phone right now. They're using a guy in Toronto too, so let's all confab together. Come on. We won't be long. Half an hour, tops. Daphne! We've got a call!' he barks in her direction, and when she comes running willingly, without protest, it's all Duke can do to look back to let Evie know he'll be back soon. But she's disappeared from view.

40

Evie

Evie taps the mic.

'Right then,' she says into it. 'I lost a bet with my best friend, and that's why I'm up here.' She gives a nervous chuckle, and everyone is kind enough to nervously chuckle with her.

'Get it, girl!' Magda shouts across the room of people, and Evie shakes her head. She's had three shots and ten minutes with a meditation app in order to be able to do this, but that was the dare: Evie lost a game of *rock, paper, scissors* over something so stupid she can't even remember now, and the forfeit was to sing a song at the wrap-party karaoke . . . and dedicate it to Duke.

'First one up, what did I do to deserve this?' She laughs, and everyone laughs again with her. God, is she really going to do this? It's safe, right? *I'm okay,* she tells herself. *I'm gonna jump, and he's gonna catch me.*

The guy on the sound system catches her eye and gives her a thumbs up, and then the lyrics to her chosen song come up on the screen in front of her.

'Well . . .' she tells the audience, too shy to actively seek him out. He'll make himself known. She knows he will.

'I once told a man that life – that love – isn't all Ed Sheeran songs and mad dashes to the airport. We're all going home tomorrow, so that's the airport bit covered, and as for love being a pop song . . . erm, here goes nothing,' she says, and the early notes of 'Perfect' come on.

Everyone cheers, and a few people turn, having guessed she's talking about Duke. She dares to look up, but then quickly glances back to the screen, knowing that she has to come in with the first line. She's all but tone deaf, so this isn't a serenade so much as it is an assault on everyone's senses, but she's trying to be cute. She's going out on a limb, here . . .

'I've found a love . . .' she starts to sing, and as soon as everyone can tell that her vocal range is akin to that of drowning kittens in a trash bag, they go *wild*. So wild that she actually can't hear herself for the next few lines, but she's enjoying it. It's kind of fun, letting herself be so bad at something. And by that, she means bad at both singing and seduction.

'But darling, just kiss me slow, your heart is all I own . . .' She continues to crescendo, and she has the confidence, now, to look up to the room. She gets louder, even more out of tune. *Yolo,* is her thinking. Before she went up Magda had said the golden rule of public karaoke is that the worse you are the more people love it, so she leans into it. She starts doing hand actions with the words. She's cooing and wooing and oohing and ahhing, and by the time she looks up again, everyone has properly started to get on board and they've all put their phone torches on and held them aloft like it's Madison Square Garden and she really is Ed Sheeran on the closing night of a multi-year international tour.

She blasts out the last line, holding the final note, spreading her arms wide. The room erupts. She feels high as a kite. She might even be happy crying? To stand there and just own it – God, she's never done anything like this in her life. She's euphoric. She is the worst singer known to man – literally, every other person who goes up there tonight will undoubtedly be able to hold a note infinitely better than she can – and yet she feels the best she ever has.

She stumbles off the makeshift stage, people grabbing her shoulder and saying well done, and good job, and oh my God you're amazing! She smiles, and nods, and rolls her eyes to signify that she gets it, she was *awful* and that's what was so brilliant, but she's looking over everyone's shoulder as she does it, searching for Duke. It was all for him. This was her grand romantic gesture, a feat never before attempted by Evelyn Bird. This will probably never be attempted again! So where is he? Can he just be in front of her already, wrapping his big arms around her and laughing, making her laugh too? *Dancing in the dark, with you between my arms* – just like the lyrics said.

But as the crowd thins out and she gets to the back of the room there's still no sign of him. And then she sees the look on Magda's face, and her stomach drops.

'What?' Evie pleads, her voice panicked. She just needs

Magda to say it: that Duke was so repelled by her, so disgusted by her voice and her audacity at even getting up there in the first place that he's sent Magda to tell her the whole thing is off. The look in Magda's eyes tells Evie she's blown it, or worse: never had it to blow in the first place. This is all a big, horrible misunderstanding and everyone is extremely embarrassed by her stupid emotional display of affection and it really would be better for everyone if she could just climb into a human sinkhole and never return to conscious earth again, please.

'Say it,' Evie says, shaking her hands like moving her body will ward off whatever is happening. 'Was it really that bad?'

Magda shakes her head. 'No. You were great. It was amazing. I've never seen you so full of joy as I just did up there! But—'

'What?'

'He's not here. I don't think he saw any of that?'

Evie drops down into a nearby booth. He missed it? It was all for nought?

'Well,' Evie says, as Magda sinks down opposite her. 'That's crushing.'

Magda pulls a face.

'You could always go again?' she suggests, and Evie gives her A Look.

'Right,' Magda notes, hurriedly. 'That was a one-time thing. I get it. I'm with you.'

The women sit, neither sure what happens now.

'I think,' Evie decides, speaking slowly, 'I'm going to call it a night. I'm gonna put on some music, pack, take one last long hotel bath . . .'

She hates how Magda looks at her then. Evie has spent her whole adult life trying to avoid the exact expression on her best friend's face right now. Magda feels sorry for her.

'Do you want me to come up too?' she offers. 'I can bring a bottle. I'm stealthy. Nobody will know . . .'

Evie shakes her head. 'Nah,' she says, and her voice is too bright. She's acting stronger than she feels. In fact, she might even cry. Not now, not even in the elevator, but she might do upstairs, once the hotel door is closed behind her. It's a lot, all this, and now it's over and she thought she was going to get a shot at a big happy ending chapter – her Happily Ever After, HEA, like Duke said, back when they first met – but she's alone. And, yes, that's better than being with the wrong person, but damn if she hadn't thought Duke could be the right one, when it came down to it.

She waits for the elevator to come down, and when the one on the right pings its doors open, she gets in.

She's already on the eighth floor by the time the elevator on the left pings its doors open downstairs with Duke getting out, looking for her.

41

Evie

'You know,' Evie says, rolling her case out to the kerb. 'I'm fine. This is fine. I'm ready to get out of here. That song can be the last thing anybody remembers of me. That's cool. I think now is a good time to call it.'

It's morning twilight and the birds are barely awake. Evie is so used to early call times after three weeks on set that she can almost enjoy it – there's a peace that permeates the air at this hour, before the sky breaks into pink and purple stripes and the business of people gets too hectic.

Magda takes a breath.

'I trust you,' she says, smiling. 'If you say it's time to go, then I say: let me get you a cab.'

Evie smiles back. Magda is a good friend. If there is a search for the love of Evie's life, maybe it's a futile one when Magda is stood beside her. She might be all the soulmate

Evie needs, and she said as much last night after she got out of the bath: ruddy-cheeked and skin-shrivelled, all cried out for reasons she couldn't articulate. Magda had understood. Evie hadn't seen Duke again, and so he was lost to the wilderness – or the upper floors of the hotel. Evie wasn't going to go up there again. It was desperate. He knows where she is if he wants her – but he hasn't sought her out, so he obviously doesn't.

'Is that everything?' the driver asks, and Evie nods.

'Just . . . one moment.' On a whim, she sets down her bag to rifle through her stuff for a pen and paper. On a small notecard she writes: *No hard feelings. All the best, Evie x*

She goes to the desk and asks them to pass it along to Duke. Then she hurries back to the taxi and says: 'Okay. I'm ready.'

It's a long drive to the airport, so they do indeed get to see the sun come up and kiss the sky, and Evie watches the cars going in the other direction, people obviously travelling to see family or friends for the holidays. There are cars packed with grown-ups up front and kids in the back – iPad screens lighting up faces and phones being peered at, trunks filled with boxes and gifts and luggage. Evie will go and see her mom on Christmas morning, and she's pushed down thoughts of her, really, even when that horrible article came out about abandoning her. She knows the truth. Evie has never abandoned her mother. She was summoned here and ended up having the time of her life. She's allowed to do that. That's okay. Evie absent-mindedly rubs a hand over her arm, where her new tattoo is. *Cite your source.*

*

'Are we doing Chinese on the 25th?' Magda says, breaking through Evie's reverie. It's natural they're both thinking about the big day, considering that's what everyone is flying home for. The adventure is over – of course they're thinking about what is next.

'A nice big sleep-in,' Evie says, looking at her lovely, kind, adventurous soulmate of a friend. 'Eggs Benedict for breakfast, then Christmas movies and Chinese with champagne for dinner? Maybe a brief walk with the dog to see the lights so we at least get *some* fresh air?'

'Perfect,' Magda says. 'My first Christmas as a divorcée. Jesus. Who'd have thought it?'

'You've not talked about it much these past ten days,' Evie reflects. 'I know you're still feeling feelings about it . . .'

'I am,' Magda says. 'But, you know . . . It was the right thing, and I'm more certain of that than ever now.'

'And Markus?' Evie asks. 'All I know is that he had to go off for work, but I never got the full story on if you're going to keep in touch, or if that was that . . . ?'

'We said we'd keep in touch,' Magda says, scrunching up her face like she's shy about it.

'What?' says Evie.

'He's coming out to visit in January,' Magda replies, and Evie squeals so loudly the driver swerves the car.

'Sorry!' Evie cries to him. 'Sorry, sorry, sorry!' She looks at Magda. 'He's coming out. To. Visit,' she says, clapping her hands to punctuate the words. 'Why am I only just hearing about this now?!'

'Stop!' Magda laughs, using a hand to bat away Evie's attention. 'It's not a big deal.'

'Not a big deal?' parrots Evie. 'You flew halfway across the world and ended up meeting a beautiful man who is going to fly out to the States to see you because that's how much he likes you? I thought it was just sex!'

Magda shrugs, and the scenery outside the car starts to change to lots of signposts for airport lanes and hubs. They're almost there.

'So did I,' she says. 'For the first ten minutes. But I knew pretty much that first night it had legs. I get that I only just signed the papers and everything, but life's short, you know? I don't want to be sensible. I want to be free.'

Evie feels like Magda has reached across the seats and snatched out her heart.

'What?' Magda asks. 'You think I'm stupid?'

Evie shakes her head. Their car pulls up to the kerb. 'No,' Evie exclaims. 'I think you're the bravest person I've ever met. You just go for it, and know you'll be okay. I worry I won't be okay and so don't do anything. And I think I just decided, right now this second, to try things differently.'

'You don't have to change who you are,' Magda says, as they clamber out at departures. 'Who knows what will happen with all this. I didn't mean to make you feel bad or anything. You're amazing too, Evie. Look what this trip has done for you! You've left some ghosts behind, you've smiled more than I've seen in years . . .'

Evie nods, excitedly.

'All true,' she agrees, and their driver finishes unloading their bags. Magda gives him a tip and they both say thank you, Evie pulling out her phone and scrolling through her emails. 'But I am just going to get Duke's email and write to him. Life's too short to be sensible, right?'

'I actually think writing to him is the epitome of sensible, but sure.' Magda smiles, and she scrolls the internet as Evie searches through anyone cc-ed in all the emails about the movie and the contracts and the fauxmance to see who could be best placed to help her. In the end, she settles for her own agent, dropping her a line to explain that she left for the airport early and would love to get word to a few key people to say thanks. *Could you hunt down contacts for Daphne Diamond and Duke Carlisle for me please?* she asks, and then the pair head inside to check in.

'No, this way,' says Evie, pointing to the queue for economy check-in. Magda was heading for first class, the check-in desk with a literal red carpet out front and no line.

Magda furrows her brow.

'No,' she says. 'We're first class, right?'

Evie looks at her friend.

'Duke got you a *first-class* ticket home too?' she says, incredulously. 'Jesus! Magda!'

Magda shrugs. 'Only because of you,' she says. 'So really it's like *you* got me a first-class ticket.'

Evie tuts. 'Okay, well. Let's see how much it is for me to upgrade.'

Magda nods. 'Excellent idea,' she says.

The check-in person announces that it is almost ten thousand dollars.

'Sorry,' Evie says. 'One-way?'

'Yes, to Salt Lake City it is nine thousand, four hundred and ninety-six dollars to upgrade your economy seat to first class.'

'But . . .' asks Magda, stuttering with her words in shock. 'Why?'

The assistant nods. 'Well,' she says. 'It's on-the-day, it's Christmas, and it's a full flight. This is the last first-class seat we have today.'

Evie looks at Magda. 'I *could* pay that,' she says. 'But it would be stupid of me.'

Magda bites her lip. 'Especially when you already have a ticket,' she agrees.

'I'm supposed to be getting savvy with my spending, right? I deserve nice things, but I also owe it to myself to be smart?'

'That's what we said . . .' Magda agrees, and Evie is waiting for her friend to say, *Screw it! Think of all that movie money!* but she doesn't, and Evie finds that she can't actually do it. She can't blow that kind of cash, even if she does, in theory, have it.

'Can I check in my bags here please,' Magda says to the assistant, and then to Evie she says: 'And then I'll come with you to check in over there, okay? I'll even sacrifice the first-class lounge to buy you your last *Weisswurst*. Come on.'

It takes Evie forty-nine minutes to get through economy check-in, and she stares longingly at the empty red carpet of first the whole way.

'You'll survive,' jokes Magda. 'And if we're allowed, maybe we can switch halfway through the flight, both get a turn.'

Evie pouts dramatically. 'Okay,' she says, in a small voice. 'Thank you.'

42

Duke

Duke stands by the cast and crew airport shuttle, waiting for Evie to come out of the hotel with her stuff, so he can finally corner her and . . . well. He isn't *totally* sure. Say words. Get reactions. Go after what he wants explicitly, because he *knows* she feels it too. He's not sure where she went last night. By the time he got back to the party she was gone, and nobody seemed to have any idea where. He tried her room, but to no answer. He thinks maybe she was in Magda's room? But he couldn't find Magda to ask either, and so he's been down here since 6 a.m. trying to catch her in the lobby, or at breakfast, and again now, as they all file out of the hotel and get their rides to the airport so everyone can catch whatever flight they're booked onto.

'You find her?' Daphne asks, walking up to him from where she's been hugging some of the lighting crew goodbye.

'No,' he says.

Daphne laughs. 'I hope for your sake she comes soon. You look like you're about to throw up.' Duke shoots her a look, and then one of the producers' assistants passes by with a clipboard, and Daphne has the good sense to say, 'Hey, Trish? You don't know where Evie is, do you? Evie Bird? The author?'

'Yeah, I know who Evie is,' Trish says, evidently more than a little stressed at being tasked with organising everyone and their check-out. She looks at her list, running a painted fingernail down the paper before announcing, 'She left earlier. Got a taxi with her friend before dawn.'

'What?' says Duke, but Trish has already lost interest and moved on. He can feel Daphne looking at him.

'That sucks,' she says. 'I know how badly you wanted to see her.'

'Duke?'

They are interrupted by one of the concierges from the front desk.

'Yes?' Duke says.

'I have this for you. I apologise – I didn't see you come down.'

He hands Duke a folded piece of paper. Inside it says: *No hard feelings. All the best, Evie x*

Duke hadn't fully understood what folks were telling him last night, all slurring their words and having their sentences run into each other or trail off. She dedicated a song to him? He can't imagine Evie singing in front of a room of people, but six different people told him it had happened. He's sorry he missed it. If anything, he'd like to see her to be able to take the piss, because it sounds brilliant. Alas. She's gone.

334

Without saying goodbye.

All he has is this note.

It blows.

But . . . wait. Something doesn't seem right.

'I feel like . . .' he says, slowly, a very fuzzy and faraway thought becoming a tiny bit clearer.

'Yes?' Daphne asks.

'I feel like . . .' he clarifies slowly. 'Real life isn't Ed Sheeran songs and mad airport dashes.'

Daphne blinks.

'Okay,' she says. 'Cool . . .'

Duke mulls over the thought. Yeah. She'd said that, right when they'd first met. And then she literally sang an Ed Sheeran song?

'Real life isn't Ed Sheeran songs and mad airport dashes . . .' he repeats, a little bit louder this time, starting to understand.

'Duke . . . ?' starts Daphne, but he's gone now; his head is somewhere else. He has to get to Evie. He needs to get to her right now this second.

His bags are still in his room – somebody else is taking care of that. He doesn't even have a coat – just a wallet, passport and phone in his pocket. That's all he needs, right?

'Taxi!' he calls to a passing cab. 'TAXI!'

43

Duke

Ninety minutes into a cab ride to the airport, the initial adrenaline has worn off and Duke is feeling angsty. One minute he was all, *let's go! Yeah!* and the next he's . . . well, an hour and a half is an age to get somewhere in order to declare your romantic intentions, once you've wasted so much time deciding to actually do it.

He fiddles with his phone nervously, catching up on his texts: Auntie Patricia, just checking in, to Daphne to say no, he's not there yet, to his publicist in LA to say he's not sure about a plus-one for the Globes yet, can he go stag? Maybe go with Daphne? What are the optics on that?

'Home for Christmas?' his cab driver says, a tank of a man who isn't afraid of the accelerator.

'Yeah,' Duke says, before, inexplicably, correcting: 'Well, actually . . . Not right now. This isn't my flight. This isn't even my airport. I'm trying to catch somebody else before *their* flight.'

The driver peers at him in the rearview.

'Woman?' he says, his accent heavy in a way that makes him almost intimidating, like Duke had better not even consider withholding the truth from him.

'A woman, yeah.' Duke nods, making eye contact with him. The man nods back knowingly. 'She's already there, you see, flying to Utah, and I *was* going to fly to London, but what's there, right? So I'll probably go to LA . . . I think. I don't know.' And then he does something even more startling: he seeks the guy's advice. He's babbling nervously. God, why aren't they here yet? 'What would you do: London or LA?'

The man shrugs. 'Nice choices,' he notes. 'You must have a nice life.'

'Yeah, I do,' he says. 'You know. Choices are good, right? So many people don't have choices.' And then he's off. 'This has been a big year for me. The end of this year has been huge. Everything that has come to pass whilst I've been in Germany feels like the culmination of years' worth of work – professionally, but personally, too. You ever had that? That work-life balance thing? We can go too far one way and miss out on what it's all about, can't we?'

The driver looks again at him in the mirror. Duke answers for him.

'Yeah, we can. I haven't always got it right. I think that's okay. We're all learning, aren't we? That's the point of it. Where would the fun be if we came here already knowing all the answers?'

'Love and fishing,' the driver says. 'That is my purpose.'

Duke laughs. 'That's cool. Yeah. You married?'

The driver takes a hand off the wheel to grab his phone off the passenger seat, showing his wallpaper to be a smiling woman and two tween boys.

'My reason for everything,' he says, and Duke peers at the screen.

'Your family is beautiful,' he admires, and then he looks out of the window, wistful and deep in thought.

He's ending the year more sure of who he is and what he wants than ever before: less people-pleasing, less outsourcing his sense of self-worth, more saying no so there's room for a really big yes . . . He's excited. But more than that he's ready to take himself seriously as a person. As a man. He's got the career he has through sheer force of will – but it doesn't keep him warm at night, doesn't look after him when he's sick or watch the sun come up over his garden with a fresh pot of coffee. You can't force that, but he also understands, now, with Evie, that there's a difference between forcing it when it is wrong and giving it your all when you know it is right. If he doesn't at least try to give this a go, to spend some proper time with her, he's a damned fool.

They don't have to do it on his terms: he sees her. She doesn't like the limelight, not really. She likes a quiet life. Okay, well, great: he can do quiet. Everything is different now. What got him here won't get him to where he wants to be, with his own family as his phone's wallpaper. Things don't change until you change them. Duke is going to change his priorities. The world might love him – and for that he is truly, honestly, so very grateful – but there's only one person who truly counts. And now he's met Evie, he doesn't see how it can be anyone but her. She's the first woman to get him, properly, outside of everything else.

'Five minutes,' the driver says, and it occurs to Duke, suddenly that he doesn't have a ticket to get to Evie's departure gate. He pulls up the departure information on his phone to see which terminal she leaves from. He'll have to buy a last-minute ticket for the same flight so he can get through security. Easy. Many a problem can be solved with the right credit card.

'Good luck,' the driver tells him, as Duke pays his taxi fare. 'And remember,' he adds. 'Love and fishing. Nothing else matters.'

'Love and fishing,' Duke repeats. 'Merry Christmas.'

Inside is chaos. It's incredibly busy, with people in big, snaking lines at check-in desks in a way that Duke hasn't seen for a long time: he's used to private check-in at the very least, if not a private plane. But he's here, and he can make it work.

Two teenage girls stood with their parents nudge each other as he passes by, looking for somewhere to buy a ticket, and he flashes a smile but doesn't stop. He's a man on a mission.

'Can I buy a ticket here?' he asks a flustered assistant at the first-class check-in for KLM. 'I need to get through security to get to . . .' Wait. What is he doing? This person doesn't need his life story. The cab driver got enough of that. 'Just one first-class ticket for the 12:10 to Salt Lake City, please,' he says, remembering to give that famous Duke Carlisle smile.

'Any luggage, sir?' she says, only barely concealing her

confusion that he doesn't seem to even have carry-on with him.

'I sent it ahead,' Duke lies, because he can't get into it.

'Excellent, sir,' she says, presenting him with everything he needs. 'Have a safe flight.'

At airport security, Duke is able to loop around the back of the longer economy queues to get to a shorter one for premium customers, but he feels exposed. He wishes he had a baseball cap or something to cover his eyes – maybe he can get one at the other side. He waits in line, pulling out his phone to have something to do with his face, because he can't see around the corner to the gate. She must be there – no way will she still be in the security line. She's probably already in the lounge with Magda. He'll go straight there. Boarding time is in twenty minutes.

Come on, come on, come on, he thinks, careful to smile at the staff, because even if he doesn't want to be one of the most famous actors in the world anymore, he still intends to be polite for the rest of his days.

'Are you . . .' a forty-something woman says as he walks through the x-ray when it is his turn.

He nods, and says quietly. 'I am,' he tells her, and then with a wink adds, 'But don't blow my cover.'

'I loved you in *The Marvellous Mrs Maisel*,' she says, and he thanks her, then is free to go. He makes a mad dash for the departure gates, not quite running, but almost. Right before he gets there he slows down, pats down his hair self-consciously.

Duke pushes through the glass double doors, ready for this moment that has been building and building, his blood thumping and his breath shallow and his heart all but singing at its chance to be given away.

But she isn't there.

He searches the room with his eyes furiously. It's busy, and people are starting to stare at him, now, one person snapping a photo drawing more attention to him, until a couple of people are taking pictures and blocking his way, and he's trying to be cool, polite, say Merry Christmas, but really this is stupid. He just needs to see Evie, say what he needs to say before she leaves, and then he knows he has fully tried to shoot his shot.

'Excuse me,' he says, picking through the crowds. 'Pardon me.'

He can see the queue for the gate up ahead, and he frenziedly tries to search her out. She's not in line, waiting to board, and he can't see her in the seating area either. He's got this wrong. This was all assumption. He assumed she was flying to Salt Lake and assumed it was from this airport and he assumed it was at this time. He actually doesn't know any of this for certain. Bugger. He feels defeated. He has no plan B. He hadn't thought of anything beyond getting to the airport. He searches for a hint or clue in the recesses of his mind about what he should do next. Somebody else takes his photo.

'Hey, I'm not who you think I am,' he says, shaking his head. 'I get it all the time, but honestly, what would I even be doing here if I was him?'

The middle-aged man with a camera phone looks apologetic.

'Sorry,' he says, gesturing to a woman standing nearby. 'My wife – she's a big fan.'

Duke waves across the way at her. 'Hey,' he says. 'Merry Christmas.'

He can't get a handle on what he's supposed to do next. She's not here. She's nowhere to be found. So . . . That's it?

He starts pacing up and down near the toilets and food outlets. He's messed this up. He's hotfooted it across the country, made out to his cab driver like he's some Hollywood hero from one of his own movies, making one last big declaration, and as it turns out, Evie had been right from the very beginning. None of this – life, or love – is an Ed Sheeran song or a mad dash through an airport. He bought into the fantasy of it, and that makes him a bloody idiot. He sinks down the nearest wall to sit on the floor.

Well . . . he tried.

That has to count for something.

'Duke?'

It's Magda. Magda! Her best friend! Magda will know what to do! Magda might even be with her!

'Is she here?' he says, in response.

'Evie?' she asks. 'Yes. She's just paying at the bar. Oh my God, thank God you're here. You *are* here for her, right?'

'Yes!' cries Duke, scrambling to stand up.

He spins around and watches Evie as she leaves the bar, shouting a thank you over her shoulder. When she sees him, she stops walking, stares, looks at Magda, then back to him.

'Evie,' he says, taking a step forward, and the ten steps it takes for her to reach him feel like seven eternities.

'Duke,' she says, coolly. 'Hello.'

'I'm going to . . .' Magda says, looking between them. 'Go.'

Evie looks at her. 'No,' she says. 'You don't have to.' She

342

looks at Duke. 'Our flight is boarding,' she says. 'I'm not trying to be cool or anything, it's just we really are going to miss the flight if we don't get a move on. We don't have long.'

'I'll walk with you,' Duke suggests, hurriedly, and Magda slips ahead to lead the way so that Duke and Evie can fall in step behind her. The waiting area has cleared out, and they join the back of the queue, only a handful of people in front of them. They really did only just make it.

'Where is your stuff?' Evie says, looking him up and down.

Duke pulls a face. 'I . . . actually don't know,' he says, and she looks at him with those eyes, those lips, that hair, that face, puzzled, and he laughs. She's here! He caught her! 'At the hotel, maybe?'

'I don't get it?' she says, puzzled.

'I realised you'd left already and I just . . . got in a cab,' he explains, and her face, when she understands that he's here for her, is a face he will remember until the day he dies. It's surprise, then confusion, then pure, unadulterated joy followed by flushed cheeks as she gets self-conscious.

'Evie, your boarding pass?' Magda says, turning to them. Evie hands her pass to the flight attendant, and Duke does the same.

'You're on this flight too?' Evie asks. 'To Salt Lake?'

'Well,' he says. 'I needed the ticket to get past security. I can just wait with you until they're closing the doors, right?' He turns to look at the attendant.

'Not really, sir, no,' she says, alarmed. 'This is kind of a you're-in-or-you're-out situation.'

Duke looks at Evie. She seems hopeful. It's a no-brainer, then.

'In,' he says.

'In,' Evie echoes. 'You're going to fly to Salt Lake?'

'Sure,' he decides. 'I mean. Look. There's things I want to say!'

'So say them!' Evie retorts.

'Okay!' He laughs, and then they're both laughing, and Magda turns around from where she's walking, up front, through the jet bridge, and smiles.

'Just wait,' he says. 'Magda – we're coming, okay?'

'We won't fly without you!' Magda shouts, boarding the plane.

'Evie,' Duke says. 'I don't know what I am doing. All I know is that I've been looking for love all my life, and all my life it's been in the wrong places. And something has happened this month, during this time in Germany, where I've realised that I had my own stuff to deal with. I've been a performer for my job, and in my real life, for so long I didn't know where one Duke ended and the other began, and I was resentful of it, but I still didn't change it, you know?'

Evie does something strange with her head, a sort of nod-meets-a-shake, like she really is trying to follow along but: what?

'Okay,' Duke says. 'This isn't coming out great. I think what I mean is: I was looking for love outside of myself, right? And then you came along, and you sort of . . . challenged me – I don't even know how. You make me want to be better, Evie. You make me face up to who I am and where my actions don't match my words and I find you so freaking stubborn, and impossible to read, and a little bit infuriating, quite frankly—'

344

At this, Evie laughs, and it's then that Duke sees the tears in her eyes, threatening to spill over.

'You are!' he repeats. 'You are infuriating. But also kind of a realist. You make me better because you force me into reality, and you know, you said love isn't mad dashes through airports but I did one hell of a mad dash for you, and I think that's because I'm kind of a fantasy guy, and that makes us a tiny bit perfect for each other. And between fake-dating you, turning into real-dating you . . . I guess I got so scared because there's nowhere to hide with you.'

'I've been told that before.' Evie giggles, and those tears are streaming, now, down her cheeks. 'But I tried!' she protests. 'I did a whole romantic gesture last night and you weren't even there! It started to feel like even if you were right, the timing was wrong, or the place . . .'

'And that's where Ms Reality comes in,' Duke agrees, taking a step towards her. He can't bear to not be touching her. He has to touch her. He wants her face in the palm of his hands, his lips against hers. 'Because we have to make this the right place and the right time. If I know anything, it's that when two people have whatever this is—' he motions between them '—that they are morally obliged to the gods and the stars to figure everything else out.'

'Okay.' She nods. 'I'm scared, but I like you, Duke.'

'I'm scared and I like you too,' he says back, pressing his nose to hers.

She laughs, and he laughs, and then they kiss, and he can taste her salty tears as he uses a finger to wipe them away.

'So we're doing this?' she says, pulling slightly away.

'We're doing this,' Duke tells her, and then the air steward manning the aeroplane door motions to the inside of the plane and says, 'Very cute, guys. But are you doing *this*?'

Evie looks at Duke.

'Come stay with me?' she says, and he nods. 'For Christmas?'

'I thought you'd never ask,' he tells her.

44

Evie

On the plane, Evie glances to the left in search of Magda, who is kneeling up on her chair looking at the exit, waiting for her to confirm safe embarking. Evie waves, and Magda lights up, too far away to shout to her without disturbing the other passengers, and so settling for a thumbs up, then a thumbs down, as if to say, *So, are you good? Or not?* Evie gives a thumbs up, and then points her out to Duke, and he laughs when Magda gives him a double thumbs up across the aisle, and then a wink, and then a mild hip thrust, much to the disgust of the woman in 7C who catches it.

'Okay then,' the smiling attendant says. 'Madam, you're just through here and four rows up there, in the aisle, and, sir.' She takes Duke's ticket, and tells him he's in the empty chair by Magda. His face falls.

'Wait,' he says to Evie. 'You're in economy?'

'Yeah,' Evie replies. She doesn't expect him to ride back there with her when he can enjoy the flight up here. If anything, she's learnt enough these past few weeks to know that nobody can't expect him to go unnoticed, and certainly not for the next fifteen hours. 'It's okay,' she tells him. 'Go. Enjoy. I'll see you both on the other side.'

Duke looks pained.

'I don't want to be apart from you,' he says. 'I just found you.'

'It's a few hours.' Evie smiles, giving him a kiss, and he lingers, and she likes it.

'I'm sorry, you two, but you really do need to take a seat now,' the flight attendant says, and Duke slips Evie's boarding pass out of her hands and gives her his.

'See you on the other side,' he says, as he makes his way down to her seat in coach. She looks at Magda, who is doing a silent but dramatic clapping action at this turn of events. Duke takes his seat and smiles at her up front. She blows him a kiss. What a guy.

'So, how was it?' Magda says, and Evie settles in beside her in first class. 'I *would* say that I can't believe he came all this way and got a ticket to freaking Salt Lake City so that he could profess his love to you, but actually, I kind of can?'

'He didn't profess his *love*,' Evie clarifies, 'but . . . I did invite him for Christmas. If that's okay – I totally get it was just going to be us, and it's your first one post-divorce, and he can totally just get a hotel or whatever if he needs to. You come first.'

Magda waves a hand. 'He cares for you, Evie. That's the most lovely present a best friend could ask for. I shall but welcome him with open arms.' She seems to have a second thought then, and adds: 'But he can get his own spring rolls. I'm not sharing with *anybody*, not even the man who makes you smile brighter than the sun and the sea and the stars.'

Evie reaches up to her cheeks. She really is smiling widely.

The seatbelt light goes on and the pilot makes an announcement about windspeeds and estimated arrival times as a woman delivers flutes of champagne to everyone in their part of the cabin and they start to taxi down the runway.

'How *long* is he going to stay for?' Magda asks, as the plane launches into the air.

'I don't know.' Evie shrugs.

'Is he your boyfriend now?' she presses.

'I don't know!' Evie repeats.

'Well, what do I call him?'

Evie finishes her bubbles and lets the drink fizz happily on her tongue.

'Same as you always have, I'd imagine,' she says. 'Just plain old Duke.'

The plane is busy, but it's so peaceful in first class that Evie feels like she could be in a private members club. She chats with Magda as they get served drinks and snacks, and flicks through the TV shows and movies on offer. None of it seems as dreamy as the story she has written for herself – even Duke aside, being away with her best friend, breaking herself open, the tattoo . . . the Evie Bird landing back in Utah isn't the same Evie Bird who took off.

'I'm proud of you,' Magda whispers once the food has been cleared away and most people have gone into a mid-flight sleep. 'I'm proud of both of us actually. Two best friends, weather-beaten by life, trying and trying again.'

Evie grins. 'We're doing okay, huh, friend?' she says and Magda nods.

'Yes, ma'am.'

As Magda falls asleep too, Evie pulls out her laptop from the overhead locker. Rereading the thirty thousand or so words of her new book, she can tell this is going to be a breakout novel for her. She just knows. The pace is different, the energy to it. She sighs happily, and then a figure appears beside her and she almost jumps out of her skin.

'Jesus!' she says, clutching her chest. 'You scared me half to death!'

'Sorry.' Duke smiles, in that way that he does. 'It's just, they closed the curtain so I couldn't see you anymore, and I was okay when I could see you, but with it closed . . .' He trails off.

'Well, aren't you cute,' Evie says, and he crouches down beside her so they're eye level and does that thing he does with his face, where his eyes sparkle and his dimples form adorable craters. Evie reaches out a hand to his cheek and strokes it, and he takes it, holding it there against his skin, sighing happily.

'Okay,' he says. 'Just had to remind myself what luxury looks like. The man beside me back there was using my shoulder as a dribble-catcher, so . . .'

'I appreciate the seat,' Evie replies. 'You're a true gent.'

He winks at her, kisses her hand, and then says, 'Okay. Going now, before I'm kicked out.'

'Bye,' Evie whispers, and she doesn't even hide that she's

watching his ass as he walks away, pinning back the curtain whilst no one is watching so that he can see her again. She has a thought: *That's my guy.* It pleases her, to think of him that way. She doesn't want just anybody, but she does want him. It feels like freefalling to admit it.

Evie returns back to her laptop, the story in front of her – the one she thought might not, this time, be a love story like the others. But isn't that just the thing? This love story isn't like the others. This is the one she finally gets to be a part of, and so she feels compelled, now, to finally write one she can believe in. She looks back to see Duke staring down the aisle in her direction, the curtain suspiciously pinned back again. He lifts a hand, does his cute half-smile. She lifts a hand back.

Something gurgles in her chest, something she knows she can trust. She turns back to her computer and starts a new chapter. One she is really very excited about.

45

Duke

Two months later

A movie set is an extraordinary place. But not, Duke thinks, as he pads through the living room, as extraordinary as being here, at home, with her. He could get used to this. Slowly, slowly, and with no rush, he can see that this would be a nice forever. You know, eventually. He's not forcing anything. He's trying, for once, to let things unfurl in their own time. So far, so good. It's funny how surrendering to the current can work out better than trying to swim upstream. If it was all leading to this, it was worth it. Staying present suits him: the past has happened, the future isn't yet written. Enjoy *this*. It isn't hard.

'Cup of tea?' he asks, getting up from where he's been planted in the living room for the past few hours with scripts and his laptop. Evie doesn't look up from her spot in the sunroom, which, in the two months he's been in Utah, has unofficially become her workspace when she's over. She's in there, listening to Cleo Wade and Bach, her little dog Doctor Dolittle at her feet, and he's in the other room, taking calls and making plans, and they work, they chat, they make love, they take walks . . . they say goodbye for a few nights when she goes back to her place and then do it all again.

'Coffee,' she hollers back, not looking up from her computer. 'Double shot, please.'

Duke busies himself pulling out mugs and teabags and putting a capsule in the coffee machine, locating the milk. It's not his house. It's rented. Over Christmas, when he stayed with her, she'd floated the idea of him sticking around for a bit, in between awards shows and visiting his mum back in Sunderland, before he's due on set in Brazil for a month at Easter – his last movie for a while, he's told his agent. When Evie asked, he said he'd like that – but that in the spirit of unfurling he'd stay nearby, not with her, to take the pressure off. It's going so well that he's just asked her if she wants to come with him to Rio. She said she'd like that, too, since it turns out a little travel is actually quite fun. It's give and take, and they're both practising the roles. Duke finds it easier to give love than receive it, and Evie says she finds the same. Together they're helping each other to be loved. It's not a bad endeavour.

Duke's phone rings. He holds it in one hand as he delivers Evie's double-shot, extra-foamy soy latte with the other, and she looks up at him, smiling gratefully. They look at each other, a beat suspended in time, as if surprised by the continued presence of the other. Doctor Dolittle stirs at her feet, and they break eye contact so she can bend over and ruffle his head. He watches the lean muscle of her neck ripple and enjoys the sing-song of her giggle as the dog leaps up to lick her face.

'Silly boy,' he hears her say into the dog's fur.

'Daphne,' Duke says, as he answers the call, still taking in the sight of his girlfriend. 'What do you think?'

He's talking about a script he's just sent her, which he got this morning. It's from a screenwriter who has been creating buzz around her latest arthouse movie, which she wrote and starred in. This new script is one she told him about in passing, at a party after the Globes – where Duke lost out on his award and didn't, to his surprise, really care. It's about a glitch in the space-time continuum that means a couple of sixteen-year-old star-crossed lovers keep meeting again and again, and he likes it. Daphne would be great to direct, and Duke wouldn't mind playing the lead's dad, which is a first.

'I'm obsessed,' Daphne enthuses. 'I just have a few notes?' she adds. 'If you've got time?'

Duke deposits a kiss onto Evie's forehead, and she receives it with a smile before exclaiming, 'Look! Snow!'

They turn to face the double window with the view out over the valley, the sky getting dark, the fire roaring, and Duke smiles.

'I've got time,' he says, and even though it's not Evie he's talking to she looks at him and pulls a face, a happy face. A contented face. God, he loves her. He knows she feels it too.

Daphne gabbles down the line with her ideas, and Duke

354

goes back to the kitchen where he rests against the breakfast bar. And when he's done, Evie comes over to him, hops up onto the counter so her legs are wrapped around him and she says: 'Duke. I'm sorry to tell you this, but, apropos of nothing and everything . . . I've fallen in love with you.'

He smiles, tipping her chin up to him, whispering right back, through a smile and an almost-kiss, that he's fallen in love with her too. Not a happy ending. A beginning.

Acknowledgements

Just for December is a punctuation mark in my author life. It's going to be different for me after this. Before now, I've been seduced into calling writing a 'dream' career, something that millions aspire to and few achieve, something I should feel lucky for and grateful for and not question too deeply, lest it be taken away and bestowed on somebody nicer or less demanding. Somebody who asks fewer questions. It's not a shift down the mines after all! What could I possibly have to complain about?

Well . . .

Call it a post-pandemic wake-up call, or parenthood, or maybe even the simple fact of growing up, but this past year has made me understand that a job, no matter how much passion you have for it, is only ever that. A job. And a job will never love you back. I know I'm not the only one to have realised this. I've been part of The Great Resignation too! Figuring out what works for me in my career, and what doesn't, precisely because if I don't look after myself nobody else will. That's capitalism, baby. (And, dare I say, the patriarchy.)

The biggest trick pulled on us is that our job should be our purpose, and it means we commodify the most precious thing we have – our time – to make other people rich. I've radicalised my thinking, and now my job isn't my purpose, but rather the thing that finances the rest of my *actual* life. It feels like freedom. I suppose that's why I'm telling you about it.

This has been a time of professional reckoning for me, supported by a personal life stuffed to overflowing with people kind enough, patient enough, and wholehearted enough to have weathered a necessary and incredibly painful evolution. (Seriously, I can't overestimate how hard I've cried, how many sleepless nights I've tossed and turned, how many emotional outbursts I've had to apologise for – not to mention my very first, very scary, panic attack.) Friends, your names here are in no particular order, and should by rights all appear on the same line because you've *all* been so amazing. You've listened and you've counselled, long after even I was bored of the whole 'WHAT SHOULD I DO WITH MY LIFE! WHAT DOES IT ALL MEAN!!' monologues – and I was the one giving them! Quite literally, I could not have done this without you:

Daniel Draper, Charlotte Jacklin, Lucy Sheridan, Sarah Powell, Sabah Khan, Meg Fee, Katie Loughnane, Calum McSwiggan, Claire Baker, Lucy Smithson, Jessica Stones, Shirley Argyle, Lucy Vine, Gillian McAllister, Beth O'Leary, Ella Kahn, Mum, Dad, Jack.

And My Darling. It's all for you, by which I mean: not the work that puts food on our table, but the boundaries that mean the work doesn't get any more time than it needs to. That would be time away from you, after all, and defeats the point of everything.

Thank you for reading. Whilst I've found a place for work outside of my heart, what I will never have enough gratitude for is the readers who continue to pick up my books and then tell other people about them too. I love hearing from you, I love meeting you, I love sitting at the computer and crafting tales of love and becoming with you, and only you, firmly in mind. If I'm indebted to anyone, it's you. Look out for my next book – it's a blinder. I appreciate you being on this storytelling ride with me, so very much. Thank you, thank you.

Until next time,

Laura x

Publishing Credits

Team Avon:

Molly Walker-Sharp – Commissioning Editor

Cara Chimirri – Senior Commissioning Editor

Elisha Lundin – Assistant Editor

Ella Young – Marcomms Assistant

Gabriella Drinkald – Publicity Manager

Hannah Avery – Key Account Manager, International Sales

Hannah O'Brien – Senior Marketing Director

Helen Huthwaite – Publishing Director

Maddie Dunne-Kirby – Marketing Manager

Oli Malcolm – Executive Publisher

Raphaella Demetris – Editorial Assistant

Sammy Luton – Key Account Manager

Thorne Ryan – Publishing Director

Freelancers:
Anne Rieley – Proofreader
Giovanna Giuliano – Illustrator
Helena Newton – Copy editor

HarperCollins:
Alice Gomer – Head of International Sales
Anna Derkacz – Group Sales Director
Ben Hurd – Trade Marketing Director
Ben Wright – International Sales Director
Caroline Young – Senior Designer
Charlotte Brown – Audio Editor
Claire Ward – Creative Director
Dean Russell – Design Studio Manager
El Slater – Trade Marketing Manager
Emily Chan – Production Controller
Georgina Ugen – Digital Sales Manager
Holly Macdonald – Art Director
Melissa Okusanya – Publishing Operations Director
Tom Dunstan – UK Sales Director

Rights and international:
Emily Gerbner, Jean Marie Kelly and the Harper360 Team
Lana Beckwith and the Film & TV Team
Michael White and the HarperCollins Australia Team
Peter Borcsok and the HarperCollins Canada Team
Zoe Shine, Rachel McCarron and the HCUK Rights Team

Nose in armpit.
Elbow in back.
Not every romance starts with flowers . . .

Penny has to choose between three.
But are any of them The One?

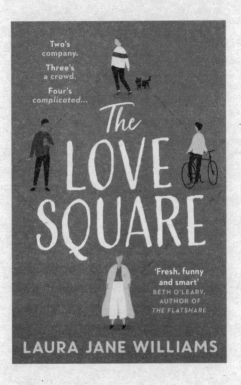

The wedding? Cancelled.
The bride? Heartbroken.
The honeymoon? Try and stop her . . .

Escape with this gorgeous read, full of effortless banter, sizzling sexual tension and, above all, an overwhelming sense of hopefulness – in life as well as love.

Available in paperback, ebook and audiobook now.

When you lose your luggage, the last thing you expect to find is love . . .

A warm-hearted novella packed with lust, longing and luggage, this is the perfect bitesize treat from the author of the smash-hit bestseller *Our Stop*.

Available in ebook and audiobook now.

**It's his first night in London.
And her last . . .**

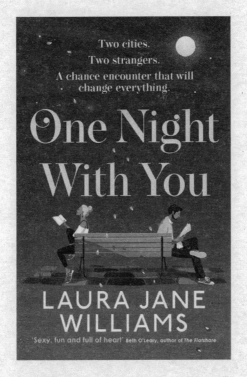

Move over Harry and Sally, sit down Ross and Rachel,
there's a new will-they-won't-they romance in town! Enter
Nic and Ruby: perfect for each other, but cross by the stars
even as they meet under them for the very first time . . .

Available in paperback, ebook and audiobook now.